## "I WISH YOU NEED NOT GO."

"So do I, but it can't be helped, Miranda."

"Sneaking about as though we are children."

"Yes, well, it is a bit awkward, but it's for the best. You know it is. One slip and you'll be the talk of London."

"She's an old maid, they'll say," Miranda said with a scowl and a wrinkled nose. "She ought to know better. Can you imagine her throwing herself at the man? At her age? Why, she's lost her mind. And to toss her handkerchief at a valet, of all things. Utterly nonsensical!" She ceased to speak and pushed herself away, a bit, from his chest so she could stare once more up into his eyes. "Josiah, are you crying?"

"Of course not. I'm perfectly fine, thank you. And I am not crying. Of all the things to say! I love you, Lady Miranda Wesley, that's all. I love you with every ounce of my being. I require a kiss."

"Then you shall have one."

# <u>BOOK YOUR PLACE ON OUR WEBSITE</u> AND MAKE THE <u>READING CONNECTION!</u>

We've created a customized website just for our very special readers, where you can get the inside scoop on everything that's going on with Zebra, Pinnacle and Kensington books.

When you come online, you'll have the exciting opportunity to:

- View covers of upcoming books
- Read sample chapters
- Learn about our future publishing schedule (listed by publication month *and author*)
- Find out when your favorite authors will be visiting a city near you
- Search for and order backlist books from our online catalog
- Check out author bios and background information
- Send e-mail to your favorite authors
- Meet the Kensington staff online
- Join us in weekly chats with authors, readers and other guests
- Get writing guidelines
- AND MUCH MORE!

**Visit our website at
http://www.kensingtonbooks.com**

# SHALL WE DANCE?

## Judith A. Lansdowne

**ZEBRA BOOKS**
Kensington Publishing Corp.
http://www.kensingtonbooks.com

ZEBRA BOOKS are published by

Kensington Publishing Corp.
850 Third Avenue
New York, NY 10022

All Kensington titles, imprints, and distributed lines are available at special quantity discounts for bulk purchases for sales promotion, premiums, fund raising, educational, or institutional use.

Special book excerpts or customized printings can also be created to fit specific needs. For details, write or phone the office of the Kensington Special Sales Manager: Kensington Publishing Corp., 850 Third Avenue, New York, NY 10022. Attn. Special Sales Department. Phone: 1-800-221-2647.

Zebra and the Z logo Reg. U.S. Pat. & TM Off.

First Printing: March 2002
10 9 8 7 6 5 4 3 2 1

Printed in the United States of America

# ONE

His honey-blond hair damp and dark from the mist and his shoulders hunched against the chill, Josiah Daniel Elliot leaned wearily against the bridge rail and gazed at the softly curving shoreline of the Thames. Not that he could actually see much of it, of course, the patches of fog as thick and plentiful as they were. But in his mind he saw it, especially the line of it that curled between Whitehall and the York water gate. "Are you standing out there somewhere, laughing at me, Buck?" he whispered into the night. "You are, aren't you? *You* would find this all a splendid adventure, would you not?"

Eleanor might never have seen him through the fog-thickened night did Donovan not whisper in her ear and set her gaze in Elliot's direction. She and her brother had paused at the very end of Westminster Bridge with the link boy they'd hired behind them. Beyond them in Bridge Street, like some great, hulking beast, its lanterns like eyes blinking lazily through the murky night, a hackney cab silently awaited their return. A ghostly tableau they made in their moment of indecision as they stood motionless among the distorted shadows made by the torch boy's flame. Had Elliot taken note of them then and there, he would have thought them specters from his past.

But then the need to proceed obvious to Eleanor and Donovan both and therefore not to be postponed, Mr. and

Miss Feebes began the long walk to the center of the bridge. Eleanor held tightly to her brother's arm lest her pink kid slippers—most inappropriate footwear for such an excursion—send her sliding downward. At one point, Donovan gave her white-gloved hand a pat. He intended it as a silent reassurance that he would allow nothing untoward to happen to either one of them or to the torch boy who followed closely, lighting their way from behind.

The nearer they came to Elliot, the more clearly Eleanor saw him. He was hatless. He wore neither cloak nor box coat to protect him from the elements. His hands were bare and his long-tailed riding coat hung imperfectly on his wide-shouldered frame. He seemed to her statuelike—a grave, pondering sort of statue—with his gaze fixed on the river below. Her heart lurched inside her as she watched tatters of fog twist around his ankles and attempt to fasten themselves in his hair. She whispered a prayer of thanksgiving that Donovan had been pressed into service by their uncle Roger and thus found it necessary to cross this very bridge this very evening. And more especially, she gave thanks that her brother had taken note of this gentleman on his way to and from Calliban's, had recognized what she recognized now, and had thought at once to seek her out at the Carlsons' dinner party. Because this stranger's very dress and posture illustrated his despair. His position on the bridge spoke clearly of his intentions. Eleanor was convinced beyond doubt, by his very presence and stance, that he was contemplating, in the midst of this damp, dark night, the beneficial consequences of writing *fini* to his life.

"I would not do it, sir, if I were you," Eleanor said in a worried but hesitant voice as she and Donovan drew within speaking distance of Elliot. "It is never the answer. I know of what I speak."

Elliot did not so much as gaze in her direction. In his heart he hoped whoever the woman was, she was merely bound across the bridge and that when he declined to deal with her in any way, she would simply pass him by.

But Eleanor, with Donovan to support her, had no intention to pass him by. "Whatever it is that compels you to so much as consider this action," she said more strongly, with less hesitation, "it cannot be truly as horrid as it seems to you at the moment. Do not pretend to ignore me, sir. I have come to speak truth to you."

"You aren't going to go away, are you?" Elliot sighed in a quiet voice.

"No, sir, I am not, nor is my brother."

Elliot straightened, though he did not take his hands from the bridge rail. He turned his head slightly to study these unwelcome intruders on his private moment. The young man was of medium height and slim. The young woman likewise. Behind them a little torch boy stood.

"I am Donovan Feebes and this is my sister, Miss Feebes," the gentleman said with great dignity.

"Just so," Elliot responded, nodding.

"And you are?" queried Eleanor.

"Weary."

"She means your name, sir."

"I know what she means, Mr. Feebes. I'm not a beetle-brain."

"Of course not," Eleanor responded in a rush. "You are merely hesitant to confide in us. As, of course, you ought to be. You don't know either of us from Adam."

"I would know you from Adam, Miss Feebes, without a second glance," Elliot replied. "Though I might have difficulty distinguishing you from Eve. No, I lie. You are much more fittingly dressed for this weather than Eve would be. However, I don't recall inviting you or your brother to join me in a discussion of the first man and woman, fashion, or the weather. So, if you are on your way across this bridge, please don't pause in your journey on my account."

"We're not bound across the bridge," said Eleanor quietly,

waving the torch boy closer and studying Elliot in the erratic light. "We came here expressly to speak with you, sir, to be of assistance to you, if you will allow it."

"Assistance?" Elliot removed his hands from the rail, tucked them into his pockets and turned the full power of his gaze on Eleanor. "Come to throw me over, have you, Miss Feebes?"

Eleanor smiled a faint smile. "You know very well we haven't. But you've not lost your sense of humor, sir. That's a very good sign."

"Is it?"

"Yes, indeed," offered Donovan. "An excellent sign."

"Actually, my brother and I have come to offer you a place to spend the night if you require one," said Eleanor. "A bite to eat, a warm bed in a safe place, a fire to take the chill from your bones."

Elliot noted, with considerable admiration, the manner in which Eleanor held herself and the direct way in which her eyes met his. "I do beg your pardon, Miss Feebes," he said after a thoughtful pause. "I hesitate to point this out to you. But there was a family once by the name of Pointerby who dwelt here in London and who were known to have made similar offers to perfect strangers."

"Oh?"

"You don't recall them? Too young, I expect. Indeed, it must have been before you and your brother were born, now I come to think of it, because I was merely a lad myself. The Pointerbys. Always willing to take a stranger in, they were. Killed them, of course. Men and women alike. Took anything and everything the poor dead people had and buried their bodies in the rear garden. Lovely garden, I think the papers noted at the time."

Eleanor stared at him, amazed. "You think that Donovan and I—that we—I daresay, you are gravely mistaken."

"Most likely so. But you will understand, will you not, why I decline your very kind offer? And I'm not without a home of my own, Miss Feebes. There is a fire burns there on the hearth even as we speak. And a comfortable bed that awaits me, though it won't be as warm as I could wish. It will be cold and lonely actually."

"You're not a gentleman who has lost all at the gaming tables?" Donovan's handsome face glowed ghostly in the torchlight.

"No, Mr. Feebes. I rarely gamble. It's one vice among many which does not appeal to me."

"Then what brings you to this—to contemplate such an action as—?"

"A woman," supplied Eleanor, interrupting her brother. "Did you not hear him, Donovan? He said his bed is cold and lonely, and in *such* a voice. This poor gentleman has lost the woman he loves and cannot bear to go on without her."

"A woman?" The amazement and disbelief apparent in Donovan's tone and on his face sent the light of laughter into Elliot's dark eyes, where it sparkled brilliantly for a moment, though Mr. and Miss Feebes did not recognize it.

"Do you mean to say, sir, that a woman has set you to contemplate the taking of your own life?"

The laughter bubbled up again at this further evidence of the young man's incredulity. This time it rose into Elliot's throat. He truly did not wish to laugh at the lad, so he attempted to force the laughter back down again. This resulted in a fit of coughing so violent that it brought tears to Elliot's eyes. With a strong hand, the young gentleman pounded him, most sincerely but unhelpfully, between the shoulder blades. "Enough," Elliot croaked when at last he found his voice again. "I—it—thank you, Mr. Feebes."

"Quite all right."

"It is grief constricts your throat so," Eleanor announced with tremendous empathy. "I've seen it before. Grief from merely speaking of your poor dead wife. But she would not wish you to throw yourself into the Thames because you miss her so. I can assure you of that."

"N-no," managed Elliot, schooling his features into an acceptable sadness. "No, she would never wish me to throw myself into the river on her account—especially since I have no wife, dead or otherwise."

"But—but you said—about your bed being cold and lonely. Oh!" Miss Feebes grew abruptly silent.

"You are thinking to drown yourself over a woman who is not your wife and is not even dead?" Mr. Feebes asked, utterly astonished. "Well, of all the peabrained things to do."

"Donovan!" exclaimed Miss Feebes.

"Well, but it is peabrained, Nora!"

"Yes, but if you persist in insulting the gentleman's intelligence, he certainly will not think to take advantage of our offer to aid him. He likely thinks himself a veritable dunderhead already, and to have you confirm it will drive him into the water more swiftly."

"Oh."

"Not to fear, Miss Feebes," offered Elliot. "I have no intention of throwing myself from this bridge into the Thames at the moment."

"You have not?"

"No."

"But you are standing here alone in the middle of the night, sir, without the least regard for the weather. You have been standing here for an hour, if not more. It did take you at least a quarter hour to reach the Carlsons', did it not, Donovan? Yes, just so. And then another quarter hour for us to make our way back here. And Donovan stood and watched you for ten whole minutes after he came back across the bridge with Uncle Roger's package. Just to be certain, you know, before he gave the hackney driver the Carlsons' direction and came to bring me to you."

Elliot, thoroughly engaged by the suppressed hopefulness

he detected in Miss Feebes's tone, studied the young lady by the glow of the torch. She was a bit taller than his beloved Miranda. The top of her head might reach his shoulder did she stand on her toes, whereas Miranda's wouldn't quite. Her hair, uncovered and growing damp now, was a deal darker than the tawny locks that he missed so dearly. And she was a good deal younger than his beloved. And yet, there was something about Miss Feebes that quite reminded him of the woman who owned him, heart and soul.

"It's her confidence in her own abilities," he murmured before he thought not to do so. "Thinks she can save me and is looking forward to the opportunity."

"What?" Eleanor queried, unable to distinguish his remark.

"I do beg your pardon, Miss Feebes," he replied. "I was merely muttering to myself."

"Muttering to himself," repeated Donovan with a knowing glance at his sister. "They'll do that."

"Yes, indeed," nodded Eleanor.

"Who will?" Elliot asked. "Who specifically, I mean. I thought everyone did so from time to time."

"Well, perhaps," replied Miss Feebes. "From time to time. But those in true despair, those at their wit's end, do it when others are present and those who aren't at their wit's end mutter only in private."

"Is that a known fact?" Elliot queried, leaning back against the bridge rail.

"Yes, sir, it is. So, you need not pretend with us any longer. You need not feel any shame about wishing to do away with yourself either. Donovan and I have been raised to understand that such things happen to people, and it is not some unforgivable sin to wish to end your life. But you must not do it. That's why we've come—to talk you into giving your life a second chance, to rescue you from such grim thoughts as must be floating about in your mind, and, if you will grant us the opportunity, to help you feel better about yourself."

"Just so," nodded Mr. Feebes. "Exactly so. What is it, sir?" he added as the most anguished look—at least, he thought it was an anguished look, but in the flickering shadows it was difficult to tell—the most anguished look came over Elliot's countenance.

"I—I—I must g-go," stuttered Elliot. "I c-cannot—" Without another word Elliot brushed past them and hurried toward Bridge Street where the Feebeses' hired hackney stood.

Miss Feebes turned to follow him, with considerable difficulty on the slippery bridge, her slippers not at all suitable for such a maneuver. Mr. Feebes and the torch boy turned to follow as well.

"What the deuce!" exclaimed Donovan, tucking his sister's arm through his own and preparing to dash after the man. "What the deuce is happening to him, Nora?" he asked in a hushed but excited voice as together they watched the shadow that was Elliot—almost invisible in the fog and the night—cease to rush away and fall instead to its knees at the north end of the bridge.

Lady Newcombe paced her drawing room floor with a vengeance, her lemon kid slippers slapping angrily against the carpeting, her hands clasped so tightly behind her back that her fingers grew white from lack of blood.

"Now, Caroline," said her husband, watching her with a sympathetic eye from his place on the gold silk settee with the enormous crocodile legs. "There is nothing in it, I'm certain."

"Yes, just what I expected to hear from you, Newcombe. 'Nothing in it.' Our niece has run off to who knows where in the dead of night and there you sit, smoking that wretched cigarillo as though she is upstairs in her bed dreaming the dreams of the innocent. Smoking that wretched cigarillo?"

she repeated and ceased to pace on the instant. "Newcombe, how dare you to light that vile-smelling thing in my drawing room?"

"I rather like the smell of it, actually," Newcombe responded, a smile twitching at his lips. "And I dare to smoke it here, Caroline, because you seem much too upset to be abandoned simply because I wish for a puff or two. I thought to myself, might as well smoke it here. Not a good idea to step outside at the moment."

"Throw it on the fire."

"I think not. Rather like tossing my favorite pudding out the window after one taste, that."

"Oh, you are exactly alike!"

"Who?"

"You and Eleanor, exactly alike. As stubborn as two peas in a pod."

Newcombe did smile at that. "Cannot say I've ever noticed that peas in pods are particularly stubborn, my dear."

"You know what I mean."

"This time I do, yes," admitted Newcombe. "Caroline, dearest, cease this nonsensical fuming. I can see the steam rising from your ears. Sit down here beside me, and attempt to regain your composure, won't you? You know as well as I that Eleanor will return home safely. Any moment now she'll come walking in through the front door, her face shining with triumph over someone or something she's rescued. You know it's so. She departed the Carlsons' with Donovan in a hackney cab, did she not? That's what you told me. Departed the premises in a hired cab on the arm of her brother. How much danger can she possibly be in with Donovan at her side?"

"Excessive danger. Especially with Donovan at her side. He's green as grass, Newcombe, and well you know it. A mere fledgling fresh from the country. Ripe for the picking. Any rascal might take advantage of Donovan and of Eleanor as well."

"Well, perhaps Donovan is a bit of an innocent, but he's still her brother, Caroline. He'll not stand by and see her harmed. Knock any fellow flat who so much as insults the girl. I promise you that." Newcombe rose from the settee and took Lady Newcombe gently into his arms, being especially careful not to set the tendrils of her hair alight with the burning tip of his cigarillo. "You worry far too much, m'dear. Eleanor is a tiny tower of strength and dependability. The female equivalent of a white knight, in charming armor."

"Yes, she is," agreed Lady Newcombe with a sigh, resting her head wearily against Newcombe's shoulder. "Yes, she is. And forever proving it in the most unfortunate ways."

"Well, but she cannot help herself, Caroline. Born to it. Takes after her mama."

"Takes after you, too."

"Yes, and me. Wretched tendencies came to m'sister and me through our mother. And what must Isabelle do but pass them on to her own children. However, m'dear, you love me precisely because of those wretched tendencies. Admit it."

"I love you in spite of those wretched tendencies," Lady Newcombe murmured, her lips quivering against the silk of his waistcoat. "But at least you don't go chasing off in the middle of the night all over London in search of someone or something to champion. At least—at least—"

"My Causes come to knock at our door."

"Just so, Newcombe. Though I wish they would cease to knock at our door from now until June. Just until I have found Eleanor a husband. Is that too much to ask?"

"Not at all, m'dear. Leave a message with James, I will. Send m'Causes to look me up at Westminster."

"You're laughing at me."

"A bit. You're so serious, you know, about finding Eleanor a husband. It's not as if the earth will tumble from its axis if you don't, Caroline."

"If only she had remained at the Carlsons'," sighed Lady

Newcombe, one lovely arm finding its way up over New-combe's shoulder, her slim, delicate fingers striving to twist themselves into the short strands of his hair, sending a series of shivers through the viscount that caused him to drop the ash from the end of his cigarillo right down onto the Aubus-son carpet. "She ought to have remained and continued to encourage Lord Dunley, but I could not convince her of it."

"Dunley?"

"Yes. Oh, Newcombe, I didn't tell you that!" The fingers ceased to play with his hair, and Newcombe's lovely wife took a step back to stare up into his eyes, her own alight with excitement. "Lord Dunley showed an astounding in-terest in Eleanor. He promenaded with her around the draw-ing room after dinner and then sat speaking with her on the Carlsons' little love seat near the windows for almost a quar-ter of an hour. Everyone was amazed at it. But then, of course, the Carlsons' footman came and whispered in Eleanor's ear and she spoke to me, excused herself and dis-appeared. Eyebrows raised, I must say, even though I did explain that her brother was at the door and required her assistance at once. Of all things, Newcombe, to abandon a pleasant young gentleman who might well prove willing to marry her in order to rush off into the night to talk a perfect stranger out of throwing himself from Westminster Bridge—which is precisely where she told me she was bound. Though I dared not say as much to the assembled company. Why, I was practically speechless. Where, I ask you, have the girl's wits gone wandering? To abandon an interested gentleman in favor of meandering about Town in a hackney cab with her brother?"

"To talk a perfect stranger out of throwing himself off Westminster Bridge?" repeated Newcombe. Ashes fairly jolted from his cigarillo. "Eleanor and Donovan have gone to confront some madman? Why did you not tell me this at once, Caroline? I must go after them. No telling but they're even now lying on that confounded edifice, their blood pooling around them.

"Oh!" squeaked Lady Newcombe. "Oh!"


The Earl of Blazingame drew the curtains of his parlor window aside and peered out into the night. The heavy mist had altered to a wind-driven rain scattering tatters of ragged fog before it as it swept through Manchester Square. "Where the devil can he be?" Blazingame wondered aloud. "If it grows much later without sight of him, I'll be obliged to go out into this wretched weather and look for the man."

"Who?" asked Wilde, peering around the side of the wing chair. "Do come away from the window, Blazingame. Makes me cold just to see you standing there. Join me here before the fire, eh? Comfortable place to be on a night like this, before the fire."

"Indeed, and I wish Elliot were upstairs even now, enjoying the warmth of his own little hearth."

"Oh. Elliot. Ought to have known. Gone off, has he? Again? I can't think why you put up with him, Blazingame. If the man were my valet, I would certainly not—"

"But he's not your valet, Wilde," Blazingame interrupted, allowing the curtains to fall back across the window and bestowing an agitated frown on his cousin. "He's my valet, and I will worry about him if I please."

"Yes, but why do you please is what I want to know. Who is the man? Where did he come from? You spent an entire month interviewing valets after Rulesby departed in a huff and could not find one man vaguely acceptable to you. If I recall correctly, you were so put out with the quality of applicants for the position that you told Doughtry to cease looking. You were contemplating the possibility of doing without a valet altogether, were you not? And then, out of the blue so to speak, you hired this perfect stranger."

"So I did. And now my perfect stranger is out there in

the midst of this wretched weather and he's like to contract the ague and die."

"Never. He's a man full-grown, m'boy. Forty if he's a day. Certainly he's not out wandering the length and breadth of London on a night like this. More likely safe and warm in some public house, drinking gin and contemplating his good fortune."

"What good fortune?" asked Blazingame, striding toward the hearth and plopping down into the chair beside Wilde's.

"Why, the great good fortune, lad, of having hired himself out to an employer who does not so much as demand that he do his work properly."

"He does his work properly."

"Ho! Of course he does! Which is why you appeared in the park yesterday in mismatched stockings."

"That was merely an—an—experiment."

"In what? Bad taste?"

"Wilde, I don't see that anything Elliot does or does not do ought to concern you at all."

"Well, it doesn't. Not actually. It's merely puzzling, dear boy. He came near to slitting your throat shaving you last week and still he remains employed."

"Who said that he came near to slitting my throat?"

"Doughtry. He was so overcome to see you bleeding, he could not but tell my own Homewood about it. And Homewood, of course, told me."

"Is there anything that goes on in my life that you don't know about, Wilde?"

"I daresay barely a thing. Well, I can't be blamed for that, Blazingame. I have looked after you for so many years that Doughtry will confide in Homewood, even now, does he think your welfare is at stake. And it's obvious to me that he thinks this Mr. Elliot is an enormous threat to your welfare. Thinks he's a threat to your life, as well."

Blazingame pouted at the fire. The very sight of that pout

warmed Wilde's heart. He smiled, and then he chuckled, and then he sipped at his wine.

"What?" asked Blazingame.

"Nothing."

"It's something."

"No, no, nothing at all, lad. Do you remember, Blaze, when first we came to know each other?"

Without the least effort, Blazingame's pout turned upward into a grin and a tiny sound escaped from between his lips.

"You were a wonder to me," Wilde said. "I never knew you existed until Doughtry came knocking that day on my front door."

"Amazed the stuffing right out of you, did I not?" laughed Blazingame. "You never even knew that Papa had married, much less produced an heir. Thought *you* were in line for the title."

"Just so. But there stood Doughtry on my doorstep, worn and weary and quite out of sorts. And there sat you, your curls barely visible, in the coach at my curb. What the deuce was I to do but what your papa asked of me in his letter?"

"You were kind to do it."

"Oh, without doubt. Don't know of another heir presumptive, barely twenty himself, who would have taken the brat born to replace him into his own home and raised him up to be the earl instead. I know some heirs presumptive, in fact, who would have done away with you in the blink of an eye. I was beyond kind, Blaze, now that I come to think of it. I was close to saintly."

Blazingame stared into the flames, remembering. "Saintly," he murmured, thoughts of his cousin's kindness through the years warming him more than did the fire. "Ha! Saintly!" he said to avoid sentimentality. "You turned pale as ashes, Doughtry said."

"Doughtry has an enormous mouth."

"He has, hasn't he? I've noticed that. About Elliot, Wilde."

"Yes?"

"He came to me with a letter from Daxonbury's valet, Whethers."

"Surely, you jest."

"No, truth," said Blazingame, raising his right hand in the air as though to vow it. "A letter from Daxonbury's Whethers. What more recommendation need a man have than that?"

"So that's why you hired him on the spot."

Blazingame glanced at his cousin. Wilde's kind gray eyes were full upon him. Those eyes had always astonished him—from the very first time they'd peered in at him through the coach window until this moment—they had always astonished him. They must be, he thought, the kindest eyes in all the world. There is never a hint of selfishness or greed or envy in them. Only sadness from time to time, and a bit of disappointment now and then. But even so, they are kindly sad, kindly disappointed. "Well, I didn't hire him because of Whethers's recommendation exactly. The letter didn't actually contain a recommendation. It contained an explanation and a request. Elliot's not truly a valet," Blazingame admitted.

"Fancy that."

"You knew?"

"Most valets, my boy, aren't quite as tall and broad-shouldered as your Mr. Elliot. That alone makes one wonder. And then, of course, he does tend to go wandering off of an evening without the least thought to your needs."

"No. He always asks if I will be in need of him before he goes."

"And if you say yes, does he remain?"

"Of course he does."

"Ah. Well, I did wonder who ruled whom."

"It isn't a case of ruling, Wilde. Not at all. It's not even a case of employing actually. It's—it's—"

"What? Do not say you won't confide in me, Blaze. I

have been your confidant for two decades now. Certainly I can be trusted with the true identity of your valet and his reasons for seeking sanctuary in your establishment."

The smell of gunpowder, the roar of cannon fire, men shouting, horses screaming, the vile taste of copper and sulphur on his tongue, all began to fade, as did his trembling. Gradually Elliot became aware of the stink of damp straw from the floor of the hackney and the buzzing of quiet voices. He blinked himself, silently, back from the brink of Hades. Across from him, Miss Feebes and Mr. Feebes came into shadowy view as the vehicle passed beneath the streetlamps. A scattering of rain whipped across the top of the hackney and rattled along its sides, distracting Elliot for an instant. Raining, he thought. When did it begin to rain? But then he returned his attention to the two young people on the seat facing him. They were speaking quite seriously to each other. Elliot declined to so much as wipe the perspiration from his brow lest he alert them to his resurrection from the trembles. They were discussing what was to be done with him and he was interested in learning what that might be.

"But we don't know, Donovan, that Uncle Roger will forbid it," Miss Feebes said in a hushed voice. "Uncle Roger is quite as tolerant as Mama about some things."

"Not about madmen."

"We don't know he's mad."

"No, but we don't know that he isn't. You saw him rush off right in the middle of a perfectly refined conversation as though the devil were at his heels, Nora. Not to mention the fact that, no matter how much he protested, it seemed quite obvious to me that he walked out on that bridge for the sole purpose of throwing himself into the Thames."

"But he did not throw himself into the Thames."

"Because we prevented him from doing so."

"Yes, we did. And for that reason alone, Donovan, we

are now responsible for him. And do we merely explain precisely that to Uncle Roger, he will allow us to keep him. I am certain he will."

"Even if he does, Aunt Caroline will stand against it."

"Oh, pooh! As if Aunt Caroline could ever prevail against Uncle Roger's wishes. Uncle Roger knows his way around Aunt Caroline very well. That's what Mama says, and it's plain she's correct. At least, it is plain to me."

"Well," sighed Donovan with a shake of his head. "Well, it isn't plain to me—or to Aunt Caroline. Now, what the deuce?" he added as the hackney trundled to a halt close beside a coach bound in the opposite direction.

"Donovan?" a worried voice called. "Eleanor? Are the two of you in there?" Rain assaulted the brim of Lord Newcombe's hat as he leaned out the open window of his own vehicle.

"Uncle Roger?" Donovan slid the isinglass window upward. "What are you doing here, sir? Frightful weather to be gadding about in."

"Gadding about? *I'm* gadding about? I came in search of the two of you, by gawd! Thank heavens you're safe. You are safe? Eleanor is safe in there with you?"

"Yes, Uncle Roger," announced Miss Feebes, leaning across her brother to present herself to Newcombe's view. "I'm in here as well and we are both perfectly fine."

"I thought to discover the two of you dead by the hands of some lunatic on Westminster Bridge," admitted Newcombe, relieved. "Come, join me in this coach and we'll go directly home."

Eleanor sat back and glanced uneasily at Donovan. Donovan glanced just as uneasily at her. Then they both glanced across at Elliot.

"I would go at once if I were you," Elliot said softly, sitting up on the rear-facing seat. "I doubt your uncle will depart without you."

"Oh! You are recovered, sir! Well, but we cannot just

leave you," Eleanor declared in a determined but hushed tone.

"Of course you can."

"No, no, we cannot," Donovan replied with a shake of his head. "You're not well. You—something happened to you on the bridge. You likely do not remember, but—"

"Donovan? What the deuce is going on? Assist your sister to exit that vehicle and enter this one at once." Newcombe peered suspiciously across at the shadows in the opposite coach and recognized a third presence he'd not noticed before. When no reply came to his latest sally, no coach door opened, neither of the young people appeared, he reached down and fumbled angrily beneath his coach seat.

"At the very least we must see you safely home," Miss Feebes declared, her chin rising stubbornly. "You did say you have a room and a bed. Allow Donovan and me to escort you there."

"What? To my bed, Miss Feebes?"

"To your room, sir. You are perfectly aware of what I mean."

"Yes, I am. I do apologize, but there is something about you that makes me wish to tease you just a bit. I should think that bodes well for me, eh? Wishing to tease an innocent young woman? Cannot throw myself off a bridge when I'm in such a wry humor as that. Do go with your uncle, both of you. I give you my word to ride home safely in this hackney and not to go out again tonight. That will free you from any imagined responsibility for me."

"You were listening to us!" gasped Eleanor. "All the while we thought you lying there, lost to the world, you were listening to us!"

"Not necessarily, Nora," Donovan pointed out.

"Well, of course he was. How else would he know that we considered his welfare our responsibility? He listened to our entire conversation. For shame, sir. You might have made a sound, said a word, allowed us in some way to realize that we were no longer speaking privately."

"He could have just surmised that we feel responsible for him, Eleanor," Donovan replied. "It's easily enough done. We took him from the bridge and put him in this hack. We're riding right along with him. What else would a gentleman think but that we felt a responsibility for his welfare? Girls," he added. "And you are generally so rational, too, Nora. Most of the time I don't think of you as a girl at all."

"You don't?" queried Elliot, a smile flitting unseen, across his lips.

And then the door on Mr. Feebes's side of the coach opened, a whoosh of wind and rain entered the vehicle and, with it, Lord Newcombe. Pistol in hand, he ducked inside, dropped down onto the seat beside Elliot, and aimed the weapon directly at Elliot's heart. "So, this is the villain detains you, is it?" he growled, rain dripping from the brim of his hat onto the muzzle of the pistol. "Attempting to abduct my niece and nephew, are you, you dastard? Foiled your plot, did I, by turning up in search of them? Well, well, and now you can't think how to get yourself out of it, eh?"

"Uncle Roger!" exclaimed Eleanor at once. "Do put that horrid thing away! It is not at all what you think. You are mistaken on every point."

"I should think so," agreed Elliot. "It's your niece and nephew who are abducting me, Uncle Roger, not the reverse."

"Uncle Roger?" blustered Newcombe. "What the devil! *You* dare to call me Uncle Roger?"

"Well, it's all I've heard you called," Elliot replied, his face a mask of innocence. "Be pleased to address you properly did I know how to do it."

"He's Viscount Newcombe," Donovan offered in an embarrassed tone. "And what the gentleman says is true, Uncle Roger. I did never think of it quite that way. I'm certain it did never occur to Nora. But in effect, sir, it is we who are in the process of abducting him."

"Not that I intend to hold it against them, Newcombe. I mean, your lordship," said Elliot. "Because I don't. They were merely attempting to be of help to me. I say, Newcombe, I'd be obliged if you would point that weapon at the floor," he added, pushing the muzzle of the gun to the side with the flat of his hand. "Actually, I'd be even more obliged if you would take the thing from this coach entirely, along with your niece and nephew. I've been attempting to convince them that I am perfectly capable of returning to my own home all by myself, but they'll not be persuaded."

"You found this man on Westminster Bridge, Donovan? Eleanor?" Newcombe queried, pointing his pistol at the floor of the coach but not for an instant removing his gaze from Elliot.

"Yes, Uncle Roger," Miss Feebes replied. "That is to say, Donovan noticed him, and when it seemed as though the gentleman was determined to end his life, Donovan came to fetch me so that we might save him from such a stupid fate."

"And do you know his name?" asked Newcombe.

"No, sir," Donovan replied. "He will not say."

"Your name?" Newcombe queried, his pistol rising again, centering on Elliot's heart. "Come now. Any honest man ought not fear to give his name."

"Not even when he has a pistol pointed directly at him?"

"Your name," urged Newcombe.

"Elliot."

"And your profession, Mr. Elliot?"

"Now, what the devil has that to do with anything?"

"Allow me to be curious. I am, after all, the gentleman holding the pistol."

"I'm a valet."

"An employed valet?"

"Yes."

"And who is it employs you?"

"Lord Blazingame."

"Blazingame? By Jupiter, you're Blazingame's man? No wonder you were considering jumping from that bridge." Newcombe lowered the pistol and gave a sad, dramatic shake of his head.

"Why? Why, Uncle Roger?" Eleanor asked in a rush. "What happened to Lord Blazingame? What has Mr. Elliot done?"

"Only sent his employer out in public in one clocked stocking and one plain one. That's all. Not to mention the waistcoat."

"What was wrong with his waistcoat?" Elliot asked, an eyebrow cocking in surprise.

"Well, it was daffodil yellow, man."

"And?"

"It was daffodil yellow and had purple hummingbirds embroidered all over it."

"How ghastly!" groaned Donovan.

"And this is something over which a gentleman thinks to take his own life?" asked Eleanor, incredulous.

"If he happens to be a valet, yes," Newcombe responded. "If he were my valet, mind you, I'd take him right back to the bridge this instant and toss him over the rail myself."

"Uncle Roger!"

"Well, perhaps I wouldn't, Eleanor. Perhaps I wouldn't. But I would seriously consider it."

# TWO

Blazingame gazed thoughtfully into space as Elliot assisted him into his coat the following morning. "Miss Eleanor Feebes," he said. "No, I don't recall the name, Elliot. Is she pretty?"

"Can't say. I think so, but it was dark and she was forever fluttering in and out of shadows."

"Fluttering? The girl fluttered?"

"No. The shadows fluttered. Miss Feebes generally stood still."

"Do you think her a part of our puzzle?"

"Not likely."

"Then why are you so interested in her?" Blazingame turned to meet his valet's gaze, curiosity evident in his jade green eyes. "I should think, Elliot, from the tale you just told me, that you're fortunate to be rid of such an interfering female."

"Did I make her sound interfering?" Elliot asked. "I didn't intend to do that. A young woman concerned for my welfare, merely. Concern for the welfare of others ought to be applauded, don't you think?"

"Yes."

"Just so. She's a bit like you, actually. You're concerned with the welfare of others. You offered me your assistance the moment you read Whethers's letter. And not once have you faltered since then, either, in your efforts on my behalf.

She would react in a like manner, I believe. Her uncle is Lord Newcombe. He knows you, he says."

"That's true. He has never mentioned the girl to me, though. What are you doing, Elliot?"

"Checking."

"Checking what?"

"Your stockings."

"No one will so much as see my stockings with my boots on."

"True," Elliot replied, "but yesterday you didn't wear your boots and—"

"I would have worn my boots had they been shined."

"Yes. I had a bit of a problem mixing the polish and—"

"It began to steam and bubble up and came near to exploding. I know. Doughtry told me. It's all right, Elliot. They're shined now. Come and give me a hand getting the blasted things on, eh?" Blazingame crossed to a straight-backed chair and seated himself on it. Elliot brought a pair of high-topped riding boots to him and knelt down before him. "Who helped you get into your boots, Elliot, when you were in the war?" Blazingame asked.

"No one. I rarely took them off."

"Not even at night?"

"Not even at night."

"I shouldn't like to be a soldier, ever."

"No, I expect not. You were never meant to be."

"Why did you join up?"

Elliot sat back on his heels and studied the younger man. "Well, I always expected to be a cavalryman, you see, and so I was—rather like you expected to be an earl and now you are."

"I wasn't old enough to expect to be an earl. My father died when I was two and I just suddenly was one."

"Oh. Sorry to hear that, Blazingame. I mean, your lordship. Damnation, but every time I think I've got it down, I forget to do it."

"It doesn't matter, Elliot. You may call me Blazingame whenever you like. It's not as though you intend to be my valet forever. No, and it's not as though I'm unaware of your situation and just who you are. But unless this Miss Feebes of yours has something to do with the disappearance of your brother and his boys, I can't think why you're so interested in her. You have mentioned her name eight times this morning already. Oh, and by the way," Blazingame added as Elliot buckled his spurs on for him, "Marley is in town. Spoke to him at Watier's last evening. Just for a moment. He and his friends were busy gloating over some rapier he discovered in an abbey in Yorkshire."

Elliot scowled. "Marley can't be satisfied with owning the thing, eh? Now he must be the one who discovered it?"

"He didn't discover it?"

"No. I sold it to him. And he was ready enough to purchase it, too. It belonged to The Buck, that rapier."

"I cannot fathom why Marley is so enraptured with all things having once belonged to that madman," Blazingame said, standing and strolling across the room to view himself in the looking glass again. "I can understand your being interested in him, but Marley?"

Blazingame set his hat at a rakish angle on his thick brown curls and studied the effect. "No matter what I do, I look like a cherub," he observed. "Still, I expect I ought not to complain. Apparently it works."

"What works? Looking like a cherub?" asked Elliot as he folded up his lordship's nightshirt and stuffed it into the clothespress.

"Precisely. No one takes me at all seriously because of it, not even the ladies, so I am generally free to go about my business at all the entertainments without any serious interruption. Looking like a cherub and dressing like a blind man do have benefits, Elliot. Of course, having you as a valet has furthered my reputation as a gentleman to be avoided enormously."

"I protest," Elliot said, gazing at the vision that was Blazingame. "I never say a word to you about what you ought to wear and what not."

"Yes, and that alone makes you perfect, don't you see? Any decent valet would slit his own throat before allowing me to exit this chamber in this mustard coat with blue braiding, this raspberry-and-green-striped waistcoat and buckskin breeches. You, however, see nothing at all wrong with it."

Blazingame turned from the looking glass and strolled, silver spurs jangling, toward the door. "Oh, by the bye, Elliot. I learned the most amazing thing last evening."

"What?"

"Marley's the one."

"I beg your pardon? Marley's the one what?"

"No, the one who, Elliot. Marley's the one who now holds the title to your brother's house."

"Marley? My cousin, Marley?" Elliot, who was just then leaning down to collect the four neckcloths Blazingame had tossed to the floor before he had managed to tie the perfectly imperfect knot in the fifth, straightened up and spun around on the instant. "Are you certain?"

"Indeed. Rents it out during the Season."

Elliot shook his head slowly from side to side in disbelief. "He swore to my stepsister that he'd no idea what happened to Nathaniel and yet he now owns Nathaniel's house? When did he purchase the place?"

"Well, I knew you'd wish to discover that, so I sent a message around to Gloom. Ought to have an answer for me this afternoon. Perfect sort of solicitor, Gloom. Never asks why I want to know anything, or what I intend to do with the information. Merely does precisely what I request of him whenever I request it. He's the exact sort of solicitor that you are a valet, Elliot."

"Is he?" asked Elliot with a slow smile. "Does that mean that he's an inept impostor, too?"

* * *

Lady Miranda Wesley paused just inside the vestibule of the house in Portman Square and gazed about her, a weak smile of acceptance on her face.

"It is a bit ornate, but the location is all, Miranda," offered Miss Markum as she removed her gloves, handed them to the butler and began to take the pins from her hat. "And considering that Lord Daxonbury had very little notice, he and Dessie have done remarkably well by us, I think."

"Glory," murmured Mrs. Harriot, "there be cherubs on the ceiling and the cornices be made of lace. Never saw such a sight in my whole life. What must my kitchen be like?"

"I have no idea, Early," Lady Miranda replied, "but if this vestibule is any indication, your kitchen likely has a chandelier, bookcases, and a silk-covered sofa for you to recline on whenever you feel the need. Honestly, Ariel," she added with a glance at Miss Markum, "this establishment looks as I always imagined a house of ill repute might."

"No, do you think?" asked Miss Markum, laughing.

"Yes. You don't think it actually was one at some time in its history, do you?"

"In Portman Square? Oh, I think not. Simply an old house redecorated by someone with extremely bad taste."

"If it was not the only house to be had within a comfortable walking distance of Manchester Square, I would turn around and leave at once," declared Lady Miranda.

"But you are not going to leave?" Miss Markum queried.

"No. Of course not."

"No. So I thought. Come," Miss Markum added as the butler took Lady Miranda's cloak, hat and gloves, "let's have a peek at Early's kitchen. I assume it is at the rear of the house, is it not Mr. Browne? It is Mr. Browne? I do remember correctly?"

"Yes, Miss Markum," the butler responded quietly. "Yes,

I am Browne and yes, the kitchen is straight back along this corridor. The second to the last door on your right."

"We will find our own way to the kitchen, then," Lady Miranda said. "If you would be so kind as to collect the rest of the staff, Browne, while we tromp off to contemplate the kitchen's excesses, I should like to make everyone's acquaintance when I return, and introduce Mrs. Harriot to you all as well."

"Indeed, madam," Browne responded. He had not expected these ladies until tomorrow afternoon at the earliest. And though the house itself had been opened, aired, scrubbed and polished, the staff had not been assembled and awaiting her ladyship's and Miss Markum's arrival in the vestibule as they ought to have been. He watched as the two women strolled off in quiet conversation with the cook they had brought with them from Yorkshire and he hoped that her ladyship's affability at his lapse in gathering the staff was a sign of her general good humor. Lord Daxonbury had assured Browne, when he requested him to assume the temporary position of butler to his aunt, that her ladyship was far from a tyrant—but then, Lord Daxonbury had been so bemused since his marriage to Miss Quiggley that he saw everyone and everything as affable and good-natured. And Browne's memory of Lady Miranda was vague to say the least. He had been but a newly hired footman in the Duke of Comestock's household when Lady Miranda, then just completing her third Season in London, had departed that particular establishment and disappeared into the hinterlands.

Quickly, Browne stowed the ladies' things away and dashed up the staircase to the first floor to sound the alarm. "Her ladyship and Miss Markum are here," he called in a hushed whisper to the young maid dusting in the front parlor. "Run quickly, Martha, and find Mrs. Holden. Tell her to gather the household staff in the vestibule, except for the footmen, of course. She must send the footmen out to help with the luggage at once, and then they will join the rest. I shall go down to the mews and fetch the grooms."


"Thank goodness, no chandelier," Lady Miranda observed, her blue eyes brilliant with unexpressed laughter as she, Miss Markum and Mrs. Harriot stepped into the kitchen. "But look at the size of the place, Early. You will need to consult a map to find your way in and out of it. Nooks and crannies everywhere."

Mrs. Harriot glanced around her. "It be extremely large, my lady," she acknowledged. "But it be merely a kitchen and nothing more. No bookcases nor sofa nor nothing."

"I expect we have a scullery maid to help at the very least," whispered Miss Markum in Lady Miranda's ear.

"Oh, I expect we must. And likely a potboy as well. Dax is fond of Early. He'd not forget to hire servants to assist her."

"No," replied Miss Markum quietly. "And if he did, Mr. Whethers would remind him. I ought to have thought of that immediately. There is considerable interest in that particular direction."

"Early and Whethers?"

"Indeed. Did you not notice that your nephew expressly requested we bring Early with us for his and Dessie's wedding celebration? It was not because he longed for her cooking, my dear. It was because he thought Whethers wished to get to know Early better."

"I vow," Miranda sighed, "put a bachelor together with the girl of his dreams and what do you get—a matchmaker. Dax, of all people!"

"When did you tell Mr. Elliot to expect us?" Miss Markum queried, changing the subject completely.

Lady Miranda stared at her as if she had just spoken the entire sentence in Greek.

"Miranda? What is it? Clearly we've arrived earlier than

Lord Daxonbury thought we would. Mr. Browne would have had the staff lined up to greet you, else. I only wondered if you had mistaken our day of arrival in your letter to Mr. Elliot as well."

"I—well, I—"

"Miranda? You did write to Mr. Elliot to tell him to expect us, did you not?"

"No."

"No?"

"No, Ariel, I didn't," Miranda replied, raising her hand to stop the burgeoning tirade she saw about to burst forth from between her companion's lips. "Please don't tell me that I ought to have done so. I know I ought to have done so. But I found that I could not. He would have protested, you know. Vehemently."

"Yes, but, Miranda—"

"He would have written back and convinced me to remain at Lavender Hill until he came to fetch me himself," Miranda continued, not allowing Miss Markum to voice her thoughts further. "Or if not that, then he would have resigned his position with Lord Blazingame and gone into hiding merely to avoid any contact between us—lest there should be a public scandal, you know, concerning a particular middle-aged noblewoman and a certain handsome valet. As if I give one fig about a public scandal! At any rate, I could not take the chance, Ariel. I could not force myself to give Josiah fair warning. I have lived for months now without the sight of Josiah Elliot's dear, dear face, and I will not live without the sight of it for another day."

In the shadow of a large rosebush growing from a pot beside the door, Eleanor waited impatiently as Donovan lifted the knocker once again and let it fall. Her fingers, encased in pale pink gloves—which matched exactly the pale pink rose on the front of her wide-brimmed bonnet—

fiddled restlessly with the strings of her reticule. "Is someone going to answer this door or not?" she murmured. "We
have been standing here forever."

"Of course someone will answer," Donovan assured her.
"But it's a bachelor's establishment, Nora, and likely Blazingame's gone off somewhere. That means that his servants
are busy doing whatever it is servants do. Bachelors' establishments are not run on the same principles as households
belonging to married men. There are no ladies of the house
forever expecting callers, so the front door is not constantly
manned."

"You make it sound as if ladies live in continuous expec-
tation of callers."

"You do."

"I do not."

"Not you, Nora. Regular ladies. Ladies like Aunt
Caroline and Miss Jennings and Lady Sebastian."

"Oh."

"I ought not to have escorted you here, you know," he
added, gazing around him to see if any of the neighbors
were taking note of the two of them standing on Blazingame's doorstep. "It's not at all proper for an unattached
young woman to pay a call at a bachelor's residence."

"But I have you beside me, Donovan."

"Even so, you've made your come-out, m'dear, and
you're eligible and it ain't the thing for eligible females to
go about knocking up eligible gentlemen in their own
houses."

"I don't care in the least," declared his sister.

"I know you don't," sighed Donovan. "Thank goodness,
someone's coming at last. I hear footsteps. Just so," affirmed
Mr. Feebes with a thankful nod of his head as the door
opened slowly inward and an elderly face, smooth shaven,
with a mere button of a mouth and curious dark eyes, peered
out at them.

"Yes?" asked the butler, his gaze lingering on Miss Feebes while his silvery eyebrows arched in surprise.

"We should like to speak with Lord Blazingame," Mr. Feebes said, handing his card to Doughtry.

"I am afraid Lord Blazingame is not at home, sir."

"Are you quite certain?" asked Eleanor.

"Quite, miss."

"Then we should like to speak to Mr. Elliot," Eleanor said, causing Doughtry's eyebrows to arch even higher.

"Mr. Elliot?"

"Just so," nodded Donovan.

The butler stared down his substantial nose at them both. "You wish to speak to my lordship's valet?" he asked again, incredulous.

"Yes," Eleanor said. "It is of the utmost importance. Summon him, please. At once."

Doughtry took one step back and then another, allowing them to enter the vestibule. "If you will wait in the chamber to your right, I will tell Elliot you're here." He gestured them toward a tiny room just to the left of the front door, bestowed on them a most disapproving look and departed.

"Probably thinks we've come to steal the silver," murmured Eleanor.

"I doubt that, Nora, but he likely thinks us mad to be knocking on an earl's door and then ask to speak to a valet."

"Ought we to have gone around to the back?"

"No. We've as much right to come to the front door as anyone. It's not as though we're servants or in trade. Honestly, we ought to have just acknowledged that Blazingame was from home, turned around and left. You don't go asking to speak to a man's valet when the man is not at home."

"Is that some sort of gentlemanly rule? But it's Mr. Elliot I really wish to see, not his lordship."

"I know. But I'll not hear the end of this for years, does it come to Aunt Caroline's attention."

"Nonsense. You have merely escorted me to where I wish to be. It's not as though you forced me to come here."

"The other way around, rather."

"I did not force you, Donovan. You said you'd be pleased to escort me anywhere."

"Yes, but that was before you said anything at all about coming here. Why are we here?"

"Precisely what I should like to know," said a voice from just beyond the threshold. "You've ruined me completely in Doughtry's eyes by coming. A gentleman and a young *female* require my presence is what he said when he came to fetch me. And he gave me such a scowl, too. Likely thinks I've taken advantage of you, Miss Feebes, and that your brother has come to beat me about the head until this entire room is awash in blood."

Elliot stepped into the room with an easy grace and offered Feebes a curt bow. "Y'r servant, Mr. Feebes," he said. "Miss Feebes," he added, bowing as well in her direction. "May I be of some assistance?"

"We've come to see if you're feeling more the thing," said Eleanor, the words tumbling from between her pretty lips in an uncharacteristically nervous rush.

Is this the gentleman we saved last evening? she wondered, her eyes wide. When did he grow so—so—interesting-looking? Her cheeks reddened the slightest bit as she considered him. Is it merely the difference between daylight and darkness that has altered his features so? And he has a fencing scar. I did never notice last evening that he had a fencing scar on his cheek. Oh, dear, he hardly looks to be the same person.

"I'm feeling in fine feather, Miss Feebes. Almost jovial. I thank you for stepping around to inquire," Elliot replied. "Was it your uncle gave you my direction?"

"Actually, no," offered Donovan, bestowing on Elliot the most put-upon glance. "He didn't *give* it to us. Nora had to pry it out of him. And then she hoaxed me into agreeing to drive her anywhere she wished to go this morning. So, here we are."

Elliot grinned and the very mischievousness of that grin set Eleanor's heart to dancing a bit of a country dance. It makes him look so boyish and endearing, she thought. Yes, most endearing. It could make a person want to hug him. But I won't, she told herself silently. Indeed, I won't. Aunt Caroline would have an apoplexy. Besides, he is not a boy at all. He's almost as old as Uncle Roger, I should think. I wonder if valets marry? He spoke of a woman last evening. I wonder if he longs to marry her and she, him, but they cannot because—

"You are not despondent any longer, Mr. Elliot?" she asked. "You seemed in despair last evening. And I could not rest knowing that Uncle Roger had sent you home, likely with a bug in your ear and not the least consideration for your nerves on top of it."

"I'm fine, Miss Feebes. Truly. I was not at all set on ending my life last evening. I attempted to convince you of that, did I not? I was merely—merely—"

"Merely what, Mr. Elliot?"

"Staring at the York water gate and pondering."

"Staring at the—the—water gate?" Eleanor could not think why anyone would stand on a bridge and stare at a water gate.

"Um-hmmm. The one at the bottom of Buckingham Street."

"You were truly not considering suicide?" Donovan asked, his disbelief evident in his tone.

"Not then."

"Oh," murmured the two simultaneously.

"Of course, now that an unattached young lady has come to seek me out at my employer's establishment—while my employer is absent from the house, no less—and knowing that word of it will fly through every household within walking distance, I may change my mind about the matter."

"But you can't possibly have seen the York water gate from where you stood. Not in all that fog," declared Eleanor abruptly, her voice filled with doubt.

"Nora's right. You couldn't possibly have seen it. Not in the dark of night," agreed Donovan, equally doubtful.

"I didn't actually need to see it," Elliot replied. "I know what it looks like well enough. My mother was accustomed to take me to see it once a week. Designed by Inigo Jones, they say. Built by Balthazar Gerbier. You'll have learned a bit about Jones and Gerbier, I expect, eh, Feebes?"

"Of course," replied Mr. Feebes with a nod.

"Most certainly," agreed Eleanor, not to be thought purely stupid. And then she steered the conversation directly back to the main topic. "After what Uncle Roger said he would do to you were you his valet, Donovan and I feared you must have suffered gravely at the hands of Lord Blazingame. That perhaps he'd turned you off without a reference or some such. And so we came to see that you were all right and to speak with Lord Blazingame on your behalf. We would have accompanied you home last evening, but Uncle Roger would not permit it, you know."

"We mean to tell Lord Blazingame that you're not at all well, too, when we get the opportunity," added Donovan. "He's an earl, after all. He can well afford to bring in a physician to see to your—to your—"

"Comfort," provided Eleanor neatly. "No, no, don't protest, Mr. Elliot," she added, raising one neatly gloved hand.

The edge of the glove had little lavender flowers stitched around it, and these caught Elliot's eye at once.

"We realize Lord Blazingame is not in at the moment, but we shall return. I intend to give him a rather large piece of my mind," Eleanor continued. "Of all things, to persecute you to such an extent that you should think to do away with yourself! And over what? Some silly mix-up in stockings! What sort of gentleman must Lord Blazingame be? What *are* you staring at, Mr. Elliot?"

"I do beg your pardon, Miss Feebes. The flowers on your gloves."

"The flowers on my—" Eleanor could feel her cheeks begin to burn. "Of all things! And just when we are being most serious, too," she managed.

"They're quite beautiful, your gloves," Elliot observed, "as are you, Miss Feebes, if I may be permitted such an observation." His eyes grew bright as he noticed the deepening blush on Eleanor's cheeks and the uneasy manner in which her fingers began to toy with the strings of her reticule. She's the one, he thought to himself. I knew it from the moment she approached me on the bridge. Righteous, courageous, impetuous, and purely innocent. Likely she's Blazingame's equal in all the things that truly matter.

Try as he might, Doughtry could not hear the conversation occurring behind the antechamber door. He lingered very near it, shuffled about, took two steps this way, then three that, leaned precariously to the right, circled, leaned to the left. But no matter what position he assumed, nothing but murmurs reached his ears.

Drat Elliot for closing the door behind him! Doughtry stuffed his hands deep into the pockets of his newfangled trousers and contemplated the checkered pattern of the vestibule floor. Truly, there was no other way. He would be forced to press one ear or the other against the oak. He'd not hear a word of what was going forward if he didn't. He must swallow his pride and do it. Lord Blazingame's peers already considered Lord Blazingame eccentric. Should anything at all scandalous come of this unique visit, Lord Blazingame might be ostracized from society altogether. At the very least his lordship would take a hearty ribbing for it and the other gentlemen would snicker behind their hands for months whenever he entered a room. Doughtry could not bear the thought. He must learn what was going on and take the offensive at once in order to protect his lordship's reputation. He must and he would.

Though it defied his very nature, Doughtry inched closer and closer to the door until, at last, his right ear came in contact with the wood. He flinched at the chill of it. Never in all his days had he done such a thing. But he would do this and more for Lord Blazingame. Lay down his life, he would, if it ever came to that. He had not escorted that tiny, sad-eyed orphan across half a continent, borne the stomach-churning currents of a February crossing, and knocked imperatively on a perfect stranger's door all those years ago to see Lord Blazingame grow up into a jest, a fool, or an object of derision. Though he could do nothing at all about the manner in which his lordship chose to present himself in public, by gawd, he could do something about this young female and Elliot! Whoever this Elliot was—and he was *not* a valet—Doughtry would see to it that the man's machinations did not in any way affect his lordship. Not in any way.

"I should very much appreciate your speaking to Lord Blazingame on my behalf," Doughtry heard Elliot say. "Not about my contemplating suicide, Miss Feebes, because I assure you, I would never take my own life. Never. But if you were to have a word with him about . . ."

Doughtry came close to leaping straight up into the air as the knocker sounded against the front door. His heart rattled against his ribs. His ear parted company with the door at once. Suicide? he thought, stepping toward the entrance. Elliot? The knocker sounded again. Doughtry took the latch in hand, tipped it upward, tugged the heavy door inward. He stood straight as a lamppost, his eyes alight as they shone down his nose at the two women who stood on the threshold before him. They had the most determined looks on their faces, as if they expected to be told to scat. Though why they should expect such treatment at his hands, Doughtry could not fathom, for they were both of them quite respectable-looking and of an age that could never bring comment to anyone's lips whether the door they knocked upon belonged to a bachelor or not. Not at all young and eligible ladies like Miss Feebes. Neither of them.

"May I be of service, madams?" Doughtry queried with a slight bow, thinking perhaps they were seeking some other establishment in the square and had forgotten the direction.

"Yes," began the elder of the two. "We should like to know if this is the residence of the Earl of Blazingame."

"Yes, madam, it is." She was a fine-looking woman for her years, which Doughtry guessed to be somewhere in the early fifties, and her bit of a smile called to him in the most unnerving manner. He was merely fifty-seven, after all. Not so old as to be beyond appreciating a lovely smile or a fine figure when he saw one. "His lordship, however, is not at home at this time. Is there something I may do for you?" he queried.

"Indeed, I believe you may," said the younger of the two.

Late thirties, perhaps forty, Doughtry guessed. And she, too, was comely.

"We've not actually come to speak to his lordship," the younger woman continued. "We've come to speak with his valet."

"Madam?" Doughtry could not believe his ears. Surely his ears were hallucinating. This could not possibly be happening again. Who the deuce was Elliot, and what the devil had he done?

"Mr. Elliot does valet for Lord Blazingame, does he not?" asked the younger of the two.

"Yes, madam."

"Good," said the elder. "Will you please tell Mr. Elliot that Miss Markum and Lady Miranda Wesley require his presence?"

"No, no, don't say that," protested the younger lady. "Say merely that someone wishes a word with him."

"Really, Miranda, Mr. Elliot will not run out the back

door if Mr.—Mr.—" Miss Markum glanced up at Doughtry with a fetching tilt of her head.

"Doughtry," the butler supplied at once, his voice beginning low and ending in a high squeak that would have signaled to Blazingame at once that the old fellow's nerves were decidedly on edge.

"Mr. Elliot will not run out the back door if Mr. Doughtry merely states that we are standing at the front. Mr. Elliot is a gentleman."

"Yes, but he is not in the least expecting us, Ariel. And you know how he feels about— May we step inside, please, Doughtry? I cannot think it quite the thing for the neighbors to see us standing about so indecisively on your doorstep."

"Indeed, your ladyship," Doughtry managed, discomposed though he was at the very idea that a true lady now wished to speak to Elliot. But then, he thought, perhaps she's not a true lady. Perhaps she merely says she is and it's all a game of sorts. He stood aside as the two entered the vestibule and studied them thoroughly. No, no game. The younger of the two was indeed a lady born and bred. Anyone could tell from the mere sight of her. And her companion was gently bred as well. No doubt of that, either.

"Mr. Elliot is—he is—in conversation with someone at the moment," Doughtry began. And then the antechamber door opened and Miss Feebes stepped out into the vestibule followed closely by her brother and Elliot.

Miranda looked toward them and felt her cheeks flush with pleasure. "Josiah!" she exclaimed. Her feet longed to carry her directly into his embrace, but she forbade them to do so, quite aware of what an embarrassment that would prove to everyone present.

"Miranda?" Elliot all but swallowed her name and came near to choking on it.

"I must speak with you," Miranda said in as authoritative a voice as possible. "It is quite urgent."

"C-come in, then," Elliot offered, still holding open the

door to the antechamber. "You will forgive me, Miss Feebes, Mr. Feebes, but— No, not at all the thing," he interrupted himself, his hand on the knob. "Best to introduce the lot of you first, I expect. Lady Miranda Wesley, Miss Markum, Mr. and Miss Feebes. Mr. and Miss Feebes are just now leaving."

"And we are just now coming," said Miranda softly. She nodded to the brother and sister, then stepped around them, took Elliot's arm and shoved him gently back into the antechamber. "Do look to everyone's comfort, won't you, Ariel?" she said over her shoulder. "I daresay Mr. and Miss Feebes would like some tea before they go. Have you tea, Doughtry? If you'll have whoever is in charge of your kitchen make some, Ariel will be pleased to pour out."

No sooner did she enter the antechamber and the door close behind them but Miranda took both Elliot's hands into her own, raised them, and held them tenderly against her cheeks. Then she stared up at him in perfect happiness. She had planned what to say to him at this moment—carefully and with great forethought—but the words escaped her in a small puff of air as she tumbled through the amazing portals of his eyes into his very soul. There was nothing to say, nothing to do. This instant was all. Everything.

The room, the house, the square, the entire city of London disappeared from Elliot's mind as her gaze held his. He felt himself spinning away to another place, another time, another life. It was a place he had known, had loved, and had left behind. It was a time he yet anticipated. And it was a life he had lived once and hoped to live again.

"What are you doing in London?" he asked at last, struggling back from his dreams. "You cannot be here, you know, Miranda. Here, at this house, I mean. If any of the neighbors should take note—if word should reach your brother—if someone you know should discover— Oh, by gawd, Miranda," he said hoarsely, interrupting his stumbling monologue, "I thought I would die from the lack of you all these months!" His arms encircled her. His head lowered. He kissed her softly, tenderly, as though her lips were fragile china and the least pressure might shatter them. She stood on tiptoe, placed her arms around his neck and kissed him back, ardently, fervently, passionately.

"By the stars above, Miranda," Elliot murmured, halting the kiss but keeping his lips so close to hers that a bit of straw would not have fit between them. "By every god the ancients ever thought of, I never expected you to come to London, much less to this establishment. I have been near mad for the sight of you, for the feel of you in my arms, for the touch of your lips on mine. There are times I can do nothing but stand and stare and think of you. I thank God that you're here."

"Do you? And to think I feared to tell you I was coming."

"But you cannot stay, Miranda. And when you leave this house, when I can finally force myself to let you go, you must not think to return here. The chance of scandal is too great. Blazingame will not be able to protect us."

"Blazingame? That child? I do not expect him to protect us."

"No, no, he's not a child, Miranda. He's twenty-three or so, I should think."

"That elderly?" Miranda could not help but smile. She smiled so sweetly, her lips a mere speck of a space from his, that he had to smile himself. Then she turned in the circle of his arms and rested against him, the top of her head barely reaching his breastbone, her hands huddling inside his own, every inch of her touching him, engulfed by him. "You need not worry about Lord Blazingame or my brother, Josiah. Or anyone else for that matter. I have merely decided to visit The Graces for a time," she said quietly. "We have rented a house, Ariel and Early and I, in Portman Square, and we plan to remain for the Season. My niece, Sophia, is making her come out, you see. A perfect excuse for a maiden aunt to return to London."

As much as he wished to protest against her visiting the city under false pretenses for his sake, he found he could not. He rested his chin on the top of her head and sighed. "Portman Square is very near."

"The nearest I could find. I intend to keep you in my sight, Josiah Daniel Elliot, and within my reach as well. I could not bear Yorkshire without you for another day."

"I think I cannot bear London without you every waking moment, but until now I found I must and so I did. You cannot come here again, Miranda. Truly you cannot. You will make yourself the talk of the town. Your brother will get word of it and storm these portals. And what will I say when he demands to know the truth?"

"You will say very nicely that though you are a valet and I am the sister of a duke, you do not hold my rank against me. That you have every intention to provide me an opportunity to rid myself of the onerous title I wish to abandon. And that you intend to make me the plain but distinguished Mrs. Josiah Elliot."

"Miranda, I couldn't."

"Well, it's a good deal better than telling him you're a highwayman and intend to carry me away across your saddle bow."

"I'm not a highwayman anymore."

"No, you're not. And a good thing, too, because you weren't very good at that particular occupation, dear one."

"Rotten."

"Just so." She released herself from his embrace, then turned back to face him, taking his hands into her own again. "You do still love me, Josiah? You do still wish to marry me?"

"Yes."

"You haven't lost your heart to someone else? Miss Feebes, for instance?"

"I don't think so." Elliot grinned down at her, his face growing younger and more enticing with each passing moment. "No, no, I'm certain of it. Miss Feebes shall never have my heart. How can I give it to her or to anyone when you own it so completely that it will not beat without it whispers your name?"

# THREE

"I cannot believe you did that, Miranda. Such audacity! Such high-handedness! I thought the poor butler would sputter himself to death. To invite perfect strangers to tea in someone else's house!" Miss Markum was quite determined to keep a responsible, disapproving frown on her face, but a bit of a smile kept twitching at the corners of her mouth as the two strolled along the sun-bright pavement back toward Portman Square. They paused for a moment at the junction of Berkeley and Baker streets and waited for the sweep to clear the way before they crossed. Miranda took a guinea from her reticule and pressed it into the sweep's hand as they passed him by. The sweep's eyes grew large as he noted the flash of gold.

"I be thankin' ye, yer highness, wif all me 'eart," he exclaimed in a hoarse whisper of amazement.

"Miranda! A guinea?" Miss Markum's frown faded completely and her dark eyes sparkled with glee. "Oh, but you've just fed that man's family for a year. Did things go so very well, then, with Mr. Elliot?"

"Very well, indeed. I am never to seek him out at Lord Blazingame's residence again, Ariel. I am not to be seen speaking to him in public or to glance in his direction if we should happen to pass each other in the street. Nor am I to gaze at him longingly from afar, or send messages around to the back door of Lord Blazingame's establishment in an effort to arrange a tryst."

"No! He never forbid you all those things. I don't believe a word of it."

"Nor should you," declared Miranda, slipping her arm companionably through Miss Markum's. "I'm giddy, is all. I have tasted the sweet nectar of Josiah's lips and it has fermented and gone to my head. He did attempt to say some of those things, but I put a stop to it at once. He is so maddeningly wonderful, Ariel! I was beginning to think that I'd imagined him to be something he is not, or that I'd dreamed him altogether. But he is neither dream nor imagining. He is precisely the proud, kind, loving gentleman who left me standing amidst the lavender all those months ago with the taste of him lingering on my lips and his image boldly engraved on my heart."

Miss Markum could not keep the look of happiness from her face or the gleam of triumph from her eyes as they strolled into Portman Square arm in arm. At last, she thought, pure joy surging through her. Oh, at long last Miranda has found true love!

Ariel had almost given up, almost conceded that Lady Miranda—to whom she had stood in the position of governess and with whom she now shared a partnership in Lucy Lavender Enterprises—Ariel had *almost* conceded that Lady Miranda would never find a gentleman capable of winning her heart. But she had *not* conceded the point, had clung relentlessly to the hope that love would find this most extraordinary woman, and it had. It had! Miss Markum's feet hesitated on the pavement, bringing both ladies to a sudden halt.

"Ariel, what is it? Oh, I have been walking much too energetically. I did not stop to think."

"Think what? That I cannot keep pace with you? Of all things, Miranda. I am not as elderly as that. No. It—I—Miranda, what on earth has Mr. Elliot to do with Miss Feebes?

Not that she does not seem an admirable young woman. I found her quite fascinating, actually. She reminds me a good deal of you in some ways. But it was quite obvious that she came to that house expressly to see your Mr. Elliot. They were closeted away together behind a closed door even as we arrived, he and she and Mr. Feebes."

"I thought Miss Feebes quite pretty and Mr. Feebes most handsome," inserted Miranda, giving Miss Markum's arm a playful squeeze. "Are you imagining, Ariel, that I might have cause to be jealous of Miss Feebes because she required time with Josiah?"

"No, of course not. It is merely that I can't think what can be the basis of her relationship with him."

"To tell the truth, neither could I," grinned Miranda, "so I asked Josiah straight out."

"You didn't?"

"I did."

"And?"

Miranda began to stroll along the walk again, taking Ariel with her. "Miss Feebes and her brother appeared on Westminster Bridge last evening prepared to rescue Josiah from despair and prevent his leaping into the Thames."

Miss Markum stared at Miranda dumbfounded and almost tripped over a crack in the pavement.

"Oops! Do be careful Ariel. At any rate, Miss Feebes came today to discover for herself whether Josiah was all right and to take a stand for him against the evil Lord Blazingame."

"Mr. Elliot? Our Mr. Elliot? Despair? Suicide? The *evil* Lord Blazingame? Miranda, what has been going on here in London while we've been frittering away our time at Lavender Hill?"

"Now he is *our* Mr. Elliot, is he?" laughed Miranda. "Well, and I think he is—yours and mine, Daxonbury's and Dessie's and we must not forget Elizabeth's. He belongs to Lord Hartshorn's Elizabeth as well, even if she is merely a dog. And soon, if I'm not mistaken, Miss Feebes will come to think of him as her Mr. Elliot as well. He has plans for Miss Feebes, Josiah has."

"Plans? For Miss Feebes? What on earth? Has she something to do with Mr. Elliot's family? Does she know something about his brother's disappearance?"

"No," grinned Miranda. "It simply occurred to Josiah, sometime during their conversation on the bridge last evening—and again today, I might add—that Miss Feebes is just the young woman to bring love into Lord Blazingame's life. It is quite like Daxonbury with Whethers and Early— only give a lonely man someone to love and poof! You've turned him into a matchmaker. Oh, Ariel, Josiah says that he is so happy being in love with me that he finds himself wishing every gentleman of his acquaintance could have the same sort of love and could feel the same joy!"

"What a remarkable thing for him to say," observed Miss Markham with considerable delight. "I do think you ought to keep him, Miranda, no matter what."

"You know very well I intend to do just that. Ah, and here we are home again. Do you know, Ariel, cherubs cavorting about the vestibule ceiling may not be just the thing, but I find I like them very much more now than I did at first. My nephew managed quite nicely for us. It is less than a ten-minute stroll from this house to Lord Blazingame's. Oh, dear. Now that I think on it, I ought to have given Josiah our exact direction. Portman Square, I told him, as if there were but one establishment here. What a ninny I am! And all because when I'm with him, my wits go flying off into some netherworld and I cannot think about anything or anyone but him."

Adolphus Gloom rarely entered his office, which consisted of two rooms above a florist shop in Oxford Street. But when he did, as he did today, every precariously balanced stack of volumes, newspapers, briefs and files trembled, slid, slumped and tumbled to the floor. "Drat!" Gloom exclaimed as the last of his paper towers collapsed. "Drat and bang! As if I'm not far enough behind on everything!" So saying, the solicitor dropped to his knees and began to sift through the scattered remains of his stacks in search of the particular papers he could not do without. "You're here somewhere, you beastly things. I sent Will to deposit you on my desk this very morning. Will! Will, where are you? Don't tell me you've gone to fetch a meat pie. I don't want to hear anything at all about food. It's all you ever do—eat, eat, eat!"

The infamous eater of meat pies and other nonspecified foods, who had been sitting quietly behind his own desk in the first of the two rooms when Gloom had rushed right past him without so much as a glance in his direction, rose from his chair, stepped across the uncarpeted floor and peered cautiously around the door frame. It was a sight, Mr. Adolphus Gloom, his chubby body encased in a puce morning coat and buff pantaloons, scrabbling about on hands and knees with his wide posterior rising toward the ceiling and his Roman nose sniffing at the floor. It was a sight indeed, and his clerk of eight long years had never grown accustomed to it. Will gulped down a guffaw, sneezed away a snicker and, schooling his features into a studious and interested scowl, entered his employer's office.

"What is it you require, Mr. Gloom?" he asked, lowering himself to the floor beside the solicitor.

"Oh, you *are* here, are you? Fancy that! It's those copies of the title and the bill of sale for Number Twelve, Portman Square that I procured from Asserby. I gave them to you this morning. Remember doing it. Outside the baker's shop. You were nibbling at some gingerbread. Got to have them, Will. Got to have them now. Blazingame awaits me at the Hen and Hunt even as we speak."

"Allow me to search for them," Will offered. "Please,

Mr. Gloom. You cannot see all that well even with your spectacles on. You'll scrape the tip of your nose like you did the last time you attempted to decipher what's on the papers without picking them up off the floor."

"No, no, I won't. No time to pick them up and sort them out. I'll be more careful this time. I cannot lose Blazingame, Will. *We* cannot lose Blazingame. He's our bread and butter, my boy. Our bread and butter!"

Just so, thought Will as he began to sort through and stack the papers nearest his knees. Without Lord Blazingame's patronage we'd likely starve to death. Did his lordship not keep Mr. Gloom adequately occupied and send along a friend now and then besides, we'd be forced to steal Mrs. Barley's flowers from below and cook them up in a pot for our dinner.

Blazingame hesitated outside the Hen and Hunt. He was too early for their appointment and he could depend on Gloom to be late. Gloom was forever late. *And I'm not at all inclined to spend an hour or so inside an ill-lighted coffee house, hidden from the world behind soot-covered windows,* Blazingame thought, staring at the place. *I'll wait out here in the sunlight instead. Turning out to be a glorious day.*

Gloom has actually procured copies of the title and the bill of sale for Nathaniel Elliot's house, he thought to himself, a smile touching his lips as he rested his shoulders against the brick wall of the coffee house. It's a veritable giant step in discovering the whereabouts of Elliot's brother. They will give us a date when Nathaniel Elliot was definitely alive and in London to sign them. Not that he isn't alive now, Blazingame added, perturbed with himself. There's no reason to assume he's dead. He's disappeared merely. Elliot's sister-in-law is dead, but Elliot already knew that when he came to me.

Blazingame's smile faded and a vertical line appeared just

above his nose as he began to ponder Nathaniel Elliot's fate. He'd thought, when first he'd taken on this puzzle, that the mystery would be easily solved. After all, according to Elliot, the family had been wealthy for centuries. Not ostentatiously wealthy, perhaps, but from what Elliot had confided in him about his childhood, they'd always been most comfortable. He'd thought then that he would simply go to the Elliot family's solicitor and request Nathaniel Elliot's new direction. Certainly a man who had investments and dealt with a number of companies, banks, and trusts would not—for any reason—move and forget to tell his solicitor. That Elliot had not thought of such an easy solution himself had amazed him. Then Elliot had informed him that the family solicitor had died in the winter of 1808 and no one seemed to know whom Nathaniel had hired to replace the gentleman.

But Gloom has discovered this title and bill of sale in Asserby's possession, Blazingame thought. So it's likely that it was Asserby whom Nathaniel Elliot hired to replace his old solicitor. And yet—and yet—Gloom says not. He says Asserby denies any knowledge of the man.

Blazingame sighed. After months of subtle investigation he'd discovered next to nothing. He had ingratiated himself, by means of his friends and his title, into almost every household where the Elliot family might have been known or welcomed. He'd sought out, too, people whose names Elliot recalled at the East India Company, at Sotheby's, at Lloyds. But no one had been of the least help. Yes, they had known the family. Yes, Nathaniel had been a fine, upstanding fellow. And, if they remembered correctly, Nathaniel's younger brother had joined the cavalry—the hussars, the dragoons, one or the other of them.

A goodly number of his friends and neighbors recalled with a touch of fondness that Nathaniel had married somewhat late in life. Married a decidedly younger woman. And hadn't it been sad that she'd died before him in spite of their ages. Died and left him with two boys to raise. He'd taken her death so very hard. They all seemed to have noticed that. Apparently Nathaniel Elliot had withdrawn from his friends and from society at large to such a degree during that year of mourning his wife that he'd seemed to disappear altogether. And then one day he did disappear. He and his boys had gone off somewhere and the house stood empty.

There'd been no hope of tracing the family through the boys. From what Blazingame had learned, the boys had never been to school. Elliot had been able to employ the best of tutors, a gentleman by the name of Michael Goingsworth, who, like the rest of Elliot's staff, had been dismissed shortly after the wife's death and now had no idea where his former charges might be.

"But I've a definite place to begin at last," Blazingame said conversationally to a sparrow pecking away at a piece of offal near the curb. "I know the house was sold and to whom, and shortly, I will know when. I can begin anew from there."

The sparrow ceased his feasting and cocked his head questioningly in Blazingame's direction. It hopped toward him and cocked its head to the other side.

"Never mind," Blazingame smiled. "It's all to do with people. I don't expect a bird to understand."

"I beg your pardon?" said a voice to Blazingame's right.

Blazingame turned in that direction at once. "What?"

"You spoke to me," replied the stranger, "but I did not quite understand what it was you said."

"No, no, I was merely thinking aloud." Blazingame gave the young man a cursory look, and then his eyes were drawn to the young woman beside the gentleman. He removed the hat he'd set so rakishly on his curls earlier and bowed quite properly. "Blazingame," he said. "Y'r servant, ma'am."

"Blazingame? Well, can you beat that?" exclaimed the gentleman, extending his hand at once. "I'm Donovan Feebes, Newcombe's nephew."

"How do you do, Mr. Feebes. Pleasure to make your acquaintance," Blazingame replied, taking the proffered hand and giving it a hearty shake.

"And this is my sister," Feebes continued.

"A pleasure, Miss Feebes," Blazingame said, his eyes altering from impenetrable jade to clear, sparkling emerald as he faced her fully. This is the young woman Elliot thought *might* be pretty? he wondered. Great heavens, was it a starless, moonless midnight on Westminster Bridge?

"Lord Blazingame." Eleanor returned his greeting with a curt nod. "I have been longing to make your acquaintance."

"You have?" asked Blazingame, surprised.

"Indeed. I wish to speak with you about your valet."

"Elliot?"

"Yes, Mr. Elliot. Do you know, Lord Blazingame, how deeply troubled your Mr. Elliot is? Or are you so consumed with yourself and your position in society that you've not a moment to spare for the welfare of your staff?"

"Nora," hissed Feebes.

"Do not 'Nora' me, Donovan. If you believed even one word of what Mr. Elliot said to us in that antechamber, the more fool you. He is a desperate man, your valet," she added, glaring at Blazingame. "Desperate and despondent. And last night he came very close to taking his own life. And he is ill, as well. He will not admit to it, of course. Likely he fears that you'll dismiss him on the instant and send him off without a reference should you discover that he's ill."

Blazingame's eyes grew round with wonder. He stared at her, his lips parted, his hands clasped tightly behind his back.

"Nora," Feebes said again, noting the sudden stiffening of Blazingame's spine.

"For goodness' sake, Donovan, don't tell me you're frightened of this—this—dandy. You cannot be so weak in your principles as to allow fashionable clothes and a title to keep you from saying what is true. Mama would be so disappointed."

"But, Nora—"

"And Uncle Roger would be disappointed, too."

"No, he would not," protested Feebes, "because I'm not afraid to say the truth to anyone. But, Nora, this isn't the time or the place to do it."

"I daresay it is. Is it not the very time and place that Fate has brought us face-to-face with this villain?"

Blazingame's spine stiffened even more.

"She doesn't actually mean you're a villain," Feebes offered at once.

"Yes, I do. To send a poor, sickly gentleman off without a reference, and when he is already wallowing in despair, is more than villainous. It is—it is—dastardly!"

"But, Nora, he hasn't once said a thing about turning Mr. Elliot off. It was you said that."

"I know how spoiled, fancy dandies think," Eleanor replied, fixing Blazingame as firmly in place with her stare as a collector fixed a bug with a pin.

Blazingame squirmed. His mind filled with the sight, the sound, the scent of her. She smelled of sunshine and lilacs. Her voice was low and breathy with a bit of a flutter to it. And she was beautiful. Absolutely beautiful! Tendrils of dark brown curls escaped from beneath the brim of her straw hat to caress her cheeks and brow. Her brown eyes flashed with passion. Her cheeks burned with righteousness. And her lips tempted him even as they condemned him.

"You're courting the Duke of Comestock's sister?" Doughtry's hand went to his heart, his knees buckled, and he sat down with a smack on the hard horsehair sofa in his tiny sitting room which connected conveniently to the butler's pantry.

"Well, I'm not courting her, precisely, Doughtry," Elliot said, taking the chair directly across from the man and leaning solicitously forward. "But I am determined to marry her. Are you all right?"

"No," sighed the butler. "My heart has stopped beating. He'll kill you, the Duke of Comestock. A valet so audacious as to court his sister? He'll walk in through our front door and throttle you to death and no one will do a thing about it. I shall be forced to drag your cold, stiff body out into the gutter lest Lord Blazingame suffer the scandal of a murder in his own establishment. Run down by a coach, that's what I shall say to protect my lordship. I will say that you were arriving home when a runaway gig knocked you into Hades."

"I ought not have told you the truth of things."

"Yes, yes, you ought. I have never spent such an upsetting day in all my life—not even the day you came near to slit my lordship's throat. A veritable profusion of ladies traipsing in and out of this establishment, sequestering themselves with you in an antechamber, ordering up tea!"

Elliot sighed. One hand came up to rub at the back of his neck. He gave himself a small shake and looked up to meet Doughtry's gaze with what he hoped was a confident gaze of his own. "There's nothing in it to fear, Doughtry. I promise you. Blazingame has merely set himself the task of discovering the whereabouts of my brother and his boys. I know my sister-in-law is dead and buried. I saw the letter Nathaniel wrote to our stepsister, Lily. I saw Meg's grave in St. Martin's in the Fields. But her grave was all I could find of the four of them. My brother has gone missing. My nephews have disappeared. And I cannot go seeking them on my own. Not in the elegant establishments, or among the bankers and the financiers at least. An earl, on the other hand, can enter establishments and speak to people in the most brazen manner. He can poke about in their minds, request them to recall the oddest things, and not be blinked at twice—especially Lord Blazingame, who has a considerable reputation for having an odd kick to his gallop.

"And while he seeks word of Nat among the wealthy, I've been searching among the shopkeepers and the laborers and the pickpockets. The nights I depart this house after Blazingame, Doughtry, are nights I spend among persons of the middle classes and the lower classes, searching for Nat wherever I can."

"I did not know," Doughtry said quietly.

"Of course you didn't. And I don't blame you for suspecting me of being someone I'm not, because at the moment I *am* someone I'm not. But once we find Nat and the boys, I'll be proved a born gentleman at least. I may not be a member of the peerage, but my birthright is not to be sneezed at. I'm third cousin once removed to Lord Marley, though he detests me and so would never speak for me to Comestock. And I am tied by blood to the Villiers."

"The Villiers?" gasped Doughtry. "Great heavens!"

"Yes, well, I shouldn't like them to hear of it, though."

"Whyever not? The Villiers are—"

"Rich as Croesus. I know, Doughtry. But our kinship began illegitimately and in secret and that particular secret we've kept from them for centuries. I'm not about to be the one to reveal it now. At any rate, once we locate Nat and the boys and the family Bible with the baptismal records in it—they date all the way back to the sixteen hundreds, Doughtry—Comestock will not think me quite so uppity to request Miranda's hand in marriage."

"He will toss you out on your ear, regardless," Doughtry said succinctly. He could not comprehend how any man short of an earl—and an obscenely rich one at that—could consider himself eligible to marry a duke's sister.

"No. Do you think? On my ear?"

"Without hesitation."

Elliot grinned. "I should like to see him try."

"He will," said Doughtry with confidence.

"Do you know, before I joined up, Doughtry, it seemed the most commonplace thing to be me. I never once thought to be required to prove to anyone that I was who I said I was. But then, I was merely a lad of fifteen and a total innocent. There's no one from my youth in London even recognizes me now, and no one I recognize either, except Marley. And Marley would as soon shoot me through the heart as look at me."

"You were a soldier?" Doughtry asked. "In the Peninsula?"

"A soldier before the Peninsula was ever thought of, but I was there as well. Would be there still if I had not been injured and mustered out."

"And why was I told none of this? Why was I allowed to wonder and worry about you for months and months?"

"I told Blazingame that we ought to confide in you, but he wouldn't hear of it. Said you were much too old. Said the truth would distress you excessively."

"Old? Too old?"

"Well, you are old, Doughtry, and Blazingame worries about you. He loves you, is the truth of it. Would not have you upset for all the world."

"And he thought hiring *you* as a valet and allowing me to wonder who you really are and what villainy you planned would *not* upset me?"

"I found them," Lady Sophia declared, her black satin jockey cap tilted distractingly down over one lovely blue eye, "and I'm going to keep them."

"Certainly not." The Duke of Comestock frowned in distaste at the grubby boys who stood wearily, one to each side of his daughter. "You don't know where they've been, Sophia, or who they belong to, or what they may have. Lice, for one thing. I should lay odds on that. Fleas for another. And there's likely some putrid sickness sitting on one of their sleeves, waiting patiently to engulf and consume us all. Take them away at once. Back where you got them."

"No, Father, I will not. I'm keeping them."

"CATH-ER-INE," called the duke loudly, breaking his wife's name into three distinct syllables. "CATH-ER-INE!"

"Well, I never," observed Lady Sophia. "Shouting for Mama as though you were some merchant living above a shop. Of all things."

"Of all things," repeated a whispery little voice. Sophia glanced down in surprise. "Who said that?" she asked. "Which one of you?"

"It wasn't me," responded the tallest of the urchins quietly.

"Yes, it was, too," the other accused.

"I beg your pardon, m'dear Jack, but it wasn't. Never said a word, I didn't."

"He lies," the shorter of the two proclaimed, staring up at Sophia with the saddest of sad brown eyes. "He didn't used to lie, but now he does."

"He does?"

"Uh-huh."

"CATH-ER-INE!" the duke called again at the top of his lungs.

"Goodness gracious," replied a voice from the doorway. "What is it, Charles? I could hear you all the way down in the vestibule. Likely people heard you out on the walk as well. What a caterwauler you are. Always were."

"Aunt Miranda!" Sophia turned and launched herself at Lady Miranda with the greatest goodwill. "You never said you intended to come to London. I thought not to see you until August, in Bath! Oh, welcome!" she exclaimed, hugging her aunt into dishevelment. In his chair, the duke groaned quietly.

"I heard that, Charles," Miranda proclaimed, peering around her niece at her brother. "My goodness, who are these young gentlemen?" she added as the two urchins caught her eye.

"This is Jack," Sophia said, leading her aunt by the hand to stand before the boys. "And this is Spinner."

"Don't touch them, Miranda," muttered Comestock. "We don't know where they've been."

"We have been walking all over London," said the shorter of the two.

"You have?" Miranda asked.

"Yes, ma'am," said the taller with a curt nod. "Because we got ourselves lost, y'see."

"You did?" Sophia stared down at them, a bit of disappointment evident on her face. "You didn't tell me that. That you were lost."

"No, ma'am. You didn't give us a chance to do it. And we have not got lice or fleas crawling on us or any putrid sickness sitting on our sleeves either, mister. We're just dirty, is all."

"And hungry," added the smaller one.

"I am not to be addressed as mister!" roared Comestock. "I'm a duke."

"He's a grace." Miranda smiled down at the boys. "You must call him your grace when you speak to him."

"Oh."

"Oh."

Miranda's smile widened. They were rather charming boys, actually—blond-headed and brown-eyed, with faces like angels. "Perhaps Sophie and I can help you find your way home," she suggested. "Do you know your direction?"

"Not precisely," the one named Jack replied.

"He doesn't. I do," declared Spinner.

"Then you had best tell us what it is," Sophia urged, "so we can take you safely home."

"It's Number Twelve, Porter."

"Porter?" asked Sophia. "Where in the world is Porter Street?"

"That's precisely what we should like to know," sighed Jack.

"It's near Newport Market," Comestock offered, leaning forward in his chair to have a closer look at the boys. "You're brothers?"

"Yes, sir. I mean, yes, your grace."

"And your father is?"

"Dead, they say," offered Jack. "Mama, too."

"Miranda!" interrupted a voice from the doorway. "Oh, my dear, what a marvelous surprise! Have you come for the Season? Do say you've come for the Season! Is Miss Markum not with you?"

Her grace, the Duchess of Comestock, held her arms out to Miranda, who dutifully crossed the carpeting and walked into them. "Yes, I've come to see Sophie launched," Miranda said, kissing her sister-in-law's cheek. "Ariel is resting."

"Resting? You did not leave her in your coach, Miranda?"

"No, Catherine. We've rented an establishment. Ariel is there with her feet up on a footstool, enjoying the pleasant afternoon sunlight."

"But we have enough room right here to house an army. You needn't have gone to the expense of—"

"I wished to do so."

"Oh."

"Don't say 'oh' in such a voice, Catherine. It is merely my independence again. Surely you've grown accustomed to that by now. Besides, you know that if I were to actually live in this household for more than a week or two, Charles and I would be at each other's throats."

"Who's Charles?" whispered a tiny voice.

"That grace," came the hushed reply, and a grubby finger pointed directly at Comestock.

In a flurry of silk and muslin, with a giggle here and a whisper there and a dimple betraying itself in her grace's cheek, the three ladies settled themselves in Lady Miranda's coach and her grace ordered the driver to be off with a clunk of the handle of her parasol against the hatch. On the rear-facing seat across from the ladies, Jack and Spinner sat, one in each corner, peering out the windows.

"I cannot think why you brought them home, Sophia," her grace said, planting the pointed tip of her parasol between her jean half-boots which had been stunningly embroidered to match her dress. "It amazes me your father didn't pick the little beggars up by the scruffs of their necks and toss them out the parlor window."

"It amazes me as well," Miranda agreed. "You were courageous to say the least, Sophie, to bring them right into your father's presence."

"Well, but I didn't know he would be home," Sophia admitted with a quick flash of a smile. "I thought he would be at his club. I merely went to Mr. Willis's in Fish Street Hill to fetch Mama's half-boots, because I did so wish to get out of the house for a bit, and—"

"He does extraordinary work, don't you think, Miranda?" her grace interrupted, poking one of her half-boots forward so that Miranda might see it clearly.

"They're lovely, Catherine."

"At any rate, the footman and I stepped out of the shop," continued Sophia, "to discover these two sitting quite dejectedly on the curb, and I thought to myself what excellent pages they would make. So I took them up at once."

"Without so much as asking them if they wished to accompany you?" Miranda queried.

"She asked did we want something to eat, and we did," offered Spinner, turning his glance from the window for a moment. "And we thank you for it, too," he added, remembering that after all the ruckus The Grace had made in the parlor, the ladies had taken him and his brother down to the kitchen and The Grace's cook had fed them royally.

"You're welcome," Sophia replied with a sweet smile.

"Sophie, you cannot just pick children up out of the gutter and take them home," Miranda scolded lightly.

"I thought them orphaned and homeless, run off from some cruel master or a factory or something. And they would make such delicious pages, Aunt Miranda. Jane Weyland has a page. He's a darling. He serves her just as if he were a grown footman. She takes him everywhere with her. And I thought—I thought how splendid it would be to have two matching pages of my own."

"Matching pages generally—" began the duchess.

"I know they do not match exactly, Mama. Spinner is a bit taller than Jack. But their faces are so alike, and once washed up and dressed in suitable attire—"

"What is suitable attire for pages?" asked Miranda, quite enjoying the thought of the boys as pages herself.

"Livery, of course. Can you not see the two of them, Miranda, in silver and scarlet—"

"With tiny little curled, powdered wigs on their heads," inserted the duchess, her eyes sparkling with laughter.

"No, of course I should not make them wear wigs like the real footmen, Mama."

"Why not?" asked Miranda. "I rather think tiny wigs would be just the thing. Unfortunately, dearest, these particular boys appear to want to go home. You truly ought to have asked them their circumstances before taking them up. Not all poor children are homeless, or unhappily circumstanced, for that matter."

"Nor are they all orphans," added the duchess.

"We're supposed to be orphans," offered Jack, who had not been paying the ladies the least attention because he was busy balancing on his knees with his head stuck out the window. But he did hear the word "orphans" when the coach wobbled, and he lost his balance and came tumbling back inside. "We're supposed to be orphans. But we don't believe it, do we, Spinner? Only that ugly mean man told us Papa was dead. We didn't actually see Papa dead and in the grave."

"You didn't actually see Mama dead and in the grave, either, Jack. You were ill with the fever when she died, and Papa and I thought we were going to lose you, too."

"But you saw her dead and in the grave. I believe you about that, Spinner. You wouldn't lie about a thing like that. But the ugly man would lie about anything, I think."

"What ugly man?" Miranda asked, captivated by the innocence which overrode the tragedy of the conversation.

"An ugly *mean* man," Jack said, clutching the edge of the seat with both hands and taking an extra bounce with each bounce the coach took. "It was he came and got us four whole years ago and sent us to live with Mrs. Dempsey."

"You don't know he sent us there," declared Spinner.

"Yes, I do. I heard the men who took us there talking about it. And he paid Mrs. Dempsey a goodly sum to keep us, too."

"And it is Mrs. Dempsey lives in Porter Street," Sophia concluded logically.

"Un-un," Jack replied. "It's us live in Porter Street. We have run away from Mrs. Dempsey and we're going home."

Porter Street turned out to be precisely where the duke had said it was, very near Newport Market, which, this being a Tuesday, was not open. Lady Miranda's driver brought the coach to a halt immediately before Number 12, and the footman hurried around from the rear to open the coach doors and let down the steps. Spinner jumped out first, followed closely by Jack. The two stood, staring up at what looked to the ladies in the coach to be a shop of some kind, though it bore no sign above the threshold.

"Oh, dear," Miranda murmured, gazing out at the building and the boys. "I don't think this place is quite what they expected."

"No, not at all," Sophia agreed, peering over Miranda's

shoulder. "Perhaps, though, it is a sight better than this Mrs. Dempsey's establishment."

"But who will there be to welcome them?" asked her grace, who was quite certain she had missed an important part of the boys' tale, though she could not think what. "Miranda, what if their father *is* dead? Who will be there to welcome them? Certainly the family had no servants. Not in such a neighborhood as this. Did they? Oh, it is so very confusing when one is forced to attempt to understand the lower classes."

"I daresay there is an uncle or an aunt or someone," Sophia offered quietly.

"Spinner? Jack?" Miranda stepped down onto the cobbles with the footman's aid to stand between the boys. She gazed down at them and placed a comforting hand on each one's shoulder. "Should you like me to go inside with you?"

"No, ma'am," Spinner replied, his voice exceptionally subdued. "I have made a mistake. This isn't our house at all. This is just some old shop."

"We're still l-lost," whispered Jack, gulping back a sob. "We're going to be l-lost forever."

"No, no, you are not," Miranda declared, going down on one knee and gathering the boys into her arms.

"Yes, we are," Spinner replied mournfully. "We have been looking for our house for a whole entire week, and now that we've found it, it ain't our house at all."

# FOUR

Blazingame returned home that afternoon to a butler run slightly mad. The elderly Doughtry took Blazingame's hat and actually tossed it onto one of the antlers decorating the looking glass over the vestibule table. He took Blazingame's gloves and stuffed them, jumbled into a ball, into the table drawer. "Of all things," Doughtry muttered. "Of all things to do."

"What?" asked Blazingame, staring at his disappearing ball of gloves as the drawer closed on them. "What is it, Doughtry? What's happened?"

"Happened?" Doughtry's face attempted composure, but one of his hands went to wander through his soft gray hair and set bits and pieces of it to standing on end. "Nothing, my lord. Nothing at all. What makes you think something has happened?"

Blazingame cocked an eyebrow at Doughtry's cravat, which canted slightly to the left as though the man had yanked at it and then forgotten he'd done so. "I don't know, Doughtry. Perhaps it's the manner in which you disposed of my gloves?"

"The manner in which . . . ?"

"Never mind. Come with me for a moment, eh? I've a need for your advice."

"Now? Now you have need for my advice? You could not ask for my advice when you agreed to take on Mr. Elliot?"

"Is Elliot at home?"

"Oh, yes."

"Good. Fetch him for me, will you? What I have to say involves Elliot. I shall await you both in the rear parlor." Blazingame ascended the staircase and strolled off down the first-floor corridor, his hands in his breeches pockets, whistling the same annoying low note over and over.

Cannot understand why Mr. Wilde insisted on teaching that lad to whistle and then did not bother to teach him a few different notes, Doughtry thought grumpily as he ascended the staircase, bypassing the first-floor landing and making his way to the second floor, where he discovered Elliot busily brushing away at one of his lordship's morning coats. "Our lordship wishes to speak with us in the rear parlor," he said, stepping into the small dressing room.

"He does? What about?"

"I haven't the vaguest idea. And it's not your position to ask the question, Mr. Elliot. As long as you are being our lordship's valet, you do not ask questions. You respond at once. Certainly Mr. Whethers taught you that."

"No, not actually. He didn't teach me much at all, Doughtry. Just a bit of this and a bit of that. We hadn't much time."

"No, well, I shall do my best to help you, Mr. Elliot, now that I know the truth of things. And I shall pray for you every morning and every night."

"Pray for me, Doughtry?"

"Yes. Pray that you'll not find it necessary to remain a valet much longer. Have you thought what you will do once our lordship finds your brother?"

"Do you mean before or after I marry Lady Miranda?" Elliot tossed the brush aside and placed Blazingame's coat carefully back into the armoire. "I was a considerably wealthy lad when I took to soldiering, Doughtry. Perhaps I'm wealthy yet. Nathaniel always used to write me that our investments were doing well. But then he ceased to write, of course, and changed solicitors, so I've no idea whether they've made me rich as Croesus or poor as some chimney sweep's climbing boy. But I've one investment that will save me from the poorhouse. Made it myself. Invested in Lucy Lavender Enterprises."

"The ones who make the pillows?"

"Precisely."

"Well, you'll not starve, then. Wonderful pillows. Cure the headache."

"Yes, I know. Once the investment starts to pay, I rather think I shall give up being a valet. That'll please you no end."

"Please the Duke of Comestock, too, if he don't kill you before it happens."

"Wait a moment, Doughtry. Don't run off ahead of me."

Doughtry, who had already exited the chamber and started toward the staircase, came to a halt and turned back to face Elliot, whose long strides closed the distance between them rapidly. "If you will allow me," Elliot said, and reached to straighten Doughtry's cravat. "There, that's better. And your hair is a bit mussed. You might try smoothing it down a bit. Yes. Now we're set."

Doughtry's eyes widened considerably as he entered the rear parlor and discovered Blazingame just replacing the top of the brandy decanter. There were three glasses poured and standing on the sideboard. The earl picked up two of them and walked forward. "Do sit down, gentlemen, please," he said, urging the men toward two of a trio of chairs moved from their original positions into a cozy conversational grouping.

"We could not possibly," declared Doughtry. "Have you gone mad, my lord? I am your butler and Mr. Elliot is your valet."

"I do recall something of the sort, Doughtry. Do get off your high horse and sit down and drink with me while we talk."

"Never! You were not raised in a stable, my lord. You

know perfectly well such things are not done. To treat us as though we are your equals! And for us to allow you to do so! Never!"

"I rather think we should," Elliot said quietly in Doughtry's ear.

"You would think that," hissed Doughtry. "You know nothing about being a servant. Nothing."

"No, but I know something about being a man," Elliot persisted. "And that particular man before us is distraught for some reason. Only look at how pale he is, Doughtry. He's in need of a friend or two at the moment. I rather think we have a duty to provide him our friendship. And if that involves sitting down in his presence and sharing a glass of brandy with him, then I think we ought to do it."

Doughtry studied his employer for a moment, then accepted the glass of brandy from his hand and perched on the outermost edge of one of the chairs. Elliot took the other glass and the chair beside Doughtry's. Blazingame returned to the sideboard, took his own glass into hand, and settled himself comfortably into the third.

"I have the most disturbing news," the earl said after a moment or two. "It's about your brother's house, Elliot."

"That will be the brother who disappeared," murmured Doughtry.

"Precisely. Doughtry? You know about Elliot's brother?"

"Explained it all to him this afternoon, Blazingame."

"You did? I thought we had agreed— Well, never mind what I thought. I have changed my mind about it. I want Doughtry to know everything. Because the thing is, Elliot, that I saw the documents and—and—"

"And what?"

"Your brother didn't sell the house to Marley. Marley purchased the title to the house from the Duke of Berinwick."

"The Duke of Berin—" Elliot's mouth snapped closed in the midst of uttering the name.

"That blackguard? How on earth did he come into possession of your brother's property, Elliot?" Doughtry asked, flabbergasted. "The Duke of Berinwick. M'gawd!"

"And there's something else," murmured Blazingame. "I haven't mentioned it. Didn't wish to alarm either of you until I was certain. Noticed last evening when I returned from the club with Wilde."

"What?" asked Elliot and Doughtry together.

"Looking out the parlor window, I was. Wondering whether you were lying dead in some gutter in St. Giles, Elliot, when I saw a fellow across the way, huddled out of the rain against the side of Crawford's establishment. Couldn't imagine why he should be there—out in the rain like that. And I think I saw the same fellow lingering across the street from the Hen and Hunt, where I met Gloom to inspect the copies of the title and the bill of sale. Left them in Gloom's care, by the way. Thought that'd be best. Difficult to know, though, if it was the same man. One was huddled against the rain in the dark, the other lounging in front of Sheridan's print shop in the sunlight. Still and all, I had no trouble recognizing him the third time I saw him."

"The third time?" Elliot asked.

"Indeed. Stepped into White's Club for an hour or so. Discovered the very same fellow waiting two doors down when I exited. Fell into step behind me, he did, on the way home. But when I stopped and turned to get a good look at him, he hurried into Harrington's haberdashery. I shall need you to be on the lookout for him, Doughtry," Blazingame added. "I'll describe him to you as best I can. No telling but he may come knocking on our door with some excuse or other to gain entrance and I should like you to recognize him and be wary of him if he does."

It was early yet for dinner, but mysterious scents emanating from Mrs. Harriot's kitchen had been teasing Miss Markum from her semi-drowsiness all the afternoon long.

Still, it had taken Miranda's return to lure her from the effects of warm sunlight and a lazy afternoon completely. Now she looked up at Miranda and laughed so heartily that tears came to her eyes.

"It is not as humorous as all that, Ariel," Miranda said, taking a seat on the sofa directly opposite Miss Markum's chair. "I assure you, Charles did not think it humorous at all. He's determined to find the house those boys are searching for before another day is out. If it's not Porter Street, he says, it will be Porter's Block or Portugal or Postern or the other Postern. There are two Posterns, apparently. Or Porridgepot. Though why he thinks a lad would confuse a Porter and a Porridgepot, I can't imagine. And meanwhile, Sophie was having them cleaned and polished and given a room under the eaves to share. She thoroughly intends to make pages of the scamps. And she will, too, does Charles not find either the place they've come from or the place they're bound."

"I rather think his grace might now be in need of one of our pillows," offered Miss Markum gleefully. "Oh, we ought to do it, Miranda. We ought to speak to her grace and convince her to purchase one of our pillows for him. And one for herself, as well. What delicious irony to that."

"Lord Blazingame possesses two of our pillows. Did you take note of it, Ariel? One lay on that chair at the end of the first-floor corridor and the other sat on the window seat in the drawing room. And they cost him a pretty penny, too, Josiah said. Bought them from Relph and Todhunter for an outrageous amount."

"Bless Lord Blazingame," Miss Markum murmured.

"No, no, bless Josiah, because it was he insisted that the pillows would cure Lord Blazingame's headaches."

"Lord Blazingame has headaches?"

"Oh, yes. Especially since he hired Josiah as his valet. That's what Josiah says. I don't believe it's true. But Lord Blazingame does swear by our dried lavender pillows now and has convinced a great number of his friends to purchase them. And his butler has been spreading the word among the servants of other households. We will be forced to hire a number of the Toadscuttle girls to help us sew when we get home. Lucy Lavender is rapidly becoming a darling of the gentlemen, Miranda, as well as the ladies. I knew we would never regret accepting Josiah as a partner."

"You knew nothing of the sort. All you knew, dearest one, was that you were madly in love with the gentleman and he with you. A situation devoutly to be wished, of course, but it had nothing at all to do with business."

"A situation devoutly to be wished?"

"Oh, most certainly. I have been wishing you into someone's arms since you were eighteen years old, you know," smiled Miss Markum. "And though I admit I was growing most impatient, you did find a pair of arms that are perfect for you at last."

"Yes, now I must simply convince him to put those arms around me and keep them there forever."

"He's already convinced he must do precisely that, Miranda. What you ought to do is to attempt to convince him that your brother's wishes have nothing to do with the matter and to still his fears of damaging your reputation. It's his need to prove himself worthy of you that keeps you apart."

"You're correct, of course. But he's a proud man, Josiah Elliot. If I could have convinced him to marry me in Yorkshire, without paying the least heed to Charles's sensibilities or to anyone else's, then we would even now be searching for his brother and his nephews together, as man and wife. But we will search for them together regardless, Ariel. I don't care what subterfuge I must use or how much sneaking about must be done. I will be standing beside Josiah when he finds Nathaniel and the boys. I vow it."

Elliot stood on the front doorstep of Blazingame's establishment looking like nothing more than a gentleman's valet out to get a breath of air now that his gentleman was properly attired for the evening. He often stood for a moment or two on the step for just that reason. Tonight, however, he was gazing about the square with studied nonchalance but with his eyes wide open in search of a stocky fellow of medium height with hair the color of carrots and a moustache to match. His surreptitious search, however, produced only the sight of Ledderley's coachman bringing a carriage around from the mews. Perhaps Blazingame had been mistaken after all. Elliot hoped that he had, for he could think of no other reason for a man to follow Blazingame about other than that the young earl's search for Nathaniel had been noted, at last, by a particular party and had aroused that party's interest to an extraordinary degree.

Above Elliot, a fair number of stars were beginning to sparkle in the darkening sky and a quarter moon glimmered softly among them. His thoughts turned to Miranda when he looked up at the sky. The heady excitement of her visit had settled at last into a soft, comfortable feeling surrounding his heart. And tonight, especially, he needed that comfort. Needed it because Blazingame's news had disturbed him more than he could say.

Berinwick, he thought, distressed. How had the Duke of Berinwick, of all people, come by the title to Nat's house? And why, having gained the thing, would Berinwick sell it to Marley? Marley! Nat would rather die than see that house go to Marley.

"Nathaniel is dead," a small voice whispered at the back of Elliot's mind. "He and Meg and the boys—all dead and gone."

"No," Elliot protested, attempting to shake the annoying thought from between his ears. "I thought that once, but I won't think it anymore."

I've waded through all the despair and self-pity I can abide, he thought. With the war and the trembles and losing everything I thought awaited me on England's shores, I fell into such a melancholy. But I've found reason to hope again.

Miranda has given me reason to hope again. And by gawd, I shall hope! Poor Meg may be dead and gone, but Nat and the boys have simply wandered off somewhere without a word to anyone. And Blazingame and I will find them.

"And once we do," he whispered to the sky, "I'll never let Nathaniel out of my sight again."

Wretched rapscallion, Elliot thought, visions of his elder brother and himself cavorting about the house in Portman Square unexpectedly overtaking him.

"Instigator," he murmured with a smile. "There was nothing you could not convince me to do. You got me into the most outrageous scrapes. Whenever we escaped the school-room, we were a devilish handful. A deucedly devilish handful. I remember the roar that went up when Mama first discovered us sliding— The deuceit!" Elliot exclaimed under his breath. "Jupiter, I haven't thought of it in years! The deuceit!"

"The what?" asked a quiet voice from directly behind him.

Elliot spun about on the instant to discover Blazingame's front door open wide and Miranda smiling at him from a mere two feet away. "You were so lost in your thoughts you did not so much as hear me open the door," she said, studying him from the depths of the hooded cape she wore. "I thought to wait until you had returned to the present, but 'the deuceit'? Who could refrain from comment after such a word as that?"

"Miranda, what are you doing here? How do you come to be exiting Blazingame's establishment? You never passed me going in. I was surely not so lost in thought as all that. You didn't stroll right past me, did you?" Every muscle in Elliot's body wished to reach out to her and take her into his arms, but he restrained himself admirably. The square, after all, was no longer devoid of traffic. Even as they spoke, the Ledderleys were stepping up into their carriage. And across the square, two riders were dismounting before the

Hartnells'. Elliot studied the riders for a moment, but neither had carroty hair or a moustache.

"Ariel and I came through the mews and gained admittance through the kitchen door."

"No."

"Yes."

"Miranda, you can't do such things. You or Miss Markum."

"I beg to differ with you, dear one, but we can and we have."

"Oh, glory, to think of it. I've driven the both of you to entering through kitchen doors like housemaids."

"You have not. We could have sent a footman around with a message, Josiah. I simply did not wish to do that. I wanted to come and invite you to dinner myself. But Ariel would not hear of my coming alone, so we both donned cottage capes and came to the kitchen door. And Doughtry let us in directly he recognized us. He is rather sweet, your Doughtry. And he cooks, Josiah."

"Yes, well, Blazingame is rarely home to dinner, so he hasn't bothered to hire a chef. Doughtry cooks only for himself and me most of the time."

"And the maids and the footmen?"

"There are no maids or footmen," Elliot replied with a soft smile, brushing a tendril of hair from her cheek with the side of his hand. "No maids who live in, I mean to say. They come only twice a week and are gone by six. But truly, no footmen at all. Only two grooms who live above the stables and generally dine at a place called the Hook and Anchor. Not especially fond of Doughtry's cooking, the grooms."

His touch had sent a distinct tingling through Miranda, and she put her fingers to her cheek where his hand had been. She thought she could still feel the heat of his touch lingering there. "This is truly a bachelor's establishment," she managed on a breath shaky with suppressed emotion. "Ariel and I were wise to come as we did. We certainly would have raised some comment among Lord Blazingame's neighbors else, two ladies coming to visit him at this time in the evening."

"You ought not to have come at all."

"Yes, I ought. Dax rented the house in Portman Square for me precisely because it is close enough that I *can* come to see you. No c-carriage needed. A-a simple walk merely."

The slight catch in her voice proved more painful to Elliot than a fist jabbed forcefully into his midsection. What the devil is wrong with me? he wondered, his heart tumbling and rising raggedly as he fought to keep from taking Miranda into his arms then and there. Why must I insist on propriety and pride, when all I wish to do is hold this woman in my heart and in my arms forever, when all I wish to do is dance with her in fields of lavender, in sunshine and moonlight, for the rest of our days?

"Come to dinner tonight, Josiah. Please do," Miranda said, despising the weakness that had made her voice tremble at first and driving it from her. "Doughtry will not. He cannot sit down to dinner at the same table with a lady of noble birth, he says. But Lord Blazingame has offered to accompany you if you should feel we require his presence to preserve propriety before the staff at our establishment. Lord Blazingame says, by the way, that you are the stubbornest, most prideful man he has ever met to so much as consider propriety at all when it comes to me. He says he cannot think how you ever came to London and left me behind you. And he says he will go so far as to introduce you to our butler as his cousin from Herefordshire, for my sake alone, because you must be out of your mind not to escape and be with me at every opportunity."

"Blazingame's a bit eccentric, you know," Elliot smiled.

"Yes." Miranda ached to put her arms around his neck and pull him down to her so she could kiss that perfectly beguiling look on his face. "Our staff will think nothing of it, I assure you. I have already told Browne that we are expecting a dinner guest or two—I did not say who. You may be known as Lord Blazingame's cousin from Herefordshire forever in Portman Square if you wish. Lord Blazingame's cousin to all our London staff, for as long as you consider it necessary."

Elliot nodded. Surely that would be safe enough. Surely, no gossip would develop belowstairs in Portman Square and be spread throughout the houses of the *ton* if Lady Miranda and her companion, both well beyond their first blush, chose to dine with the young Lord Blazingame and his cousin from Herefordshire. Nothing unreasonable or improper in that. Nothing to be remarked upon by anyone.

"I am sorry to seem so unreasonable, always, Miranda. I love you with all my heart. And I do long to be with you at every opportunity, but I can't bear to bring you low in the eyes of your peers. And there will come a time when I will not."

"And until then you will visit me as Lord Blazingame's cousin?"

"Yes. Yes, I will."

"Then step inside, Mr. Elliot, and prepare yourself to accompany Lord Blazingame around to Portman Square and a dinner near ready and waiting for you." The tips of Miranda's fingers touched his coat sleeve and lingered there a moment. And then she was gone. He watched her through the open door as she crossed the vestibule and traversed the long corridor leading to the rear of the establishment, the hooded cape disguising, in its boxiness, her trim figure, and its hood hiding from sight the tawny tresses that he longed to touch.

Lady Newcombe tasted the soup and bestowed the most superior gaze on her husband as he watched from the head of the table. "I knew Henri would be the very best of investments, Newcombe," she said. "One can never go wrong with a French chef."

"No, m'dear. An excellent chef, Henri. One or two dinner parties and we'll be the most envied household in London."

Eleanor's eyes crinkled at the corners in response to a quick, knowing grin from Donovan, who sat directly across from her. It is quite abominable of Uncle Roger, she thought, to go on pretending that our chef is French. Thank goodness Henry Footfellow has learned to affect that quaint accent, or Uncle Roger would be searching for a position for him still.

Henry Footfellow was one of Lord Newcombe's Causes. Both his niece and nephew were well aware of it, but neither would betray their uncle or the faux-French chef to their aunt. One never knew, after all, when a Cause of one's own might require just such silence from Uncle Roger.

"Have you had any word of your Mr. Elliot, Eleanor?" Lord Newcombe asked. "I caught a glimpse of Blazingame today leaving the club. It seemed apparent to me he had not switched valets in midstream, so to speak. Never saw such an assortment of colors on a gentleman in all my living days."

"A-assortment of colors?" Eleanor had not noticed anything at all odd about Lord Blazingame when she and Donovan had met the gentleman outside the Hen and Hunt. "He merely dresses like a dandy. What assortment of colors?"

"Well, let me think. I believe I glimpsed that dastardly yellowish-brown color Montemartre has introduced, and some Sardinian blue, a bit of raspberry, green and buff. Blazingame's taste never ceases to amaze me. Born under a rainbow, I think."

"And black and silver," Donovan added as the footmen came to clear the soup plates. "His boots were black and his spurs silver. Did you see him in sunlight, Uncle Roger, or in the shade?"

"Well, for goodness' sake! What difference if you see the man in sunlight or in shade?" Eleanor asked.

"In the shade, Nora, he is colorful, but in the sunlight, he lives up to his name," Donovan responded. *"Blaze*—in-game."

"You have met Lord Blazingame, Eleanor?" Lady New-combe queried as the second course entered in the footmen's hands. "When was this? I do not recall—"

"It was I introduced her, Aunt Caroline. This afternoon, as a matter of fact," Donovan inserted in a rush. "Met the man in Oxford Street quite by accident. Nora was on my arm. Could not avoid introducing him."

"I thought the two of you had decided to take the landau to Green Park and then stroll—" Lady Newcombe began.

"Yes, precisely what we intended," Donovan interrupted. "But Nora finds parks dreadfully dull, you know, so I thought she would enjoy to walk a bit in Oxford Street and look through some of the shops." Donovan watched his aunt's face anxiously. It sounded to him like a feasible tale. And they had actually gone to Oxford Street after the stop at Blazingame's establishment. And they had actually met Blazingame there, too.

"Well, perhaps it was for the best," Lady Newcombe said after a thoughtful moment. "Though I do not care for it when the two of you propose to do one thing and then do another. Still, Lord Blazingame. I expect the diversion was worth it this time. Lord Blazingame is amazingly available."

"Amazingly available?" Newcombe gazed down the table at his wife with the most guarded expression. "What does that mean precisely, Caroline?"

"You know perfectly well what it means, Newcombe. It means he is young, handsome, wealthy, titled and without a wife."

"I was afraid of that. You are mistaken, Caroline. He is not amazingly available. He is amazingly unavailable. You've only to look at the way he dresses to know he's two teacups short of a set. Yes, and he's a perfect innocent to boot. Doesn't know the first thing to say to a girl after how d'ye do. Wilde is constantly in despair over him. You are not thinking of a match between Eleanor and Blazingame,

I hope. I can't think of anything more humiliating than to be forced to admit that that boy is one of my family."

"A match? Between Lord Blazingame and me?" Eleanor stared at her uncle in disbelief. Then she transferred that exact gaze to her aunt. "Oh, I daresay it is a jest of some kind," she offered at last. "Certainly no sensible woman would look twice at Lord Blazingame. There is not the least bit of character in his face. He is much too handsome to be taken at all seriously. And he is cruel besides," she added, applying the tines of her fork to a sprig of broccoli.

"Cruel? Lord Blazingame? What makes you think him cruel, Eleanor?" Lady Newcombe asked, her brow furrowed. "I cannot think I have ever heard anything spoken against the man—other than your uncle's meaningless criticism of his manner of dress. Certainly I have never heard him called cruel."

"Well, I expect that is merely because no one realizes how cruel he is. He hides it very neatly behind his dimpled cheeks and shining eyes. But I know him to be cruel beyond belief. Did Uncle Roger not tell you, Aunt Catherine? About last evening? The gentleman Donovan and I convinced not to throw himself off Westminster Bridge last evening was Lord Blazingame's valet."

"Lord Blazingame's valet?"

"Yes, and well you may set your pheasant aside and stare so. Came very near to drive poor Mr. Elliot to suicide, Lord Blazingame did, and when I told Lord Blazingame that he had done so, he was not the least bit penitent for it. You will not believe what he said to me, that—that—evil snake."

"Oh," sighed Lady Newcombe. "Please don't tell me any more, Eleanor. I don't want to know."

"Know what, Aunt Caroline?" Donovan asked.

"That your sister gave Lord Blazingame a severe scold in the middle of Oxford Street with anyone and everyone looking on. She did, didn't she?"

"Well, yes, she did, but there weren't many people about.

I doubt anyone actually heard her call him a villain and a dastard."

"Oh," moaned Lady Newcombe, setting her fork aside and pushing her plate from her. "What am I going to do with you, Eleanor? I promised your mama that I would do all in my power to find you an acceptable husband and already there are two very eligible gentlemen who can be counted on to avoid you at all costs."

"Two?" Donovan cocked an eyebrow in question.

"Lord Blazingame," his aunt replied, "for reasons now obvious to us all, and Lord Dunley."

"Dunley? What the deuce did you do to Dunley, Nora?" Donovan gazed across at his sister, the corners of his lips twitching upward despite the accusing tone he used to please his aunt.

"Nothing. And I am going to apologize to him for it the very next time I see him."

"She abandoned the man at the Carlsons' without the least explanation," Lady Newcombe said. "That was your doing, Donovan. They were getting along perfectly well together until you came to carry Eleanor off with you to Westminster Bridge."

"And I will explain it all to Lord Dunley and beg his forgiveness, Aunt Caroline," Eleanor replied quietly, pushing her food about on her plate in a lackadaisical fashion. "Surely Lord Dunley must understand that a gentleman's life was at stake, that I had a much higher obligation, a more pressing task, than to sit about conversing with him and keeping him entertained."

"No, no, don't tell him that," protested Lady Newcombe heartily. "Good heavens! Tell him you had the headache, or word came to you that your brother was ill and you did not so much as pause to await my company on the way home. Yes, yes, that will do nicely. It will show him how dedicated you are to family and how much you care for those you love. Do not tell him you ran off to prevent a perfect stranger's suicide. He'll think you mad."

"Yes, all right, Aunt Caroline. I shall apologize to Lord Dunley and tell him a regular whopper of a lie."

"Eleanor!"

"Well, but that's precisely what you've just requested me to do. And I will do it, too, if it's what you wish. But I will not apologize to Lord Blazingame for what I said to him. I care not whether I ever speak to that villain again. The man is a care-for-nobody! A veritable fribble of fashion! Certainly there is nothing in him appeals to me or ever will. And I shan't lower myself to beg his forgiveness for words I truly intended."

Blazingame drew Elliot to a halt and stood looking at the house a moment in silence. There were lamps alight in almost every room on the first floor, all shining a welcome through newly washed windows. "Quite a sight compared to all the other times we've peered at it, eh, Elliot?"

"Someone's moved in," Elliot murmured. "Why didn't you tell me, Blazingame? I haven't passed by here since Thursday last and then the shutters were still closed and the knocker gone from the door. You don't suppose it will be those Percivalls?"

"They were the ones turned you away, denying any knowledge of your brother, were they not? When you first arrived in London from the Peninsula?"

"Yes. Never heard of Nathaniel Elliot, their butler told me, and when I protested that he must have heard of Nat, because the house was Nat's and had been in our family for fifty years and more, he called Percivall to the door, and Percivall threatened to have me thrown in jail if I did not disappear from his sight at once."

"Just so." Blazingame spun the silver-headed cane he carried in a small circle just above the pavement. "Let's go knock on the door now, Elliot."

"Now?"

"Um-hmmm. Right now."

"But we are bound for dinner at Miranda's."

"And do you know in which of these houses your Lady Miranda resides?"

"Oh, damnation!" cursed Elliot under his breath. "She left without giving me her direction again."

"Never fear, Elliot. Miss Markum gave it to me. Doughtry, in fact, scribbled it down for me, though I didn't require him to do so. I doubt I will ever forget it for as long as I live."

"Why?"

"Because your Lady Miranda and Miss Markum have taken up residence at Number Twelve, Portman Square," Blazingame replied with a wide smile and a tip of his hat in Elliot's direction.

"Here? They're living here?"

"Indeed. Do you remember when we decided—if all our probing about came to naught—that we would be forced to break into this place some dank, still night and search about for something resembling a clue? Well, tonight's the night, Elliot, and I think the breaking in part is like to prove a good deal easier than we imagined."

It was one of Lady Miranda's newly acquired footmen who met them at the door, took hats and gloves and Blazingame's cane, and led them to the drawing room. He attempted to lead them to the drawing room, at least, but was foiled time and again because Elliot would apparently not abandon the vestibule and then he would not abandon the bottom step of the staircase. And then his hand appeared to become adhered to the round polished cherrywood ball atop the first newel post. Not until Blazingame hissed at him "Cease acting like a country bumpkin, Cousin. Our hostesses await" did Elliot force his feet to ascend the gracefully curving staircase.

"Lord Blazingame, Mr. Elliot, welcome." Miranda greeted then, quite formally, for the benefit of the footman.

"It has been so very long since last we met, my lord. And, Mr. Elliot, it is a great pleasure to make your acquaintance."

Blazingame's eyes sparkled and he bowed over Lady Miranda's hand with a mischievous glance up into her eyes that almost set her to laughing. "The pleasure is all ours, my lady," he replied. "Elliot and I are delighted to be here. What a unique house you've taken for the Season. My cousin is apparently enthralled with your vestibule. Could barely persuade him to leave it. Must be the cherubs on the ceiling. Good evening, Miss Markum," he added, passing Miranda's hand to Elliot and stepping up to bow before Ariel. "It's a treat to see you again. All of London will be more interesting now that you and Lady Miranda are here."

"Indeed," Miss Markum said. "I am expecting this to be a most interesting visit myself. Arthur, you need merely serve the wine and then you may go," she added, prompting the new footman to action. "I cannot recall. Are you an intimate of Lord Daxonbury's, Lord Blazingame? Arthur came to us through Lady Miranda's nephew, you see. You and your cousin are the first guests he has ever received as a footman. You are an experiment of sorts for our entire staff this evening, the two of you. We did warn you of that when we met this afternoon, did we not?" she said loudly enough for the footman to overhear every word despite the fact that he was pouring wine at the sideboard across the room.

Blazingame seated himself in the chair beside Miss Markum's with aplomb and smiled widely at her.

Really, this young lord does have the most engaging smile, Ariel thought. I only wish it were not Miranda's and my machinations that provoke it at the moment. Why on earth do Miranda and Mr. Elliot not sit down? she wondered then, taking a glass from the tray the footman offered her. It is not as if we're going to run into dinner on the instant.

"You ought not worry overly much, Miss Markum," Blazingame said softly when the footman had returned the empty tray to the sideboard and left the room.

"Pardon me?"

"I said you need not worry. You explained our presence here quite properly and subtly before your footman. He will doubtless repeat all he's heard without error. Rumors will not fly, I assure you. Unless, of course, Elliot discovers he can't restrain himself any longer, sweeps your lovely Lady Miranda up into his arms and rushes off to Gretna Green with her to marry her over the anvil. Which, I assure you, he will not do. Not Elliot."

"No, I know he will not," Ariel replied with an engaging smile of her own. "He is too much of a gentleman to do it. And besides, I will have his guts for garters if he does."

"Miss Markum! Such language!" exclaimed Blazingame, laughing. "I never would have expected it of you."

"Nor would I have expected someone like you to be sauntering about London, nonchalantly burrowing into this and that, sticking your nose into things that don't concern you, to help a perfect stranger discover what remains of his family."

"Oh, but he's not a perfect stranger now, Miss Markum."

"He does become a friend quickly, does he not? I find, Lord Blazingame, that there are not many things I would not do for Mr. Elliot, but allowing him to sweep Miranda off to Gretna Green? Does he ever attempt such a scandalous answer to his problem, I *will* have his guts for garters. You may count on it."

# FIVE

"*That's* a deuceit?" Miranda chuckled.

"That's a newel post," observed Blazingame unnecessarily, for they could all see it was a newel post as they gathered behind Elliot on the staircase.

"Yes, well, but it's only this part above the bannister here, with the ball on the top, that's the deuceit," Elliot explained.

If Ariel and Lord Blazingame were not here, Miranda thought, I would kiss him this instant for that blush blooming on his cheeks. How can he have fought so fiercely, suffered so very much and yet prove so endearingly boyish? Blushing. A grown man. Of all things.

They had dined simply, had conversed only on the safest of topics while the footmen and Browne were present, had withdrawn together, the gentlemen declining to linger over their wine, and had discussed most seriously the likelihood that some clue to Nathaniel Elliot's disappearance might lie in this house. But the house had been altered greatly since last Elliot had strolled its corridors. Cherubs, he told them as they'd come down the staircase, had not cavorted across the vestibule ceiling. Elliot had recognized none of the furnishings or paintings throughout the establishment. The paper on the walls had changed and the paneling had been replaced as well.

Blazingame had started at the mention of replaced paneling. "Surely they were looking for something hidden behind the stuff, Elliot. Why else take down all the paneling and replace it?"

"Looking for what? A buried treasure? My family's fortune is composed of investments, Blazingame— was composed of investments. I'm almost certain that the investments failed somehow. Well, a goodly number of them must have failed or Marley wouldn't own this house. No, and Lily told me that a number of mementos—little things— that once belonged to Buckingham and once dwelled in this establishment now decorate the walls and shelves of Marley's manor house in Yorkshire. It makes me think Nathaniel must have lost a good deal of money in the funds or some such. He'd not have parted with The Buck's things else. Certainly wouldn't have sold them to Marley."

"Did you not tell me, Elliot, that your brother and Marley muddled through fairly well together? That it was only you whom Marley took into extreme dislike?" Blazingame asked now.

"Just so," Elliot nodded, one hand caressing the round knob on the top of the newel post. "But Nat would not have sold anything that once belonged to The Buck. Not to Marley. Not unless he were in dire straits. Because all we owned that was Buckingham's belonged to me, you see. It was left to me in our grandmother's will. It's one reason Marley despises me, I think. Because as a child, I was heir to what he coveted."

"And the reason you think Nathaniel would never have willingly sold Marley this house is the same?" asked Miranda.

"No. The house belonged to Nat. But he'd not have sold it to Marley unless he was in great need because Marley was always saying that the best thing that could be done with the old place would be to tear it down and build a modern house in its place. And Nat loved this house. He loved it with all his heart."

The sadness that appeared in Elliot's eyes thoroughly

overwhelmed Miranda. Her hand went to his cheek and then one long finger traced the line of his jaw gently, all the way to the cleft in his chin. "But he didn't sell it to Marley, dear one," she murmured. "You said yourself that it was the Duke of Berinwick, not Nathaniel, who sold the house to Lord Marley. And even if what you say—about the extent of Nathaniel's losses—is true, Josiah, the loss of a fortune is not beyond bearing. Nathaniel is a fine, noble gentleman, you tell us. Well then, he will not have given up merely because he lost a fortune. He will have attempted to recover all he lost, and likely he has."

"But why did he never tell me what happened?" whispered Elliot, thoroughly bewildered. "Why write me letters filled with good tidings if things here at home were so very bad? Did he think for one moment that I'd not do something to help him? I would have sold out and come home if only he'd told me that he needed me. Or did he think I would despise him? I could never despise him, Miranda. Never. He's my elder brother."

"Perhaps he thought to spare you, Josiah," Miranda said, her heart filled with pity for the disappointment in Elliot's voice, the grief that spilled across his face. "He knew you lived in the midst of war and he had no wish to add his troubles to the horrors he imagined you suffering."

"And it *is* likely he believed he would come about," added Ariel, she, too, overcome with pity for Elliot, "so he saw no reason to set you worrying needlessly."

"And perhaps, when he saw he had to leave the house, he left you a message, Elliot. You said yourself that he might have written something and put it in the deuceit. What sort of things did you have that belonged to Buckingham?" Blazingame added, hoping to lighten the moment, if only a bit.

Elliot looked at him and smiled a sad smile. "All sorts of things. None of them significant except for their history—a rapier, a foil, a most remarkable old pistol that never would fire. Ledgers, a saddle, spurs, a pair of gauntlets, a wig."

"A wig?"

"Indeed." Elliot's smile lost some of its sadness. "A vile wig with dark curls that must have hung all the way to the man's shoulders. You'd have laughed out loud to see it, Blazingame. It was the day of the cavaliers, you know, when The Buck was young and likely most gentlemen wore such things."

"However did you know it was his? A wig?" Miranda asked.

"Because he scribbled on the inside of it."

"What did he scribble?"

" 'Death to Cromwell' and signed it 'Buckingham'. We used to run about the back garden, Nat and I, with that wig on my head, fencing with sticks and shouting 'death to Cromwell!' whenever we got the chance. And we used to slide down this bannister as well. I'm relieved to find they didn't replace the bannister." Elliot slipped a small knife from his coat pocket and began to pry at a piece of the newel post slightly below the cherrywood ball.

"Why is it called a deuceit?" Miranda asked, watching. "Are you going to tell us, Josiah, or make us guess?"

"What? Oh, no. It is merely—when we slid down this bannister we never did manage to jump off before we hit this post."

"At which point you'd yell, *deuce it!*" Blazingame finished for him.

"Precisely, and so my mother came to call it the deuceit and we did as well. Ah, here we go!"

Please, Miranda prayed silently as Elliot lifted two thin squares and the ball from the remainder of the post. Please, God, let there be something inside for Josiah to find. Something that will help him discover what happened to Nathaniel. A message that says where Nathaniel and the

boys have gone. Please don't let it be empty. Josiah is counting on this so very much. Please don't let it be empty.

"What the devil?" mumbled Blazingame as Elliot took a
black velvet pouch from the shallow space. "I beg your
pardon, Lady Miranda, Miss Markum, but—what the
devil?"

"I don't know," Elliot replied, working at a knot in the
strings that held the pouch closed. "It's heavy, whatever it
is. Not a note, unless there is one in here with it. I was
hoping for a letter."

"Perhaps it's something more meaningful than a letter,"
Miss Markum offered. "Perhaps it's something from your
childhood that Nathaniel hopes you will recognize and as-
sociate with a particular place."

"Yes," Miranda agreed as Elliot fumbled with the knot.
"Perhaps Nathaniel thought to leave you a message that you
alone can decipher. Anyone might read a letter, but perhaps
this says something only you will understand."

"Ohmigawd!" Blazingame exclaimed on an indrawn
breath as the knot came untied and Elliot dumped the con-
tents of the pouch into his hand.

Miranda's eyes widened. Miss Markum gasped. Blazingame muttered "Ohmigawd" again and reached out with
one finger to touch the thing.


Eleanor bid her brother, aunt and uncle good night and
with Maria Edgeworth's *Vivian* in hand, she took herself off
to her bedchamber.

"I don't know how you can be reading tonight, miss,"
her abigail said as Eleanor set the book on her night table
and turned to allow the girl to undo the tabs at the back of
her dress.

"I read every night, Mary. I love to read. And Mrs. Edgeworth does write the most interesting stories."

"Yes, miss, but there is not another young lady I know would even think to be reading on such a night as this."

"And why is that, Mary?"

"Because of tomorrow, miss," Mary replied, lifting the dress over Eleanor's head. "Tomorrow is Wednesday."

"Yes, I know. Wednesday generally follows Tuesday. No, not that silly thing, Mary. My flannel nightgown. I want to be warm and cozy. I can't think why Aunt Caroline even bought such a thing as that for me."

"It's silk, miss."

"Yes, and cold and slippery. I detest it. What is it about Wednesday, Mary, that should keep me from reading?" she called after the abigail who was just then disappearing into the adjoining dressing room with the silk nightgown over her arm.

"Wednesday nights is Almack's, miss," replied Mary, returning with the requested flannel gown and assisting Eleanor into it. "When her ladyship had your cousins to fire off, they were each so excited to receive vouchers to Almack's that they could do nothing but pace Tuesday night away in anticipation."

"Of what?"

"Pardon, miss?"

"In anticipation of what?"

"Why, of appearing at Almack's, miss."

"It's merely a dance, I thought."

"Oh, no, miss, not merely. Every Wednesday night the most elegant of the aristocracy attend the dancing at Almack's. The most eligible bachelors in London can be found there. Yes, and only the most acceptable of young ladies, too."

"Oh?"

"The finest of alliances begin there, miss. There is no telling who you'll meet, what gentleman will set eyes on you and fall into love with you on the instant. Oh, but it's so very exciting! You will come home worn to a frazzle from all the dancing and wake to a vestibule filled with flowers from all the admirers you have gained."

"I will?"

"Oh, yes, miss. All the cousins have."

Eleanor smiled a wistful smile. All the cousins have, she thought. Charity and Priscilla and Beth danced the night away at this Almack's and woke to Uncle Roger's vestibule overflowing with flowers. She took a tiny dance step; the skirt of her nightgown swirled around her ankles. "Thank you, Mary. You may go," she said. "I've no further need of you this evening."

"Yes, miss," the abigail replied, and with a slight curtsy she exited the chamber.

Eleanor waited until the door had closed firmly behind Mary and then she took a second dance step and a third. She took Mrs. Edgeworth's book into her hands and, smiling at it, pretended it was a gentleman and allowed it to lead her in a waltz around the room. And then she stared at it, her eyes aglow with imagining.

It was the most secret dream of Eleanor Feebes's heart that she would one day meet a gentleman who loved her, a gentleman of worthy stock, with broad shoulders and curly hair. A titled gentleman whose glance alone would thrill her to the very core of her being, whose voice would send her heart to pounding and whose innate goodness would lay such a claim on her soul that they must live forever in each other's arms or die.

We will marry, of course, Eleanor thought dreamily. And raise a fine family. But in the midst of the doing of it, he and I will travel all over England, from the mightiest cities to the smallest villages. We shall pause where we're needed and dispense with kindness whatever might be required of us. We will recruit any number of worthy Causes just as Mama and Uncle Roger do. But it will not be the same for us as it is for Mama and Papa, and for Uncle Roger and Aunt Caroline. No, not at all. We will be a perfect match, he and I. We'll work together as a pair, and when they are old enough, our children will join in. He won't grouch and complain like Papa that Mama's Causes take up all her time. No, and he won't be like Aunt Caroline, either, always attempting to understand and always falling short. He will know what it is that drives me to stand and fight for people who cannot stand and fight for themselves at a particular moment in their lives. My gentleman—my husband—will be of a like mind with me and together we'll search for and discover and invent ways to save a goodly portion of the world from destruction and despair.

"Perhaps," Eleanor whispered, climbing up into the bed and carrying the book right along with her, "perhaps I will meet him at Almack's."

"It's a diamond," Miss Markum whispered, her hands clasped tightly before her in an effort to keep from touching the jewel. "I have never seen such a diamond in all my life."

"Only see how it glitters and glows," murmured Miranda. "But surely it cannot be real."

"A diamond as large as that—where would it come from?" Blazingame muttered, his finger unable to refrain from stroking the cold, hard gem. "How could it exist anywhere and the entire world not know of it? It's as large as a lady's fist."

"It's The Heart of a Queen," Elliot said softly, staring down at the jewel. "It can't be, but it is. By Jove, whatever possessed Nat to fetch the thing from where I hid it and put it here? Did he lose his mind?"

"Fetch it from where?" asked Blazingame. "Perhaps that's the clue, Elliot. Perhaps he and the boys have gone to wherever the gem came from."

"No. It came from a ruin on the moors of Yorkshire. No one would go there to stay."

"If he was in need of funds, why did he not—" Miss

Markum began, but then her voice faded and her hand went to her lips. "How beautiful it is," she said from behind that slightly trembling hand. "Such beauty as that hidden away in a newel post."

"Yes. But why hide it away when he might sell it? Perhaps Nathaniel wasn't in need of money after all, Josiah," Miranda offered quietly. The thing shone so in Elliot's hand that she could not resist the lure of it. She stepped down a stair and moved in beside Miss Markum. She reached out to touch it. Elliot tossed the velvet pouch into the newel post at once and captured her hand in his.

"No, Miranda, don't touch it. Nor you, Miss Markum. Blazingame, it is likely too late for you, but I should remove my finger from the thing at once just in case. It's cursed."

"Cursed?" Miranda stared at him in disbelief as Blazingame's finger moved unobtrusively from the diamond into his coat pocket accompanied by the rest of his hand. "Surely you don't believe in such things as curses, Josiah?"

"I do. I believe that this particular jewel is cursed, at any rate. It came to The Buck's father from Queen Anne of France. 'A great diamond to wear over the heart that loves diamonds and me' she wrote when she sent it to him. It was The Buck's father named it The Heart of a Queen. And shortly after he received the thing, he was assassinated by a disgruntled ruffian with a tenpenny blade."

"Oh!" Miss Markum inhaled with a bit of a squeak.

Miranda's hand nestled comfortably in Elliot's. "One death does not a curse make, dearest," she said with a bit of a smile.

"No, but there were a great many more lives lost after that. It was hidden away during the Great Rebellion and certain people met grisly deaths in the attempt to rediscover it. Curse or no curse, Miranda, it hasn't a very pretty history and there's no one in my family who's at all fond of the thing."

"Your family? This diamond has been in your family

since the Great Rebellion?" Blazingame stared at him in wonder.

"Only now and again. It comes and it goes. I did tell you at the first, Blazingame, that we're related to the Villiers."

"But you're not a Villiers."

"I am by blood but not by name," Elliot replied.

"Did anyone know? About this diamond, I mean?" Blazingame asked. "I mean to say, Elliot, might this be why all the paneling was replaced? Because someone thought the thing might be hidden in some nook behind the old paneling?"

"No. No, I can't think who would—Marley. Marley and his brother heard tales of it from my mother, but his brother is dead and Marley would know the diamond was never kept in this house. You don't keep a cursed thing in the very house where you raise your family."

"Josiah, what is it?" Miranda asked as his hand closed more tightly over hers and a frown furrowed his brow.

"I can't think why Nat brought it here and put it in the deuceit when he might simply have left me a letter instead. He must have known I would come home from the Peninsula eventually. He must have known I would come here expecting to find him. And he had to know that a word or two written in his own hand would mean more to me and tell me more than this stupid stone."

"Are you certain there's nothing else inside the deuceit, Josiah? Perhaps there *is* a letter. Perhaps it was under the pouch and you did not feel it at first."

Elliot freed her hand and reached down into the deuceit again. He fished about in the shallow hiding place, but he found only the pouch he had tossed back inside earlier.

Sophia was in alt. She spun about the drawing room in a gown of willow-green silk beneath a fitted robe made entirely of Bruges lace. The soft green of the gown peeked through the leaves and petals of the white lace design and flared out from the high waist of the robe through the up-side-down V of the front opening in the most alluring fashion. Around her neck she wore an ivory cameo on a fine gold chain and on her feet, dancing slippers that matched perfectly the willow green of her gown. Her hair, as deeply auburn as her brother Daxonbury's, had been clipped short and her curls threaded through with a string of pearls. "Is it not the most beautiful ensemble you have ever seen, Papa?" she asked, twirling to a halt before him.

"Quite lovely," his grace adjudged from his favorite chair beside the dieffenbachia.

"It's for tomorrow night, Papa. For Almack's."

"Aaarrrgh! Almack's! I'd forgotten." He had been looking forward to spending the evening playing whist at his club. The aspect of a dull time in Almack's card room playing for absolutely chicken stakes appalled him. The knowledge that he must dance at least one dance with his daughter and one with his wife or they would feel dreadfully abused hovered threateningly over him. The idea of squeezing himself into outmoded silk stockings and proper velvet knee breeches proved daunting.

"You'll like to appear at Almack's, will you, Sophia?" he asked, forcing a sparse joviality into his voice. "Well, and what young lady would not? An enviable thing, to be allowed into Almack's on Wednesday nights. You are not planning on taking those two urchins with you, I hope."

"Oh, Papa, of course not. Spinner and Jack will remain here."

"Unless I discover their house sometime during the day. I will find the place, Sophia. I promise you. And then you will be forced to give them up, so do not become attached to those boys."

"No, Papa. I won't. I have resigned myself to the fact that I am not to have matching pageboys."

"Not even one unmatched pageboy."

"I am not to have any pageboys, even if Jane Weyland

does have one and goes about with him trailing after her as if she were the Queen."

"I don't care what Lady Jane Weyland does," proclaimed his grace with a good deal of majesty. "She may go about pretending to be the Prince of Wales for all I care. But you will not, Sophia."

Sophia, whose cheeks had dimples quite like her mama's, smiled prettily at him, then leaned down and kissed the tip of his nose. "You are a veritable tyrant, Papa," she whispered. "I love you dearly."

"Yes? And you think I don't mean a word I say, but I do."

"Of course you do, your grace. You always mean precisely what you say. I am not such a goose as to think otherwise."

From the opposite side of the dieffenbachia, her grace laughed quietly.

"Don't laugh, Catherine," the duke said. "I do mean what I say and it's about time Sophia came to realize it. She's practically a woman grown. Off to Almack's in search of a husband, she is. Time for her to understand that every man is king in his own castle."

"Yes, Charles," came the reply. "Do your knee breeches still fit? I asked you to be certain of that two full weeks ago. Did your valet help you try them on? You can't enter Almack's without them, you know. And it would be such a shame should you miss your only daughter's debut there. She's like to steal every gentleman's heart away before the night is done."

"She stole my heart away long ago," his grace replied, taking his daughter's hand into his own and giving it a squeeze. "Eighteen years ago. You look exquisite, m'dear, and your mama is correct. By the end of tomorrow evening there will not be a gentleman who has set foot in Almack's whose heart you do not own."

\* \* \*

Elliot and Miranda stood before the drawing room windows in the house in Portman Square holding each other's hands. Their eyes spoke so clearly, their lips need not move at all. Their hearts understood everything without the least confusion. Blazingame attempted to avoid looking at them, to allow them that minimal privacy at least, but try as he might to keep his gaze focused on Miss Markum, he could not manage it.

"You don't approve?" Miss Markum asked him quietly.

"Approve?"

"Of the coalition that strengthens even now between Miranda and Mr. Elliot."

"It's not my place to approve or disapprove."

"Just so. I expected you would think that or else you would not have agreed to take Mr. Elliot into your household and aid him. But then, it occurs to me that you have another reason entirely for coming to his aid. You enjoy searching about and poking your nose into things, do you not, Lord Blazingame? Good heavens, why can you not keep your gaze from them?"

"Because I haven't my back turned to them as you do, Miss Markum."

"Are they kissing?"

"No, no, merely holding each other's hands and staring into each other's eyes. Can love truly be like that, Miss Markum? So silent? So still?"

"Indeed, it can. Have you never been in love, Lord Blazingame?"

"No. Nor have I any wish to be."

Miss Markum smiled. "I see. You despise females, do you?"

"Not at all. I merely cannot think why any man would wish to play the fool just to get one."

"Mr. Elliot is not playing the fool."

"No, he isn't. But he and Lady Miranda are—are—"

"Old?"

"Well, I don't precisely mean to say that. She is very beautiful, you know, and intriguing. But she's not the youngest chick to leave the nest. And Elliot— Well, I should say Elliot is in the prime of his life. At least, it would be the prime of his life if it were not marred by his illness and the loss of his family and now his need to prove himself worthy of a duke's sister."

"You know of his illness?"

"Yes, ma'am. He got the trembles last week while he was shaving me and came near to slit my throat."

"Oh!"

"Ought not have said that," Blazingame added immediately, seeing the color fade from Miss Markum's cheeks. "He *might* have slit my throat is what I ought to have said, but he merely nicked me before he dropped the razor and turned away. He knows when they're coming upon him most of the time. Lady Miranda knows about the trembles?"

"Yes."

"And she loves him in spite of them. I can't think of one of the young ladies I've met who would love a man with the trembling, falling-down illness. Run from him, they all would."

"You do not run from Mr. Elliot."

"No, of course not."

"Why not?"

"Why not?" Blazingame's hand went to wander through his hair and then rub at the back of his neck. "Why not?"

"Yes, Lord Blazingame. Why not? He is barely acceptable as a valet. I know that to be true, for it was in our house he attempted to learn his skills. He departed before he learned anything much at all. You owe him no great debt, do you? You had never met him, had you, before he came to your door to request a position? You were not obliged in any way to take Mr. Elliot on?"

"Well, no, but I had a letter from Whethers explaining about Elliot's situation, you see. And—and—I am rather fond of solving puzzles. The thought of helping to discover what happened to his brother appealed to me very much."

"And?"

"And, Miss Markum?"

"And when you discovered he was not only a barely adequate valet but had a most annoying illness, and then you discovered that he is in love with a duke's sister who has just lately made you part of a plot to allow them to meet secretly, what makes you keep him on?"

"I have grown fond of him, Miss Markum. A man doesn't turn away a friend simply because he's ill and in trouble and in love."

"No, of course not. Nor does a woman, Lord Blazingame. You are mistaken in your estimation of our sex. You see only the frivolous members of it, I think, and you measure us all by their actions. You ought not. Women, like men, are individuals. Some of us are not worth the ground we stand upon and others of us are priceless."

*"You're* one of the priceless ones," whispered Elliot with a wide smile as he took Miranda into his arms.

"Ariel's voice does rise when she's teaching," Miranda replied, cuddling against his chest. "I wish you need not go."

"So do I, but it can't be helped, Miranda."

"Sneaking about as though we are children."

"Yes, well, it is a bit awkward, but it's for the best. You know it is. One slip and you'll be the talk of London."

"She's an old maid, they'll say," Miranda said with a scowl and a wrinkled nose. "She ought to know better. Can you imagine her throwing herself at the man? At her age? Why, she's lost her mind. And to toss her handkerchief at a valet, of all things. Utterly nonsensical!" She ceased to speak and pushed herself away, a bit, from his chest so she could stare once more up into his eyes. "Josiah, are you crying?"

"Of course not."

"But your eyes shimmer as though there are tears standing in them. And your eyelashes are wet."

"It's nothing. Smoke from the lamps."

"It's something. Josiah, what is it? Are you not well?"

"I'm perfectly fine, thank you. And I am not crying. Of all the things to say! I love you, Lady Miranda Wesley, that's all. I love you with every ounce of my being. I require a kiss."

"Then you shall have one."

As Blazingame's gaze returned to the couple, Miranda stood on tiptoe. Her hands grasped the lapels of Elliot's coat. She touched his lips softly with hers and then more passionately. In a moment she freed his lapels. Her arms went around his neck and tugged him down to her and she kissed him with such a need and such a longing that Blazingame's eyes grew wide and his face red from the sight of it. He was that astounded. But he did think almost at once to reach out and take both Miss Markum's hands into his own to keep her from turning around to see what Lady Miranda and Elliot were doing to cause such a reaction in *him*.


"I thought the both of you would collapse from lack of breath," Blazingame said as he and Elliot strolled back toward Manchester Square. "And then I thought, perhaps you would squash the poor woman to death, as big as you are and as tiny as she is. Great heavens, Elliot, I have never seen such a kiss as that in all my days."

Elliot shoved his hands into his breeches pockets and kept his gaze on the pavement before him. "You don't know much about women, do you, Blazingame?"

"I beg your pardon?"

"Don't sound so offended. I don't intend it as an insult

to your manhood or anything like that. It's merely an observation. I've been observing you for months now and it seems to me that you don't know much about women at all and that's why you avoid them at all costs."

"I do not avoid them at all costs," Blazingame protested, dragging the tip of his cane along the pavement behind him. "Do I not attend dinner parties, breakfasts, musical evenings in quest of news about your brother, Elliot? Do you think there are no women at these entertainments? I assure you, there are. More than enough of them to teach a man all he needs to know."

"About kissing?"

"Well, no, not about kissing, but about everything else."

"I see. You know everything a gentleman needs to know about women aside from the kissing part."

"Exactly so."

"And what Miss Markum said to you tonight about women—yes, Miranda and I heard her lecturing you, Blazingame—what she said, you already knew?"

"Well, no. I'd never heard that particular lecture before. I expect it's not in Wilde's collection. Besides, I think Miss Markum was wrong in what she said. There may be one or two women who are not just like all the rest, but they're sparse, Elliot. A man would have to go very far out of his way to find one. You, for instance, had to go all the way to Yorkshire."

"Just so."

They walked on in silence for a number of steps, Blazingame tapping his cane against the pavement. "A gentleman has to be very careful, Elliot," Blazingame said at last. "Especially a gentleman who's an unmarried earl and wishes to remain that way. That's one of the reasons I resort to it."

"Resort to what?"

"Dressing the way I dress. The kinds of young ladies I know don't like it when gentlemen wear colors brighter than their own. Or lace. Or jewels. Well, generally they don't, and so they go off and pester someone else and leave me alone."

"And that's why all that lace at your collar and cuffs tonight, and lavender knee breeches, shoes with silver buckles and a coat the color of flowing blood? Because you thought Miss Markum would pester you and you wished to keep her from it?"

"Of course not."

"Well, but it must have been Miss Markum you feared, Blazingame. You certainly didn't think Miranda would set her cap at you."

"It hadn't to do with them at all. I just—I expect it won't matter if I admit it to you—I like all the colors and the lace and the shoes with silver buckles, Elliot. I began dressing this way to turn the young ladies away and discovered I like it. Don't like all this black-and-white business Brummell began. Feel like an undertaker in black and white. Besides, you never know whom you'll meet," Blazingame replied stiffly, scraping his cane along behind him again. "Only this afternoon I was accosted in Oxford Street by the most aggravating young woman."

"You were?"

"Indeed. Your Miss Feebes, it was."

"Miss Feebes? Accosted you in Oxford Street? Despite the way you were dressed? Well, leave it to Miss Feebes not to run with the rest of the pack. Your extraordinary taste in clothes didn't put her off as it does the others, eh?"

"I should think not. Gave me a tremendous scold, all on your account. Called me a villain and a dastard."

"She did? Well, it only goes to show you."

"Only goes to show me what?"

"That Miss Markum *was* correct. All women are not alike. And those who are different aren't as sparse as you think, Blazingame. Sometimes a gentleman need merely go as far as Oxford Street to find one."

They walked on, Elliot staring silently off into the night

and Blazingame whistling his one low note and playing with his cane. Just as they turned right into the square, Elliot caught at Blazingame's arm and tugged him off the pavement, forcing him down behind a grouping of bushes against a low wall.

"What?" asked Blazingame in a whisper.

Elliot nodded in the direction from which they'd just come. A man of rather stocky build, a tall hat set rakishly on his head, just then turned into the square. He paused a moment and looked around him in puzzlement. Then he passed them by and hurried toward Blazingame's establishment.

"He followed us to Portman Square and followed us home again," murmured Elliot. "Didn't notice, did you?"

"No. I can't think why, but his very existence slipped my mind. What did you do with the diamond, Elliot?"

"In my pocket. Well, but he can't be after the diamond, Blazingame. He began following you before we ever discovered the thing."

"Still, you ought to have left it in Portman Square, I think."

"No. No telling what might happen to Miranda or Miss Markum or anyone in the household if I left it there," muttered Elliot. "Let's go back around the corner, through the mews, and in the kitchen door, eh?"

"Excellent idea," Blazingame agreed. "You truly believe that the diamond's cursed, do you?" he added once they exited the square the way they'd entered.

"If you'd been raised in my family and heard all the tales, you'd believe it, too, Blazingame. The blessed thing has caused so much blood to flow, it's a wonder it doesn't glow red itself from the stain of it. Not a thing I'm likely to leave under Miranda's roof. Not at all." Elliot lowered his head, fixed his gaze on the toes of his shoes. "I didn't wish to admit it in front of the ladies, but I think Miranda was correct, Blazingame. I think Nat left the diamond in the deuceit as a message that only I would be able to decipher. Better than a letter which anyone might be able to read. The Heart of a Queen says everything to me and nothing to anyone else."

"And what does it say to you?"

"It tells me to be afraid, Blazingame. To be very afraid. It tells me that Nat was caught in dangerous straits and the danger will persist regardless of what has happened to him. The diamond's a warning that whatever dire threat hovered over my brother, hovers over me even now. And because you and Miranda and Miss Markum are linked to me, it hovers over all of you as well."

# *SIX*

The following evening descended on London with as much refined elegance as had the evening before it—clear, cool, bright with starlight and not a hint of fog, not even along the Thames. Blazingame had spent most of the day thinking and puttering around his study. He had popped out each time a name occurred to him, to discuss the possibilities with Doughtry, though he would not do so if Elliot were anywhere about. Then he would sequester himself again and delve into his memory for someone else he'd spoken to in the past few months about Nathaniel Elliot. One of them must have a secret but overwhelming interest in that gentleman's whereabouts, he thought, because that's the only reason for the carroty-haired man to be set the task of following me around London. Someone wishes to know as soon as possible if and when I find Nathaniel.

It made perfectly good sense, actually—if Elliot were right about the message intended by The Heart of a Queen, if Nathaniel Elliot had been in danger, if the danger persisted to this day. Then certainly, the man or woman who was the source of this danger would be searching for the missing Elliot brother still. And what better way to increase the likelihood of finding him than to search separately and yet keep an eye on Blazingame's efforts as well. Two separate, yet secretly combined, searches. One of them ought to produce results.

"But I can't say as much to Elliot," Blazingame muttered, "because then he'll think whoever it is has put the carroty-haired man onto me means to kill all of us once Nathaniel's found. I can't have him thinking that. He's been fretting over that wretched diamond all day. Worried to have it in this house. Worried that Lady Miranda and Miss Markum and I are already cursed. Worried that Doughtry will end up cursed along with us. He'll worry himself into a severe case of the trembles if I can't find some way to ease his mind. Perhaps if I knew more about the history of the stone—"

Marley. The name popped into Blazingame's mind most abruptly. Marley's a cousin of Elliot's. Perhaps he's heard tales about the stone, Blazingame thought. And he's interested in historical artifacts from the Great Rebellion. Perhaps he knows more about The Heart of a Queen than does Elliot. Perhaps he can give me some clue as to how to convince Elliot the thing isn't cursed at all.

Marley, he thought again, a frown appearing suddenly on his handsome face. Marley knows the Elliots. Marley knows about the diamond. Marley owns the house. With each realization, Blazingame's frown increased. "Glory, what a fool I am!" he exclaimed under his breath. "When the devil did I speak to Marley? Was it before or after the advent of the carroty-haired man? And what the deuce did I say? He was boasting about that old rapier at Watier's. And I had a look at it. And I said it was in admirable condition for as old as it was. And then I said— Oh, Jupiter! I had best have another conversation with Marley. And I'd best have it tonight if I have to set foot in every club and every gaming establishment in the city to find him."

Lord Newcombe, looking particularly dashing in knee breeches, a sparkling white neckcloth, and a long-tailed dress coat, grimaced despite the pleasantness of the weather. He stared up at the bland façade of Almack's assembly rooms with considerable distaste as his coach moved on along King Street, St. James's, without him. Lady Newcombe took his arm and urged him forward. A mere three steps behind, Donovan offered an arm to Eleanor.

I ought to be accustomed to this by now, Newcombe thought, contemplating the visual dullness of the Ionic doorcase. Fired off three nieces in three years, a fourth Season ought to be nothing. But there is something about Almack's always makes me wish I could turn around and run.

Newcombe handed Mr. Willis the tickets at the door and led the small procession up the staircase and into the ballroom with its six arched windows and hideous dance floor. He paid his respects to the patronesses, introduced Eleanor and Donovan, and then took Donovan by the arm and tugged him away from the jabbering ladies.

"What, Uncle Roger? You barely gave me time to bow to them."

"You'll bow to them enough before the Season is over. Did your aunt warn you?"

"Warn me?"

"That you'll be expected to dance, Donovan."

"Oh. Yes. But I'm not one of the eligible bachelors, you know. I've neither fortune nor title. I doubt I'll be forced to dance at all."

"Are you male, Donovan?"

"Yes, sir."

"Are you married?"

"No, sir."

"Then you'll be expected to dance. Best thing is to hide in the card room and peek in at the dancing from time to time to see that your sister and your aunt are going on quite happily."

"Is that what you do, Uncle Roger?"

"Indeed. Dance a man to death even if he is married, these women. But if he's not married, they'll keep him dancing beyond the grave. Devil, if it's not Comestock!"

"Comestock, Uncle?"

"Yes, yes, just there. The Duke of Comestock and his duchess and his daughter. Ought to have known."

"Ought to have known what?"

"That he'd not talk his way out of Almack's on opening night, either. Daughter is making her come-out this Season. Both his boys are married and gone. Stuck with the duty."

Donovan followed his uncle's gaze to see who the Duke of Comestock might be, and discovering the duke, also discovered Lady Sophia. He inhaled raggedly. "That's Comestock's daughter beside him, Uncle? In the white and green? Do—do you know him to speak to, Uncle? The Duke of Comestock?"

"Of course I know him. Went to university with him. See him often in the House of Lords. Devil of a man. Born condescending. He and his duchess both. The Graces, their children call them, for their manner of descending from the heights to bestow their favors. Ha! The Graces! Tickles me, that!"

The Duke of Comestock was not in the least tickled, though he did smile politely as several of the patronesses fawned over him. His feet already hurt. His neckcloth was strangling him and his legs were cold because he'd had to forgo his boots in favor of the knee breeches. Sons! he thought while bowing charmingly over some patroness's pale hand. What good are sons if they're never around when you need them? Daxonbury could be standing here in my stead, and I could be playing cards at White's. But no, Dax must go off on some fool wedding trip.

The very thought of his eldest son and his newly acquired daughter-in-law brought a good-humored smile to Comestock's countenance. Give one hundred pounds to see Daxonbury and his Desdemona here, he thought. Yes, I would. Most likely can't dance at all, that wife of his. But she can use a sling and a stone to excellent effect. That she can.

"Papa? What are you thinking?" asked Sophia quietly in his ear. "You're smiling the most beguiling smile. I believe Princess Esterhazy thinks it is meant for her."

"No, does she?"

"Yes, and Mama is beginning to glare."

"I was merely thinking of Daxonbury and Desdemona."

"Were you? So was I. I wonder what Dessie would think of such a place as this?" Sophia took a step to the side and, peering past her father, contemplated the room and the people occupying it for a very long moment. Dessie would be appalled, she thought, a smile as beguiling as her father's appearing on her face. And then she noticed him. Well, she felt him first, felt his gaze upon her, but she noticed him within an instant of that. "Papa, there is a young man staring at me from across the room."

"All the gentlemen will be staring at you tonight, m'dear. Is it someone we know?"

"It's not a face I find familiar, but—he's standing beside Lord Newcombe, Papa."

"Newcombe? Newcombe's here?" Visions of playing cards fluttered happily through Comestock's mind. "Well, yes, of course Newcombe's here. I'd forgotten all about this one. Fired off three nieces in a row, Newcombe has. And there's still one to go. Isabelle's girl, she'll be. Last of the lot, I believe."

"Yes, Papa, but it's not a girl staring at me as though I am some delicacy set out on a golden plate. It's a gentleman."

Lady Newcombe and Eleanor freed themselves at last from the conversational tangle in which they'd become entrapped and crossed the floor to join Newcombe and Donovan. "Do you see, Newcombe," Lady Newcombe said with a triumphant smile. "You're not the only married gentleman here this evening. I told you that you wouldn't be. It's the first of the balls, after all."

"Quite right, m'dear. Forgot about Comestock."

"Yes, and there are several other fathers wandering about."

"Who?"

"Let me think. Did someone not mention Lord Covington, Eleanor? Yes. And Lord Marley returns again with that dreadful Angela. And Mr. Davis-Bowes-Templeton."

"Davis-Bowes-Templeton. Lord, what a name," sighed Newcombe. "Did you ever hear such a name, Eleanor? That's what comes of marrying money, m'dear. If you join fortunes, apparently you must also join names. That's better," he added as Eleanor smiled nervously. "Can't have you strolling about with a frown. Not this evening, we can't. What do you think of the place?"

"I think it's very shabby, Uncle Roger, for a place with such a reputation. I expected something quite different. Somehow, I can't believe that great alliances have ever been formed here."

"Oh, but they have, dearest!" protested Lady Newcombe. "Just you wait. Once the musicians begin to play and you begin to dance, these rooms will acquire an entirely different aspect. Donovan? Who on earth are you staring at?"

"What? Oh. I don't know, Aunt Caroline. She is the Duke of Comestock's daughter, Uncle Roger says, but he doesn't say her name."

"Lady Sophia," his aunt provided at once.

"Lady Sophia," repeated Donovan, tasting each syllable of it tenderly.

Eleanor's eyes widened on the instant. She stepped hurriedly from between her uncle and aunt, directly to Donovan's side. "Lady Sophia is a duke's daughter," she hissed anxiously in her brother's ear.

"I know."

"Donovan, for goodness' sake!" she exclaimed with hushed frustration. "Take that gleam from your eye and that look from your face. Do not tip heels over head in love with that particular young woman. She will break your heart."

"Why do you say that?"

"Because a duke's daughter is not allowed to fall in love with any man beneath the rank of—of—earl. It's forbidden. Don't go anywhere near her. If she scorns you, you will be humiliated. And if she doesn't scorn you, you will lose your heart to her and then have it broken when she discards you for some titled gentleman."

"I've already lost my heart to her, Nora."

"No, no, no! You cannot have done. She is not like Lillian or Clara or Sally."

"Not at all," whispered Donovan, who was slowly turning himself and Eleanor in a complete circle because he could not disengage his gaze from Lady Sophia as she strolled on her father's arm from one group of acquaintances to another. "She is not like the girls at home at all."


Elliot, in buckskin breeches, high-topped boots and a burgundy morning coat, looked most unlike any valet in the city of London. He helped Miranda down from the hackney and sent it on its way. Together they strolled down Buckingham Street, she with a comfortable hold on his arm, he with a comfortable look on his face.

"I am pleased you confided in me," Miranda said.

"So am I. I ought to have told you everything last evening, but I was so overwhelmed by the mere sight of the diamond that I barely managed to express myself to Blazingame on our way home."

"Which translates, I believe, into you did not wish to worry Ariel and me until you had sorted it all out in your mind." Miranda gave his arm a firm squeeze. "I love you,

Josiah Elliot, but you need not be so careful of me. I am not some young, delicate flower."

"No. You're a lavender plant in full bloom," Elliot murmured, bringing them both to a halt beneath a streetlamp and staring down at her, losing himself in the clear, honest depths of her eyes. "Intoxicating, seductive, soothing," he whispered after a long silence. The very tip of his index finger went to trace the soft bloom of her cheek, the strong curve of her jaw. "You're the essence of my existence. Balm for my soul. My Lady of the Lavender."

Miranda's lips parted the slightest bit, but no words came. None at all. And for a moment she was home again at Lavender Hill, dancing in his strong arms beneath the shining sky, the summer sun. She and this most frustrating gentleman, waltzing together amidst the rows of lavender. Someday it will happen, she thought. Someday it will be more than a dream. We will dance together, Josiah and I, before everyone, before no one. It won't matter as long as he is the one guiding my steps. How could I have allowed him to leave me? she wondered. And yet I knew I must. "But never again," she said, her voice wrapped in the velvet of the night. "Never again."

"Never again what, Miranda?" asked Elliot, his own voice sounding odd and husky in his ears.

"Never again will I allow you to run off without me. No matter where, no matter what, no matter why."

He smiled then, the glow of the lamplight softening his features, shadowing the cleft in his chin, obscuring the fencing scar on his cheek. And that smile filled Miranda with such joy that she thought she might soar into the sky and burst into glowing sparkles like the fireworks at Vauxhall Gardens.

"We had best walk on, Miranda," Elliot managed, his voice grown hoarse. "We had best not stand and stare so at each other any longer or I will lose myself to you so completely that I will never find *me* again, much less find Nat."

"You aren't angry that I came to London, Josiah?" Miranda asked as she once again took his arm and they continued their stroll along the pavement.

"Angry? Never. Thankful. Overjoyed. Filled with the certainty that all I dreamed in Yorkshire was not a dream at all but real and true."

"Just so. And I am not some interfering old tabby?"

Elliot laughed, and the laugh sent ripples of bliss shivering through Miranda.

"I do wish you had spoken to me of the import of the diamond before you spoke of it to Lord Blazingame, Josiah," she said.

"Why is that?"

"Well, because now Lord Blazingame—if he believed you—is wandering about thinking we are all of us in the gravest danger. And he's such a young man. And when young men think their friends are in danger, one never knows what they'll do."

"As opposed to more elderly men like me, do you mean?"

"Yes. You are to be counted upon to think things through, you know. To be quietly circumspect."

"Dull."

"No, I don't mean dull. Or boring. And you know it, too."

"Blazingame won't do anything foolish, Miranda. At least, I don't think he will. He's skilled at finding answers and solving puzzles, and he'll think of the diamond as a clue, nothing more. I doubt he believes in curses any more than you do. And he's proved most subtle and prudent so far. But I'll tell him as soon as I can that I no longer believe the diamond was left there to convey the message I derived from it. I'll set his mind at ease on that point at the first opportunity. This is it," he added, bringing her to a halt before the York water gate.

"Oh, Josiah, how lovely!" she exclaimed, gazing at the

small, square building before her. "To think I have been to
Covent Garden Theatre any number of times and have never
once come down this way to see it."

"I expect the gentlemen who escorted you never thought
to invite you to see a water gate. Much too common. It's
the lions I like the best," Elliot added with a laugh. "With
all the intricate work gone into the design and the building
of it, I find my preference for the lions despicable. But ever
since I was a boy I've thought those lions at the top are the
very best part of the entire thing."

"You love this place," Miranda observed as he led her
through to the other side of the ornate little building and
down the worn stone steps to stand on the lowest of them,
right above the river. "I can hear the love for it in your
voice. And if the streetlamps were brighter and not behind
us as they are, I've no doubt I could see the love for it in
your eyes, too."

"I love it all," Elliot admitted, placing his arm around her
waist. "This gate. Buckingham Street. Villiers Street. Duke
Street. You."

"Me?"

"Yes. You've recently been added to the list of the things
I most love, my lady. You're at the top, actually."

"Oh?" Miranda's cheeks dimpled. "Tell me about this
gate, Josiah."

"My mother brought Nat and me here often when we
were boys. She would sit on the steps above the Thames,
gaze out over the river, and tell us such stories. They were
so vivid that I could actually see Buckingham House as it
must have been before they destroyed it. A great glowing
palace on the Thames, each room elegant, exquisite. The
Rubenses, the Titians, the Tintorettos hanging on the walls.
The diamonds lying about on the tables."

"The diamonds lying about on the tables? Oh, Josiah,
surely that part is from a faery tale."

"No, I think not. Tossed them anywhere and everywhere,

The Buck's father did. That's what my mother said. Though she never actually saw Buckingham House herself, mind you. She heard the tales of it from her father, and he from his mother and—"

"And your idol, The Buck? Was he as mad for diamonds as his father?"

"Mad, yes, but not for diamonds."

"Where did you put it, The Heart of a Queen?" Miranda asked abruptly. "Somewhere safe, I hope."

"It's in my pocket."

"Josiah!"

"Well, I did think to find a place to stow it safely away at Blazingame's, but I decided against it."

"Then you shall give it to me and I will put it back in the deuceit."

"No."

"Josiah, why not?"

"Because—"

"I thought we had talked it all out and that you no longer believe that Nathaniel left it there as a portent of all-encompassing evil? I thought we agreed that just because your brother thought to hide the gem from someone, we are not all suddenly surrounded by terrible danger?"

"Yes, we did, but—"

"But what?"

"But I still believe the thing is cursed, Miranda. And I'm not about to let you dwell in the same house where a gem awash in blood is stowed neatly away. We're lucky beyond belief that I remembered the deuceit, discovered the thing and got it out of there." In the silence of the night, something splashed at their feet and tiny ripples silvered by moonlight appeared on the water.

"A frog, most likely," Elliot observed. "Swim, you scoundrel. Swim for your life. No telling but what we're French and eat frogs for dinner."

Miranda laughed softly and Elliot thought it sounded like

angels singing. Such a lovely, deep, thrilling sound, her laughter. Did he never hear it again for as long as he lived, he would not forget it.

"You're impossible, Josiah Elliot," Miranda whispered huskily, turning to him, placing her hands on his shoulders and standing on tiptoe to kiss the cleft in his chin. "I cannot believe you're capable of such childish fears. A cursed diamond! Awash in blood! Eating frogs!" She turned within the circle of his arms then and rested the back of her head against his chest. She smiled at the silver ribbon of moonlight traveling along the Thames. "Of all things. You're a strong, rational gentleman of considerable years, a gentleman who has braved the horrors of war, a gentleman who has done what he must to survive in the most demeaning circumstances. And yet, here you stand, spouting nonsense. If ever I attempted to describe the contradictions of you, not one person would believe me."

"If I were you, my charming Lady Miranda Wesley," he replied, his arms going more tightly around her, holding her snugly against him. "If I were you, I wouldn't say one word about *my* proving contradictory." He kissed the top of her head lightly. The scent of lavender that lingered in her hair carried him for an instant to the fields of Lavender Hill. He saw her, standing among the endless rows of blooming plants, sunlight sparkling in her hair, and sighed at the vision. But then he recalled himself to the present. "Indeed, my dearest love," he continued after a long, silent moment, "I'd be most careful what I said about other people. A duke's sister who transforms herself into a woman of business has no cause to be judging others."

"I know," Miranda replied, her mind filling with memories of Elliot as highwayman, hero, friend, her heart swelling with love for the very fact of his being. "You're correct, of course. I've certainly no right to judge and no right at all to call anyone else contradictory. But you *are*," she added with a giggle that was almost girlish.

And then she felt the muscles in Elliot's arms stiffen. His head bent low over hers. "There is someone here," he whispered in her ear. "Someone watches us, Miranda."

"Where?"

"Close. Inside the water gate, perhaps. Very close. I can feel him, feel his eyes on us, cannot you?"

"N-no."

"Only be still a moment and you will hear him breathe. The sound is like reeds rattling in the wind or rats scrabbling in the walls, but it's neither. It's someone breathing just out of sight."


Blazingame parted from the patronesses and peered intently around the ballroom. One dance had just ended. Another would begin shortly. He'd barely made it here before the doors closed for the evening. Where the deuce was the man? He'd been to White's Club and Watier's and every other gentlemen's club, and had not got one sight of Marley. Finally he'd resorted to going around to Marley's establishment and knocking on the door, only to be informed by Marley's butler that his lordship, her ladyship and the young miss had gone to Almack's for the evening.

Of all the places I didn't wish to come tonight—or don't wish to come on any night for that matter—Blazingame thought grumpily. And then his attention was abruptly caught by a young woman dressed in white muslin, with golden hair piled high atop her head, blushing cheeks, and blue eyes appearing and disappearing rapidly behind fluttering eyelashes. Obviously she was unacquainted with his reputation, or she didn't recognize him in the sober black and white that an appearance at Almack's demanded, because she was attempting to lure him to her from across the room. Ye gods, he thought, and turned his back on her at once. He fixed his attention on the small groups of gentlemen gathered here and there. They were all busily discussing one thing or another, waiting for the orchestra to strike up again before going to claim a dance with this miss or that.

"I say, Loring," he called quietly, recognizing an old school chum and strolling as rapidly as he could away from female charms and to that gentleman's side.

"Blazingame?" Viscount Loring's eyes squinted the least bit. He tugged on the ribbon that attached his quizzing glass to his buttonhole, held the quizzing glass before one eye and made the most remarkable show of looking Blazingame up and down. "By Jupiter, it is you, Blazingame. I should never have recognized you in that coat and those knee breeches. They're both the same color, old fellow!"

"Black," added the gentleman to Loring's right. "Didn't realize you knew there was such a color as black, Blazingame."

"Well, obviously he does," Loring said, letting the quizzing glass fall to the end of its ribbon. "But he upholds his reputation with that waistcoat, Ditwalder. If there were any rules for waistcoats in this establishment, that one would keep him out."

The frown on Blazingame's face altered into a smile. "Loring, you can never just say how d'ye do, can you?"

"No."

"I've come looking for—" Blazingame began.

"A young lady to marry," provided Ditwalder in a voice so resembling that of Lady Drummond-Burrell, the most intimidating of the patronesses, that every gentleman within hearing distance turned to see if the lady was standing among them. "Preferably pretty and rich, but pretty will do. You don't require her to be rich, do you, Blazingame? After all, you are not without funds."

"Doesn't require her to be titled, either," chuckled Loring. "Has titles enough for four people, Blazingame does."

"I do not," protested Blazingame.

"Yes, well, the rest of us think you do. But at least you're smiling now, Blaze. What brings you here of all places?"

"I'm looking for Lord Marley. His butler said he brought his wife and daughter here, but—"

"Marley's in the card room," Loring replied as the band struck up the notes signaling the start of another dance. "I must be off now, Blaze. Don't get caught standing about by one of our beloved patronesses, eh? Have you tripping through a contre danse with some spotty-faced wallflower if one of them catches you standing about with your hands in your pockets."

Miranda, with great deliberation, stood on tiptoe and placed her arms around Elliot's neck, pulling him down to her, pressing her cheek against his. "I hear the breathing," she whispered in his ear. "He is in the gate above us."

"Don't be afraid, Miranda," Elliot whispered back, and he kissed her softly, tenderly. And when their lips parted, he straightened and lifted her up with him until her feet dangled above the worn stone step. "When I put you down again, my dearest, pretend to stumble and fall to one knee so I can bend over you as if to help you up. There's a knife in my boot. I wish to reach it without our watcher guessing what it is that I'm about to do."

He kissed her again wildly, passionately, until she was actually forced to struggle in his arms for breath, and then he released her and she did stumble. She didn't need to pretend. He bent over her, stood tall again, and stepped between her and the water-gate doorway.

Behind him on one knee, Miranda saw nothing but Elliot—his broad back, his wide shoulders, his strong legs spread wide, his hands down at his sides—and in his right hand, a blade glittering in the moonlight. A blade he turned slowly, deliberately.

"Come for us, then," he said in a steady, bored tone. "If you intend to attack us, do so. My lady and I await your pleasure."

Footsteps shuffled on stone. Cloth brushed against a column. A low voice muttered. And then a figure, backlit by streetlamps, loomed over them like the specter of death itself. It stood silent, threatening, and then it emitted the most bloodcurdling scream, low and loud and terrifying. It lurched a bit forward, turned, and stumbled away, back through the doorway, and scuttled like some mad spider out of the water gate and up Buckingham Street, seeking the shadows as it did. Elliot's first instinct was to give chase, but he suppressed the urge and turned instead to Miranda, helped her to her feet, kissed her cheek. Then he leaned down and placed his knife back into the nearly invisible scabbard in his boot.

"Some ruffian after our valuables," Miranda said as he straightened and placed his arm around her shoulders.

"Are you all right, Miranda? You're not harmed?"

"What? From falling to my knee and hiding behind you? I think not."

"No, of course not. What was I thinking? That you'd scraped your knee, perhaps? You did not scrape your knee or tear your stockings?" A smile flickered across his face in the moonlight.

"My lady and I await you?" Miranda said, noting that smile and the touch of pride it contained.

"Just so. Knew better than to take on the both of us, did he not? Knew he could not best two of us. Probably thought you would turn to a mass of quivering jelly, and be more of a detriment than a help, but we corrected that misconception."

"I might have become a mass of quivering jelly."

"No, not you," Elliot drawled, wondering if this man and the one who had been following Blazingame about were one and the same, wondering if he ought to tell Miranda about the man with the carroty hair. But he couldn't conceive of any reason that a man sent to follow Blazingame should suddenly be following him, and so he declined to mention it to her. "A mass of quivering jelly? The brave lady who fought her way through wind and rain into the Forest of Wynde to save my hapless life? I think not."

"As a matter of fact, I did scrape my knee and tear my stocking," Miranda murmured, remembering with a grateful heart that bitter night she and the others had found Elliot trapped beneath fallen tree limbs. "But neither is of any consequence, Josiah. I shall not die because of it."

"No, you'll not die because of it. I ought not have brought you here so very late in the evening, I expect," he added, as they started together up the worn steps. "It used to be a safe neighborhood, this. There was a time when no ruffian would dare to wander these streets."

"Things change, Josiah, and not always for the better."

"True. But sometimes for the better," he added as they reached the top step. He swept her up into his arms without the least warning and spun in a circle with her cradled there. "Sometimes for the better," he laughed as they spun.

"Josiah, have you run mad?"

"Yes. Mad. Mad with love for you and admiration for you and pride in you. With you beside me, I can conquer the world."

"You've no need to conquer the world," Miranda whispered, tucking her head neatly between his chin and his shoulder, allowing the fingers of one hand to play with the knot in his neckcloth. "You've merely to once again make a place for yourself in it."

He ceased to spin that instant, became like a statue of fine moonlit marble. She raised her head and gazed into his eyes. "You've merely to make a place for you and me together," she whispered as her fingers left his neckcloth to caress his jaw, while the fingers of her other hand twisted themselves into the honey-blond curls thick on the back of his neck. "A place where you and I can be together forever, Josiah."

\* \* \*

Blazingame left the card room thoroughly frustrated. I've managed to ferret out nothing, he thought, frowning. If I've done anything, I've made Marley and every gentleman at his table curious. Can't tell Elliot that. That will make him more uneasy than he already is. "I cannot like Marley," he muttered to himself. "I find he sets my teeth on edge. What the—? Jupiter, I do beg your pardon," he added more loudly as he grabbed for the young lady he'd walked smack into, attempting to keep her from crashing to the floor. "Clumsy of me," he said, stooping to pick up the tiny reticule she'd dropped. "I'm frightfully sorry." And then, as he handed her reticule to her, he actually saw her face for the first time and his own face turned positively gray, as gray as a pigeon's chest feathers.

"Blazingame! Fancy meeting you here!" exclaimed Sir Francis Danvers, who had been in the process of escorting Blazingame's victim from the dance floor. "Miss Feebes, may I make Lord Blazingame known to you?"

"We have already been introduced," Eleanor replied, feeling her cheeks flame. She attempted to shake open the pretty hand-painted fan attached to her wrist by a fine gold chain so she could hide behind it and peer at the odious Lord Blazingame from over its top. Unfortunately, the fan had been in her hands when she'd brought them up to stave off the collision, and now every thin ivory stick of it was bent absurdly to the left. It refused to open. Aggravated, she shook it more heartily. Still it would not open. Tears of frustration rose to Eleanor's eyes. *Surely everyone in the room is staring at me this very moment,* she thought. *I have not the least hope of bringing this ludicrous encounter off with the least aplomb. Even my fan is against me.*

It was the final blow to Eleanor's hopes for the evening. What had begun promisingly, with introductions to a number of likely gentlemen, had dwindled away into this just-ended dance with Sir Francis and their silent retreat from the floor. She had had many partners, some of whom had remarked upon the sweetness of her smile, the flash of her eyes, the splendid turn of her ankle. Handsome, well-spoken, affable gentlemen had taken note of her and led her out onto the floor. But not one of them had proved to be interested in any Causes. They had all been quite pleased to discuss their prowess at this and that, their likes and dislikes, their fortunes and titles. Flirtatious flattery had dripped from narrow lips and wide. Admiration had mounted into several sets of smiling and seductive eyes. But every pair of eyebrows she'd encountered had risen in horrified amazement as she'd attempted to converse with their owners about the need for the education of England's poor or the despicable propensity of the upper classes for gaming or the havoc wreaked upon cottage industries by the continuing advancement of factories. Bit by bit her hopes, her dreams of discovering a gentleman to share with her the joy of aiding the unfortunates of the world collapsed around her. And now, this—Blazingame—stood openmouthed before her, preventing her from hurrying back to the little rows of chairs, where she might hide beside her aunt Caroline. And Sir Francis was not making the slightest attempt to lead her around the man either. No, he was helping to fence her in instead.

Eleanor instinctively lifted one small hand in a sweetly embroidered glove to swipe at a tear in the very corner of her right eye. Unfortunately, this tear was followed by another, which rose in her left. Sir Francis, seeing the tears, stared helplessly at Blazingame.

"They are striking up a waltz," Blazingame heard himself say as if he were standing at a great distance from his own body. "Has one of the patronesses approved you to dance the waltz, Miss Feebes?"

"N-no."

"Oh."

"Why must s-someone approve me?" Eleanor managed around a tiny sob she could not avoid.

"I haven't the vaguest idea. Rules. Sir Francis, Lady Jersey is standing right over there. Trot over like a good fellow and beg her to give Miss Feebes and me the nod."

"What? Oh! Oh, surely, Blazingame!"

And in the time it took to flick a flea, Eleanor found the fence post of Sir Francis gone from her side and her way clear to escape the dance floor. But Lord Blazingame was taking hold of her arm. What was he thinking to do? "Release me at once," she demanded, though the authority of the demand lost something for the tears now rolling slowly down her blushing cheeks.

"No, Miss Feebes, I won't," Blazingame heard himself say. "You cannot leave the floor with tears flowing and sobs in your voice. You'll be the talk of the town for a week at least."

"I shall already be that."

"Not at all, Miss Feebes. Anyone who saw realizes that it was I walked smack into you and not the other way around. And no one has seen your tears as yet except Sir Francis and me. It is I shall be the talk of the town—not only for setting foot in this place tonight, which I never do, but for having walked straight into a lovely young woman and nearly knocked her to the floor. I am sincerely sorry for it, Miss Feebes. I had not the least intention— Ah, there, Sally Jersey is waving her hand in the air and nodding at us."

He ceased to speak, took her tiny reticule and tucked it into his pocket, placed one hand on Eleanor's back and swept her into a graceful if somewhat unnerving turn— swept her into the midst of the other dancers—swept her into the waltz.

"You must attempt to stem your tears, Miss Feebes," he heard himself whisper. Jupiter, what was wrong with him? He felt as if he'd nothing at all to do with his own body, had no control over what it chose to do. His legs moved without his say-so; his lips spoke without his mind urging them to it. And all the while his heart beat wildly, most uncomfortably, within his chest and the feel of Miss Feebes so near to him made his collar wilt.

They waltzed on in silence for a bit, Eleanor stemming her tears and swiping the stain of them from her cheeks with the back of her glove.

"I know you don't care for me overly much, Miss Feebes," Blazingame said at last when he thought he had managed to put himself back into his own body once more, "but I could not simply stand by and watch you rush, sobbing, from the floor. Especially not when I was the cause of it."

"You were not the cause of it."

"I wasn't?"

"Not solely."

"You were not having a perfectly grand time here at Almack's this evening, Miss Feebes, until I ruined it for you?"

"No."

Blazingame gazed steadily down at her with such a light in those eyes of his. Eleanor could not fathom the meaning of that light. And yet, even as she watched, the cold, solid jade of them warmed and shimmered and transformed themselves into flashing emeralds. The very impossibility of such a metamorphosis deprived Eleanor of speech entirely.

# SEVEN

For the longest time he sat in the lumpy wing chair before the cold hearth listening to his heart ratchet against his ribs. It would take him forever, it seemed, to catch his breath after that dash up Buckingham Street, through the rear door of Number 15, up the back stairs and along the corridor into his rented rooms at the front of the house. He was amazed, in a vague way, that he had made the dash at all. He'd not thought it possible that he possessed the energy to run. Perhaps it had been a dream merely and he hadn't run at all. What was the dream? What was the reality? To distinguish between the two had become nearly impossible. But his heart was beating madly. He could hear it. He could feel it. And if he had not been running, as he imagined, then it beat so because of Josiah.

Had he actually seen Josiah standing with a woman beneath the streetlamp in that moment he'd gazed from his window? Had he actually gazed from his window? But he must have done. And he must have gone down into the street, followed the two to the water gate, felt his stomach scream in pain as Josiah's face stared up at him, splashed with moonlight. It had seemed so real. So very real. Even now Josiah's voice echoed in his ears. "My lady and I await your pleasure. My lady and I await your pleasure."

His fingers scrabbled unnoticed through his long grayish-blond hair and tugged at this clump and that as he felt himself sinking further and further into the nightmares of his mind. Ought to have stepped out and faced him, he thought. Ought to have stepped down into the moonlight and called him by name. Ought to have descended the steps and welcomed him. That would have sent the damnable haunt back to his grave. That would have ended the vision, freed me from the terror.

But he'd not found the courage to do it and it was that which prompted him toward despair—his realization of how he'd faltered on the very edge of courage. He did not remember his scream, not at all, but he remembered the shock, the horror that had come directly before it.

Boys spend their days anticipating futures filled with heroic deeds, honor, nobility, he mused in silence, his breath coming more easily now, his fingers ceasing to plague his hair and relaxing on the arms of the chair instead. Boys spend every waking hour desiring manhood so they can prove themselves, show the world the mettle they're made of, and then—and then—the world turns around and bites us all soundly in the posterior. He giggled madly at that thought—the world clinging to his own posterior. "Has huge, sharp teeth, the world," he observed as the giggle faded. "Greater and sharper than I ever imagined. Who ever guesses when they're young that the world can eat men alive?"

He forced himself to rise, persuaded himself to walk to the window, to stare down into the street. And Josiah and the woman were just then strolling along the pavement below as if his thoughts of them had summoned them up. He felt a scream rise in his throat, but it did not come. Nothing came. "How can I see a dead man walking? Nothing is ever as it seems. Nothing." He made his way back to the chair, sat down in it and reached with trembling hands for his pipe. He filled it awkwardly, hurriedly, lit it with fumbling fingers and put it to his lips.

At the top of the street Elliot hailed a hackney cab, assisted Miranda to enter and they drove off. In the sky above, one lone cloud whispered around the moon.

Miranda dismissed her maid and settled herself between the sheets. Four pillows at her back, the lamp on the night-stand turned high and a volume of poetry in her hands, she sat comfortably amidst the bedclothes and stared at the wall. Her mind could not be easily captured by Keats this night. Her thoughts focused instead on the ride home in the hackney, on Josiah's touch—the strength and protectiveness of his arm around her shoulders, the warmth of his hand on her own, the sweet, gentle whisper of his breath along her cheek and the tickle of it in her ear. "Surely his wishing to prove himself to Charles is all nonsense," she murmured. "I am a fool to let it go on. There must be some way to make Josiah see that he need not prove anything to anyone. Not for my sake. Not even for his own. Oh, to have him beside me now, in this very bed, discussing that ruffian at the water gate, encouraging each other in the possibility that perhaps tomorrow we will discover Nathaniel's whereabouts, taking hope and courage from each other's embrace as we settle into sleep. What difference to Charles if his sister marries a valet? No difference. None. Whomever I choose to marry, it is not my brother's concern."

But it's of concern to Josiah, she reminded herself silently. He's a good man, Josiah Elliot, and proud. And he's determined to prove to Charles's satisfaction that he is not merely some rugged fellow I've plucked from the streets because I'm desperate for a husband. He remains determined to win Charles's approval of our marriage in spite of all I say to him.

And yet, it would be rather nice to have Charles and Catherine at our wedding, she thought. To see them smile as Josiah and I become husband and wife. And I ought not be so judgmental of my brother. I was quite as snobbish and *tonnish* as he and Catherine once. I remember. I was positively loath to make the acquaintance of any man beneath the rank of earl.

"Oh, I almost cannot believe it!" She laughed a full-throated, husky laugh that warmed the chamber more than did the little coal fire on the hearth. "Of all things! Lady Miranda Wesley, dreading to dance with a viscount, turning up her nose at barons, dismissing all second sons on sheer principle! Fate *does* make fools of us all. To think I was once so overwhelmed with my own importance and now, quite without the least warning, I have willingly and cheerfully given my heart to a commoner. Once a soldier, once a highwayman, now a mere valet. Yet he is the man with whom I dare to share the deepest secrets and most intense yearnings of my heart."

Enough, she thought then. I am burning with longing for Josiah. I shall never get to sleep this way. Keats, Keats, Keats. There's the answer. Think of Keats and not Josiah. At least for a short time. At least for the time it takes to slip into dreams.

Elliot had abandoned the idea of slipping into dreams altogether. Instead, he paced the floor of the tiny sitting room beside Blazingame's bedchamber and mumbled. What he mumbled made not the least bit of sense. Bits and pieces of thoughts, merely. Disjointed, disconnected, and so random that when Blazingame walked in on him and attempted to make sense of the snatches of words he heard, the earl was fairly certain his valet had gone mad at last.

"I do beg your pardon, Elliot," Blazingame said as Elliot continued to pace, not once taking note that he was no longer alone in the chamber.

"Eh? What?"

"I said, I do beg your pardon, Elliot, but is there something wrong? I mean to say, if it's the diamond from Hades that has you in such a state, I'm certain—"

"No, no, not the diamond. I am not worried about the diamond."

"You're not? But I thought—"

"I *was* worried about it, but Miranda has convinced me that I was wrong. Not a portent. Not some dire warning. Nat likely hid the thing in the deuceit to keep from losing it along with everything else. Though why hide it in a house that he had already signed over to the Duke of Berinwick, I can't comprehend."

"Perhaps he hadn't. Perhaps he had not given up the house at the time."

"I expect that must have been it. That's precisely what Miranda said. But why not go back for it then? Once the house is lost?"

"And that's what you've been mumbling about?"

"No."

"What, then? Help me off with this dratted coat, Elliot."

"My pleasure."

"It's your job, actually."

"Yes, well, my pleasure and my job," Elliot acquiesced as he began to peel the close-fitting garment from Blazingame's shoulders.

"So what is it that has you all upset, Elliot, if it's not the diamond?" And then Blazingame's eyes widened considerably and he turned to stare at Elliot just as Elliot had gotten the coat off his shoulders and down to the earl's elbows. "I say, have you had word of your brother? Ouch! What the deuce?"

"Turn back around," Elliot ordered. "Tug your arms all the way out of the sleeves before you turn back again. No, no word of Nat. Not so much as a whisper. It's—it's Miranda."

"Lady Miranda has set you to pacing and mumbling and not even noticing when someone enters the room?"

"Yes."

"Why?"

"Why?" Elliot was now in full possession of the coat and he tossed it halfway across the room onto the window seat. "Why? Because I cannot live without her, yet I have vowed not to have her—not until I discover what's happened to Nathaniel. Not until I prove that I come from a family worthy to be joined with hers. Lord love a cat, Blazingame, I'm going stark raving mad! When I'm near her, I cannot refrain from touching her. I shove my hands into my pockets one moment and the next I find they've crept back out of their own accord and one or the other of them has taken to holding her hand. Or my arm will find its way around her shoulders without my ever thinking to let it do so. Or I am drawing her into my arms and kissing the top of her head when I had every intention of keeping at a respectable distance. And when she rests against me the way she's wont to do, all of me starts jerking and jumping about inside even though my outside is as still as it can be. And my heart—my heart will not beat without it mimics her name with its rhythm. I have got to learn what's happened to Nat soon. And I've got to discover where the family Bible has gone soon, or I'll die for wanting Miranda and not having her. I swear I will."

Blazingame undid the buttons of his waistcoat and untied his neckcloth. He sat down in the nearest chair and took off his dancing shoes. Then he padded in stocking feet into his bedchamber and returned with his nightshirt in hand to find Elliot pacing again.

"Is all this anxiety and restlessness and muttering a sign of true love, Elliot?"

"Yes."

Blazingame sat back down in the chair, his nightshirt clutched in his hands. "How can it be? You've but recently shown me that love is quiet, silent even, that it can be so deep that two people need not speak to converse with each other. I have just begun to think true love is like beautiful poetry, like bluebirds singing in the orchards, like the sun rising above the hills on a summer day. It's joyful and peaceful, and fills a man with wonder."

"Sometimes it's precisely like bluebirds singing in orchards," Elliot said, coming to a halt and rubbing at the back of his neck with one hand as he studied Blazingame thoroughly for the first time since that gentleman had arrived in the sitting room. "And sometimes, Blazingame, it's like rooks cawing in the tower, setting your teeth on edge. What's happened to you?"

"Happened? To me?"

"You don't look quite the thing, Blazingame. I mean, my lord. No, deuce it, I mean Blazingame. I haven't the least notion why I must call you my lord when no one is about. At any rate, you look—subdued."

"Subdued? What sort of word is that for the way a fellow looks? Pale, perhaps. Out of sorts. Even quiet isn't too awful. A fellow can look quiet, I expect. Especially if he is."

"Never mind my choice of words. Out with it. What happened to you tonight? You weren't at all joyful when you came and changed your clothes for Almack's, but you were at least filled with a certain energy. Now you're just sitting there twisting your nightshirt slowly into one unidentifiable lump," Elliot declared, his hands fisted on his hips as he stood over the earl.

Blazingame's jade-green eyes gazed up into Elliot's brown ones and then away again. "Nothing happened. Not really. I played some cards and spoke with Marley and danced with Miss Feebes. About Marley—"

"You spoke with Marley again? You didn't mention the diamond to him, did you?"

"Well, I might have mentioned it in—in—passing. Said he's known about it since he was a child, but he's certain there's no curse on the thing. Done a bit of study on it, he has. Pooh-poohed the curse completely. All fabricated nonsense, the deaths connected with it. History doesn't bear the story out. None of the others at the table had heard of it at all. Elliot, about Marley—"

"Marley doesn't believe The Heart of a Queen is cursed?" Elliot could not believe his ears. "And none of the others at the table had ever heard of the diamond at all? None of the others at the table? How many others were at the table, Blazingame? What the devil were you thinking, to mention the dratted diamond aloud in public?"

"I wasn't playing cards in a den of thieves, Elliot. I was playing cards at Almack's. None of the gentlemen with whom I spoke is likely to break into this establishment in search of your diamond. Not that I said it was here, or intimated that I'd even seen it, because I did not. About Marley, Elliot—"

"How do you know who's a thief and who's not, Blazingame? Do you think just because a man holds a title that he's bound to be honest and honorable? Well, it isn't so. I've known an aristocrat or two in my time I wouldn't have trusted not to steal a paper of pins. What about Marley?"

"Huh?"

"You have been saying 'about Marley' forever. What more about Marley do you want me to know?"

"Oh! Yes. Well, it occurred to me that the person who apparently has gained the most from your brother's disappearance is Marley. He's come into possession of the mementoes you mentioned and the house in Portman Square. And it occurred to me that it was shortly after I spoke to him at Watier's that the carroty-haired man began to follow me about."

"What did you say to Marley at Watiers?"

"I said—I said—that I had recently discovered papers of my father's that listed an unpaid debt to a gentleman by the name of Elliot and that I wished to attend to the matter."

"Yes?"

"And then I said that I realized he despised you, but that Nathaniel was the Elliot involved and I asked if he could point me in Nathaniel's direction. That was when he told me he owned the house and rented it out, but he'd no idea where Nathaniel had gone or why."

"So?"

"I *said* that I knew he despised *you*, Elliot. How the devil would I even know you, much less know you and Marley did not get along? Marley had to know I was lying from the start. And it was shortly after I spoke to him that the carroty-haired man began to follow me about."

"Damnation," mumbled Elliot, beginning to pace again. "And all this is what has made you so—pale and quiet? You sound worse than you look, by the way. All whispery, sort of."

Blazingame shook his head and sighed. "No. Actually, dancing with Miss Feebes has made me what I am at the moment."

"Dancing with Miss Feebes?" The most enchanting grin appeared on Elliot's face despite his upset over Marley. He felt it there, the grin. He erased it at once. "Well. Do you want to talk about it, Blazingame?"

"Talk about what?"

"About—dancing."


The following morning Eleanor departed her chamber and descended the staircase all the way to the ground floor to discover exactly what she feared. The butler was not busily answering knocks at the door. The footmen were not dashing back and forth in an effort to keep the vestibule clear of posies. The silver salver on the table was not overflowing with gentlemen's calling cards.

"A vase of flowers arrived for you earlier, miss," Laughton said quietly. "Very pretty flowers. I placed them in the morning room. A small package accompanied them. I set the package beside the vase."

"Thank you, Laughton."

"Yes, miss. It is early times yet, you know, miss. Most of London's gentlemen are still abed."

Eleanor nodded, though she knew full well that Laughton's words were intended merely to take away the sting of her failure. He had butled for her uncle Roger for years. He had seen the floral offerings garnered by each of her three cousins. Laughton pitied her. It was obvious from the look on his face.

"I expect I did not take, Laughton," Eleanor managed from behind a forced smile.

"Much too soon to draw such a conclusion as that, miss, if you'll pardon my observation."

"You needn't attempt delicacy with me, Laughton. I assure you, it doesn't matter if I took or not. Not in the least. I did never expect to become all the rage."

Well, I *didn't* expect it, Eleanor told herself as she climbed back up the staircase to the first floor and made her way along the corridor to the morning room, where breakfast awaited the family on the finely crafted Italian sideboard. I merely hoped to find—someone. I am not as pretty as Charity or Priscilla or Beth. And I do never say anything fetching or delightful. And my cousins are all blond and petite and charming as can be, whereas I am like Mama—a chirping brown sparrow merely allowed to share the nest with the colorful songbirds.

"And there is nothing wrong with being a sparrow," she whispered as she entered the morning room. "Sparrows have their place in the world. Oh!" she exclaimed as her gaze abruptly filled with color.

"I should say 'Oh!' again, and a bit louder," offered her brother from the breakfast table. "I've never seen such a bouquet in my entire life. Can't think where he got them, and so early in the morning, too."

"Who?" Eleanor asked, crossing to the round table at the center of the long row of windows that welcomed in the morning sun.

"The gentleman's card is right beside them, Nora. Atop that package."

"Oh, Donovan, are they not the most beautiful flowers you've ever seen? It's like having a rainbow alive and dancing before me." Eleanor took the small rectangular card into her hand and discovered she had to actually force herself to look away from the reds and pinks, yellows and violets, to read the gentleman's name. "Oh!" she exclaimed softly. "Lord Blazingame? Lord Blazingame sent them?"

"Yes, well, there can't be much doubt of that, can there?" declared Donovan. "What else would a gentleman who dresses like a living rainbow send but a living rainbow? He was my first guess, actually, when I walked in and saw the things."

"Lord Blazingame," Eleanor murmured, holding his card out before her. " 'To the Belle of the Ball,' it says."

"Open the package, Nora, and see what else he's sent."

"He ought not to have sent anything else. Not to a young woman he barely knows. Whatever it is, I shall be forced to return it to him."

"Open it regardless," urged Donovan.

"I should wait for Aunt Caroline and ask—"

"No, open it now, Nora," Donovan interrupted, rising and going to stand beside her. "You may not be the least bit curious, but I am. I've been sitting here staring at that package for the past quarter hour. Been debating what it could be since my first bite of bacon."

It was a long, slim package wrapped in silvered paper and tied with a red ribbon. Eleanor's hands trembled the tiniest bit as she lifted it from the table and began to unwrap it. Why would Lord Blazingame call me a belle? she wondered. Why would he send such beautiful flowers and this package as well? He doesn't even like me. Well, how can he after I said what I did to him in Oxford Street and then turned around and made a complete fool of myself in front of him last evening? "Oh!" she exclaimed as the wrappings came completely undone. "Oh, Donovan, look!"

She held out an elegant little fan for his inspection, an

exquisite piece of craftsmanship. Unlike most of its counterparts, its sticks were fashioned from narrow strips of silver. Small rubies fastened fine crocheted lace to the sticks at top and bottom, and the whole had been created to dangle from a slender silver-linked chain.

"Well, Aunt Caroline won't allow you to keep that," Donovan observed. "Ought to know better than to send a young woman such a gift on such short acquaintance."

"But a fan is nothing extraordinary, nothing intimate."

"Perhaps not intimate, Nora, but that particular fan is most extraordinary if you ask me."

"I expect you're right, Donovan. Aunt Caroline will doubtless consider it such. But there is a perfectly good reason for—Lord Blazingame walked right in front of me and I was not watching at all and we—we—bumped each other. My fan broke on the instant. Doubtless he merely thinks to replace that one with this one. He assumes the responsibility for our little impact and means to make amends."

"He does? Blazingame? Accepts responsibility? Hopes to make amends? I thought Blazingame was a villain and a dastard—that there was not the least virtue to be found in him. I thought you despised Blazingame."

"I—I—perhaps I was mistaken in him, Donovan. I did not give him the opportunity, after all, to explain his treatment of Mr. Elliot and— Do you not think, Donovan, if I explain to Aunt Caroline why he sent this fan, she will allow me to accept it?"

"No."

"But it is not as though—"

"Aunt Caroline will return it to him at once and no doubt inform him that it is far from some little trifle. You know she will, Nora. I think those are real rubies."

Miranda sat at the breakfast table, toast and tea before her, a doubtful frown creasing her brow. "Do you think so, Ariel?" she asked after a moment's pause.

"I am not the only one who thinks so," replied Miss Markum, tapping the top of a soft-boiled egg with a silver spoon. "Early thinks so as well. Though whether you wish to speak to him or not is, of course, your decision to make."

"It seems such an odd thing to do, to bring Charles into it. And why you should think the Duke of Berinwick has anything at all to do with Nathaniel or Josiah— Certainly neither Josiah nor Lord Blazingame mentioned the man to us."

"No, but Mr. Doughtry mentioned the man loudly and clearly to me last evening and I thought—"

"Mr. Doughtry?" The frown on Miranda's face vanished and her eyes widened the slightest bit. "Lord Blazingame's butler? *That* Doughtry?"

"Precisely. Lord Blazingame and Mr. Elliot have taken him into their confidence just as they have us. And Mr. Doughtry says the Duke of Berinwick once held the title to this house and it was he who sold it to Lord Marley."

"You spoke with Doughtry last evening, Ariel? Where?"

"W-where?"

"Yes."

"H-here."

Never before, in all the years she had known the woman, had Miranda seen Ariel's cheeks color up as they did now.

"He came rapping at our kitchen door last evening shortly after you departed, Miranda. He introduced himself to Early and requested to step inside. Early allowed him to do so."

"I see."

"He is quite a nice gentleman, Miranda. And he is most fond of Lord Blazingame and concerned about him."

"He told Early this?"

"No, no, he told me. I—we—the three of us shared a cup of tea around the kitchen table and—"

"You do realize that you're not a governess any longer, Ariel?" Miranda interrupted, a smile playing at the corners of her mouth.

"I beg your pardon?"

"I said, you are not my governess any longer. You're a gentlewoman of independent means now. You need not have gathered with a cook and a butler for tea in the kitchen. You might well have invited the both of them up to the drawing room."

"Miranda, don't tease. Of all the things for Mr. Browne and the staff to see. Me entertaining a neighbor's butler and our cook in the drawing room. Besides, he would not have come up to the drawing room."

"No. I gather he is very conscious of his position and has no intention to overstep. Did he bring flowers with him?"

"What?"

"Flowers, Ariel. You remember, those long, green, stick-like things with prettily colored tops. Oh, he did! I can tell from the increasing flame in your cheeks. He did!" Miranda's smile came near to lighting the entire room.

"Enough," Miss Markum declared. "You are a worse tease than your brother could ever hope to be. And this is serious, Miranda. I think Mr. Doughtry's idea is not without promise. Your brother knows the Duke of Berinwick, does he not? And if we could get his grace to have a conversation, to pry just a bit—on a duke-to-duke basis of course—he might discover something of how Berinwick came to have the title to this house in his possession. It may have been payment for a gaming debt or repayment for some particular boon, you know. Something not at all sinister."

"Yes, that's true. But is Berinwick in London?"

"There was an article in the *Times* only yesterday affirming that he is. He despises a particular bill presently being discussed in Parliament and has come to town to talk as many of the lords out of voting for the thing as he can. The man is a frightful Tory, you know."

"More strongly Tory than Charles, if I remember correctly."

"It would be simple enough, don't you think, for your brother to seek out the Duke of Berinwick on the pretense of wishing to discuss the bill? Indeed, that would work exceedingly well. And I expect it would prove no great trick, once he meets with the man, for his grace to steer the conversation in other directions."

"If Charles feels so inclined, I expect it would prove no great trick at all."

"Just so. I know you don't wish to ask favors of his grace, Miranda. I know your independence from him is dear to you. But you would not be losing any of it by simply asking him to speak to the Duke of Berinwick. If the duke can provide us with the merest hint of what actually occurred— well, but it's your decision. You must do as you will."

"Still, how would I go about it if I wished to do it? Charles knows nothing of my relationship with Josiah. What excuse would I give him for my unusual interest in the problems of Lord Blazingame's valet? I realize, Ariel," Miranda replied quietly, "that a mere valet like Josiah has no likelihood of gaining a face-to-face meeting with the Duke of Berinwick, and so I can see someone must do it on his behalf. But why must it be Charles? Lord Blazingame is an earl. Cannot he arrange to have a word with the duke?"

"He can. And Mr. Doughtry fears that he will."

"Oh, I see." And Miranda did see. Very clearly, too. "The Duke of Berinwick is a demon to be sure, Ariel. What was the last rumor we heard of him? That he branded a tavernkeeper as a highwayman and then had him hanged, all in order to bed the man's wife? No, no, that was not the last. But that's the one I remember as the most appalling. And your Mr. Doughtry fears to have his lordship confront this particular hellion, does he?"

"He is not *my* Mr. Doughtry."

"I do beg your pardon, Ariel. I cannot seem to keep from teasing you." Miranda's brow furrowed again, this time with apprehension. "Oh, but I don't like to think that Josiah's brother disappeared because he made some misstep in regard to the Duke of Berinwick. I would much rather believe in the curse of that dratted diamond. But if we must go up against such a devil as Berinwick to set things right again, we will. I *will* speak to Charles about it, Ariel. I will think of some way to broach the subject. Charles is certainly older and wiser and more capable of coming away from that demon of a duke with all his body parts intact than is Lord Blazingame. Your Mr. Doughtry is correct in that. I will go to Charles as soon as possible."


"You can't have sent Miss Feebes a silver and ruby fan," Elliot observed, one eyebrow raised slightly, the small fencing scar on his cheek more evident than usual in the morning light.

"I can and I have," replied Blazingame, studying the shelves of books in his library. "Well, I broke hers last evening, Elliot. It was my duty to replace it, was it not?"

"Not with a fan worth a small fortune, no. Some chicken skin thing with a painted scene, bought in one of the little shops, perhaps, but this one you described—"

"Elliot!" Blazingame interrupted. "Cease and desist with your rules of propriety! Anyone would think you were my nanny instead of my valet. I sent her flowers and the fan and that's that. It's done. I've an appointment with the Duke of Berinwick this afternoon. I intend to ask him, in a roundabout manner of course, how he came to possess the title to your brother's house. Getting the answer to that ought to make you smile a bit."

"I have been smiling right along."

"Have you?" Blazingame, who had begun nervously picking through book after book, turned around to gaze at Elliot, who stood nonchalantly with one arm resting along the fireplace mantel. "You're not smiling now," Blazingame observed.

"No. Only smiling until you mentioned this business of

Berinwick—I don't want you to go fishing about in that particular stream on your own, Blazingame."

"I'm not afraid of the Duke of Berinwick."

"You ought to be."

"He can't possibly be as black as he's painted, Elliot. No man can be as black as that."

"Possibly not. But he's still a devil in his own way. I wish you will put off any meeting with him for a day or two. Give us both an opportunity to think the thing through. Miranda and I were almost attacked at the York water gate last night. Did I tell you that?"

"No. Attacked? By whom? Not the carroty-haired fellow. He was following me all over London. Even waited for me outside Almack's. I can't believe he's so stupid as to think I don't know he's dogging my every footstep."

"I've not the vaguest idea who it was stood pondering the idea of assaulting Miranda and me. He stepped out to confront us, but then he screamed, turned and scurried away. Likely just some ruffian after our valuables and nothing more." Elliot shrugged his shoulders nonchalantly. "About Berinwick, however, I should like to think about that for a time before you go off and arouse his interest in you and this household. And I've been thinking, too, Blazingame, about Miss Feebes. You ought to go and pay Miss Feebes a call."

"Miss Feebes? How did we get back to Miss Feebes?"

Elliot's smile returned. "I can't say. I expect my mind is running hither and thither like a mouse in a maze. Do you intend to pay her a call today?"

"I was considering it, Elliot." Blazingame's hand went to rub at the back of his neck. "I can't think I'll be exceedingly welcomed. Not after the debacle of last evening. Still, I should like to see how she does. I made her cry, you know."

"Yes, you told me that. Ought to call on Miss Feebes. But you ought to change your clothes before you do."

"My clothes? But I donned these barely two hours ago."

"Yes, and I expect they were fine for jaunting off to the florist. But for a visit to Miss Feebes—"

"You're not striving to become a true valet, Elliot, are you? Please don't. I couldn't bear to have you become a true valet. At least, not one with *taste*."

"I was merely thinking," Elliot replied, his eyes sparkling, "how fine a cherry-red cravat would look with that particular coat and waistcoat you have on. I happen to have purchased a cherry-red cravat only yesterday."

"You did?"

"Indeed. And Miss Feebes is coming to like bright colors, I think. You *do* want her to like you? I'm not wrong about that?"

Aristotle Gaylord Marley stood in the front parlor of his house in Russell Square and stared with considerable thoughtfulness out the window. He did not see the sun shining brightly over the lovely new façade of the house opposite him or take note of the robin singing on the lowest branch of the oak in the middle of the square. He did not so much as notice Elsinore's high-perch phaeton as Elsinore tooled off toward Gray's Inn Lane. In truth, Marley saw nothing of this particular morning at all. It was another morning that held his attention—a morning gone quite beyond his reach—a morning in another place, in a time long since past. In his mind he watched in silence as his younger brother, Darius, mounted a flashy chestnut, waved a cheeky farewell and rode away from Marley Manor in the shire of York toward Crystal Pond and the marshes beyond. The dew had laid heavy on the grass that morning and the sun barely risen. The air had smelled of sheep and rotting wood, and the wind whistled down the chimneys of the ancient house.

"The Heart of a Queen," Marley whispered as the vision of his younger brother faded into the distance. "How many years since I've heard lips other than my own speak of it? Dare was the last. But how long ago? Damnation, I cannot so much as remember the year. Gone, off into the wild to make his fortune, he said. To bring home The Heart of a Queen for Nat and share in its sale. And I thought him a fool.

"He was a fool," Marley mumbled then, turning away from the window and the memory. "Rode off in search of a fortune and never rode back home again. Dead. Buried in the marsh. And even if Mama will not have it so, it is so. You would think even Mama must admit Dare is dead, let go his memory and die herself. Been ten years at least and he's never once returned or sent word of his whereabouts. Even Mama must admit he's dead sometime soon."

Marley had never much liked his younger brother. Too bold. Too beautiful. Too much of a braggart. As a matter of fact, Marley had never much liked his mama either, for the same reasons. But the dowager Lady Marley had vowed not to die until she at last discovered what had happened to Dare, and she was even now keeping that vow. Marley had thought to escape her this Season as he had the last by bringing his wife and daughter to Town, but his mama had insisted upon accompanying them this time. At this very moment she was upstairs, speaking in the most extraordinary voice to her dresser and pounding on the floor above Marley's head with her cane. "Old she-devil," Marley muttered, stuffing his hands into his pockets and glaring at the ceiling. "Wretched old she-devil!"

But then her pounding ceased and his mind slipped away from her and skidded into last evening at Almack's and his conversation with that young dunce Blazingame. What possessed the boy to ask me about The Heart of a Queen? he wondered. As if he hadn't already aroused my suspicions enough by speaking earlier of my dislike for Josiah Elliot, there he came last evening, wondering innocently about some tale he'd heard about the blasted diamond and its being cursed.

"I'm right," Marley mumbled. "It's a good thing I set O'Riley to following the lad. Because where else could Blazingame have heard about The Heart of a Queen and the curse but from Josie? Won't have heard about it from Dare, certainly. Dare is dead. Likewise, the lady who spun us all the tales of Buckingham, Elliot's mama. She's dead. Nathaniel? No, no, not Nat. The boy cannot possibly have heard these things from Nat, because he's still looking for Nat. It's Josiah who's told him these things and set him to questing after Nathaniel. Has to be. Everyone else who even knows about The Heart of a Queen is dead and gone."

A rugged, bewildered countenance rose up in Marley's mind unbidden. "He was somewhat alive the last time I saw him, Josiah was. Mad as a hatter, hostling at the inn, but breathing. Has he come to London then, trembling madness and all?"

The thought of Josiah Elliot somewhere in London, somewhere near him, had the same bilious effect on Marley's stomach that it had had that night at Watier's when Blazingame had first intimated the likelihood, and for a moment Marley thought he might need to sit down and rest his head on one of his wife's new lavender pillows. But he fought against the sudden illness and in the end merely burped. "But how would that lunatic come to know an earl," Marley wondered aloud, "much less succeed in convincing him to ask after Nat on his behalf? Disappeared from the cottage at Crystal Pond the night Carpenter was murdered. Thought he believed he'd killed Carpenter himself and went to put an end to his worthless life. Expected him to hang himself on the moor. Still, there's no one else. Josie must be alive and in London. And he must have gained Blazingame's ear somehow. But how? How? And what in Hades am I going to do about him when I find him?"

# EIGHT

"You intend to marry whom?" The Duke of Comestock sprang from his chair as though propelled upward by a catapult. "Are you mad, Miranda?" he bellowed. "Have you lost all sense of propriety? All sense of what is due yourself?"

"I knew I ought not tell you," Miranda sighed. "But I could think of nothing else powerful enough to make it clear to you how important my request is. Truth is the most powerful of all tools. It was you who taught me that, Charles."

"You've lost your mind," Comestock declared, pacing back and forth in front of her. "All those years on your own in Yorkshire have deprived you of sense and sensibility! I ought to have gone after you at once and dragged you back here, kicking and screaming if need be."

"And I ought to have married Josiah in Yorkshire and never said a word to you about it. And I would have done precisely that if he had not insisted that we wait. Do sit back down, Charles. You impress me not at all by strutting before me like some cock before his hen and you'll give me a crick in my neck from needing to look up at you besides."

His grace came to an immediate halt before his sister and glared down at her through eyes as fierce as a charging bull's.

"Honestly, Charles," Miranda said, uncowed by his glare, a glare she had watched him practice over and over again before the looking glass in his youth. "Sit down and attempt to set aside your innate ability to rate yourself and your family higher in value than almost anyone on earth. I have a much larger problem at the moment than whether you approve of the gentleman I intend to marry. This could become a matter of life and death. I would not have confided my matrimonial intentions to you at all, else."

"Life and death?" Comestock's glare altered at once into an expression of puzzlement. "Whose life and death?"

"I don't know precisely."

"Merely attempting to arouse my curiosity, Miranda?"

"No, Charles. It is simply that I don't understand it all myself at this point and so I can't guess what has happened or may happen. I think there may have been a murder and I fear there may be another if things are handled badly. There's information we lack—well, we lack any information at all, actually. We're simply proceeding on hypotheses—but there's someone who can point us in the right direction. And you, dear brother, are the most qualified gentleman I know to confront that someone and uncover that information."

"Me?" A touch of pride incorporated itself into the curiosity on the duke's countenance. With three long strides he returned to his chair. He sat down in it and crossed one knee gracefully over the other. He rested his elbows on the chair arms and made a steeple of his fingers. "Proceed," he commanded with a touch of royalty.

Miranda found it difficult not to smile at his tone, his posture and his sudden interest—he reminded her so very much at this moment of his younger self—but she schooled her features into a most serious frown. "Whether or not you approve of Josiah, Charles, I don't believe you will withhold your assistance from him or from me once you hear his story. I will admit that I did hesitate to bring you into it—because Josiah has no intention of so much as introducing himself to your notice until he can prove to you his worthiness."

"A perceptive member of the Great Unwashed? Unbelievable."

"He is not a member of the Great Unwashed!"

"Not quite. But the man is a valet, Miranda. You said so yourself. He can never be worthy of my notice."

"He can. He is. You don't know him, Charles. He fought on the continent and in the Peninsula for ten years and more. He's courageous, honorable, admirable—"

"And a commoner at best."

"I did not come to argue with you about Josiah's class. I came to beg your assistance. Ariel and I have discussed it and we think you can help us enormously. Lord Blazingame intends to help, but he is so very young and inexperienced and—"

"Blazingame? That fop?"

"He is not a fop. And I am not going to sit here and argue with you about Lord Blazingame any more than I am going to argue with you about Josiah. Listen to me very closely, Charles, and please don't interrupt again. Josiah fought last in the battle of Salamanca, where he was gravely injured. He was mustered out. He returned here, to London, to discover that sometime during his long absence, his elder brother, Nathaniel, and Nathaniel's sons disappeared. Someone else now holds title to the family's London residence and none of the neighbors have the least idea what happened or where Nathaniel and the boys have gone.

"Josiah's stepsister, who lives a considerable distance to the north of me in Yorkshire, has not had a letter from Nathaniel in years, and Lord Marley, who is a cousin of sorts, will not so much as speak to Josiah, much less betray any knowledge of Nathaniel's disappearance. And there is no rumor, no gossip among the neighbors to explain it."

"Most likely dead, eh? The entire family taken off by some fever?"

"Yes, just what Josiah thought at first, and why he rode off into Yorkshire to find his stepsister and her husband—

but they could not say yea or nay to it. They had a letter from Nathaniel saying that his wife had died of a fever several years before and that he buried her. One of the boys was ill as well, he wrote, but no word ever came following that."

"Well, then, it's likely the entire family succumbed."

"I would think so as well, Charles. But then, would not the neighbors be aware of it? Why does no one say, 'Indeed, the Elliots lived here for decades, but the younger son went off to war and the elder and his family died of a fever in the winter of '09 or '10 or whatever year?' "

"I can't imagine. Seems reasonable they would."

"Just so. Josiah searched but could find no direction for Nathaniel. The family solicitor was elderly before Josiah ever joined the Hussars and—"

"He was a Hussar?"

"Yes."

"Well, there's some hope in that—for his social standing, I mean."

"I do not care a fig about his social standing!" Miranda declared in frustration. "Have you not listened to a word I said? Nathaniel and his sons are gone. The house was eventually purchased by Lord Marley, who is a third cousin once removed and who, though he would not speak to Josiah, has told Lord Blazingame that he has no idea where Nathaniel went. The family solicitor is dead, all records of Nathaniel's assets are missing. There's not so much as a will to be found."

"Assets? A will? Are you attempting to tell me that this Nathaniel Elliot had considerable money, Miranda?"

"Josiah says the family has always been well off. But now Josiah's investments have disappeared along with Nathaniel's investments, because Nathaniel had control of them all, you see."

"I do see, actually. An abominable situation. What did

this valet of yours do, eh, when he discovered his brother's disappearance?"

"Well, after his first inquiries—which he had to make without anyone's assistance and which gained him nothing—Josiah went to Yorkshire to live in a cottage near his stepsister. He thought to begin his life anew there, to earn a living and establish a new sort of existence for himself. But he—he—he suffers from a certain peculiarity because of his war injuries. It's a trembling actually. It comes upon him without warning and he has no control over what follows. His mind drifts away when the trembling seizes him and—"

"Jupiter, Miranda! He's not only a commoner but a lunatic?"

"He's not a lunatic! It's an illness—an illness that kept him from being of any value to any employer. He attempted to hold any number of positions, Charles, but he was always let go because the trembles caused him to do something extraordinary. At last Whethers took him on—"

"Whethers? Daxonbury's Whethers?"

"Yes."

"Taught him enough to become Blazingame's valet, eh?" Comestock murmured. "Good for Whethers. Of course, he didn't need to teach the man much. One look at Blazingame and you can't help but know—"

"Never mind about Lord Blazingame's fashion sense, Charles. We are not discussing fashion. Whethers sent Josiah to Lord Blazingame because Whethers knew something about the earl that Daxonbury and you and I did not. Blazingame is mad for solving puzzles. And I must say that he has apparently thrown himself into the solving of this puzzle of Josiah's disappearing brother wholeheartedly."

"And what, so far, has Blazingame discovered?"

"That Nathaniel's wife is truly dead and buried, but there are no graves for Nathaniel or the boys in the same graveyard. That a solicitor by the name of Mr. Asserby was placed in charge of selling Nathaniel's house to Lord Marley. And that Mr. Asserby saw to the sale at the request of the Duke of Berinwick, who was at the time in legal possession of the title to it."

"Berinwick? Why would Berinwick be interested in some hovel previously owned by a nobody?"

"It is not a hovel and the Elliots are not nobodies. They can trace their ancestry as far back as the fifteenth century, Josiah says."

"Which explains why the man is now a valet and why I never once heard of him or his brother, eh, Miranda?"

Comestock's tone brought a most forbidding scowl to Miranda's countenance. "You needn't be scornful," she said quietly. "Josiah does not lie. If he says his family is of ancient stock, then it is. Will you never change, Charles? Always with you, rank equals worth. Any gentleman beneath the rank of earl, you taught me once, was not worth my time. No matter how handsome he was, no matter how kind he seemed, no matter, even, if he was wealthy—if a gentleman were not a duke, a marquess, or an earl, he was not worthy of my attention. Those were the lessons you taught me, Charles, when you prepared me to make my come-out. And I learned them well. Second sons were to be dismissed from my mind immediately. Gentlemen born on the distaff side of good families were to be considered beneath my notice. If a man did not hold a title outright or were not in direct line, I was not to waste my precious time with him."

Comestock nodded. "It's what Mother and Father taught me, and I can see nothing wrong with it, Miranda. Royalty unites with royalty, nobility with nobility, and so on down the line. It's the way of the world."

"The way of the world for Mother and Father. The way of the world for you, perhaps. But not for me, Charles. I wanted—I needed—to love someone and be loved by him. It was not the position of duchess or marchioness or countess that I craved, no triumphant alliance between two noble families. I paid strict attention to your lessons because I thought you knew best how to find the love I craved. I depended on you and your lessons. I believed that love could exist only within the lines you had drawn for me, that to step outside those boundaries would bring only disaster. I followed your teachings in my first Season and in my second and in my third. But I found no one to love, no one to love me. Not even a man I could *hope* to learn to love."

"You did not try—"

"I tried."

"You turned down every offer."

"Every offer? Yes. Because that is precisely what they were. Offers. As if I were something you had put on the auction block, something for the gentlemen to fight over, something to be sold to the highest bidder. There was no love involved in any of those offers. They saw before them only the sister of the Duke of Comestock, and therefore a link to you."

Comestock stared at his sister in disbelief. "I never—" he began, and then he lowered his gaze and studied the toes of his boots for a long moment. When he looked back up at Miranda, there was a dullness in his eyes she had never seen there before. "Did it truly seem so to you? That you were being sold to the highest bidder? I only wished for you to be married and for that marriage to be the very best it could be, Miranda. And I have always believed that the best of marriages is based on similarity of rank, power, fortune. Well, but it makes sense. People raised alike, who think alike and desire the same things—and are capable of getting what they desire—they have every hope for an excellent union, don't you see?"

"Yes, I do see. And I saw then how much sense it made, too."

"Just so. And Catherine and I had then, as we do now, a very happy marriage, Miranda."

"I believe you. But you and Catherine love each other, Charles."

Comestock smiled softly. "I fell in love with her the day we met. She was strolling in Green Park with her mama when her parasol blew away. I was merely passing by, but she seized my arm, spun me about and ordered me off in pursuit of it. I can't explain why, but I fell in love with her on the instant. Chased that damnable thing all over the park. Caught it finally. We were both laughing so hard when I returned with it—"

"That's just the thing," Miranda interrupted. "You love Catherine and she loves you. It may be your similarities that make your marriage a prodigiously workable union, Charles, but it's the love that makes your union worthwhile. It's the love between you that makes every day worth living, don't you see?"

"I—I never thought of it quite that way. I mean to say, if two people are much alike, do they not just simply come to love each other? Is it not the similarities that promote their love, that make their love possible?"

"Perhaps for some. But in three Seasons, Charles, I discovered no gentleman who could bring a smile to my face like the smile you were smiling just a moment ago. No one who did anything that caught at my heart or stirred my soul as Catherine does yours. And since I wished so much for love and could not find it in anyone of my own class, and since I believed it quite beyond the pale to step down from my titled heights, I simply decided that I was destined to live out my life alone and unmarried."

Comestock nodded gravely. His hands formed fists on the arms of his chair. From the day she'd demanded her inheritance and they had quarreled bitterly over her ability— any woman's ability—to live independently, to manage her own funds and her own life—to this very moment, Comestock's heart had been filled with concern for her. He had spoken so unwisely; their quarrel had been so caustic, that Miranda had lived without his aid, his guidance, without so much as a word of his advice for the past ten years and more. In desperation, at one point, he'd written to Miss Markum and begged the girl's former governess to go to her in Yorkshire. He'd insisted that his wife and his children keep up a steady correspondence with her. For years, he'd sent Catherine and Sophia to Bath each summer without him, just so Miranda would meet them there and spend time with them. Through these others, he had assured himself of her safety and well-being. Truth be told, he cared deeply at this very moment about what would become of her—though he would never say as much to her. He did not know how to say such things to her.

"All this time, I have longed for love. Hoped for it. Prayed for it," Miranda continued quietly. "Often I wondered what it would be like to share my most intimate thoughts and desires with a man I loved, with a man who loved me. I thought myself likely to die without ever knowing that, Charles. But I won't, you see, because I've found Josiah. He is everything I have ever dreamed of. I love him heart and soul. I have waited an excessively long time for Josiah Elliot to find me, Charles, and no one, not even you, will keep us apart."

Comestock cleared his throat and squirmed a bit in his chair. He looked at his sister, looked away, looked back again. "I'm sorry," he said at last in a low, husky voice. "You will likely not believe me after all the shouting I did when you took control of your life and drove off to Lavender Hill. And after all I've said this morning, you'll think me an enormous liar. But I am sorry, Miranda. I tried to do right by you, but I could not. I never intended for—for—things to happen as they did. And yet, I never could think how to undo them. You've not been unhappy?"

"No. I have been happy, Charles. As happy as a woman can be who has never known a husband's love. And my lack of a husband is not your fault. None of it is your fault, actually. You must not think it is. I have a mind of my own now and I had a mind of my own then. I was simply as blinded by rank, power and fortune as you were. The only difference is that I have had my eyes opened and now I see beyond those limitations, and you do not."

"Then I will learn to see beyond them," Comestock murmured. "I can't promise I'll be gracious in the doing of it, Miranda, but I'll try. Tell me what it is you want from me on behalf of this valet of yours."

"I want you to meet with the Duke of Berinwick, Charles. To meet with him on some pretense—perhaps a need for information about this bill he wishes to halt in Parliament—and to discover, without making him suspicious, how he came to hold the title to Nathaniel Elliot's house for a period of time."

Comestock nodded. "I can do that. Where is this house, Miranda? I've no doubt Berinwick has owned many and he may not recall—"

"It's the house Ariel and I have rented for the Season, of all things. Number Twelve, Portman Square."

Comestock's sky-blue eyes, so like his sister's, widened considerably. His hand went to his forehead. He sighed and muttered.

"Charles? Charles, what on earth is wrong? Have you taken ill of a sudden?" Miranda was up and beside him, taking his hand in hers before he could so much as answer. "Charles, shall I send a footman for Catherine?"

"No, no, no. I'm not ill. Number Twelve, Miranda. Number Twelve, Portman Square. Not Porter Street. Not Porter's Block or Portugal or Postern or the other Postern. I had those boys driven all over town and it was not any of them. Why did I not think of Portman Square? Because I saw them as mere urchins, that's why. Blind. I am blinded by class just as you said."

"Oh! Spinner and Jack! But if Number Twelve, Portman

Square is the house for which they search, that would make them—"

"—Elliot's nephews? What were the boys' names, Miranda? Did he tell you?"

"One was Nathan and the other—the other was Jack, Charles!"

"Yes, well, there you are! Jack! And what is Spinner but a fond sort of name between brothers? Well, any lad would rather be called Spinner than Nathan. Dull sort of name, Nathan."

"Charles, do you think it can be? Where are the boys? Are they here?"

"Out," Comestock replied, rising from the chair, keeping his sister's hand in his own and leading her toward the front window to peer out at the street. Having long missed the feel of her hand in his, he enjoyed now the sense of protectiveness and responsibility and love it sent jolting through him. "Catherine left word that should any gentlemen from last evening come calling, they must return at three. Gone out shopping for something, Sophia and Catherine. Took the boys with them. All dressed up in matching little scarlet suits with silver trim."

"You allowed Sophie to make pages of them after all?"

"What else was I to do? How was I to stop her? Could not find the blasted house no matter how I tried. And Sophie— All the while I searched she was cleaning them up, feeding them full, having them measured for livery in her mind. So in the end I allowed it. Well, Catherine and I allowed it. It was that or send them off to some institution or back to this woman from whom they ran away. It would have ruined Sophia's Season to have done either. Ruined mine as well," he added much more quietly.

"Pardon, Charles? I did not hear you."

"I said that it would have ruined my stay in Town as well, to think of those rascals slaving away in some workhouse or returned to the care of some woman they detest. Grow on a fellow, those lads do."

Blazingame stepped into the Newcombes' drawing room directly behind the smiling butler. He made his bow to Lady Newcombe and then to Eleanor. He took note of his flowers, which had been hurriedly moved to a small table near the piano. He was extraordinarily relieved to find them there and not given away to the scullery maid or tossed out into the gutter. Resplendent in a lime coat, buff breeches, black boots, a striped waistcoat of peachy-pink and lime, and silver spurs, Blazingame wanted nothing more than to tug nervously at the cherry-red neckcloth Elliot had tied awkwardly around his neck, but he refused to do it. He took the seat offered him instead and sat on the very front of the chair cushion, his back straight, his hands folded on his knees, and an unruly lock of brown hair just preparing to tumble down over his brow. "I do hope you are well, Miss Feebes," he said. He said it quite distinctly. He knew he did because he was listening most seriously to himself.

"I am very well, thank you," Eleanor replied. "How kind of you, Lord Blazingame, to pay me a call. I must thank you for the flowers. They are perfectly splendid."

Blazingame's relief was evident on his face. "You don't find them too—too—colorful?"

"No. Certainly not. They're lovely."

"And the fan is lovely as well, Lord Blazingame," Lady Newcombe said, taking it from the cherrywood cricket table beside her. "But Eleanor cannot accept it."

"Elliot said you would say that."

"Elliot?"

"Mr. Elliot, Lord Blazingame's valet, Aunt Caroline. You remember. Donovan and I told you about him."

"Oh, yes. Elliot. Well, your valet was correct, Lord Blazingame. The flowers are most welcome, but you must take this fan back. It's not the sort of thing, you see, for a gentleman to give a young woman he barely knows."

"No, I realize it isn't, but there are special circumstances, Lady Newcombe. I broke Miss Feebes's fan, you see. Last evening at Almack's. And I think it is my responsibility to replace it. I wish you will allow her to keep the thing. It's a trifle, merely."

"It is not a trifle," Eleanor said, much to her own surprise. "Oh, dear. I was to allow you to settle it between you, was I not, Aunt Caroline? But it is not a trifle, Lord Blazingame. Uncle Roger says the sticks are of real silver and the stones are actual rubies."

"Only very small rubies. But they're as red as cherries, don't you think? You do like the color red, Miss Feebes?"

"I— yes."

"I thought you might. At any rate, it is a mere trifle. Picked it up at my jeweler's this morning. He has kept it for me for years now."

"Kept it for you?" Lady Newcombe cocked an eyebrow in Blazingame's direction, the fan in her outstretched hand.

"Yes. It was my mother's."

"Oh, now truly you must take it back!" Lady Newcombe exclaimed. "You ought not go about bestowing heirlooms on young women you have only just met!"

"Well, ordinarily, I wouldn't," Blazingame admitted, refusing to notice the fan though Lady Newcombe came close to tapping his knee with it. "But I could never think what I ought to do with it, ma'am. I have had it for years now, and a gentleman has no use for such a thing. It was fate that Miss Feebes's fan broke last evening. I have been wanting to give the thing to someone worthy of it. And certainly, Miss Feebes will do it honor whenever she makes use of it."

"It is a prize to be saved for the woman you intend to marry, Lord Blazingame. It must remain in your family. It must always remind you of your mother."

"Not hardly," Blazingame murmured. "I mean to say, it

cannot remind me of my mother because I haven't any memories of her at all. She died when I was born."

"Oh," Eleanor sighed softly, compassion stirring in her heart.

"Then you must keep it to honor your father."

"Well, I didn't know Father very well either. He died when I was two. But from what my cousin Wilde has let slip, I don't think my father was precisely honorable."

Lady Newcombe heard Eleanor sigh in sympathy again. She felt her poor old heart beat at an increased rate. The most frightening of all thoughts leaped into her mind. A Cause. Eleanor was sitting across from this gentleman—who was an earl of all things—and viewing him as a Cause. She was certain of it. She'd heard such sighs as those before—from Newcombe himself, from Eleanor's mama.

"You did not know your father well, my lord?" Eleanor asked quietly.

"No. I was merely two when he died, as I said. So you see, Miss Feebes, Lady Newcombe, there is really no great significance to the fan for me. And I did not run out and purchase it, after all. No one will take note of it and remember having seen it for sale at this place or that. It was merely lying about in my jeweler's safe and I requested that he deliver it here. It seems only fair that I replace what I broke. And no one need know it came from me, Lady Newcombe, if that's what you fear. I certainly won't let on and I'm sure Miss Feebes can be trusted not to reveal its origin."

"You are an orphan, my lord," Eleanor said, rising from her chair and taking the fan from her aunt's hand. "How dreadful for you." No wonder, she thought, returning to her seat, that he seems so—so—bewildered by some things. He has not the least experience of a normal life. Well, how can he, without mother or father to raise him up properly? And he's wearing a cherry-red cravat. It bewildered her that the color of his cravat should suddenly seem of importance to her, but it did. No other gentleman of her acquaintance—not

even in Liverpool—would so much as own a cherry-red cravat, much less think to wear one in public. "I will accept
the fan, then, will I not, Aunt Caroline? Certainly, I must.
You see that I must."

Lady Newcombe nodded. She had not actually intended to
nod, but her mind was so filled with the awful prospect of
Eleanor making a Cause out of an earl that she had no thought
any longer for such a minor infraction of protocol as the man
presenting her niece with a fan worth a small fortune. And
she had lost her voice besides. Not one of her other nieces
had managed to do as much as lure an earl into cantering
across Hyde Park to speak to them in their carriage, much
less managed to bring one in through the front door, up the
staircase and into the drawing room to pay a morning call.
And Eleanor was going to frighten him into scurrying away
like a rat before a terrier by making a Cause of him. The mere
thought of the size of the possible loss was overwhelming.

"I thought, perhaps, you would like to join me for a drive,
Miss Feebes," Blazingame managed to say with something
approaching confidence. "I have an appointment later today
and so cannot take you to the promenade in Hyde Park, but
if you would care to drive about London for a bit and see
some of the sights—or have you seen all of the sights already?"

Have you seen all of the sights already, Blazingame
thought in despair. Does that sound as beetlebrained as I
think it does? "Oh, I do beg your pardon, Miss Feebes," he
added abruptly. "I am not thinking at all. You cannot possibly drive out with me."

"Why can I not?" asked Eleanor, noting the confusion
apparent on Blazingame's cherubic countenance.

"Well, because you must be here to greet your other gentlemen callers. It was Elliot's idea, actually, that I invite you
to see the sights in place of the promenade, but he was not
thinking any more clearly this morning than I, I fear."

"But I should like to go driving about London with you, Lord Blazingame," Eleanor said with a soft smile.

"You should?"

"Indeed. It's most unlikely there will be any other gentleman callers, you see. I did not—I was not—an enormous success last evening."

"Eleanor." Lady Newcombe found her voice at last. "You cannot drive about Town with an eligible gentleman without a chaperone, my dear."

"Should you like to join us, Aunt Caroline?"

"I cannot possibly this morning. I have so many things to see to and— Surely Lord Blazingame will understand and ask you for another time." When I have had time to speak to you and disabuse you of the notion that this particular gentleman requires any sort of saving, she added silently, hoping that her niece would read the desperation in her eyes. But it was not Eleanor at whom she ought to have been staring.

"You need not accompany us, Lady Newcombe," Blazingame said, never once noticing the desperation in Lady Newcombe's eyes because they were not fixed on him at all. "I'm driving my curricle, you see, and my tiger is with me. He will stand propriety for us. And it's an open carriage as well. No one will make the least fuss over it."


Her grace, the Duchess of Comestock, and Lady Sophia were just stepping out into New Bond Street from the last of the shops they'd intended to visit—George Michell, Stationers. Followed by one extraordinarily tall footman and two little pages, all three of whom had arms near to overflowing with packages, the ladies paused at the sound of raised voices near Maude Filigis's perfumery a mere three doors up.

"What on earth?" queried her grace, peering up the street at a rapidly gathering crowd of spectators.

"I expect there has been an accident, Mama," Sophia replied. "I hear men shouting, and all the traffic has come to a halt. Look. There's John Coachman waving at us from down near Ballentine's. He cannot come any nearer at the moment. Goodness, what a clutter of vehicles."

"James, Spinner," her grace commanded, glancing over her shoulder at her entourage, "take our packages to the coach and remain there. Lady Sophia and I will join you shortly. Jack, my boy, give your packages over to James and come with us. Perhaps we may be of some help, Sophia," she continued, taking Sophie's arm and urging her in the direction of the perfumery. "Such clutter as this requires a clear head and a voice of authority to set it aright."

"Yes, Mama," Sophia agreed, knowing full well that her mother's voice of authority could always be depended upon to produce order from the midst of chaos. "I hope no one has been injured," she added as she and Jack followed the duchess, who moved through the gathering crowd completely unjostled, her aristocratic bearing alone clearing a path for the three of them.

"Devil," Jack whispered as the cause of the shouting appeared before them. A cart brimming with coal stood crosswise in the middle of the street while its driver occupied himself by bellowing at a slender young woman in a tweed carriage dress, jean half-boots and a wide-brimmed straw hat with blue ribbons. Jack would not ordinarily have noticed the hat's ribbons, but just at the moment the carter was threatening to strangle the woman with them.

"I think you will not," replied a gentleman's voice loudly and angrily.

Jack looked around hastily for the speaker and discovered the gent striding hurriedly up behind the woman. The gent's coat was askew and his hat looked as if he'd just jammed it atop his head without the least consideration for how it looked there. And behind him a visibly quaking boy was holding to the reins of an empty carriage which Jack thought must be the gent's.

"And you will apologize to Miss Feebes immediately if you know what's good for you," Blazingame added.

"Me? Me apologize to that woman? And why for, I ask ye? I didn't do nothing. I were merely leading m'Dexter up this here street, minding my own business."

"Ha!" said Eleanor with great significance, her hands on her hips, a scowl on her face as she stood fearlessly, stiff and straight, before the man.

"You know I were minding m'own business," the carter declared loudly to Blazingame. "You know, 'cause you was passing by me just as easy as can be when she grabbed your reins. I seed her grab your reins, I did. Sent you careening almost into me. Sent me and m'Dexter scooting aside to avoid you. You know I ain't lying. You done bellowed at her the minute she did it. And you bellowed again when she jumped down from your fancy little carriage and came charging after me, too! What does she be, a madwoman?"

He was a short, broad sort of man, the carter, with heavily muscled arms. And he was covered from top to toe with soot. His breeches, his vest, his shirt and boots, all covered with soot, and his hair was black with it—what hair he had. But soot aside, he was covered with something else—righteous indignation. Every word he'd spoken was the truth. Blazingame could not deny any of it. He couldn't understand any of it, either. One moment Miss Feebes had been exclaiming over the lovely collection of little shops in the neighborhood and the next she had flown into a fury.

"Regardless," Blazingame said, fixing the carter with a scowl of his own, "you have no business to address a gently bred young woman in such an uncouth manner. You will apologize for your language at once!" he demanded, placing his hands protectively on Eleanor's shoulders. "What is it has angered you so?" he asked quietly, looking down at her. "What has the fellow done? Only tell me and I will see all set aright."

It was like the sun itself descending from the heavens to

encompass her wholely. The warmth of his touch, the strength of him centered firmly behind her, the support for her in his words. A great wonder seized Eleanor on the spot. Can it be? she wondered, amazed. Can it truly be that Lord Blazingame is not only in need of my help but that he is the gentleman destined to stand beside me in my efforts to help others? Can he be the gentleman of whom I've dreamed for so very long? Lord Blazingame?

Just as the carter was taking a deep, frustrated breath, preparing to shout at Eleanor again, another voice rang clearly through the afternoon.

"If one more bellow erupts from between your lips, sir, I shall have you taken off to Newgate on the instant," her grace declared to the carter as she strolled into the midst of the confrontation, Sophia and Jack beside her. "Only see what a muddle you've made of the street with that cart of yours. Why, our coachman cannot so much as approach us through such a mess as this. And to be threatening a gentlewoman with strangulation. Of all things! Good morning, Lord Blazingame," she added, cocking an intimidating eyebrow at him as she noted his hands on the young woman's shoulders. "Fancy meeting you here. And this young woman is—"

"Miss Feebes, Mama," provided Sophia instantly. "She and I met last evening at Almack's. We danced together in a set of country dances, did we not, Miss Feebes? It was your brother with whom I danced. Such a fine young gentleman."

"Good morning to you as well, then, Miss Feebes," the duchess said with a nod. "Now, what precisely is the trouble?"

The carter looked the duchess up and down in silence. Then he opened his mouth. Then he closed it again.

"Yes, what has the fellow done, Miss Feebes?" Blazingame queried. "Her grace and I are both willing to set things right. But you must tell us what is wrong first or we won't know how to go about it."

# NINE

Eleanor could not keep the triumph from her eyes. It had taken a good deal of negotiating on Lord Blazingame's part, and his tiger was even now trudging sullenly behind them rather than sitting on his little perch on the curricle. And, to be sure, Lord Blazingame was forced to drive his horses at nothing exceeding a walk, but still, she had succeeded in rescuing the beast.

*We* have succeeded, she corrected herself in silence. Lord Blazingame and I. And to think the Duchess of Comestock and Lady Sophia were willing to take a hand in it as well! I never thought to see the day that a duchess—

"A penny for your thoughts," Blazingame said, scattering every one of them to the wind.

"Oh! You startled me, Lord Blazingame! I was merely thinking how delighted I am that we have saved the poor beast from such a dreadful fate. Can you imagine! Such a tiny animal forced to pull such a tremendous load! I could not believe my eyes when I saw it. Why, that coal was stacked higher than the beast is tall. And to think he would be forced to pull it every day of his remaining life if we had not taken a stand and put a stop to it."

"Mooooo!" said the beast in a thunderously echoing voice from a short distance behind them.

Blazingame smiled. "I am considerably out of pocket because of that beast, you know. Two guineas, Miss Feebes, not to mention what my tiger paid to purchase a horse to pull the fellow's cart for him. He wasn't happy about being sent to purchase a cart horse, Tommy wasn't. Never has gone off to purchase a horse alone before. Still, he did manage to return in a reasonable time with a reasonable animal."

"Yes, he did. And I am so grateful to you. I feared you would not bother, Lord Blazingame."

"Not bother? To see something upset you enough that you face down a common laborer in the middle of a public thoroughfare, and I not bother to help you? Your opinion of me must be even lower than I imagined."

"No! I assure you, my lord, you rise in my opinion with every new thing I discover about you. I was so very wrong to have condemned you out of hand for what I imagined to be your treatment of Mr. Elliot. I did not know then what I know now—that you are kind at heart and courageous and care nothing for what others may think of you."

Miss Feebes's smile shone like the sun on the Thames as she beamed at him and Blazingame knew, beyond doubt, that his whole self was warmed by it. He placed his free hand over hers as he directed his team around a corner. "Not care what others may think of me? Oh, you mean the crowd that gathered in New Bond Street. Well, but most of them I don't even know, Miss Feebes. Why should I care whether they see me dealing with a carter for the release of his beast? Which begs the question, Miss Feebes—what are you going to do with it? The beast. You persist in referring to it as 'he', but it's a cow, you know, not a bull."

"It is? A cow? Named Dexter?"

"Not a country girl, are you? I guessed as much."

"I have never been to the country, actually. I was born and raised in Liverpool."

"And your household purchases milk, no doubt, only after it has left the cow."

"Yes," Eleanor replied. "After it has left the cow. I am

truly thankful, Lord Blazingame, that you did not blanch at the idea of freeing that poor animal from such abuse."

"You mean blanch like I did when you suggested we free the leopards from the menagerie at Exeter 'Change?"

"Well, I knew, actually, that we could not do that. I am not quite so innocent as to think I can save everyone and everything from their fates. What would I do with leopards? Where would I put them?"

"What will you do with this Dexter? Where will you put her?"

"How can it be a cow, Lord Blazingame, with such a name as Dexter? I thought surely it was a bull. Well, no, actually, I thought at first it was some horridly misshapen pony. And I grew so angry when I imagined it had gotten that misshapen form from having been forced all its life to pull such enormous loads. I was not thinking clearly at all. I was so very upset."

Blazingame studied her face for a moment. As pretty as it was, peeking up at him from out the shadow of her hat brim, it was also purely innocent. Best not to laugh, he told himself. She may be offended if I laugh. Best just to explain. "It is not *named* Dexter, Miss Feebes. It is a Dexter. That's why it's so very tiny. They're a breed developed in Ireland, the Dexters."

"Ireland?"

"Yes. I can't believe there's one of them here in England, actually. And in the possession of a mere carter! My cousin Wilde and I journeyed to County Tipperary just to see them once when I was a lad."

"No, did you?"

"Yes, indeed. I had read a bit about them and grown most curious. There are all sorts of tales as to their origin, you know. One of them suggests they are the offspring of Kerry cattle who wandered down to the sea centuries ago to graze on the seaweed. They became enamored of the sea lions playing on the beach, the tale goes, and mated with them.

Of course," Blazingame added, glancing back over his shoulder, "I don't see any resemblance to a sea lion in this particular one."

Eleanor giggled. It was the first time Blazingame had ever heard her do so and, inexplicably, it made his heart swell a bit with pride to have brought her to it.

"Another tale says the breed was established by a Captain Dexter who was an agent for Lord Hawarden as short a time ago as 1750," he continued, smiling widely.

"I expect that is the more likely of the two."

"Not actually, because the title of Hawarden didn't exist until 1793. Nonetheless, they are called Dexters and unless there was a particular sea lion by that name, I expect a man named Dexter had something to do with them. But this is the only one I have ever seen on our shores. I don't doubt some smuggler carried it here along with a load of Irish soap, thinking to keep it for a milk cow for his family or some such. How it came to be pulling a cart of coal on New Bond Street, I can't think. Pleasant, intelligent little beasts, but quite small. The fellow will be much more satisfied with the horse Tommy purchased for him."

"I should think so. Why, that horse was a positive giant compared to our poor little dear."

"Just so, Miss Feebes. And that horse will haul coal from morning till night without once needing to stop and be milked."

He tugged at the wide brim of his hat, bringing it down lower, almost covering his eyes. The sun was too brilliant, the noise of the shoppers too loud. Each rattle of a wheel over the cobbles magnified itself a thousand times, a million times. Each click of a heel on the pavement did the same. With great care, so as not to feel them brush against the cloth—a feeling he detested, though he couldn't think why—he put his hands into his pockets. With shoulders slightly hunched against the exceedingly disturbing street scene in which he was inadvertently taking part, he made his way—in what to others must have seemed a stupor but was much more an intense sensory experience—past Philip Metivier's haberdashery in New Bond Street.

His heart, which had seemed to him to have ceased to beat entirely at one point, lingered now in his throat. He could feel it there, a beating mass of muscle stopping up the passage, making it all the more difficult for him to breathe. In the corner of one eye he could feel a bit of wetness, but this he ignored as best he could, fearing that to give it the least attention would bring upon him a great rush of tears. A waterfall of tears so mighty and so vicious that he would drown in them on the instant. He groaned under his breath, and the sound of it echoed in his ears so mightily that he could not imagine why every head on the entire block did not turn and stare in his direction.

Too much, he thought. Too much. Ought never to have left my rooms. Ought simply to have waited for Marley's man to arrive.

The more he contemplated the bewildering villainy of the vision that had assaulted him, the more he could not believe it. It had not happened. Could not have happened. Specters, shadows, ghosts. He had not been herded toward the perfumery by an overwhelming crowd of people as he'd exited the apothecary. He had not stood, unnoticed, and watched as an obviously demented young woman had taken on a carter for no reason but the preservation of a cow. And yet their words had come soaring, like screeching peregrines, into his ears. And each participant had stood lighted, as though center stage in some great theatre of the gods, the sunlight shimmering around them, glowing and gleaming from their faces, making lightning of their hands, setting fire to the clothes they wore. A young woman, a gentleman, a carter and a cow. And no sooner had he convinced himself that all of these were imaginary, than in what seemed a mere blink of an eye his heart had ceased to beat and had come lurching up into his throat as more and different players had wandered onto the stage.

He mumbled to himself as he made his way to the corner and signaled for a hackney cab to take him home to Buckingham Street. "Can't be. Can't be. None of it. Bits of flotsam floating to the surface from the wreck of my sea-drowned mind," he muttered. He was certain it could not have happened. None of it. He had not seen Josiah at the water gate last evening. Never. A dream and nothing more. And this present apparition, this tremendous realization that had crashed against him with the force of a cannon ball, that had smashed into him and set him reeling, was nothing more than a nightmare into which he'd wandered, a most unfortunate dream from which he'd wake. He prayed with all his heart that he would wake soon. "Betrayed," he muttered. "My trust betrayed? No. For what reason? It was nothing to him, what I asked. The mere twitch of cat's whisker. And he not quibbling to do it. Not for a moment hesitating to do it. He'd never dishonor his word to me, not Berinwick."

Miranda slipped her hand into Elliot's and led him quietly away from Ariel and Mr. Doughtry, out into Blazingame's walled rear yard and the kitchen garden. Her heart thrilled with the thought that she and Charles might well have discovered Josiah's nephews, but she dared not tell him. Not yet. Not until the boys returned home with Catherine and Sophie, and Charles could make certain the lads were who she and he assumed them to be could she tell Josiah. But her brother had promised to send a footman here, to Manchester Square, as soon as he ascertained the truth.

"Miranda? What is it?" Elliot asked, pausing just beyond the rows of carrots and smiling down at her. "I didn't expect you so early in the day."

"But you did expect me?"

"Oh, yes. And if you didn't appear, I intended to go for a short stroll, as far as Portman Square, to rap upon a particular door and invite your butler to announce that Lord Blazingame's cousin from Herefordshire must speak with you."

"You like being Lord Blazingame's cousin from Herefordshire."

"Indeed. I find I like anything that allows us to spend time together. Did I tell you that Blazingame proposed to meet with Berinwick sometime soon?"

"He did?"

"Yes, but I thought about it a goodly bit and I told him I won't have it."

"You won't?"

"I know Berinwick."

"You do? You *know* him? Josiah, he's a duke. How could you come to know him?"

"Never mind that now, Miranda. It doesn't matter. The fact is that I do know him and Blazingame is too young and inexperienced, despite his talents for investigation, to take on the likes of Berinwick. Discriminating conversation and polite inquiries won't do with that particular demon. He'll cut the lad off at the knees without a second thought. No, I'll not have Blazingame tread on tippytoe in Berinwick's parlor for me. I'll tread in Berinwick's parlor myself, thank you, and not on tippytoe either. If Berinwick knows anything of Nat, I'll have it from his lips without a go-between. I find I can't bear it anymore, standing about, being forced to depend on Blazingame while I do what seems like nothing at all."

"Oh, dear."

"Oh, dear?"

"I—" Miranda had thought, when he'd first begun to speak of Berinwick, to tell Josiah that she had already petitioned her brother to take up his cause with the disreputable duke. However, in the face of his statements and his determined glare, she could not quite find the words to do it. "Does Doughtry know?" she asked instead. "That you've forbidden Lord Blazingame to meet with Berinwick?"

"No, but I expect I ought to tell him, eh? Yes, I ought.

Doubtless he's wandering about in fear that Berinwick will lop off Blazingame's head the instant Blazingame crosses his threshold."

"Indeed," Miranda said. "He's so frightened of what the Duke of Berinwick might do to his lordship that he stepped over to our establishment last evening to discuss it with Ariel."

"No, did he?"

"Yes."

The smile that replaced the scowl on Elliot's face and the feel of his hand as it disengaged itself from hers and went to rest at the small of her back forced a soft puff of air from between Miranda's lips. A sense of anticipation rippled through her from top to toe. She gazed down at the little garden and then up into Elliot's warm brown eyes—and found she could not gaze away. She turned without the least thought into the circle his arms readily provided her. She watched dreams wrap around him and settle like clouds in his eyes. And though she was unaware of it, her hopes and dreams rose up and enveloped her as well—dreams Elliot recognized, dreams he tasted with the utmost delicacy as he lowered his head and kissed the fine lines beside each of her eyes. And then his freshly shaved cheek was touching hers and he was whispering in her ear. "You're my life, my love, Miranda Wesley, and I will marry you no matter what comes of all this. I've had enough of vaporous fears and stupid pride. If you don't hesitate to be known as the noblewoman who married a nobody, then who am I to quaver at the thought on your behalf? I'll marry you, Miranda, regardless of what comes. Do I prove my ancestry or not, I'll marry you. Neither your brother's outrage nor Society's wagging tongues will keep me from it. Whenever you please, we'll sign the forms and take the vows and from that moment forward we'll travel together down whatever roads life leads us."

"We will?"

"Indeed. Though I pray to God life won't lead me down into Hades once more and you with me. No, that'll not happen. With you beside me, I'll never glimpse the shores of Hades again. Only the bright, shining stars of Heaven can lie before me if we're together. I *will* marry you, Miranda, before the altar in St. Martin in the Fields, or over an anvil in a Scots blacksmith shop, or in the glade near the deerkeeper's cottage in the Forest of Wynde. Whatever happens. Whatever I discover or don't discover about Nat and the boys, believe that I shall have you for my wife whenever you choose. Tomorrow if you say, or four weeks from Sunday if you prefer. I'm the one man among all men who loves you truly, Miranda, and will love you until death—and even death won't part us if I have the least say in it."

The boys were very merry as they trudged into Comestock House, their arms stacked with packages. "Did you ever see such a thing, Spinner?" Jack asked. "I did never see such a thing in all my life."

"You're so lucky, Jack. You got to be right there," Spinner pointed out. "Right in the midst of it. Devil, but that lady had the carter shouting. I expected to see smoke coming out of his ears. It was wonderful!"

"Did you see how her grace knocked the air right out of the fellow? And with words only. Someday I'm going to learn to speak like that, with my nose up in the air and my chin all aquiver. She was exceeding impressive."

"We all saw," nodded Spinner. "Even James climbed up on top of the coach to watch. We couldn't hear, though. I wish we could've heard."

"You would've shouted hurrah for every word," Jack assured him as they climbed the stairs to place their parcels in Lady Sophia's chamber. "Her grace was absolutely splendid."

"There was a peculiar gentleman in the crowd staring at the lot of you," Spinner informed his brother as they trudged along the corridor. "Did you take note of him? Wearing a dark box coat he was, and a big old floppy hat pulled down near over his eyes. Looked like a regular highwayman."

"How do you know? You never saw a highwayman."

"Yes, I did, too. Papa showed me a drawing of one once. Black Jack Wald, it was, and he was wearing the same sort of coat and hat. Of course, a lot of regular gentlemen wear the same things, I expect, but they don't go pulling their hats down over their eyes like that. He was most impressive. I'm going to get me a hat exactly like that one and wear it just the way he did and all the other lads will know to be wary of me. Think I'm dangerous, they will."

"Me, too. I'm going to look dangerous, too," Jack proclaimed, setting his packages down on Lady Sophia's bed. "And I'm going to learn to strut like a dandy, as well. Only it will be a dangerous strut 'cause of the way I'm dressed. Will you draw me a picture, Spinner, so I can see how I'll look?"

"Certainly," Spinner agreed affably, tossing his parcels onto Lady Sophia's bed and then strutting considerably like a dandy around the room. "Be pleased to draw a picture for you, Jack. Whenever you like."

"But not at this very moment," declared Sophia as she entered the room, her eyes bright with laughter because she'd arrived just in time to see Spinner's imitation of the dandy strut. "His grace wishes to speak with the two of you at once."

"He does? His grace?" asked Spinner, flabbergasted.

"What did we do?" Jack queried.

"I have not the vaguest idea," Sophia said, "but he's not to be put off for a moment. Come. I'll accompany you. That way Papa won't begin by bellowing at you straight off."

They descended the staircase to the first floor and Sophia shepherded the boys into the front parlor where the duchess as well as the duke awaited them. "Come here, lads," the duke urged from where he stood before the window. "Step in all the way. Come stand right here before me."

"Why?" asked Jack, backing up into Sophia.

"What did we do wrong, your graces?" Spinner queried. "We didn't mean to do anything wrong. We'll fix it."

"No, boys, do as his grace says," the duchess urged. "Go and stand before him. I'm fairly certain he's not going to assault you."

"Assault them?" the duke repeated, perplexed. "Great goodness, Catherine, when have I ever assaulted anyone? Never, that's when. Oh, perhaps a ruffian on the street when I was young—but never in my own home. Come here, rascals. Jack, Spinner, cease clinging to Sophie's skirts and step lively. I don't have all day."

"I ain't clinging to no lady's skirts," mumbled Spinner, stalking across the Aubusson carpeting fearlessly, followed a bit less audaciously by Jack. "We haven't ever hid behind a lady's skirts, Jack and me. Let us have it, then, your grace. Roar away."

"Nathan," the duke said. "Nathan and Jack Elliot. Number Twelve, Portman Square. Father's name, Nathaniel. Mother's name, Meg."

The boys blinked up at him in silent wonder.

"Well? Am I correct or am I not? Your real name isn't Spinner, is it, m'lad? It's Nathan."

"Y-yes, but—"

"Old lady Dempsey has come for us," Jack sighed in despair. "I told you as how she would find us if we weren't careful, Spinner. She's a wily one, she is, and determined, too."

"Has she, your grace?" asked Nathan, blinking up with worried brown eyes at the duke. "Because if she has, we aren't going back with her. We will run away again."

"Why, Spinner?" Sophia asked. "Is this Mrs. Dempsey cruel to you?"

"No, my lady. She's rather nice, actually, but she's got lots of boys already. She doesn't require us. And besides, we decided that we're going home. And we are, too, as soon as we know where the house is."

"Our papa might be there," Jack said. "The man told us

Papa was dead, but I think he was lying. He only had just one eye, but it looked frightfully odd—like he lied a lot."

"Is our house in Portman Square, your grace?" asked Nathan, formerly Spinner, quietly. "I remembered it was Portsomething. Portman might be it. Is there a Portman Square with a house in it that looks like ours?"

"I believe so, Nathan," Comestock replied, placing one hand on the lad's shoulder. "I do believe so. We'll go and take a look at the place, shall we? Just the three of us."

"Papa, I should like to go along," Sophia said at once.

"And I," declared the duchess.

"No, no. Can't. Callers coming for Sophia in less than a quarter hour. Rude of you to instruct them to return at three and then send them away again when they appear. And the girl can't receive them without you beside her, Catherine. Most unacceptable."

"Just so. I had forgotten," the duchess replied with a decisive nod. "Sophia, you must hurry upstairs and change into the ivory dress with the pink stripes. That will be just the thing. Likely an entire flock of young men pacing the pavement of London waiting for the hour to come around."

"Hundreds of them if the arrival of flowers at our door is anything to go by," said Comestock. "Entire drawing room is filled with offerings. Off with you now, Sophia. I don't intend to take the lads and return without them. Not part you from them as abruptly as that."

"But you knew they were named Elliot, Papa," Sophia said softly. "Has someone who knows them come to speak with you?"

"No, no, it's someone known to your aunt Miranda spoke of them to her. But I'm not about to hand them over to anyone I don't know, Sophia. Never fear. Perhaps the name's the same, but our Jack and Spinner aren't the particular lads this man seeks. See if the boys recognize the house, I will, and then the three of us will pay your aunt Miranda's friend a visit."

* * *

"No!" Lady Newcombe was as adamant as Lord Newcombe had ever seen her. She stood just on the threshold of the kitchen door with arms crossed at her breasts and glared at him and at Blazingame and at Eleanor as well. One little foot shod in an elegant kid slipper tapped in agitation, and her cheeks glowed pink with emotion in the sunshine.

"But, Caroline, it is merely—"

"A cow! It's a cow, Newcombe! We will be the laughingstocks of the neighborhood, keeping our own cow as though we cannot afford to purchase milk like respectable people. And where would we keep it? Here? There is barely room for the kitchen garden and the three of you. Even now the gate is open to allow its rump a place to stand."

"Merely because Blazingame's tiger has not led it all the way into the yard, Caroline. You frightened the poor lad when you flung open the kitchen door and shouted 'Halt where you are right this minute.' Frightened Blazingame and Eleanor as well, I should think. There is all this grass, Caroline," he insisted, waving his arm around to point it out to her. "All grass from this garden to the old privy, m'dear. A cow would keep it down. It would give the gardener more time to attend to your roses along the wall—actually give him time to plant you a real flower garden. And it's a tiny cow. No bigger than a large dog, actually. The Eisners have *two* very large dogs merely two houses down." One of Newcombe's hands went to stroke the cow's wide red velvety nose companionably.

"The Eisners have two setters, Newcombe," Lady Newcombe declared, her hands forming into fists and going to sit on her hips, setting her arms akimbo. *"Setters,* which do not come near to weigh fifty-three stone apiece, which is what Lord Blazingame just said he thinks that animal weighs."

"But it's merely three feet high, regardless of its weight, Caroline. I grant you, the setters are not as heavy, but they are nearly as tall. And Eleanor did rescue the thing. It would be most unjust to return it to the man who abused it in the first place. You cannot be so heartless as to condemn a poor, unfortunate animal to a life of sheer torture. You have never before denied assistance to one of my Causes, Caroline. You ought not deny assistance to one of Eleanor's. Not when it is so terribly at risk."

Lady Newcombe's eyes blazed; her cheeks flamed from pink to scarlet; she took a thunderous breath. "It's a *cow!*" she roared in a voice more appropriate to a fishmonger's wife than to the wife of a peer of the realm. "A *cow* is not a *Cause!*"

"Moooo," said the unfortunate object of her observations agreeably, as though it understood the particular word "cow" and none of the others and wished to assure her that it was actually pleased and proud to be one.

Blazingame stared down at his boot tops thoughtfully. Miss Feebes was clutching his left arm so tightly that he had lost all feeling in his left hand. He had watched her face grow paler as the debate between Lord and Lady Newcombe escalated. She had not said one word—not one—to further her own desires. But then, she need not voice her feelings to him because Blazingame knew precisely what they were. Had he not stood beside her in New Bond Street, a witness to the enormous depths of her caring heart? Had he not understood in those few frustrating, yet now precious, moments what a loving, tender, innocent soul this young woman possessed? And so his heart went out to her. Not because she pleaded with him to help her, because she did not. Not because tears stood in her eyes and she shivered woefully against him, because neither was the case. It was simply because he realized from the increasing pressure of her grasp that Newcombe stood no chance at all of overcoming his wife's objections and that Miss Feebes had pinned her every hope for saving the animal on the belief that Newcombe could.

Blazingame raised his eyes to study Lady Newcombe most

seriously, and then he opened his mouth. "I do beg your pardon, madam, for interrupting, but you need battle for the integrity of your garden no longer. I shall be pleased to take the creature home with me. And if you are not opposed to it, you may bring Miss Feebes to visit it whenever she likes."

Newcombe bit his tongue to keep the reply he was about to offer his wife from escaping his lips. Eleanor grasped Blazingame's arm even more tightly and took a step forward so that she could more easily gaze gratefully up into the splendid green sparkle of his eyes. That gaze said more to him than her words might have done and he blinked with considerable astonishment at the realization that it did. Lady Newcombe's fists abandoned her hips, diminished to hands with nowhere in particular to go, and fluttered about her neck, her cheeks and her heart most distractingly.

Oh, my, she thought, what came over me? To cause such a scene in the presence of an earl—an earl who is obviously interested in Eleanor. Gracious heaven, what have I done? I have forced the Earl of Blazingame to take a cow into his own household, that's what I've done. "I—I—" she stuttered helplessly, unable to find the words to keep Blazingame from feeling as greatly put upon as she thought he must. "I—I—" I am *not* going to add that beast to *my* household, she thought as she fumbled for something to say. Not even the possibility of Eleanor reeling in an earl will convince me to do that.


There was no arrival of the expected footman with the news. No word delivered from one establishment to the other. No warning whatsoever. One moment Miranda was strolling with Elliot around the enclosure at the rear of Blazingame's establishment, digesting the presence of a man with carroty hair who had taken to following Lord Blazingame everywhere, and the next she was clinging tightly, silently, to Elliot's arm and staring at her brother, Charles, at Ariel and Doughtry, and at Sophia's two little pages all tumbling out through the kitchen door into the sunlight with eager faces.

Beside Miranda, Elliot turned to cold, smooth marble. Not a muscle of him twitched. Not a breath passed in or out of his lungs. His gaze fastened on the crowd of people moving toward him and remained there without one blink of one eye.

"Slow down," called Comestock in a deep, commanding voice as the boys dashed ahead of him. "Try for a bit of decorum, rascals. Remember whose livery you're sporting."

A perfectly dignified walk was beyond the boys, but they did slow to a gallop that carried them up before the statue of Elliot just as surely, but took a moment or two longer. Two pairs of dark chocolate eyes stared up at him from faces filled with wonder. Unruly locks of fine golden hair blew in the gentle breeze and rippled across brows quite as proud and noble as Elliot's own. Two square little chins with tiny dimples in them quivered the least bit in anticipation.

"He don't look precisely like Papa," whispered Jack after a long silence.

"Un-un."

"But his hair is the same color."

"Uh-huh."

"And his nose is just as long."

"Almost."

"Why doesn't he say something?"

"Because he's flabbergasted, I expect," Spinner murmured. "He hasn't ever actually seen you before, Jack. And he hasn't seen me since I was an infant. I expect he's overcome at the sight of us. He doesn't look precisely like Papa, but he looks just like the miniature of Uncle Josiah that Papa carries about in his waistcoat pocket. Older though, and his moustache has disappeared." Spinner reached out and took his uncle's hand, the one that belonged to the arm to which Miranda did not cling. "I'm Nathan, Uncle Josie, and this is Jack," he announced, giving the hand a decisive shake. "I'll wager you're amazed as a toad in a turtle's nest to see us."

The hand Spinner held began to twitch awkwardly. The arm to which Miranda clung seized and trembled. Elliot took a great gulp of air and whispered, "No, no, not now."

The glorious smells of the English spring altered abruptly, became the smell of muck and moss, sulphur and copper. Muskets, pistols, cannon fire, exploded in Elliot's ears, drowning out all the voices around him. Miranda, the boys, the garden, all vanished, and the battlefield at Salamanca loomed before him littered with bodies, drenched in rain and blood and mud. His sword crashed against the sword of a French dragoon. His shoulder ached. Beneath him, Morning Star quivered and listened to the language of his knees. And then, around them, the air throbbed, pulsated, like a thing alive, and the French dragoon blew away like a leaf on the wind, the dragoon and his horse both, flying away before Elliot's eyes. And then Elliot was soaring after the Frenchman, he and Morning Star, soaring like birds toward the horizon, and then falling, all of them falling, down, down into the mud, into the blood, into a pit so dark and deep that not even Elliot's soul could comprehend the depth of it or the length of his stay there.

When at last the sunlight returned, Elliot blinked wildly, blinked until the shadows above and around him resolved themselves into solid figures, blinked shakily up at Miranda, at the boys, at Miss Markum and Doughtry, at a gentleman whose face bore a strong resemblance to Miranda's, at Blazingame and a cow.

*A cow?* Elliot brought his fists up and rubbed at his eyes. "A c-cow?" he mumbled as the animal refused to disappear.

"Thinks he's lost his mind completely now, I'll wager," Blazingame said as he attempted to shove the Dexter away from Elliot. "Believes he's cracked every plate in his cupboard. But you haven't, Elliot. Here, Doughtry, let's get him out of this sun and into the parlor, eh? Plenty of room in the parlor for everyone."

"N-not the cow," murmured Elliot disjointedly. "D-don't invite the cow."

"No, dearest," Miranda assured him as Blazingame and Doughtry helped him to his feet. "We wouldn't think of having the cow in to tea. Not when you're ill."

"It's all my fault," whispered a tiny voice as Elliot shook off Blazingame's and Doughtry's able assistance, and took a determined step all on his own.

"Who said that?" he asked, turning slowly to his right to where the boys stood.

"I did," murmured Spinner, his head lowered, his fingers fiddling with the bottom of his coat.

Miranda watched, her heart overflowing with love as Elliot lowered himself, a bit unsteadily, to one knee and tugged the boy to him. Then he reached out and tugged Jack to him as well, making a circle of his arms and holding them both tenderly captive within. He smiled up at each of them and beneath the smile Miranda could see the awe that had come over him before he'd been stricken by the illness. It lingered still. The very air around the three of them pulsed with it.

"You're Nathan. And you're Jack. I cannot believe you're here any more than I can believe I opened my eyes to see a cow. And yet here you are, alive and well and as much like your father as ever I imagined you would be. It was not your fault that I—that the trembles took me, Nathan. I assure you of that. It's something happens to me from time to time. Had nothing to do with you gentlemen at all."

"Are you certain? Because I did take your hand and give it a shake and call you Uncle Josie and—"

"No, no, had nothing to do with that. Ask Lord Blazingame if you don't believe me. Why, he didn't do or say anything at all to me when I got the trembles a week or two ago and cut him with the razor. Came near to slitting his throat and sending him to meet his Maker, I did, and he wasn't a bit responsible for it."

Two pairs of chocolate-brown eyes opened very wide.

"Exactly so," confirmed Blazingame at once, plucking a red cow hair from the sleeve of his coat and dropping it nonchalantly to the ground. "Simply sitting quietly, enjoying my shave, and then—blood everywhere and Elliot white as a ghost and trembling and falling toward the floor. I will tell you the whole of it one day, lads. Messy. Very messy. Come, Lady Miranda, let me be your escort this once, eh?"

Miranda took Blazingame's arm and with her other hand reached out and gave the duke a tug. "Come in with us now, Charles," she hissed. "Let the three of them have this short time alone together. He wants to crush them to his chest, but he'll not do it if we all stand about watching."

"Well, I expect it will be all right to leave the boys alone with him. He's not likely to have another fit, is he?"

"No, I shouldn't think so. Never has had two in a row that I've seen," Blazingame replied.

"Just so. I expect he'll not do them any damage then. I want to know more about your slit throat, Blazingame."

"And I'll tell you," Blazingame responded, "as soon as we're settled in the drawing room. Look, Miss Markum and Doughtry are at the kitchen door already. Hurrying back to raid the wine cellar so we can lift a glass to the reunited gentlemen, I should think. Have some fine wine in that cellar, Comestock, I assure you."

"Yes, well, never have turned down a glass of fine wine," grinned the duke, taking his sister's free hand and tucking it away in his. "I find I like this fellow, Miranda. Knows just how to go about distracting a duke from his perceived duty. Are you certain you can't force yourself to love Blazingame instead of his valet?"

# TEN

The Duke of Berinwick was not a happy man. He'd made the trip from Twickenham to London ostensibly to beat back the advancing liberal notions of the Whigs by disposing completely of Wright and Abbercombe's fool Education of Orphans bill. If the Earl of Wright wished to use his own money to build schools for orphaned boys and the Duke of Abbercombe wished to join in, that was their business. But to suggest that such schools become the rule in England, be supported by taxes and established across the length and breadth of the country, well, that was going too far, much too far. The very thought of it set Berinwick to grinding his teeth.

The bill, however, was not the prime reason for his visit. No one would doubt that the bill had compelled his presence, and so it made an excellent excuse, but he had other reasons—more important reasons—for this particular sojourn in Town. Two, actually. Two quite small but truly annoying reasons. One of them was named Nathan and the other Jack. And right this moment he wished them both at the devil. Berinwick rested his elbows on his study desk, cradled his chin in his hands and sighed.

"I'll be deviled if I don't chop them up into little pieces and use them for fish bait once I get them back," he mumbled. "Damned rapscallions. If anyone knew I was here searching for boys, they'd laugh till their noses fell off."

Nevertheless, I *am* here searching for those boys, he

thought. And I'm doing a wretched job of finding them, too. How the deuce *does* one go about finding two particular urchins in a city filled with urchins? I can't very well put an advertisement in the papers. He smiled to himself, envisioning the ad he might place: Lost, two blond-haired, brown-eyed boys possessed of considerable impudence. One barely as high as the Regent's middle. The other might reach to Napoleon's belt buckle if he stands on his toes. Neither of them worth a farthing, but will pay five pounds for their return. If found, contact the devil's own, Berinwick.

He'd thought, at first, that his search would end quickly. Jack had confided in little Guy, after all, that he didn't believe Elliot was dead and that he and Spinner were bound for London to find their papa. And where else would they think to find their father but at their old house in Portman Square? "But they aren't there," Berinwick muttered. "House is rented out to some ladies. Only one boy there, according to the butler, and he's got hair as black as midnight, is called Billy and is employed to scrub pots." Berinwick smiled again, remembering the look of abject fear on his solicitor's face when the man had returned with that information only four short days ago. "Shuttlefield thought I'd strangle him on the spot," chuckled Berinwick. "Certain he'd breathed his last for delivering such unwelcome news. Perhaps I won't chop the rapscallions up after all. Almost worth the trouble of having to search for them just to have seen that look on Shuttlefield's handsome face."

Berinwick was not a handsome man himself, having lost his right eye and gained a considerable amount of scarring around the empty socket. The empty eye socket could be covered by a patch, but the scars could not. They extended far too low on his cheek and all the way up across his brow into his thick black hair. It had happened in his childhood, The Accident. His mother to this day called it The Accident. And though he hadn't the least memory of it, nor would anyone ever discuss it with him other than to say The Accident had been unavoidable, he did remember clearly years of taunting by other schoolboys and visible distaste in the eyes of all who looked on him, children and adults alike. In his early years, he'd pleaded with his father, whenever he returned home, not to send him back to school again, to allow him to remain at Blackcastle and study with tutors, but the old duke had refused to consider such a thing.

"Learn to be a man" had been his father's final word on the matter in the boy's eleventh year of life. "Stand up for yourself. Show the world you're bred of guts and glory. You're not some insignificant little twit to be cowed by looks and words. You'll be the Duke of Berinwick one day. Act like it."

And right there and then, the eleven-year-old heir to the title of Berinwick had taken up acting.

"For all the good it did me with the Elliots," he muttered now as he sat back in his chair and thumped his fist on the desk. "Even as ill as Nat was that last time we met, he knew I'd take his boys. Knew I'd keep my word about them, too. And by gawd, I am going to keep my word! I'll find those scamps and take them back to Twickenham. I'll scoop them up from beneath the noses of every dandy in St. James's Street, toss them across my saddle bow, and ride out of London with a pack of Bow Street Runners and righteous citizens on my heels if I must."

"Who?" Elliot asked, confused by the story his nephews were excitedly relating to him. "What was the lady's name?"

"Mrs. Dempsey. She is called Mrs. Dempsey and she lives in an elegant little cottage in Twickenham," explained Jack.

"Mr. Dempsey lives there, too," offered Spinner, who had pleaded not to be called Nathan unless his uncle was certain he was genuinely angry with him. "It's Mr. Dempsey teaches us Latin and mathematics and Greek and the like."

"And Guy and Davidson and Congreve live there too."

"And Harold and Archibald."

"My goodness, but poor Mrs. Dempsey has a considerable cottage full, does she not?" observed Miranda, who had gone back out to the garden to shepherd the three of them into the house to share in the celebratory toast. Enthralled by the perfect glow of Elliot's smile as he sat on the grass with the boys cross-legged before him, she had immediately forgotten the toast and remained to listen, settling beside Elliot, whose arm went possessively around her. "Wherever does she put all of you, this Mrs. Dempsey?" she asked.

"It's a very large cottage," offered Spinner. "Enormous, actually."

"But we're not going back," Jack declared.

"No. Never. You won't make us go back, will you, Uncle Josie?" Spinner asked, the happiness in his eyes dimming a bit. "Because we've come to London to find Papa, you see. The man who came to take us away said Papa died, but Jack doesn't believe him, and I don't know that I do either. Mrs. Dempsey said Papa was dead as well, but Jack heard the men who took us to the cottage say Papa wasn't dead at all."

"The man who came to take you away?" asked Elliot. "A man you didn't know came to Portman Square and just took you away?"

"Uh-huh," nodded the boys simultaneously.

"When?"

"Four entire years ago. In the very middle of the night," Jack replied. "Dark as pitch it was, and he, all dressed in black, his face glowing deathly white in the flame of the candle he held. 'Up, boys,' he ordered in this great, mean voice. 'Get dressed at once. You're coming with me.' And then he set the candle on the table and tugged us out of bed and hurried us into our clothes and out the door into an enormous coach with six outriders, or perhaps eight."

" 'Never mind the rest of your things,' he said to Jack when Jack wanted his toy soldiers," added Spinner. " 'My men will see your things packed and brought after us.' Which I didn't think was the truth. But then he did send

Jack's toy soldiers and all our other things to Mrs. Dempsey two days following the one we got there. He must have an entire brigade works for him."

"You were abducted from your own beds?" Miranda could not believe her ears. "Where was your father? Where were the servants?"

"I don't know," said Spinner. "Before the villain left us in the charge of his men, he told us Papa was dead and now we belonged to him. Said we'd better do just as we were told, too. But then Jack overheard his men say that Papa was still alive."

"Do you think he killed all the servants, though?" Jack asked in a whisper. "He *must* have killed them, Spinner, because there wasn't anyone to be seen. I didn't even see Mr. Goingsworth. Not for as long as a blink of an eye, I didn't."

"No, and there wasn't a sound from anywhere," Spinner offered, thinking back.

"I expect the villain waited until Papa was gone out, then came and killed all the servants and Mr. Goingsworth—each and every one of them. We were abducted, Spinner. I never even guessed we were abducted!"

Elliot felt Miranda shiver against him and the arm he had around her held her a bit more tightly. "Abducted. All the servants and this Mr. Goingsworth killed and the two of you taken away to an enormous cottage to be tutored in Latin and Greek and mathematics?" he asked with a cock of an eyebrow. "Deucedly odd villain if you ask me. Did he give you his name?"

"Yes, sir," Spinner replied, "only we were so frightened that neither one of us remembers it. He lives in a castle. A dreadfully ugly castle. You can see it from Mrs. Dempsey's cottage."

The Duke of Comestock stood at the kitchen door, wineglass in hand, and studied the quartet seated on Blazingame's little patch of lawn. He did not overlook the arm Elliot had placed around his sister, nor did he doubt the possessiveness and supportiveness of it.

"Are they never coming in?" Miss Markum queried, the unexpectedness of her voice behind him startling the duke into near catastrophe with his wine.

"Sooner or later, Miss Markum. Sooner or later." He raised the glass to his lips and drank the wine down in one great gulp.

"Is something wrong, your grace?"

"Wrong?"

"Yes. You have never—I mean to say, to gulp your wine in such a fashion is not—"

"No, no, nothing wrong," Comestock interrupted her, stepping across to set the empty glass on the kitchen table. "Merely remembered an appointment, Miss Markum, for which I am like to be very late. Tell Miranda I have toasted them all, eh? I must go."

"But, your grace—"

"And if—if Elliot wishes to keep the boys here with him, you must give him my permission to do so, eh? But not for a day or two, he must not. Sophia cannot be parted from them so abruptly. Put them in a hackney and send them back to Comestock House, when the times comes."

"Yes, your grace, but—"

"He loves Miranda a great deal, does he not? This— valet—of hers?"

"I believe he does. Yes, your grace."

"Then whisper in her ear, Miss Markum. Tell her, if she has not already mentioned it to him—and from the way they sit together I cannot believe she has—warn her not to say a word about importuning me to speak to Berinwick for him. This Elliot's a proud man, she tells me. He'll not appreciate her asking my help behind his back."

"I hadn't thought of that," Ariel murmured, her hands fluttering, seeking a place to alight. "I think Mr. Doughtry did not either."

"No, and neither did Miranda, I'll wager."

The Duke of Comestock's rear drawing room was so crowded with young men and young women that Mr. Feebes thought to turn right around, make his way back down the staircase and dash out the front door. The footman who had led him to the drawing room would look at him askance, of course, if he did. But what did he care for the raised eyebrow of a footman? And then he heard that very footman announce his name. The babbling of the crowd lessened and from across the room Lady Sophia's gaze fell full on him. Transformed beneath that gaze, Donovan's fears departed and he fairly floated across the carpeting, through the crowd, to bow before Lady Sophia. With the grace and audacity of a cavalier, he took her hand into his own and raised it to his lips. And when his lips tasted the smooth, tender inside of her wrist, he thought he'd cease to breathe, his heart would stop and he'd fall down dead right at her feet. The touch and taste of her was such ecstasy to him.

"I do not think we have been introduced, Mr. Feebes," a sharp voice cut into his ecstasy, causing him to release Sophia's hand at once.

"Oh, Mama, indeed you have. Last evening at Almack's. Mr. Feebes is brother to the young woman who rescued the cow in New Bond Street this morning," said Lady Sophia with a wide smile.

Donovan's eyes widened considerably. A cow? What had she said? Something about a cow?

"Is that so?" replied the duchess, looking him up and down as though he were a gander and she considering the purchase of him for tomorrow's dinner. "You are brother to Miss Eleanor Feebes, sir?"

"Y-yes, your grace," Donovan managed.

"And are you fond of cows as well?"

"I—I beg your pardon, your grace? Cows?"

"Yes, Mr. Feebes," Sophia interjected. "Mama and I met your sister earlier today. She was in the midst of rescuing a cow from what she considered frightful abuse by a carter."

"A very determined young woman is Miss Feebes," observed the duchess. "I never thought to see the day that anyone of the female persuasion could convince Lord Blazingame to part with so much as a quarter hour's attention on her behalf, much less two guineas plus the price of a cart horse. You had best beware. Lord Blazingame is in love with your sister, I think, Mr. Feebes."

"T-two guineas? And the price of—of a cart horse?" Donovan could not seem to gather his wits about him. Were Lady Sophia and her mother speaking in tongues that he could not comprehend their meaning?

"Mama, do cease teasing Mr. Feebes," Sophia said, noting the confusion in Donovan's eyes and the flush on his freshly shaved cheeks. "He's not yet heard the tale of his sister, Lord Blazingame and the cow, I think. No, of course he hasn't, or he would understand every word you say to him, which I can see he does not."

"C-cow?" was the only word Donovan could manage, and in such a tone that it set both the duchess and Sophia to laughing softly.

"Do come and stroll with me around the room, Mr. Feebes. I expect there are any number of people here you don't know. Let me introduce you to them," Sophia said, rising and taking his arm. "And I'll explain all about your sister and the cow," she whispered in his ear as they turned away from her mama.

At that very moment, the Duke of Comestock was ensconced in an oversized armchair in Berinwick's study, a glass of port in his hand and a most perplexed look settling on his face as he turned to look over his shoulder at the gentleman just then paused in the doorway.

"Surprised, eh, Comestock?" Berinwick asked gruffly.

"Didn't expect to see this man in my house, did you? Truth to tell, neither did I. Never so much as nodded to the puppy, I haven't. Damnable Whig! Well, don't just stand there, Blazingame," he added. "You sent up your card. I allowed you entrance. Step in and take a seat. Tyler, fetch the gentleman a glass of port and then get out."

Blazingame selected a chair with crocodile legs and carvings of the sphinx on its arms and slipped into it hastily. He accepted the glass of port Berinwick's footman offered him and watched in silence as the man turned and exited the room.

Silence. No social niceties continued the conversation during the footman's presence or for a good two minutes after his departure. No further welcome emanated from Berinwick's lips. A crooked upturn of one corner of Berinwick's mouth was all that acknowledged Blazingame's addition to the company.

An ominous silence, Blazingame thought with a gulp. Makes a man feel like he's about to be invited to dinner and he's the dinner. I wonder if Comestock feels the same? What the deuce is Comestock doing here? He never said a word about paying a call on Berinwick. Drank m'wine, bade me farewell, and off he went, leaving the boys behind him.

Berinwick stood, stalked to the study door and peered into the hallway. "Tyler's gone," he announced as he turned back into the room. "Don't particularly trust that man. Looks like a spy."

Blazingame's lips curved upward. He attempted to hide the smile behind his hand until he could wipe it from his face, but his eyes betrayed him.

"You think it's humorous, Blazingame? A gentleman forced to be wary of spies in his own household?"

"No, no, of course not. I merely—that is to say—what does a spy look like exactly?"

"Like Tyler," Comestock replied, edging toward laughter himself.

"They look like common ordinary people," muttered Berinwick, stalking back to his chair. "And it's not humorous. Laugh, either one of you, and I'll cut off your ears here and now. Having to watch for spies in your own household is aggravating beyond belief. Unfortunately, old retainers die, and whether a man wants to or not, he's forced to hire new ones. Never do know for a certainty whether the new ones work for you or for someone else."

"Who else would they work for?" Blazingame asked, his smile fading, his green eyes blinking innocently at Berinwick. "I mean to say, I have never once supposed that a servant I hired might be collecting my moneys and be working for someone else."

"Might work for one of the scandal sheets. Might work for Bow Street. Might work for the Prince Regent for all I know. You don't protest Comestock's presence, eh, Blazingame? Nothing secret about your visit here? Been discussing the bill, he and I. The note on your card said you wished to discuss it as well."

"Don't wish to discuss the bill. I lied," Blazingame said brazenly. It was something about Berinwick drove him to such an utter lack of diplomacy, and he wondered at himself.

"Lied? You lied?"

"Came to ask you one question, Berinwick, and then I'm gone. Won't keep after you. But it's important to a friend of mine, your answer."

Berinwick glared through his one dark eye at the young earl. "Get out," he said.

"No, no, no! Don't toss Blazingame out on his ear," Comestock protested at once, thoroughly amazed at Blazingame's audacity, impressed with his straightforwardness and guessing precisely what the earl wished to ask—the same thing he wished to ask and hadn't yet worked into the conversation. "Let Blazingame ask the question first, Berinwick. Might be important. Might have something to do with the bill. You know the Whigs, always doing things in the queerest fashion."

"Odd you should use those particular words in regard to Blazingame," muttered Berinwick, eyeing Blazingame's turquoise coat and the lace at his collar and cuffs with an almost-smile. "All right, Blazingame, since Comestock's curious, ask away. Now what the devil is it?" he added as Tyler appeared on the study threshold once again.

"I beg pardon, your grace, but there is a gentleman demands to speak to the Duke of Comestock and—"

"And he's going to do so whether you wish it or not," growled a low voice from the corridor. "And then I'm going to speak to you, Berinwick."

"Elliot?" Blazingame nearly leaped from his chair as Elliot appeared behind the footman, put a hand on each of the man's shoulders and set him aside. Comestock did leap from his chair and turned at once to face Elliot.

"Blazingame? What the devil are you doing here when I told you not to come?" Elliot continued, stalking into the room. "You're Comestock," he added, coming to a halt inches from the duke. "I remember glimpsing your face at Blazingame's when you brought the boys. Miranda said it was you who brought the boys. I wish to speak with you privately. Join me in the corridor."

"Elliot?" Berinwick's voice sounded like horses' hooves on gravel. "Josiah Elliot, is that you? I thought you were dead."

As he exited Comestock House, Donovan's feet stepped down onto the pavement but his head floated among the clouds. Not only was Lady Sophia the most beautiful woman he'd ever met, but she had proved herself kind, pleasant and thoughtful as well. She'd laughed a bit as she'd told him about Nora and the cow, yet it had not been unkind laughter. Not at all. She'd actually said, "I admire Miss Feebes so, Mr. Feebes. You must be very proud to have such a caring and forceful sister. And you are very like her, I think. Concerned for the welfare of those less fortunate than yourself. You and she both are to be much applauded."

"I'm to be much applauded," murmured Donovan as he floated along the walk in the direction of his uncle's house. "She kept hold of my arm for a full quarter hour. A room full of titled gentlemen yearning to sit beside her, or stand beside her, or promenade with her around the room, and she kept hold of my arm the entire time, introducing me to this group of people and to that and never once releasing me. Never once."

Well, that shows how much Nora knows, he thought then. I wouldn't call that scorning me. No, I wouldn't. And she won't discard me for an earl or a marquess or a duke and break my heart either, do I court her properly. By Jupiter, how does one go about courting the daughter of a duke? Very carefully, I should think. I must ask Uncle Roger about it when I get home. He'll know. He's a viscount, after all. I expect he's courted a daughter of a duke or two in his day.

"But then—he married Aunt Caroline." The sound of those words falling from his lips brought Donovan's head down from the clouds and his feet to a standstill on the pavement. If Uncle Roger actually fell in love with and courted a duke's daughter or two, whyever did he settle for Aunt Caroline? Donovan wondered. Not that Aunt Caroline isn't a fine woman, because she is, but—

"I'll ask him," Donovan whispered. "Perhaps a duke's daughter led him on and then discarded him for a gentleman of higher rank. Perhaps that's where Nora got the idea and why she warned me about it. Although, all dukes' daughters can't be alike. They aren't made from pattern cards, one after the other. Are they?"

Eleanor sat gazing out the window down into the square with the most thoughtful look on her face. In her lap lay a scrap of lovely lace-trimmed lawn on which she'd been embroidering an elegant capital L. She intended it as a present for the little scullery maid her mama had hired. Not that the Feebeses had needed another scullery maid. They possessed two already. But Louisa had come 'round to the kitchen door of the house in Liverpool—a tiny child, thin and pale—and requested a position. Her mama was ill, she'd said, and her papa such a drunkard that he was not to be depended upon. And her friend, Annie, who attended the penny school run by Mrs. Feebes and three other matrons, had suggested that Mrs. Feebes might be in the way of hiring a girl who was willing to work hard and could be trusted not to steal the silver. That had been the very morning that the traveling coach had stood outside the front door, packed and ready to transport Eleanor and Donovan to London. And Eleanor's mama, all abuzz with cautions and commands and warnings, the collar of her dress askew and unmatched slippers on her feet—so preoccupied she was with sending her chicks off to London Town—had marched into the kitchen, listened to Louisa's story, taken one very long look at the girl and hired her on the spot.

"I am certain she'll be thrilled with a lace-trimmed hand-kerchief," whispered Eleanor to herself, "but a cow would be so much more practical. Louisa and the other maids and the children at the penny school could all have fresh milk to drink every day. I expect they could. She's a very small cow, but they're very small children and won't drink much."

"What is it you say, Eleanor?" asked Lady Newcombe from the love seat, where she was busy with a bit of sewing all her own.

"Nothing, Aunt Caroline. Merely mumbling to myself."

"Not at all the thing," replied Lady Newcombe. And then she set her sewing box aside, stood, smoothed the wrinkles from her skirt, and crossed the room to where Eleanor sat on the window seat. With gentle hands she removed the handkerchief and threads from Eleanor's lap and set them aside. Then she took both of Eleanor's hands into her own and held them there. "You are not to be disappointed, my dear," she said softly. "Gentlemen do not always pay a call after they have danced with you at Almack's. Some of them are quite shy, you know, and must dance with you time and again before they are brave enough to come to the house. You must not despair, Eleanor. Truly, you must not."

"I'm not, Aunt Caroline."

"But you are so very quiet, and the look in your eyes is quite, quite dismal."

"It is? Well, I expect it's because I was thinking of Mama's new scullery maid. She's such a thin, tiny child and has suffered so much in her short life—and there are so many children like Louisa in Liverpool and even here in London."

"You cannot save them all, dearest. No more than your mama and your uncle Roger can take up all the Causes in England. It can't be done."

"I know, Aunt Caroline. But—"

"Now, if you were to meet and marry a titled gentleman, you might do more for these unfortunates than your mama does at present," Lady Newcombe continued, brushing a stray wisp of hair from Eleanor's cheek. "Money is always helpful in such matters, but power—the power to change old laws and make new ones—is where the answer truly lies. Do you know that even now there is a bill being discussed in Parliament that would make a share of government funds available to support the building of schools for orphaned boys?"

"There is?"

"Yes, Eleanor. It's in all the newspapers. You must learn to read the newspapers more often. You'll be surprised at all that goes forward in London without the least public fuss being made about it. Of course, you don't want to let your beaux know that you've an interest in anything but the gossip columns if they should come upon you with a newspaper in your hand." Lady Newcombe laughed a small, quiet breath of a laugh.

"They would label me a bluestocking if they thought otherwise, would they not, Aunt? That was one of the warnings Mama gave me before I departed."

"Just so. And most gentlemen don't wish to align themselves with young women of an intellectual bent. Of course, most gentlemen actually require a young woman with an active intelligence. They are merely too stubborn to admit it."

Eleanor was genuinely astounded at her aunt's words. To this very day, Eleanor's own mama considered Aunt Caroline nothing but a beautiful featherhead who had captured Uncle Roger with flashing eyes and innocent phrases.

"But, back to Causes," Lady Newcombe said. "If the bill of which I speak could be passed into law, Eleanor, think of the good it would do. Your uncle Roger is solidly behind it, of course, as are a number of other gentlemen. But they are, I fear, a minority."

"Those who wish to do good to others appear always to be in the minority," Eleanor observed with a sigh.

"No, you're wrong there, my dear."

"How can you say so, Aunt?"

Lady Newcombe smiled a knowing smile. "Because I have lived a while longer than you, Eleanor. And lived with my eyes wide open, too. It is not that the majority of people don't wish to do good. It's merely that they disagree on the best way to go about it. For instance, I am perfectly aware that Henri, our French chef, is truly Henry Footfellow, formerly of St. Giles."

"You are?" Eleanor's eyes widened in surprise.

"Oh, yes. Please don't tell your uncle Roger so, though, will you, dear? He does so enjoy believing that I don't realize our Henri, with his funny French accent and his well-groomed demeanor, is the same disheveled man for whom Roger's heart bled so much that he was willing to hire the fellow to stand about in a stable, shivering every time a horse entered the place."

"Uncle Roger meant to make Henry Footfellow a stable hand? But Henry's frightened to death of horses, Aunt. He will not even walk near one in the street."

"Just so. But you see, when first your uncle wished to

give Henry Footfellow a position, the man was completely incompetent at everything. The only place he could do no harm was cleaning out the stables. And so I declared I would not have him. Not in my house. Not in my stables. Not anywhere. 'Too uncouth, without one saving grace,' I told your uncle. And I told him loudly, too, so he could not misunderstand a single word."

"Just as you told him about the cow," offered Eleanor.

"Yes, but that cow is another matter. I have other motives for the attitude I adopted about that cow. At any rate, Eleanor, my protests set your uncle and Henry to thinking what Henry could *learn* to do to make himself acceptable and employable. And Henry thought he would like to learn to cook. Your uncle arranged for him to study with the Duke of Abbercombe's chef, and *voilà*, Henry Longfellow has a position and I have a pseudo-French chef who might go anywhere else and obtain just as fine a position should we suddenly become unable to employ him. He need no longer depend for his salvation on our money and our sympathies. And that, I think, is a better way to do good for him than your uncle Roger's original intent."

Eleanor nodded. "I do see, Aunt, what you mean. And I begin to suspect that you are a river that runs much deeper than anyone suspects—a wily woman with a kind heart who knows precisely how to get what is best for everyone."

"Oh!" Lady Newcombe blushed becomingly. "I'm sure that's not true at all, Eleanor. I am perfectly selfish and shallow about any number of things. And there are times when your uncle's Causes drive me quite out of my mind. And your tendency, my dear, to save every lost lamb you find, I cannot like."

"But, Aunt Caroline, it is in my very nature. And surely you cannot be opposed to my wishing to do good for others. Surely not. You have betrayed yourself to me now, you know."

"Ordinarily, I would not be against your adopting Causes, but this is not the time for it, Eleanor. This Season in London is a time for you to fix your mind on finding a husband—a husband who will be kind and generous to you and able to support you in all things. This is not the time to focus your energies on rescuing sad-eyed cows and orphaned earls."

"Orphaned earls? You do not like Lord Blazingame, Aunt Caroline?"

"I do like him, Eleanor. And I like it exceedingly much that he's an earl and came to call and took you driving with him. But my heart came near to failing when I discerned you were beginning to see the man as a Cause."

"I never did," protested Eleanor.

"No? You did not think how much he stood in need of someone to teach him the ways of the world—poor orphan that he was?"

"Well, perhaps I did have a thought or two in that direction."

"You did not think to change him in some way for the better? To teach him not to wear cherry-red cravats, for instance?"

"But, Aunt Eleanor, he cannot realize—that is to say—he is an orphan, raised by a bachelor gentleman. He cannot know much at all about—"

"Just so," interrupted Lady Newcombe, releasing one of Eleanor's hands to give the other a pat. "A Cause. You will frighten him away, Eleanor, if you view him as a Cause. I warn you of it. It is not a lady's prerogative to change a gentleman who courts her into what she wishes him to be. Never. *He* may alter himself for her sake *if* he chooses to do so, but she is not to go about rescuing him from himself. Not only is it foolish, but it's near to impossible."

"Well, you needn't fear my wishing to rescue Lord Blazingame from himself for another moment, Aunt Caroline," Eleanor said most sincerely, her eyes alight with memories of Blazingame taking a stand beside her and dealing with the carter on her behalf. "I don't see Lord Blazingame as a Cause any longer, Aunt Caroline. I assure you, I don't."

\* \* \*

"Who the devil do you think you are, ordering me out of Berinwick's study!" hissed Comestock angrily, ceasing to pace up and down the corridor, crossing his arms across his chest and resting his shoulders against the wall opposite Elliot.

"I'm the man who's going to be your brother-in-law sooner or later. That's who the devil I think I am," Elliot hissed back. "I'm the man for whom Miranda begged your aid."

"No, no, no," declared Comestock as quietly as he could manage. "Miranda never begged me. My sister does not beg. Not anything of anyone. If you love her, you ought to know that."

"I do love her and I do know that. But she told me she *begged* you to come to Berinwick on my behalf and to discover discreetly how Berinwick came to possess the title to my brother's house, and I despised you for making her beg on the instant."

"A faulty turn of phrase, then, on Miranda's part. She *requested* that I do so. I complied. There was no begging involved in it."

"Oh? Well. Perhaps my thoughts colored the words I heard."

"I promise you, they did."

"But she went to you on my behalf when she would not even apply to you on her own behalf. Certainly—"

"Not apply to me on her own behalf? When? Oh! That muck-up at Lavender Hill, you mean."

"You know about it?"

"Indeed. It was a misunderstanding between Miranda and me, Elliot, that made her refuse to come to me then. But today she came. Not on bended knee so that I'd forgive her and consent to give you my aid. Drive such a vision as that from your mind. She came with back straight, chin up, and a perfect glare in her eyes and told me everything. It was I who was humbled, Elliot, not she. Now, may I return to Berinwick and discover what I've come to discover?"

"No."

"No?" Comestock cocked an eyebrow in disbelief. "And why not, may I ask?"

"Because I intend to confront Berinwick on the matter myself."

"You're a nobody, Elliot. You can't just stroll into a duke's study and—"

"I thought I just did. Well, perhaps *stalked* would be the better word."

"Um-hmmm. And if you do that again, he'll put a pistol ball through your forehead."

"No." Elliot grinned lopsidedly. "Won't do that. He'd like to have people think he would, but he won't."

"How can you be so certain?"

"Because we knew each other once, Berinwick and I. Knew each other fairly well," Elliot confessed in a very quiet voice. "At any rate, I refused to allow Blazingame to come here on my behalf and I won't have you do it either. I may be more suited to making inquiries about Nat in St. Giles and Seven Dials, but I'm tired of being confined to that fruitless search. I will speak for myself before Berinwick."

"Then you'd best be about it before Blazingame beats you to the punch."

"Blazingame is in there! I forgot!" Elliot exclaimed, and started back up the corridor toward the study at once. Behind him, a thoughtful, bemused and curious Comestock followed at a more decorous pace.

# ELEVEN

O'Riley ran trembling fingers through his carroty hair and turned from Marley to gaze nervously out the window. "I don't see how it can be so, Lordship," he repeated. "But it must be so. I asked a neighbor's footman who was standing on Blazingame's front step the evening I followed the two of them to Portman Square—"

"And the footman did not say 'Elliot'," growled Marley.

"No, sir. No, Lordship. The footman didn't know the fellow's name. But he did say as the man was Lord Blazingame's valet, and so I dismissed the idea of his being Elliot at once."

"But now?"

"Well, I have been thinking on it, your lordship. Why, I ask you, would a gentleman stroll the streets of London with his valet beside him? Why take his valet to dine at a lady's house? Well, it must have been dinner. They were there for hours."

"Why, indeed," mumbled Marley, stroking his chin. "And why did you not tell me his valet accompanied him to Portman Square?"

"Because I didn't think much about it at first, Lordship. I thought it odd, you know, but then, Lord Blazingame has got a reputation for being a bit odd."

"Deservedly so."

"Indeed. And the valet hasn't got a moustache, like you

said this Elliot fellow would have. And he looks much more like a gentleman than you led me to believe Elliot would."

"And so—"

"I haven't followed Blazingame to any secret meetings with any mysterious, poverty-stricken gentlemen anywhere, Lordship. You ought to know that. He doesn't go near St. Giles, Lord Blazingame, or Seven Dials or any other place a man fallen as low as you say this Elliot has fallen would be expected to reside. I just now left Lord Blazingame, in fact, inside the residence of the Duke of Berinwick."

"Berinwick?" Marley asked, astounded. "Blazingame went to visit Berinwick?"

"Just so, Lordship. And mere moments after he was admitted, there came his valet, leaping from a hackney cab and demanding entrance to Berinwick's house himself."

Marley took a very deep breath. "Blazingame's discovered from whom I purchased the house," he whispered to himself. "That's what sent him to Berinwick—the confounded house!"

"But what will have sent his valet charging after him, Lordship?"

"Eh? What? No, no, wasn't speaking to you, O'Riley. Go. Take the parcels and go. They're late already and no one to take them but you."

"And then, Lordship?"

"Then go find that cousin of yours—Will, is it? the one you're so fond of?—and have an ale or two at the Swan. I'll discover for myself if Blazingame's valet is Elliot or not. And if I need you to follow Blazingame some more, I'll send for you to do it. If no message from me reaches you by seven tonight, you need merely appear on your usual day at your usual time."

Marley watched O'Riley distribute the tightly wrapped packages among his pockets and depart. He watched him from the window as the man exited the front door and hurried off in search of a hackney. His eyebrows drawn together above his nose in a thoughtful frown, Marley then walked to the sideboard, took a three-barrel box lock pistol from it, and tucked the thing into his coat pocket. It was already loaded. Marley unloaded, then freshly loaded this pistol every night. He had been enthralled with it since first he'd purchased the thing, years before, but he'd only actually fired it twice. Once at his brother, Dare, and the second time at a traitorous groom by the name of Carpenter.

Berinwick looked from one to the other to the other of them as though they were all mad. "If one of you does not put this question to me at once, I'll do away with the question and the lot of you at one and the same time," he drawled, opening the drawer in the table beside his chair and taking a pistol from it. His fine, well-manicured hands held the thing gently, as though it were a lover's hand. He stroked it sensuously with his fingertips before pointing it at the three gentlemen who had ceased arguing among themselves in the center of his study to stare at him. "I'm serious," he said softly. "My patience is at an end."

Blazingame's eyes were wide with disbelief. That any gentleman would so much as jest about such a thing was beyond his experience. And Berinwick didn't look as if he were jesting.

Comestock frowned and cocked an eyebrow.

A smile twitched at Elliot's lips, and then he laughed. "Always appreciate getting straight to the point, don't you, Berinwick?" he said when his laughter faded. He fingered the fencing scar on his cheek. His smile lingered like a ghost between them until, at last, Berinwick smiled and murmured "Touché."

*"He* gave you that scar?" asked Blazingame in a hushed voice.

"Indeed," nodded Elliot.

"I should think so," agreed Berinwick. "Likely saved his

life, too, by the doing of it. Thought he was such an excellent fencer. Discovered he wasn't. Worked harder at it after that. I've no doubt any number of Frenchies might have run him through had I not focused his attention on improving his technique. What is it, Elliot, that you want from me? What's the question causes all this hubbub? And why aren't you dead? Nat told me you were dead."

"Nat told you that? When?"

"When he asked me to do him the favor."

"What favor?"

"No, no, Elliot. What's the question you were all fighting about first?"

"That particular question is, how did you come to possess the title to Nat's house?"

Berinwick stroked the pistol once more, then replaced it in the drawer. "He gave it to me," he said, stretching his long legs out before him, sinking farther back into the chair. "Nat gave me the house free and clear. Signed it over to me. Nothing scandalous about it; nothing illegal about it, either."

"But why?" asked Blazingame, unable to keep silent. "We need to know why he gave it to you."

"Yes, and Miranda says to discover why you then sold it to Marley," Comestock added.

"Miranda? Who the devil is Miranda?" Berinwick asked.

"My sister," answered Comestock.

"My betrothed," answered Elliot simultaneously.

"You have a sister betrothed to this rogue, Comestock? Are you out of your mind? Or simply without any authority in your own house?"

"Miranda is of an age—" sputtered Comestock.

"Don't bother excusing yourself to this miscreant, Comestock," Elliot interrupted. "It's none of it his business unless we decide to invite him to the wedding. And even then he'd best not try to stir the pot, or I'll serve him chopped and roasted for the wedding breakfast."

"Nat gave me the house," Berinwick drawled, expressing not the least concern over becoming a possible breakfast meat, "in recompense for the favor he sought from me. He wanted me to take his boys and raise them up as I would raise my own sons, did I have any. Which is never likely to happen, eh? I gave him my word I would do so; he signed over the title; I stuffed it into my pocket and we parted ways. I've not seen him since. Sit down, Elliot. You look pale suddenly."

"He does?" asked Blazingame, directing his gaze from Berinwick to Elliot at once. "Come and sit over here, Elliot. Are your hands shaking? No, they're not. Not yet. But there's no telling."

"Is that how it begins?" asked Comestock, his hand abruptly grasping Elliot's shoulder, urging him toward a chair. "He grows pale and his hands begin to shake?"

"I am not going to have a fit!" Elliot declared. "Lord, what a bevy of mother hens!" But he did cross to the chair and he did sit down in it, gratefully. "Nat asked *you* to raise his boys, Berinwick?" he asked in disbelief, rubbing one hand across his brow. "*You?* It was you abducted them in the dead of night?"

Miranda, Miss Markum and Doughtry were in the midst of filling the boys with toast and jelly when the door knocker sounded. Doughtry excused himself at once and hurried off to answer the thing. "That will be Uncle Josie," announced Jack happily. "Why did he rush off, Lady Miranda? One minute you were whispering together and the next he was gone."

"It's not your business," Spinner replied. "And it's not polite to ask about things that aren't your business. If they'd wanted us to know, they wouldn't have been whispering."

"Well, it's not polite to whisper," Jack declared, spooning a large helping of jelly onto another slice of freshly toasted bread. "Not in front of other people who are right there."

"Precisely so, Jack," proclaimed Miss Markum. "You must remember that when you're grown." Whereupon, she tugged Miranda aside and whispered in Miranda's ear. "What did you say to Mr. Elliot that sent him dashing in through the kitchen door and out through the front door in such a rush, Miranda? He had the most harried look on his face when he departed."

"I told him that I'd asked Charles to go to Berinwick and learn what he could about the house."

"Oh, Miranda."

"I thought better of it, Ariel. But then, I could not be easy in my mind, you know. It seemed like lying, to keep silent."

"But his pride, Miranda."

"Was not damaged in the least. It was my pride he got upset about. He called himself a selfish dastard for forcing me into such a position as to have to beg my brother's forgiveness and plead for his aid. Which I did not do, I assure you, Ariel."

"No, of course not."

"No, and how Josiah ever got such a notion from my words, I can't think. Why, Mr. and Miss Feebes," she interrupted herself. "How pleasant to see you again."

"I told them my lord was from home," grumbled Doughtry, stepping into the kitchen behind the brother and sister, "but in she came regardless, and him behind her. Like ruffians! Demanded to know the way to the rear door, she did! Traipsed down this corridor without so much as a by-your-leave and he after her!"

Mr. Feebes had the good grace to look decidedly shamefaced, but Miss Feebes merely turned to glare at the butler. "It doesn't matter in the least whether Lord Blazingame is at home or not," she said. "I explained it to you, sir. I've come to visit Susan. Lord Blazingame said I might come to visit her at any time. If he did not explain as much to you, that is not my concern. I will not be deterred because of a lapse in household communication. And only see, this kitchen is filled with visitors. It's perfectly obvious that others may visit when his lordship is out. How pleasant to see you again, Lady Miranda, Miss Markum," Eleanor added in a belated attempt at politeness.

"Apologize," murmured Donovan in a barely audible voice. "Bee in her bonnet. Couldn't stop her."

"I do not have a bee in my bonnet," Eleanor protested. "I simply must see—I must know— There are plans to be made for her, Donovan. Aunt Caroline and I together have plans for her. I told you. Certainly Lord Blazingame will understand when I explain it to him, and he will help us to send Susan to Mama, as well. I have no idea how that can be done. If only she is large enough—if only she will prove to have milk enough for more than one person at a time—"

"The cow!" exclaimed Miss Markum, at last enlightened. "You have named the cow Susan, have you, Miss Feebes, and come to visit with her?"

"Stupid name for a cow," muttered Jack.

"Women," mumbled Spinner.

"Apologize," Mr. Feebes said again more loudly. "M'sister has hopes that— No excuse, really, for bursting in where we're not wanted, but she— Regret disturbing you," he added, his hands searching for a place to hide and settling for his pockets.

"You wish to see Susan as well, Donovan. You know you do."

"Yes, but there was no pressing need, Nora. Might have seen her any day Blazingame was at home. Merely want to see what Lady Sophia and her mama were talking about."

"Lady Sophia? Lady Sophia told you about Susan?" asked Eleanor in surprise. "Oh, Donovan. I told you not to pay her a call. I warned you of it."

"You warned him not to call on Sophie? Why?" asked Lady Miranda. "Have you something against my niece, Miss Feebes?"

"Your niece? Oh, I am so sorry. I didn't know she was

your niece. No, no, nothing at all against her. I think she's the nicest person. She and her mama helped to rescue Susan, you know. But—but—she's a duke's daughter and Donovan is merely a mister, and if he should lose his heart to her—"

"You fear she'll break it," finished Miranda with a smile.

"Yes, I do. And I don't want that to happen. Truly, I don't. She is so far above Donovan that they can never make a match of it, and—"

"That's not true," protested Donovan. "It could happen."

"Actually, it could," Miss Markum agreed, stepping across the room to where Mr. Feebes stood, his ears bright red, his head lowered, the hands in his pockets turned to fists. "There is one particular story I could tell you even now, Mr. Feebes," she said quietly, "about a duke's daughter and a—"

"I hear Susan mooing," Miranda cut in without the least regard for the laughter bubbling in Ariel's eyes. "Let's go outside, shall we, and cheer her up a bit? I expect she's lonely."

"Lonely," mumbled Jack, licking the jelly from his fingers and rolling his eyes all at one and the same time. "A cow."

"Requires milking more like," Spinner said. "Do you know how to milk a cow, Mr. Doughtry?"

"A cow? Milk a cow?" Doughtry sputtered. "Of all the things required of me in my lifetime, I have never—"

The sound of the door knocker interrupted him, and Doughtry ceased what might have been a most enlightening tirade to tread off in a righteously disturbed fashion toward the vestibule. He paused for a moment as he reached for the latch in an attempt to place a bland look on his countenance. Then he lifted the latch, studied the gentleman before him and scrabbled through his memory for a name. This particular face had not entered the Blazingame establishment in several years at least. "Lord Marley," he said with confidence after several desperate moments, "how pleasant to see you again. I'm afraid my lordship is from home at the moment."

"Don't require Blazingame," Marley replied, peering over

Doughtry's shoulder into the vestibule, his right hand curling around the grip of the pistol in his pocket. "But I should like a word with Elliot, if you please."

"Elliot, your lordship?"

"That *is* the name of Blazingame's valet, is it not? Elliot?"

"Y-yes, your lordship, but—but—Mr. Elliot is from home, as well, I'm afraid."

Amazement and triumph flashed together in Marley's eyes. Not only was Elliot in London as he feared, but he actually *was* Blazingame's valet. Where the devil did that dastard find the nerve to do either after all I did to him? Marley wondered. Did I not leave Josiah Elliot totally humiliated, penniless and unconscious beside Carpenter, believing himself a murderer as well as thoroughly useless and completely mad? And yet here the wretch is, delving into matters that don't concern him in the least. Searching for Nat. Asking questions about The Heart of a Queen. No—no—causing Blazingame to ask questions about The Heart of a Queen and right in front of Newcombe, Comestock and the others.

How could I have been so mistaken about Josie's state of mind? he wondered, his eyes growing dark with frustration. Damnable Elliot ought to have ridden off into the wilds and hanged himself. That's all there was left for him to do. Any reasonable man would have done it. Damnable dastard.

Marley's grip on the pistol tightened.

"Haven't the foggiest notion where he's gone," Berinwick replied. "Not seen or heard from him since that night. Never told me not to sell the place, Elliot. Never told me not to deal with Marley. Marley's name never entered into it, that I recall. You say you've found the boys? I want them back."

"You want them back?" Comestock's eyebrows both lifted at once. "You?"

"What do you mean by that final 'you', precisely, Comestock?" asked Berinwick quietly.

"Nothing. He didn't mean anything," Elliot muttered.

"I meant precisely what he thinks I meant," declared Comestock, rising from the chair into which he'd finally settled and beginning to pace the study. "And you're the most audacious son of a seagull I've ever met, Elliot, thinking to speak for me in my presence."

"I do beg your pardon, your grace," Elliot replied, gazing up at Comestock as he paced past. "Go right ahead. Dig your own grave and place yourself in it."

"No, don't dig your grave just yet," said Blazingame, turning from the window to study them all, especially Berinwick. "There's something I wish to know before Berinwick shoots you, Comestock, and before they hang him for it. Berinwick, you said he wasn't ill, Elliot's brother, when he came to you?"

"He didn't seem ill."

"Melancholy?"

"No, not at all."

"How did he seem?"

Berinwick frowned, attempting to recall that particular evening. "Odd," he said at last. "He seemed very odd. Told me he'd had word that Josie had lost his life at Talavera. I expected some immediate outburst of sorrow, because he was always fond of you, you know, Josiah. But it didn't come. He didn't seem at all sad about you dying, in fact. He kept staring at the lamps in my parlor as though he'd never seen such things before and spouting a good deal of nonsense about the war, the opera, the Prince Regent, the boys. Total nonsense. At least, I couldn't make heads or tails of it. And once he'd signed the house over to me and got my word about the boys, he—"

"He what?" Blazingame queried anxiously, noting the somewhat astounded look on Berinwick's face even now, as that gentleman recalled the incident.

"He kissed my cheek. There I was growling at him for being a perfect lunatic by giving his boys into my care, and he came to me and kissed my cheek, and told me I would not regret my kindness. He was off on a great adventure, he said. A great adventure."

"Was he drunk?" Blazingame asked.

"No. Always can tell when Elliot major is in his cups. Has trouble standing when he is, much less walking and talking. Even when he's merely had a few glasses of wine, he hasn't the least stability. Lists to the right. But it was the strangest thing that evening. He ought to have been mourning Josie's death, but his eyes were alive with—with—joy, I think."

"He'd just had word his brother was lost in battle; he was asking you to take charge of his sons; and his eyes were alive with joy?" Blazingame shook his head in disbelief.

"Lost his mind," grumbled Comestock. "Obvious."

"Perhaps, but he didn't strike *me* as mad," Berinwick offered.

"But then, how would *you* know?" Comestock queried, pausing for a moment to glare significantly in Berinwick's direction.

"I don't give a fig what he says," Comestock grumbled as he settled into his coach beside Blazingame and across from Elliot. "No man in his right mind would leave two innocent young boys in Berinwick's charge. Berinwick's a devil."

"He and Nat were friends," Elliot offered. "We were all three friends, as a matter of fact, when we were lads. And Dare—I cannot believe I've almost forgotten about Dare."

"Who the deuce is Dare?" asked Blazingame, tugging his waistcoat into a more comfortable position. "Don't tell me he's another piece to this puzzle."

"No, no, surely not. We were simply friends, Nat and I and Berinwick—Berinwick was Hodencourt then—and Marley's brother, Darius. No one else cared to befriend Berinwick when he was young. I was amazed Dare did, actually. But Dare was odd in his own way."

"Where is he, Marley's brother? Perhaps he knows something about your brother, Elliot," Comestock suggested, fiddling with his pocket watch.

"I shouldn't think so. Dare's dead. At least, I think he's dead." Elliot's face grew pale again. "Lily said he was dead. Said Marley told them as much. Disappeared on the moors, Dare did."

"Oh, good lord, another disappearing gentleman," sighed Comestock. "Is there anyone you know, Elliot, who hasn't disappeared?"

"Any number of people," Elliot replied with a frown. "My stepsister Lily and her husband, Henry, Marley, Carpenter—"

"Who's Carpenter?"

"Marley's groom. That is, he was Marley's groom."

"Dismissed?" asked Comestock.

"Dead," murmured Elliot, remembering himself awakening naked, except for his boots, beside Carpenter's body, stealing the man's clothes, and riding like a bat out of Hades away from the cottage at Crystal Pond, away from Marley Manor. He'd been sure he'd killed Carpenter himself somehow, during a bout of his trembles. But after a while—after he'd achieved a period of calm—he'd reconsidered that. Carpenter had been shot to death. There'd been the unforgettable hole made by a pistol ball in his forehead. *And I didn't have a pistol then,* he reminded himself again. *I had only The Buck's lovely little Italian dagger in my boot.* "The dagger," he said aloud.

"What dagger?" Blazingame asked.

"What? Oh. I was always used to carry this lovely little Italian dagger with me—in my boot—ever since I was a lad. And the night Carpenter got himself murdered, someone stole it."

"Whoever took it didn't murder this Carpenter with it?" Comestock stared at Elliot aghast, shades of his sister marrying an accused murderer closing around him.

"No. Shot Carpenter in the head, someone did. But I

never did see my dagger again. Had to settle for this one instead. It's rather like, but not nearly as grand," Elliot added, withdrawing the weapon from his boot.

Comestock looked from the dagger to Elliot to Blazingame, horrified. "Do you know your valet runs about with a dagger in his boot, Blazingame? What sort of household do you keep that you allow such things? It's an establishment filled with barbarians, I'll wager. Likely your butler keeps a guillotine in the cellar and your cook makes stew from—"

"That's quite enough," interrupted Elliot, turning the dagger in his hand to make it catch the sun. "You'll cease insulting Blazingame, your grace, and Doughtry. They're friends of mine and it offends me to hear you say such things about them."

"You're not marrying my sister," Comestock roared, his gaze fastening on the slow turn of the knife, perceiving a dire threat to his life at the hands of a madman. "Never! John, stop the coach!" he yelled, pounding at the hatch with his cane. "Stop the coach at once!"

Miranda laughed. She couldn't help herself.

"It wasn't funny," Elliot protested. "I frightened him so badly he turned white, then red, then purple." Elliot was escorting her home from Blazingame's without the least thought as to who might notice them, so upset was he with himself. Miss Markum and the earl sauntered along behind them, deep in conversation.

"Oh, I should like to have seen it, Josiah," Miranda said, wondering why he abruptly glanced back over his shoulder. "I expect it was the first time Charles has ever been discomposed in his entire life." Miranda gave the arm she held a squeeze, directing his attention back to her. "Don't look so glum, dearest. You did nothing wrong. You certainly didn't intend to gut my brother in his own coach on the way home from the Duke of Berinwick's."

"No, of course not. I never even thought of it. I was merely staring at the blade—watching it sparkle in the sun—and then he said what he said and I requested that he not say anything further. I realized what he saw and what he thought the moment he roared at me. But now I've set him against me, Miranda. Made a sworn enemy of him, I should think. That's why he swooped down and absconded with Spinner and Jack without a word to anyone. And now he'll oppose our marriage with a vengeance, do I prove my birthright or not."

"Which won't make a bit of difference," Miranda said. "Or did I mishear you earlier, sir, when you vowed you'd marry me no matter what?"

"No, you didn't mishear me. But I've made a complete muddle of everything, Miranda. I was just beginning to like your brother—"

"You were?"

"Um-hmmm. And now—"

"And now he thinks you some sort of villain. You should have seen him, Josiah. He came charging into Lord Blazingame's establishment and shooed the boys into his coach without a word of explanation, overriding all of Lord Blazingame's opposition and the boys' opposition as well. Charles has always been so utterly composed, in every situation. I've seen him this upset only once before in all our years—when I left his house, you know. Oh, but I was thoroughly impressed with his power, his dominance, this afternoon. It was the finest show. You managed to lower him from one of The Graces bestowing gifts on us poor humans, down to an ordinary man."

"Nevertheless, I've landed all of us in the briars where he's concerned, and now I must think of some way to patch things up." Elliot glanced back over his shoulder once more, then returned his attention to Miranda, his eyes betraying a good deal of anxiety.

"It will take a deal of patching, yes," Miranda agreed. "Charles thinks you as mad as the Duke of Berinwick and he's decided neither of you will ever lay hands on Spinner and Jack again."

"As mad as Berinwick?" A smile twitched at Elliot's lips. "Well, there's hope, then, because he's a savvy one, your brother, and he's like to see through Berinwick does he have many more dealings with him. And he will have more dealings with him, you know, because Berinwick gave Nat his word about the boys. Berinwick will not give them over to your brother's care. Never."

"See through Berinwick? Do you mean to tell me, Josiah, that the Duke of Berinwick is not the devil we all imagine him?"

"Well, no, I don't mean to tell you that precisely. In fact, I don't mean to tell you anything at all about Berinwick. I ought not have said what I did. But he lives by his word. And he gave his word to Nat. He'll take the boys back from your brother. I doubt he'll even give them into my care without a good deal of discussion and endless assurances, even if I am their uncle. Look back over your shoulder, Miranda, and see can you spy a gentleman with carroty hair trailing along behind Blazingame, eh? I can't get a glimpse of him myself."

"Oh! I had almost forgotten about the man with the carroty hair. No," she added as she looked over her shoulder a moment and then faced forward again. "There are any number of strollers, but no one with carroty hair at all."

"Now, that's odd," Elliot mused as they stepped from the corner into Baker Street, the sweep busy with his broom midway across. "Blazingame said the fellow followed him all the way to Berinwick's establishment today, but neither of us saw the man when we departed the place. What the deuce!" Elliot exclaimed abruptly as a loud clattering, a prolonged screeching and the pounding of hooves sounded to his left. Blazingame shouted Elliot's name. Miss Markum screamed, "Miranda!" And the sweep ahead of them came charging back toward them, broom in hand, waving wildly. It took an instant, no more, to spot the danger. A panicked chestnut, eyes rolling

in its head, ears flattened against its skull, charged straight up
Baker Street at them. Harnessed between the traces of an overturned hackney, it dragged the squealing carcass of the cab
behind it. The sound of the vehicle screeching and scraping
along the cobbles, whipping first to one side of the street and
then to the other, panicked the horse all the more.

Elliot swept Miranda up into his arms, ran back to the
curb—beyond it—to where Blazingame had shoved Miss
Markum into the safety of the nearest doorway. "The
sweep!" Miranda cried as he set her down. Elliot turned to
see the man had tripped on the cobbles and fallen in the
path of the horse run wild and the scraping, screeching carriage. He dashed back and grabbed the fellow by the collar
and the seat of his pants, lifted him and literally tossed the
sweep toward comparative safety.

Behind Elliot the sweep's broom cracked beneath the
horse's hooves, and then the hackney was swinging to the
side, coming directly at him.

The roar of cannon fire shattered the air all around Elliot
as he leaped up onto the side of the cab to keep from being
caught and dragged beneath it. Smoke and haze brought tears
to his eyes, the smell of sulphur, copper, blood and gunpowder
came near to smother him, and he saw the French dragoon
falling away before him—the French dragoon and his horse
being blown away like leaves in the wind. And the dragoon's
horse was screaming. All around him, horses and men were
screaming. And he screamed. Elliot screamed at the top of
his lungs. And then he slid from the hackney, stumbled
raggedly, his arms pinwheeling. The battlefield disappeared
as quickly as it had come. He found a precarious balance,
accepted it gratefully, and ran, his long legs pumping—not to
the other side of the street, not to the far corner and safety,
but toward the terrified, laboring horse.

In six swift strides he came close enough to catch at the
animal's collar. He forced his fingers under it. The hack's
hame tug tortured his chest. His arm twisted. His fingers

strained to keep hold as his legs battled to keep pace. He turned an ankle and was dragged for a short distance. Lost a boot. He regained his footing, seized the top of the collar with his other hand. All around him, pedestrians huddled in doorways and against buildings. Curricles, phaetons, drayers' carts swerved aside, up onto the pavement, some of them, to avoid being hit. But Elliot saw none of it.

Sweat stung his eyes. The smell of frothing horseflesh assaulted his nose as he reached the center of balance he needed. With one extraordinary twist-pull-leap, he gained the horse's back, swung a leg over. He freed his hands one by one from the collar, catching first at the blinkers, then at the cheek straps. His knees tightened against the horse, telling the animal to stop. His hands worked themselves down the cheek straps to the bit, telling the animal to stop. "Enough," he whispered in one flattened ear. "Whoa, now, m'dear. You're safe. You're safe." Telling the animal to stop.

He thought for a moment, as the horse slowed, how much the beast felt like Morning Star beneath him. Morning Star, who had stumbled and gone down in that Hades called Salamanca, who had been blown away like the French dragoon and the dragoon's mount and he, himself, on that fiery plain called Salamanca. And he rested his head on the horse's neck as it halted and stood silent, its sides heaving. Elliot's hands began to tremble, his ears shut out the shouting around him, and tears flowed from his eyes to mix with the horse's sweat. He remembered. He remembered it all. He remembered for the first time where it was he went when the trembling overtook him.

"Come down now, dearest," Miranda said for the third time, her heart firmly embedded in her throat, causing her to rasp the words. "Let go the bit, Josiah. Swing your leg over and slide down here to me. I'm terrified, you know. I require your arms around me."

Elliot's eyes blinked open. Through the blur of his fading

tears, she shimmered in the sunlight like a glorious spirit descended from the clouds above the firmament. In a moment he was standing on the cobbles, his arms around her, holding to her as tightly as to a rope tossed him from the shore in the midst of a raging stream.

She almost disappeared in his arms until her own arms found their way around his neck and she stood on tiptoe to kiss him. And then her neatly gloved fingers were gently wiping the remnants of tears from his eyes, his cheeks, his chin. "Oh, Josiah," she murmured. "What is it? What happened to bring so many tears and such sobs as heaved in your chest mere moments ago? I thought you'd been gravely injured. We all thought as much."

"I saw," he whispered. "Saw it and lived it and breathed it all over again. And I was not in the midst of the trembles when I did, either. I was not, was I, Miranda?"

"No, you could not have been, my dear."

"I did not fall down on the cobbles like a fool and lay there trembling, all unaware, while life went on without me?"

"No, Josiah."

"There was a horse wild with fear dragging an overturned hackney behind it?"

"Merely glance over your shoulder, see for yourself."

"Now I know," he whispered, pressing his cheek against hers. "Now I know where the trembles take me, Miranda. To Salamanca. To that instant at Salamanca when one particular cannon roared and I fell before it. The French dragoon and his mount, Morning Star and me, all whisked away like leaves in the wind before it. Dead, all of us dead and gone."

"Except that you are not dead, dearest. You're alive and brave and strong as ever you were."

"I am, am I not?" he said, a sudden smile lighting his face. "To the devil with the trembles! Pardon me, Miranda, for my language, but to the devil with them! They can be got through, or around, or somehow shuttled aside if the need is great enough. I never knew. I never thought it possible."

"No, neither did I," responded a voice from close beside the two of them. "Never seen the like, Elliot. Excellent job," Blazingame declared.

"Quite nicely done," Miss Markum added. "Now release Miranda, if you please, because absolutely everyone in London is staring at the two of you."

"I doubt it's everyone in London, Ariel," replied Miranda. "And I don't care if it is."

But Elliot released her from his arms and took her hand instead. "The crossing sweep?" he asked, looking around, amazed at the crowd that had gathered.

"His name is Talley, and he's fine," Miss Markum said promptly. "Lord Blazingame dashed out and caught him before he smashed straight into the corner building. I can't guess who was the most surprised, Talley or our Lord Blazingame."

"Me," Blazingame offered at once. "I sent Talley to Bow Street a moment or two ago, by the way. Shall we all get out of the middle of the street, do you think? Go back and await the Runners on the pavement? A deal more civilized."

"You go," Elliot said. "Miranda, go with them."

"And what do you intend to do?" Miranda asked.

"Stay with the animal," he replied, freeing her hand. "See if I can't get some of these fellows to help me unharness the beast from the hackney. She's shivering something fierce. Needs to be walked."

"I'll give you a hand with her, if the ladies will excuse us," offered Blazingame. "Will you be all right by yourselves?"

"We shall be perfectly fine," Miranda declared. "As if anyone would think to accost us in the midst of such a public spectacle as this has become."

"I'll watch over her very carefully," Miss Markum assured Blazingame, bestowing upon him the most knowing of looks. And then she smiled a competent smile at Elliot, intended to erase the sudden worry from his brow, and urged Miranda toward the pavement.

"The Bow Street Runners?" Elliot asked as he and Blazingame turned and approached the horse. "Why call in the Runners, Blazingame? Surely it was an accident." His hand went to the horse's nose, stroked it lovingly. "It's all right now, m'dear. You'll be fine as fivepence in a moment. I'll take this side of the harness, Blazingame, if you'll take the other."

The lad who had rushed out to grab the horse's reins once Elliot had brought the animal to a stop accepted a coin from Blazingame and stayed where he was. A gentleman in a puce morning coat stepped from the curb to help them, and another handed the reins of his horse to a boy and went to lend his aid as well. In a matter of moments, the hackney horse was free of the traces, and Elliot, tossing the boy at the reins a coin from his own pocket and thanking him for his assistance, took hold of a cheek strap, and whispering softly to the mare, strolled forward, leading her up Baker Street at a walk. Blazingame fell in beside him. They trudged through the havoc her wild run had caused to the next corner, where Elliot gave her into Blazingame's care for a moment, stripped off his coat, and laid it across her back. Then he took her again and the three of them turned and walked slowly back.

"Where's the driver?" Elliot asked abruptly. "Was he badly injured? Is that why you sent for the Runners?"

"Actually," Blazingame murmured, studying the cobbles before him, "Miss Markum and I went to find the man. Discovered him in the gutter. He's dead."

"Broke his neck in the fall from the vehicle, I expect."

"Yes, but I don't think that's what killed him, Elliot."

"Well, of course a broken neck would kill him, Blazingame."

"No, I mean to say, Elliot, I believe he was dead before he fell."

"What makes you think that?"

"A hole the size of a pistol ball in his forehead."

# TWELVE

Marley sat in the parlor of Number Fifteen, Buckingham Street, one knee crossed over the other, arms folded across his chest, and waited most patiently for an answer. Already the sun had set and one by one the lamps had flickered on in the street below under the lamplighter's deft attentions. The fog had been stealing in off the Thames for an hour and more, and for equally as long Marley had sat in the Queen Anne chair, uncomfortable but determined, waiting for an answer. He'd done a perfectly stupid thing. So stupid as to prove embarrassing, and he had no intention of losing control in such a fashion again. Therefore he called all his patience to the fore and waited without complaint.

He'd wished to kill Josiah Elliot, of course. At that very moment in time, when he'd been riding down Baker Street and actually seen the man strolling along with a woman on his arm, smiling and talking as though all was right with the world, he'd lost all patience. Now he was quite aware of the mistake he'd made because of it. If anyone had noticed him hail that hackney in the middle of the street, if anyone had noticed him ride up to speak to the driver, take out his charming little pistol and shoot the man in the head, he might, even now, be forced to take his sweet three-barrel box lock pistol for a stroll down to the river and toss it in. And that would make him sad, to be sure.

But no one had taken note of his tiny *faux pas,* he was

certain of it—because it had all happened so quickly, without the least warning. He'd seen Elliot approaching the corner; he'd seen the hackney cab not all that far away from the corner and traveling in the correct direction, and he'd simply gone and shot the cabbie on the chance that the panicked horse, with no driver to control it, would catch Elliot in the middle of the street and end his life for him. Not a head had turned along the mildly crowded thoroughfare when he'd done it. His little pistol had made no more than a slight pop. So slight as to be nearly inaudible amongst all the clip-clopping of hooves, the varied conversations, the clacking of heels and the singing of spurs. Why, it hadn't even disturbed the horse. It had been the driver, a look of sheer astonishment frozen on his face, loosing the reins and pitching forward directly onto the horse's posterior that had set the animal off. And then the blasted vehicle had tipped on its side.

"Slowed the damnable horse just enough to make a hero out of Elliot instead of making him a dead man," Marley mumbled. "Still, it was a close thing. It might have done the trick."

At the sound of Marley's voice, the gentleman whose guest he was stirred a bit. "Taking my name in vain, are you, Marley?" he asked, allowing his long legs to stretch out before him as he sat in the lumpy armchair which he'd positioned before the window. "Elliot, Elliot, Elliot. Sounds like the fluttering of angels' wings when you say it over and over again like that. Elliot, Elliot, Elliot. Elliot, Elliot, Elliot. Look," he murmured, pointing toward the darkening sky. "By Jupiter, Marley, there goes an angel fluttering by this minute. I expect it's Josie. I've been having the most terrible nightmares of late about Josie. Josie and the boys, too. He's come back from the dead, my brother. Come to stare up from the pavement at me and flutter by my window. Finds some great satisfaction in it, no doubt. And the boys—my boys are running about London all decked out in livery, like tiny footmen."

"You're sputtering nonsense again, Nat."

"Yes, I know," replied the gentleman with a slight nod of his head. "Must be nonsense. Cannot possibly be real. Yet, I can't seem to drive any of them from my mind. Must sputter on and on about them, nonsense or not."

"Well, make the attempt to cease sputtering about them for at least five minutes, can't you, Nat?" Marley prodded. "I've been sitting here for hours and I haven't got a sensible answer from you yet."

"An answer? There is no answer. You don't understand, Marley. It's all so complicated and exhausting."

Marley had the strongest urge to stand, to walk quietly up behind Nathaniel Elliot and tip the chair he sat in forward. "Send you fluttering, Elliot, right through that window," he growled under his breath. But then he caught himself and ordered himself to be patient once more. Wouldn't do to go killing the goose who laid the golden eggs, especially when the largest of the eggs was yet to be had.

"I should like to go to the opera," Nathaniel Elliot declared quite loudly. "Yes, indeed. I should like that of all things. The music is most extraordinary, you know, Marley. Most extraordinary. And the opera house ceiling—a paradise!"

"You can't go to the opera, Nat."

"Why?"

"Because you can't afford it and because I'm not inclined to purchase a ticket for you with my own money. I've told you three times already that your funds require replenishing. There's no more cash to hand. That crown you spent today at the apothecary was the last of them. I've no more of your money to give you and I'm certainly not giving you mine, not when you've a veritable fortune in the funds. If you would merely put me in sole charge of your investments and your accounts, I'd not need to keep disturbing you about such things, Nat. You would always have moneys to hand. But as it is, you must sign a note to your bank in order for me to retrieve adequate moneys on your behalf. Don't stare at me with such a puzzled look on your face, Nathaniel. You understand perfectly well what I say to you."

"But there must be moneys to hand," Elliot murmured. "I signed a note to you for a thousand pounds no longer ago than last Tuesday."

"A year ago, that was. You've got no sense of time at all these days."

"Yes, I do. I've a sense of time. I sense it scurrying around my feet and draping itself over my shoulders. I sense it whispering in my ear. I can feel it advance every moment of every day, Marley. Every moment of every day."

Marley sighed. He truly couldn't afford to lose his patience with Nat. Josiah was eminently expendable, but Nat wasn't. At least not yet. "Very well, Nathaniel," he said, fishing his purse from his pocket. "This one time I'll treat you to the price of an opera ticket—only for the pit, mind you. But I'll not accompany you. I despise all that posing and screeching—from the performers and the audience alike."

"I thank you. I do, Marley," Elliot replied, taking the bills Marley offered and tucking them safely away. "I realize I don't make things easy for you. I'll stop by m'solicitor's tomorrow or the next day and have m'funds transferred into your care. I cannot keep my mind on such stuff as investments anymore. I'm grateful to you for wishing to take over the responsibility for me. You're the finest cousin a man could have. It is merely that you've been looking after me an unconscionably long time now, and I had hoped not to burden you further."

"How many times must I say it, Nat? It's not a burden. You're family. I'm fond of you. But I do get the impression, you know, that you don't trust me. You're forever promising to stop by your solicitor's, but you never do. And you will not tell me where the stone lies, though you know it would be a great deal safer did it lie with me than in some moldy old hidey-hole somewhere."

"I can't seem to think any of it important," Elliot replied, staring, enthralled, at the lamp shining up at him from across Buckingham Street. "All of it seems too difficult. Not worth the least effort. Nonsense, in fact."

And why should it not seem so, Marley asked himself forlornly, when these days, in Nat's mind, everything is either ecstasy or terrifying apparitions? Nothing as puerile as money can possibly concern him. The diamond cannot concern him. Why the devil did I allow him to lose so much of himself before I had everything safely in my hands? And then Marley had the most inspired notion. A notion quite beyond compare.

"I don't see why you won't tell me where The Heart of a Queen lies, Nat," he said, abandoning the uncomfortable chair, crossing to the window and hunkering down beside Elliot. "Just think of the pleasure it would bring you to have it here, in your hand, glistening and glimmering in the light of the lamps. What a sight it would prove, wouldn't it? A mystical, magical thing. No telling but you could travel through it to another time, another place."

Marley stayed very still, attempted to breathe as little as possible as a series of expressions that might pass for thoughts trailed across Elliot's countenance. "Better than the opera, Nat," he said after a time, when the expressions ceased. "Better than the opera house ceiling. Better than Covent Garden on a rainy night. More glorious, I'll wager, than holding the sun itself in the palm of your hand. You need only tell me where it lies and I'll fetch it for you on the instant."

"Dare has it."

"No, Dare doesn't have it. Dare's dead."

"He was buried with it, then."

"No, he's not buried with it. He went to fetch it but he didn't have it with him when he died. He must have given it to you, Nathaniel."

"Did he? I don't recall. Doesn't matter really. Dare won't miss it if he's dead. And it ought to belong to Josie. He's the one hid it away again to begin with. All The Buck's toys belong to Josie. But Josie doesn't want the stone. Thinks it's cursed. Doesn't want to so much as touch it. But I'll touch it. Yes, I will. Glorious thing. Big as your fist. And it speaks to you when you hold it in your hand, Marley. It whispers the most amazing things to you in your mind."

I'll whisper things to you in your mind if you don't give it up soon, thought Marley, scowling. "Devil it, Nat," he said aloud. "Josie has no use for that diamond. Never did have and he certainly doesn't now. Josie's dead. Lost at Talavera. I told you that. I've told you that over and over. How can Josie be fluttering outside your window dressed in angels' garb if he's not dead? Answer me that."

"Josie's dead. Dare's dead. Meg's dead. I will go to the opera," murmured Nathaniel Elliot. "I do so enjoy the opera when I've had a bit of a smoke beforehand. The music wraps around you like thick sweet smoke, clings to you, smothers you almost. I will go to the opera and then wander through the streets, and then I'll come back here and hold The Heart of a Queen in my hand and lose myself in it forever."

"It's here?" asked Marley, thoroughly amazed.

"What's here?"

"The Heart of a Queen."

"No, no, but you'll bring it to me, won't you, Marley? Perhaps it's what Josiah wants of me, to keep the diamond for him and take pleasure in it. I shall tell you where it lies and you'll fetch it to me, won't you, Marley?"

Eleanor sat beside her aunt Caroline in the crowded drawing room, her eyes focused on nothing in particular, envisioning again and again, with enormous happiness, the two buckets of milk that Spinner had coaxed from Susan. Two whole buckets, she thought, pleased and proud. And excellent milk. The most delicious milk I've ever tasted. Oh, I know it will work! It has to work!

"Eleanor? Eleanor, dearest?" Her aunt's voice slowly made its way into her thoughts.

"Yes, Aunt Caroline?" she asked, popping into the present.

"Lord Blazingame has said 'how do you do' to you three times now, Eleanor. I do think it would be kind to give him some reply."

Eleanor's gaze fell at once on buff breeches and the embroidered pockets of a gold and aqua waistcoat. She tilted her head upward to discover Blazingame smiling down at her.

"How do y'do, Miss Feebes," he said once again. "You've been off in dreamland, I think."

"I—I—It is a pleasure to see you again, my lord," Eleanor managed.

"I hoped it would be. I happened to—come upon—your uncle at White's club tonight and he said that you and your aunt were attending this particular soiree."

"He did? Uncle Roger?"

"Indeed."

"How kind of you to seek us out, my lord," Lady Newcombe said when Eleanor said nothing, merely stared up at Blazingame, seemingly nonplussed. "You are known to the Herolds, Lord Blazingame?"

"Yes, ma'am," Blazingame replied. "Lord Herold is a cousin of sorts to my cousin, Wilde. I wondered," he added, "would you care to take a stroll through the Herolds' garden, Lady Newcombe, Miss Feebes? It's quite—festive—with all the little paper lanterns hanging from the bushes and the trees."

"Of course they'd like to take a stroll," said another,

deeper voice. "It's the finest garden in all of London. Not to be missed. And it's an absolute squeeze in here. I don't see how anyone can get a serious breath."

"Lady Newcombe, Miss Feebes, may I present my cousin, Mr. Wilde," Blazingame said, his green eyes focused intently on Eleanor. "Wilde, Lady Newcombe. Miss Feebes."

Wilde bowed quite elegantly before them. So elegantly, in fact, that Blazingame was inclined to kick him—surreptitiously, of course, a simple crossing over of his toe to Wilde's calf.

"I expect you will lose your chairs, ladies, if you join us, but I assure you, Herold's garden is well worth the loss. Come, Lady Newcombe," Wilde urged, offering his arm. "Join me in exiting this crush of humanity and entering the much more pleasurable world of nature, eh? Blazingame, give Miss Feebes your arm and come along."

"Give Miss Feebes your arm and come along?" repeated Eleanor as they exited the drawing room by way of the French windows and descended the veranda stairs into the garden.

"He's a bit intent on being a commanding presence tonight," Blazingame replied. "I was afraid this would happen when I sought him out and requested his aid. But I didn't have an invitation, you see, to this particular soiree, and Wilde did. It's Wilde's invitation that got me through the front door. I'm his guest. Of course, he wasn't coming either, but—"

"He wasn't coming?"

"No. Says he's too old and tired for such things. But then I mentioned that you would be here with Lady Newcombe and—"

"Me? You mentioned me to your cousin?"

"Yes, you're precisely why he came. To make your acquaintance and to keep your aunt occupied so that we can—so that you and I can—"

"So that we can what, my lord?"

"G-get to know each other better."

In the shadows cast by the Chinese lanterns which drifted lazily above them on a soft breeze; amidst the sweet smell of roses, lilacs, dogwood; as tiny streamers of fog—only now making a tentative approach this far inland—nipped at her toes, Miss Feebes was such a delightful vision beside him on the garden path that Blazingame could not keep from drawing her to a halt, taking her hands into his, and looking her up and down. She was so exquisite in her white muslin gown with its cherry-red ribbons that Blazingame thought he must be dreaming.

"We have not had a goodly amount of time in which to come to know each other, Miss Feebes," he managed, after his eyes had feasted on her for a full minute or more. "Not as yet, we haven't. And I—I— Do you know you are like a flower yourself, standing here in the lantern light?"

Eleanor blushed. She knew she did. She could feel the color rising into her cheeks. Inside her cherry-red slippers—which she had rushed out and purchased only today, along with the cherry-red ribbon around her waist—prodded to it by the fondness she'd abruptly developed for that particular color—her toes curled the slightest bit with embarrassment and with something else. "I am pleased you came, my lord," she said, freeing her hands from his, once again taking his arm and urging him to take a step forward along the path and then another and another, until they were strolling along together quite nicely. "My brother and I paid a call on you this afternoon. You were not at home and—"

"You brushed past Doughtry and strolled with the utmost impertinence down my corridor and into my kitchen. I know, Miss Feebes. Doughtry told me all. You came to see the Dexter?"

"Susan."

"Yes, Susan. Well, even though it does upset Doughtry a bit and Wilde says you ought not come to my establishment at all, you are welcome to visit Susan whenever you please. I have no misgivings about it, Miss Feebes."

"That's very kind of you, my lord," Eleanor responded, "but I fear I must not visit your establishment ever again. Not even with my brother beside me. I am very sorry about the dreadful scandal that I almost caused, my lord, and I shan't take the chance that such a thing may happen again."

"A dreadful scandal, Miss Feebes?"

"Yes. The dreadful scandal. Fortunately my uncle Roger put an end to it at once but—"

"Well, that's good news," Blazingame interrupted. "I should hate for there to be a dreadful scandal involving you, Miss Feebes. You are a young woman who deserves the utmost respect from everyone. How anyone could imagine that you would do the least thing contrary to morality—"

"B-but the scandal concerned you, my lord, not me."

"Me?" Blazingame drew to a halt again and stared down at her, his face concealed in shadow. "I was almost involved in a dreadful scandal? What sort of scandal was it, Miss Feebes, from which your uncle saved me?"

Eleanor had not expected to be asked what the scandal was precisely. She had thought, though he had proved gentleman enough not to mention it, that Lord Blazingame had already heard the tale. Truly, it had upset her to hear of the thing from her uncle Roger earlier, but not nearly as much as it upset her now, to be asked to reveal what had gone forward to the perfectly innocent gentleman who might have been harmed by it. And yet, if he wished to know, then it was her duty to tell him. She dithered about, looking down at her reticule for a bit, playing with its strings, looking up at Lord Blazingame, rocking from heel to toe once, twice. "One of your neighbors, the Dowager Lady Ledderley— That is to say—" she began hesitantly. "I daresay she is quite old. Is she an elderly lady, my lord?"

"The Dowager Lady Ledderley? Jupiter, yes! Eighty-five if she's a day."

"Just as I thought, because she—apparently, she was peeking out her window both times Donovan and I came to your house and she— Evidently her eyes are not as good as they once were and she—"

"She has trouble recognizing her own son and daughter-in-law if they're not within three feet of her."

"Just so. Well. She saw Donovan and me arrive at your establishment both times we came, but she did not recognize us as the same two people each time. And somehow she got it into her head that—that—"

"That, Miss Feebes?"

"Well, I expect there is no delicate way to say it. The Dowager Lady Ledderley thought at first that you had taken a mistress, but then she couldn't understand why your mistress should have a man escort her into your establishment and remain there. Apparently, she also thought she saw some man follow you home and watch your house and she imagined he must be a Runner. And she—she concluded from these things that you had—that you had gone into the business of buying and selling young women as—love slaves," Eleanor finished on a great gulp.

All her joy, all her happiness over the milk Susan could give and the number of children who would benefit from it once she devised a way to get the little cow from London to Liverpool, evaporated as the sheer ugliness of the scandal that might have landed on Lord Blazingame's broad shoulders and ruined his good name settled over her. She sought some clue from the expression on Lord Blazingame's face, from the light in his eyes, as to how he was taking the news, but he remained in the shadows. He did nothing, said nothing, stood motionless, staring down at her.

"It is all my f-fault," Eleanor whispered when she could bear his silence—which she deduced to be shock and grief—no longer. "Donovan told me I ought not walk up to a bachelor's establishment, much less go inside. Even your Mr. Doughtry attempted to tell me—over and over again.

But I didn't believe them. What business is it of your neighbors, after all, who pays you a c-call and who does not? That's what I thought."

Still Blazingame did not respond, not with so much as a sigh or a groan.

"I'm a terribly stubborn woman and I never learn until it's too late," Eleanor began again. "I'm frightfully adamant when I perceive injustice. And I did think that Mr. Elliot—And I did so want to see Susan again, to be certain she was—"

A veritable lump of regret grew in Eleanor's throat as she stared up at Blazingame. She squared her shoulders, forced herself to get on with it, because unless she did, poor Lord Blazingame would continue to think himself ruined forever. And he was not ruined forever.

"You are not forever ruined," she managed around the lump. "Please don't think you are. Uncle Roger explained to Lord Ledderley and everyone else at White's club who was listening to the story that the two people were Donovan and I. He said that he had sent us to deliver a number of papers having to do with one of his Causes. And everyone believed him, because they know how he is about his Causes. So the rumor did not truly spread all over London as it might have done and the scandal was stopped from happening. Even Aunt Caroline has had no word of it. I am so very sorry, my lord. I assure you I am. As sorry as I know how to be. Aren't you going to say anything at all? Ever?" asked Eleanor.

Blazingame did not reply.

"You may turn around and leave me standing here alone if you wish, Lord Blazingame. You needn't continue to escort me farther. No, and you needn't ever see me or speak to me again if you don't wish to do so."

Eleanor's eyes, which had been lit all this time by the same lamplight that set Blazingame's in shadow, began to glisten with unshed but truly penitent tears, and perhaps that was why he did it. Blazingame didn't know exactly. But without a word, he took the two little hands that fiddled with the reticule into his own, drew Miss Feebes to him, leaned down, and kissed her slowly, carefully, gently, on those most enticing lips.

"Love slaves?" he whispered when their lips parted. "I buy and sell love slaves, Miss Feebes?" He smiled the most charming smile. "Whatever has that old harridan of Ledderley's been drinking?"

"I—I am sure I don't know," replied Eleanor, flustered. Her cheeks burned more than ever, but the lips he'd kissed felt cool and caressed. She licked each of them separately, stroking them, tasting them with her tongue. The sweet flavor of brandy lingered there, and an enticing hint of cherries.

A goodly distance down the path, Wilde ceased glancing restlessly over his shoulder and returned his attention to Lady Newcombe, steering her farther away from the couple with a smile on his face and a rather delightful emotion flitting somewhere around his heart.

Lady Sophia stepped into the Earl of Windom's box at King's Theatre, her auburn curls glistening beneath the chandeliers. In a gown of gold silk with a black cameo on a velvet ribbon at her throat, she was a vision so exquisite that a ripple of whispers began in the pit, rose, and trembled through the gallery and all five tiers of boxes and resulted in a profusion of opera glasses being focused in her direction and a multitude of male hearts ceasing to beat for an instant. One of the hearts that ceased to beat belonged to Mr. Donovan Feebes. He'd been forced to take up residence in the pit because the gallery had been filled and his uncle was not fond of opera and so did not have a box at the Opera House in Haymarket. Mr. Feebes, however, consoled himself by noting that Lady Sophia was not as far above him as he had expected her to be, Windom's box being nestled, as it was, in the first tier. Why, with his opera glasses, he might gaze on the lady who owned his heart at any time and see her as clearly as if he sat beside her.

Except, it was Windom who would sit beside her. Windom who, under the watchful eye of Lady Sophia's mama, would share Lady Sophia's delight in the elegance of the theatre. Windom who would trade confidences with her about the company assembled within the theatre walls and would delight with her in the beauty of the music. And it was Windom who would whisper in her ear, too. Donovan's smile at his good fortune trembled just a bit at the thought of Windom whispering in Lady Sophia's ear. But then he focused his opera glasses on the Earl of Windom and noted how elderly the man was, and his budding jealousy of that particular gentleman faded. *Certainly Lady Sophia can never bring herself to love a man as old as the Earl of Windom,* he thought. *Why, he must be thirty-five if he's a day. Likely he is nothing more than a good friend of her papa's and not one of her beaux at all.* And with his smile once again steady on his handsome young face, he focused his glasses once again on Lady Sophia herself and kept them there until the performance began.

Surreptitiously, he raised the opera glasses to gaze up at Lady Sophia even in the midst of the performance and was amazed, at one point, to actually catch the Earl of Windom whispering in her ear, and to see Sophia laugh in response to it. In truth, Donovan was so preoccupied with what might be happening behind and above him that he did not so much as consider the performers on the stage or actually listen to the music. Nor did he notice when, just after the beginning of the second act, a gentleman entered and sat down beside him. Didn't notice at all, because he was busily condemning himself just then for being a fool. He ought to have gone up to Windom's box and paid his respects to Lady Sophia during the first intermission, but he'd not done so. Windom's box, when he'd looked up to check, had been overflowing with gentlemen, all of them hoping to make a splendid impression on the woman he loved, and his heart had failed him at the sight.

"But I will go and speak to her at the next break," he told himself quietly. "I will." And so deciding, he turned around at last, prepared to enjoy what was left of the second act. Except, he did not enjoy the remainder of the second act. He found himself distracted time and time again by the stranger who had taken the seat beside him. He was a tallish gentleman in a long black cloak with red silk lining. A floppy-brimmed hat sat low on his brow and he whispered to himself as he sat staring at the stage. He whispered constantly. So much so that he began to arouse Donovan's curiosity. *What the deuce was the man whispering to himself about?* Donovan leaned a bit closer and was amazed to discover that the man was actually whispering every word the singers sang and said, and at the same time, too. This so amazed him—that a gentleman would know every word of an opera—that he began to think perhaps the gentleman was a composer himself.

Perhaps he's someone I ought to know, Donovan thought excitedly. Perhaps his name is legend in London. Perhaps, do I make his acquaintance and take him with me to Windom's box and introduce him to Lady Sophia, it'll prove an enormous coup and she'll be exceedingly impressed with me. "I beg your pardon, sir," Donovan said quietly, "but I cannot help but notice that you know every word of every song."

The gentleman turned and stared at him, his lips frozen open on the last word he'd been about to pronounce.

"I merely wondered, are you, perhaps, the composer of this fascinating entertainment?"

"Dead," the gentleman whispered in return.

"I beg your pardon?"

"The opera is by Handel. He's dead. Doubt I'm dead."

"Oh! No, no, of course not. I am Mr. Feebes, Donovan

Feebes," Donovan offered, feeling a bit foolish because he knew the composer, Handel, was dead. It was merely that he knew nothing at all about opera and had not taken any note of what was to be presented. And so he had never guessed that this particular opera was by Handel. But it was still possible—likely, too—that the gentleman beside him *was* a prominent composer—a living one. "Elliot," the man mumbled in reply, graciously but most distractedly, and then he leaned back a bit and gazed up at the ceiling. He continued to stare at the ceiling in complete silence for the remainder of the act and on the final note whispered, "Paradise."

Elliot? Donovan thought, glancing from time to time at the silent ceiling-watcher beside him. Can he be some relative of Eleanor's Mr. Elliot? But then he decided not, because there were so many families with the surname of Elliot, and Eleanor's Mr. Elliot had never mentioned having a relative in London. And besides, Eleanor's Mr. Elliot was a valet, and this man—this man was obviously an artiste. Anyone could see he was by the eccentricity of his dress and the complexity of his actions. And he knew every word the singers sang and said!

"I wonder, Mr. Elliot," Donovan said as the second act came to a close and people began to move about. "I wonder if you would care to join me for a bit of a stroll? There is a young lady in one of the boxes I wish to visit and I think, perhaps, she would be intrigued to make your acquaintance."

"Intrigued?" Elliot's glance left the ceiling reluctantly. "Young lady?"

"Yes. That's her, right up there. The exquisite creature in gold with the auburn curls." Donovan offered Elliot his opera glasses, aiming them in the right direction.

Elliot took them and peered through them at the Earl of Windom's box, whispered to himself, and then handed the glasses back to Donovan.

"Time for me to depart, young sir," he said. And then the gentleman stood and bowed most graciously. He swept his hat from his head in the doing of it. He sent his cloak billowing about him. "Fare thee well," he said just as clearly, and he was almost immediately lost among the now roving members of the pit.

Donovan was startled at the oddly ancient sound of his words and the immediacy of the gentleman's disappearance and wondered if somehow he had fallen asleep during the performance and dreamed the gentleman. Or, perhaps, the gentleman had been Handel's ghost, haunting the theatre in which his works had been so very much applauded. But then he dismissed all thoughts of the strange encounter from his mind and hurried from the pit up the staircase to the corridor which provided entrance to the first tier of boxes.

They stood together on a deserted Westminster Bridge, a hazy moon blinking fitfully down at them, fog swirling around their ankles, the lights and clatter of the city turned solemn and vague in the distance. Miranda, tucked in the safety and warmth of Elliot's arm, rested her head against his breast and listened with a particularly fond feeling to the familiar, muffled beating of his heart.

"I was accustomed to come here often when I was a lad," Elliot said after a long, comfortable silence, his gaze fastened on the Thames. "Nat would come with me and we would stand gazing down at the Thames for what seemed like hours and hours."

"Did your mother accompany you here as she did to the water gate? Did she tell you stories about Westminster Bridge and Whitehall and the Tower?"

"Oh, she told us tales about all those places, but she never accompanied us here. We came here alone, Nat and I. Sneaked out a window, climbed over a rooftop or two, shimmied down a trellis and scuttled like rats through the mews and the alleyways as fast as we could scuttle, for fear that some ruffian might take note of two boys alone and seize us. Of course, no ruffian ever did. What genuine villain would think to bother with two lads who looked to be no better than filthy urchins after all that climbing and shimmying and scuttling?" Elliot smiled at a vision Miranda could not see but one she thought she understood well.

"This is the very best place we could discover to come and dream our own dreams, Miranda. This bridge at night in the fog."

"And what was it you dreamed of, you and Nat?"

"Well, Nat almost always dreamed of traveling on the tall ships—to other worlds, you know. Worlds he'd read about in his books, where strange and brilliant plants pushed up their heads and animals beyond description roamed a landscape formed before the beginnings of time."

"And you, Josiah? What did you dream?"

"You'll think me a barbarian, do I tell you."

"Never."

"Yes, you will, but it doesn't matter any longer. I'm grown now and my boyhood dreams are far behind me. I dreamed of war, Miranda. I dreamed of being a cavalier like The Buck, of proving my courage and my skill in the defense of England and my King, of performing heroic deeds, of engaging in victorious campaigns, of meriting all manner of honors on any number of battlefields. But I was very young."

"Very young, with a head stuffed full of knights and cavaliers and the like."

"Precisely."

"But now you've grown older."

"A good deal older."

"And what do you dream of now? What were you dreaming mere moments ago, Josiah? Because you were dreaming. I could tell."

"Tonight? This very night? Mere moments ago?" Elliot asked with a perfectly enchanting grin.

"Um-hmmm."

"To tell the truth, I was dreaming of how it will be for the two of us once we're married."

Miranda smiled up at him. "Truly? And I did not once feel you shudder, Josiah."

Elliot laughed quietly. And then he studied her with great deliberation.

"What?" Miranda asked. "Josiah? What are you thinking now?"

"Hmmm?"

"You heard me perfectly well. Why is the moon sparkling in your eyes in such an impish manner?"

"I'm merely imagining what it would be like to be a cavalier in this particular day and age," he said softly. "To be wild and elegant and filled with pride, and at the same time to know the steps of the waltz."

"To know the steps of— What has that to do with—" Miranda's smile widened considerably. "What has the waltz to do with anything at all?"

"It is everything, the waltz," Elliot replied, taking his arm from around her, backing away one step then another. "If men like The Buck had known to dance the waltz, all of England would be a very different place today. Only dream, Miranda," he whispered. "Only dream it with me." And he gracefully extended his right leg before him, raised his right hand in the air as though sweeping a plumed hat from his head and bowed the most elegant courtier's bow. Miranda could see the wide-brimmed plumed hat sweep across his body, could feel the slight breeze from his long scarlet cloak as he brushed it aside.

"My lady," he said in a voice that rustled with promise. "My sweet and beautiful lady, Miranda. Shall we dance?"

"I would be delighted, sir," Miranda replied, steadying herself on the hand he held out to her and performing the deepest of curtsies. A stray flicker of moonlight touched a loosed strand of tawny hair that brushed across her proud brow. An entire moonbeam jostled the fog aside and set her eyes afire as she smiled up at him.

Eyes like sapphires burning in the night, he thought as she rose from the curtsy. All our hopes, all our dreams alive and flashing in those eyes. His right hand touched the small of her back. His left hand took possession of her right. He began to hum softly, sweetly, and he led her into a waltz. He sent the fog swirling up around them as he waltzed with her in the darkness and the seclusion that was Westminster Bridge after midnight. It was not the strenuous, bouncing waltz of English ballrooms that she had come to know. Not that waltz. But the slow, sensual, scandalous waltz of the Continent.

And then, deep into the dream, Miranda's breath caught in her throat once, twice. This is not simple pretending, she thought, the very reality of him overwhelming her. This is not a dream. He's so dear, so strong, so real. How can I bear to let him go? When this dance ends and the truth of who we are and where we are returns, how will I bear to drive home with him to Portman Square, to allow him to escort me to my door, and then to close it behind me, between us, separating us once again?

A glint of moonlight touched his eyes at that moment, and Miranda came near to stumbling at the extent of the love she saw there. Her heart fluttered like a captured bird. She was suddenly terrified at the strength of that love—so strong, so deep, so endless. But then a calm washed through her and her mind filled with wonder as she felt herself melt into him, felt the two of them meld together, one to the other, until she could not discern where she ended and Josiah Elliot began. Now the dance—each slow step, each sultry turn, each intoxicating movement—now the dance became the motion not of two separate beings but of one. The night, the fog, the fear of closed doors between them, all were as nothing while they danced together into dreams.

And then Elliot ceased to hum and they slowed, stopped. Miranda gazed up at him, and he lowered his head until his lips pressed against hers. She could feel his heart beating in her own breast and she knew beyond all doubt that her heart was beating just as truly and strongly in his.

"I had best take you home, Miranda," he whispered as their lips parted. His hands came up to touch her cheeks while his thumbs traced twin lines from the corners of her eyes, out to her hair line, down past her ears. And as his hands fell away, his thumbs lingered along her jaw, and then came to rest beneath her chin, tickling it, tilting it upward. "I *must* take you home, Miranda," he said in a voice that was a mixture of gravel and velvet, "or marry you here and now without one more second passing away."

"Marry me here and now," Miranda whispered. "Let Westminster Bridge be our chapel. Let the Thames be our curate. Let the fog be our witness and the stillness of the night our marriage bed."

Elliot bent to kiss her again, his heart wild with passion, but no sooner did their lips meet than the sound of hooves clattering and wheels rattling over the cobbles boomed like thunder in their ears. They parted and looked to the foot of the bridge, where a landau, illuminated against the night with four lanterns, was just then being reined to a halt.

"My lady! My lady!" cried a most familiar voice. "Do that be you? I cannot see you through the fog so well."

"Early?" Miranda could not believe her ears. "Early? Is that you?"

"My lady!" the cook cried, her voice high and pulsing with anxiety. "You must come and bring Mr. Elliot with you! Miss Markum has been injured, my lady, and Mr. Browne has been murdered!"

# THIRTEEN

Apparently Mr. Browne had not been murdered, because it was he who opened the door to them when they arrived at Portman Square. "Browne, what happened?" Miranda asked fearfully. "Where is Miss Markum? Is she seriously injured?"

"And what about yourself?" Elliot added, discerning the ungainly manner in which the butler's waistcoat bulged.

"Oh, madam! And Mr. Elliot, how kind of you to come as well! Oh, madam! Miss Markum is upstairs in her bedchamber and Mr. Gibbs, the surgeon, with her. She fell, my lady. Fell on the stairs in the most heroic attempt to save my life."

Miranda paused only long enough to give Elliot's hand a quick squeeze, and then she rushed up the staircase to see just what had happened to Ariel. John Gibbs, the surgeon, she thought. Gracious heaven, please let her not truly need a surgeon. Please let the groom simply have thought to go to this man first, and Ariel merely have bruised herself.

"I see Miss Markum is to be depended upon as usual," observed Elliot, stepping farther into the vestibule. "You're not dead by any means, Browne."

"No. No, sir. But only because Miss Markum came hurtling down at the villain and utterly destroyed his aim. Hit me in a rib, merely. Took a bit of flesh and a bite of bone, but the ball fell right out again."

"Early said you were dead."

"Did she, sir? Well, I expect she thought I was. I—I am sorry to say that I fainted dead away, Mr. Elliot. Dead away."

Alone in the vestibule with a butler he barely knew and with Miranda gone quite out of his reach, for he could not think to enter Miss Markum's bedchamber, Elliot felt the least bit off balance, out of step with himself, unsure of what he ought to do next. Well, no. He knew what he ought to do next, he ought to hand this pale-faced butler his hat and gloves and take up residence in the parlor until Miranda returned to advise him of Miss Markum's condition. He ought to be available in case either of the ladies required his aid. But he had neither hat nor gloves with him to hand to the butler and he didn't wish to cause Browne any further anxiety by forcing the man to look to his comfort while he waited. "Early—Mrs. Harriot, that is—has gone 'round to the kitchen door," he remembered abruptly.

"Oh! It's locked," Browne exclaimed, his hands fidgeting with the waistcoat that would not lie perfectly. "I must go open it for her at once, sir."

"I'll do it for you, Browne," Elliot offered at once. "You ought not be dashing around the house. Most likely you ought not be standing around the house. Go into your parlor, eh, and sit in the most comfortable chair you have. Or better yet, go to bed," he added, accompanying the butler toward the rear of the establishment. As they reached the kitchen, one strong hand prevented Browne from heading for the kitchen door and directed him instead toward his quarters.

"But, sir," Browne protested. "It is merely a few more steps to the kitchen door."

"Which I will take for you, Browne. Go. Sit. Do not get up again. I'll come speak with you in a moment or two."

"But, sir, it's not your position to be—"

"Think, Browne," drawled Elliot in the calmest, coolest tone he could manage. "Mrs. Harriot is even now standing outside the kitchen door. Mrs. Harriot believes you to be dead. What is she going to do when you open the door to her?"

"Oh! Yes, yes, you're correct, of course, Mr. Elliot. She will scream most likely and run off into the night. The kitchen door is just beyond that jog—"

"Yes, yes, I know where it is, Browne."

"You do, sir?"

"I lived here once when I was a boy."

"You did?"

"Yes. Now off with you to your own parlor, Browne. Mrs. Harriot is likely near panic at not being able to come inside. Was it a burglar?"

"Just so," murmured Browne, wandering off toward his quarters. "A burglar. A burglar came right inside our house."

Upstairs on the second floor, Miranda discovered the door to Ariel's tiny sitting room open wide. The sound of voices carried to her from the bedchamber beyond. Her heart beating somewhat raggedly with fear for her dearest friend, Miranda hurried to the bedchamber and discovered a tall, thin gentleman with gray mustachios sitting quietly in a chair beside Ariel's bed. Ariel, herself, was on the bed, atop the bedclothes, her hair loose and disheveled, falling far down over her shoulders, the hem of her nightgown torn. She had a bandage around her head and another around her right wrist and a third fastened around a toe. But her eyes were bright and she called to Miranda the moment she took note of her on the threshold.

"Miranda, dearest, come in. Come in. This is Mr. Gibbs. Mr. Gibbs, Lady Miranda Wesley."

Mr. Gibbs stood and offered his chair to Miranda. "She will do quite nicely, I think, my lady. You do not wish for me to notify Bow Street, then, Miss Markum?"

"No. Miranda and I will look to see what is missing and contact them tomorrow, first thing," Miss Markum replied as Miranda settled into the chair the surgeon had abandoned. "I cannot bear to have Runners traipsing all over and asking all manner of questions this late in the evening. I've had quite enough nonsense for one night."

"Just so. I will stop by tomorrow afternoon to check on you and your butler both," the surgeon replied. He smiled down at Miranda. "Attempt not to look quite so apprehensive, my lady. Neither of the brave defenders of your household is likely to expire. I've left some laudanum drops for Mr. Browne, though he would not take them until he knew you were safely home. And I had to force this stubborn woman here to drink some down. I have left the remainder and written down the dosage. I bid you good evening. No, no, stay here with Miss Markum, my lady. I am perfectly capable of finding my own way out."

"He is, too," Miss Markum said once the gentleman had left the room. "I have never seen such a gentleman for taking charge. Don't you think his moustachios are rather dashing, Miranda?"

"I don't wish to discuss his moustachios, Ariel," Miranda replied, sitting forward in the chair and taking one of Miss Markum's hands into her own. "Are you in pain or is the laudanum working? Great heavens, you are practically swathed in bandages like an Egyptian mummy."

Miss Markum giggled at the thought, which was precisely what Miranda had hoped she would do.

"Do you feel well enough to tell me what happened?"

Miss Markum leaned her head back against a lovely lavender-filled pillow and sighed. "It was the most amazing thing."

"Amazing?"

"Yes, I expect that's the word I want. I was up here in my bed, reading and waiting to hear you come safely home, and I heard a noise from the vestibule, and then I heard Mr. Browne rushing from his quarters toward the front of the house. And I surmised that you had forgotten your key, Miranda, and knocked quietly for him—for I didn't actually hear a knock. And just as I was setting my volume aside and beginning to turn down the wick on my lamp, I heard the most dreadful commotion. So I slipped on my robe and went to see what was going on. Well, I dashed to see what was going on, actually, which I shouldn't have done."

Miss Markum paused and yawned and her eyes blinked closed for a moment. However, she fought off the urge to sleep and continued. "Mr. Browne was standing in the vestibule, his face as white as a sheet, Miranda, and a gentleman with a fine beaver hat was just then stepping down the last step of the staircase."

"A gentleman? Stepping *down* the staircase?"

"Yes. And I was just about to demand to know what on earth was going on, when I—tripped. Oh, I am so embarrassed. But I was actually running at the time. I had run down the corridor and I was galloping down the staircase as if I were a girl of seven. And when I attempted to bring myself to a halt I—tripped."

"Oh, my poor Ariel! You might have broken your neck!" Miranda was aghast at the thought.

"I expect I might have done, but I merely tore the hem of my nightgown, stubbed my toe, and sprained my wrist. The gentleman in the beaver broke my fall admirably. He didn't intend to do it, I'm sure, but he was intent on dealing with Mr. Browne, and I think he did not take note of my approach until I landed on him."

"And that pristine bandage around your brow? You haven't mentioned that particular injury as yet."

"It is merely a lump. A particularly ugly lump if you ask me, but Mr. Gibbs says it is nothing at all. I landed flat on the gentleman, Miranda. I expect I was stunned because I did not think to get off him at first. In fact, he pushed me from atop him. Struck me with something in his hand when he did, too, though not terribly hard."

"Great heavens. A burglar."

"Well, that's what Mr. Browne told Mr. Gibbs, but the gentleman was not at all my idea of what a burglar ought to be, I assure you. I saw him only from above and behind, but he was dressed quite nicely, Miranda. Which is why I call him a gentleman," Miss Markum added, and yawned once more. "Because he looked like a gentleman."

"I never saw the man before," Mr. Browne replied as Elliot helped him out of his coat and waistcoat. "A perfect stranger. And coming down the staircase in *our* house!"

"That must have been startling," replied Elliot, who had reassured Early that Miranda was even then seeing to Miss Markum and that he, himself, would look after Mr. Browne and had sent the cook off to her bed. "And he pointed a pistol at you, you say?"

"More than pointed it. He pulled the trigger, Mr. Elliot."

"Where do you keep your nightshirt, Browne? No, no, simply tell me and I'll fetch it for you."

"It's in the clothespress."

Elliot discovered the nightshirt on the first attempt and returned to help the butler divest himself of the rest of his clothes and slip into the thing. He then turned back the bedclothes and ordered Mr. Browne into the bed.

"I ought to have d-done something," said Browne quietly. "She saved my life, Miss Markum did, and I—I—"

"You what?" asked Elliot, tugging the bedclothes up around the butler.

"The man escaped through the front door before I got my wits about me. I did think to chase after him, but Miss Markum was lying very still on the floor, so I thought instead to get up and go to her, but I—but I—"

"You fainted."

"I am so ashamed," murmured Browne. "I am so very ashamed."

"Well, but you ought not to be ashamed," Elliot said, recognizing the anguish in the man's eyes. He knew that particular anguish intimately. He'd seen it many times before in scores of other eyes, and others, he knew, had seen it in his eyes, as well. Elliot sat down on the edge of the bed. "It is not a shameful thing to have fainted, Browne. It doesn't mean that you're faint of heart. It is merely something to do with your body, not your mind. You got up to go to her and your body could not bear the movement. That alone tells me that you're a brave man who sets the welfare of his mates—well, in this case, of Miss Markum—before his own welfare. You wished to help her despite your own situation. That's laudable, Browne, nothing of which to be ashamed."

"But I did not help her."

"Only because your body would not allow it."

"I ought to have forced my body to allow it."

Elliot smiled a sad smile. "Sometimes, no matter what we think or what we feel, our minds cannot overcome our bodies."

"Soldiers do," Browne replied, his hands forming themselves into fists atop the counterpane. "Our brave men in the Peninsula do so every day."

"But you're not a soldier, Browne. You're a butler, and your body is not accustomed to such treatment as a pistol ball to the ribs. Most unaccustomed to it, I should think. Unless, of course, there is more to being a butler than I have heretofore imagined. You're not generally shot at, wounded, battered about, are you, Browne?"

"N-no."

"No. Well, soldiers are, you see. I was a soldier for a goodly long time, Browne, and I must admit that my body became accustomed to small wounds and learned to continue on in spite of them, but not always. Not always. There were times I fell and attempted to rise, but fainted, just as you did tonight. There were times when, without the aid of my compatriots, I might have been killed where I'd fallen, because I could not rise again. There are times in all of our lives, Browne, when our hearts and our souls are willing, but our bodies are simply unable to respond. So, don't be

ashamed. Please don't. You did a remarkable thing. You saw
a man invade your establishment and you rushed to confront
him, to protect your mistress and your staff from harm at
great risk to yourself. That took remarkable courage,
Browne, and I applaud you for it."

As do I, thought Miranda, who had left Miss Markum
very near sleep and hurried downstairs to check on Browne,
only to pull up short at the sound of Elliot's voice as he
described his experiences in battle. I applaud you both, she
thought. Two courageous men in my house at one and the
same time and neither of them, I think, aware of just how
extraordinary they are.

"I don't like to do it, mind," whispered Spinner. "Everyone here has been most kind to us. But I think we're obliged
to go live with Uncle Josie."

"Just so," Jack agreed, slipping from his cot. "Obliged
to live with Uncle Josie. Do you remember how to get
there?"

"Perfectly," Spinner replied. "As long as we set out from
the front of this house and not the rear. No, don't be putting
on your red breeches, Jack. Find your old ones. Those
breeches don't belong to you. They belong to his grace."

"He'll never fit into them."

"Doesn't matter. It was he paid for them, and the new
coats and shirts and waistcoats. That makes them his."

"All right," mumbled Jack unhappily, pulling his leg out
of the red breeches and scampering about in his bare feet
in search of his old breeches. "Are you certain Uncle Josie
will have us? It didn't look like a very large establishment
to me, Spinner. Perhaps he won't have room for us."

"Then we'll sleep in his stable."

"I didn't see any stable. All I saw was that tiny cow
chomping on that little bit of grass."

"There's always a stable," Spinner declared confidently.

"In the mews, most likely. And if there's not, we'll sleep on his grass with his little cow. And we won't be the least trouble to him. You've got to remember that, Jack, because I'm going to give him my word on that. We're not going to be the least bit of trouble."

"Not the least bit of trouble."

"And the three of us will find Papa together. You've my word on that, too."

"You've my word on that, too," Jack agreed, having gotten into his breeches and now tugging his shirt on over his head. "And we will both give our word to Uncle Josie about finding Papa and he'll give his word to us."

"Just so," Spinner agreed, donning his boots and going to fetch Jack's coat for him. "Hurry, Jack, before someone wakes and hears us."

Jack hurried as best he could, but even so, it took them another ten minutes before they unlatched the little window under the eaves and climbed carefully down a trellis rich with ivy. Together they scampered as silently as they could through the narrow space between Comestock House and the house beside it and emerged into the square and the light of the streetlamps. "This way," Spinner hissed, and together they set off for the corner of the square. Taking great care not to scuff their heels against the pavement, just in case the noise it made might wake someone, they reached the corner and turned left. Outside the square, the streetlamps were not quite as bright, one or two of them had gone out, in fact, and the farther along the boys went, the more eerily shadows and fog seemed to creep up around them.

"Are you certain this is the correct way?" Jack asked in a whisper. "I don't remember it looking like this."

"Things always look different in the dark," replied Spinner, shortening his stride.

"What?" asked Jack. "Why are you slowing down?"

"Did you hear that, Jack?"

"What?"

"A sound like leaves whispering."

"It'll be the trees."

"There aren't any trees here, Jack. There it is again. Listen," Spinner urged, coming to a complete halt.

Jack's eyes grew wide as the sound, barely a sound at all but present regardless, reached his ears. "Run!" he shouted. But before the boys could get their feet started, one large hand descended on each of them, seizing them by their coat collars.

"What a delightful gift from the gods," breathed a low, terrifying voice from behind them. "Two little chicks escaped from the henhouse and not a rooster around to defend them. No hungry old fox could wish for more."


Donovan stepped from the hackney cab, handed his money up to the driver and stood staring up at his uncle Roger's house. Nora is correct, he thought, his hands stuffed in his pockets, his coat collar raised against the damp. I am not equal to any of those gentlemen who were standing about in Windom's box paying court to Lady Sophia. I've never seen such splendidly dressed gentlemen in all my life. No, and I've never heard such conversation as they're capable of before, either. Lady Sophia will have thought me a beetlebrain, standing there speechless and staring like an owl at the lot of them. I don't belong in such company. Not at all.

But Uncle Roger has a title and he is nothing like them. I don't recall Uncle Roger ever complaining of the dullness of the world, the worthlessness of making the least effort at anything, the stupidity of everyone except himself.

"Perhaps life is very different if you're merely a viscount," Donovan whispered sadly. "And if there's such a gap between a viscount like Uncle Roger and those earls and marquesses and dukes, then how much wider the gap between a mere mister like myself and a duke's daughter like Lady Sophia."

"Who is Lady Sophia?" asked a voice from the shadows,

causing Donovan to spin on his heel, his fists at the ready. But in a moment his fists were simply hands again and back in his pockets, and he was merely staring in amazement at the reincarnation of the gentleman who had sat beside him through the second act of the opera.

"Where did you come from, Mr. Elliot?" he asked quietly. "I did not so much as hear you approach."

"No, no, I'm like a ghost floating just above the ground sometimes. Not a sound. Not a whisper. I was leaning there against the fence in the middle of the square, attempting to make some sense of the world, when you pulled up in your carriage. Who is Lady Sophia?"

"The woman I love," sighed Donovan. "But I shall never have her. She's very kind and charming, and has twice made the attempt to include me among her friends, but I don't fit in with them, you know. Likely she feels a great pity for me if she feels anything. I expect, though, that she doesn't think of me at all unless I'm standing right there before her. I expect I don't so much as enter her mind until then. I'm a fool to lose my heart to someone so far above me as Lady Sophia. My sister, Nora, told me as much. Warned me how it would be, but I had already seen Lady Sophia then, you see, and I'd already allowed myself to hope."

"Is she very beautiful, this Lady Sophia?"

"The most beautiful woman I have ever seen."

"Well then, you must forgive yourself for falling in love. We all fall in love, whether it's good for us or not. Rather like catching a chill, love is. Catch it without the least thought and can't get rid of it until it takes it upon itself to leave. Such an exhausting emotion. I wonder, lad, do you perchance . . ." Elliot's quiet voice faded away completely as a streamer of fog disengaged itself from one of the streetlamps and the lamplight shone boldly down on the two of them. Everything about the gentleman went silent. He did not so much as blink an eye as his gaze fixed on the brass buttons of Donovan's coat just now gleaming in the lamplight.

"What?" Donovan asked, looking down at himself, attempting to discern what had so consumed Elliot's attention.

"Like tiny fires," whispered Elliot. "How they dance."

"What fires? What dances? Mr. Elliot?" But Donovan received no answer. The gentleman simply stood, spellbound, staring at Donovan's coat. He stood there for a goodly long time and ceased to stare only when Donovan at last moved aside and took the gentleman's arm. "Are you not well, Mr. Elliot?" Donovan queried. "Perhaps you ought to step into my uncle's house for a moment or two. Perhaps a glass of brandy—"

"I'm lost," breathed Elliot softly.

"Lost, sir?"

"I have been wandering the streets of London since last we met and I cannot find my way home. I do not recognize this place. I cannot seem to recall any of the streets through which I wandered. They all look alike and yet they all look so very different. I've lost my way completely."

Donovan could not imagine how a gentleman could lose himself completely in London. Why, one need merely step inside a hackney to get safely home from anywhere in the Town. Hackney drivers knew every street, every alleyway.

But perhaps he has no money for a hackney, Donovan thought. Perhaps he spent all he had to attend the opera tonight and was forced to depart early in order to walk a long distance home.

"Where is it you live, Mr. Elliot? Do you know your direction?"

"Yes. Number Fifteen, Buckingham Street. But where is Buckingham Street? It is not here. This place looks nothing at all like it."

The bewilderment in the gentleman's voice so touched Donovan's heart that he placed a supportive arm around Elliot's shoulders and said softly, "You're in Hanover Square, Mr. Elliot. Come with me, sir. We will walk a little way, merely, to Bond Street, and there we'll hail a hackney cab and I will take you safely home."

"You will?"

"Indeed, I will. We cannot have you wandering the streets the remainder of the night, can we? No, we certainly cannot. Not good for your constitution, for one thing. I can't think how you come to be so very far from your destination and so very far from the King's Theatre."

"Looking at things," the gentleman in the cloak and the floppy-brimmed hat murmured as he began to move in the direction Donovan urged him. "Looking at things," he repeated very softly.

It *is* as though he's floating, Donovan thought in amazement. As though his feet barely touch the ground. And another thought touched Donovan's mind as well. I daresay I have found a Cause of my own, he thought, astonished. Is this what it feels like for Mama and Nora and Uncle Roger? I'll wager it is. No wonder they keep doing it. By Jupiter! I have found a Cause of my own!

Marley arrived at his own establishment just as his coach drew to a halt before it. He went at once to the vehicle, opened the door, lowered the steps himself, and helped Lady Marley and Angela to descend. His own horse he sent off in the care of one of the footmen.

"Oh, Papa, we had the most wonderful evening," Angela declared as Marley ushered both ladies into the house. "You truly ought to have come with us."

"To a musical evening at the Clarenbighs'?" asked Lady Marley with such a droll expression on her face that it made Angela giggle. "I think not, my dear. Your father would expire at the sounding of the first note."

"No, do not say so, Mama. Papa is fond of music. Well, he must be. Did he not always applaud most enthusiastically each time I played a new piece for him on the pianoforte when I was a child?"

"You're still a child," offered Marley, removing Lady Marley's evening cape from her shoulders and handing it to a footman who'd just performed the same service for Miss Marley.

"I am not a child," Angela declared with more vehemence than Marley ever expected of her. "I am a young woman now, and into my second Season."

"Yes, and doing very nicely at it, too," said Lady Marley agreeably as the three of them climbed the staircase. "You will not believe it, Marley, but there were seven young men intent on impressing our Angela this evening. Four baronets, two viscounts and an earl."

"Who was the earl," Marley asked. "Not Windom?"

"No, not Lord Windom. He was not present. It was the Earl of Rockinghamshire."

"What? Rockinghamshire? That old dastard?"

"He is not an old dastard," proclaimed Angela, halting on the staircase to turn and face her father. "He is at least ten years younger than you, Papa, and very much a gentleman. He said I had eyes like gemstones."

"Gemstones. Bah! If he thought them gemstones, then he was likely estimating their weight and how much he could get for them, too."

"Marley, what a wicked thing to say!" exclaimed Lady Marley.

"Yes, yes, I apologize for it. Shall we continue up these stairs, my dears? Or do you both intend to stand there glaring down at me for eternity? I don't want you encouraging Rockinghamshire, Angela," he added as they began to move upward again. "He's much too experienced for the likes of you."

"But, Marley, the man has ten thousand a year," Lady Marley exclaimed, "and our Angela would be a countess."

"I should love to be a countess," Angela announced enthusiastically. "Only think, Papa, of all the money I would have and the enormous staff at my beck and call. And I would rule an entire county."

"Two counties," muttered Marley. "Rockinghamshire has two estates in two separate counties and you'd likely be the highest-ranking woman in each of them."

"Oh!"

"But I won't have it. Do you understand me, Angela? I will not have Rockinghamshire as a son-in-law, no matter what. There are things I know about him that you do not. Trust me, m'dear. He's a dastard, and marriage to him is not to be contemplated. However," he added as a warning sniff sounded above him from one of the noses preceding him up the stairs, "I believe you would make an elegant and competent countess, Angela, and I do believe I have just thought of the perfect earl for you."

"Who?" asked Angela and Lady Marley simultaneously.

"Blazingame."

"The Earl of Blazingame?" asked Angela as she reached the second-story landing and turned to face her father again. "Papa, have you lost your mind? Why, he—he is the most eccentric gentleman in all of London."

"Is he? Why do you think so? Because of the way he dresses? You must learn to see beyond a gentleman's outward appearance, Angela. A great many gentlemen hide themselves behind audacious façades precisely because they don't wish young women to see them as they truly are."

"But, Papa, he—"

"—has fifteen thousand a year, four profitable estates, and you would still be a countess. Besides which, Angela, he's a decent man and his age is much more suited to yours."

"Fifteen thousand pounds a year?" asked Angela in a hushed voice. "Are you certain, Papa?"

"Well, no. It may be twenty thousand by now. Wilde has been investing and reinvesting on Blazingame's behalf for as long as I can remember, and Wilde is the luckiest man on the face of the earth when it comes to investing. Now, off to bed with you. The sun will be up before you know it."

"What on earth happened this evening, Marley?" asked Lady Marley as they turned toward the master bedchamber at the front of the house. "Rockinghamshire is a dastard? Why, he's one of your closest friends, I thought. And Lord Blazingame? You wish to interest our Angela in Lord Blazingame? She's much too savvy for that innocent young man. Fifteen thousand pounds a year or not, I should think Angela would do better with Rockinghamshire. At least her shrewdness doesn't frighten him off, which it is very likely to do to such a shy, uneasy colt as Lord Blazingame. Truly, Marley, you don't seem at all yourself. No, and now that I pause and look at you, you don't look at all yourself, either. There's a smudge on your cheek, dear heart, and your neckcloth is partially undone, and you're pale, Marley. Did you lose a considerable sum at the tables tonight? Is that it?"

"One might say," Marley muttered, "that I lost a veritable fortune, Theophania. But I didn't lose it in any gaming establishment."

"Oh, dear!"

"No, no, don't be upset. My pockets are just as deep as they always have been, my love. It was merely a most seductive and expensive gem I was intent on having that got away, not any money of my own."

They separated then, she going to her dressing room to be made ready for bed by her abigail, and he going to his dressing room, where he sent his valet packing and donned his nightshirt and cap on his own.

The truth was, Marley hurt everywhere. He had pains in the most peculiar places. There must be bruises. Large bruises. And he had no intention of letting his valet see any of them.

Never know what goes through servants' minds, he told

himself as he entered the bedchamber. Sees me bruised and battered, he'll likely imagine some horrendous tale and spread it about below stairs. Then it will take off and sail through the neighborhood like a schooner through open waters. Devil it, but I hope Theophania is completely exhausted and wants nothing more but to lie down and go to sleep. I don't wish to be forced to explain to her why I wince every time I move. At least I was able to refrain from wincing or groaning all the way into the house and up the staircase. At least there are no scratches on my face and my nose is all in one piece.

Damnation, he thought as he tied his nightshirt at the neck, I should like to kick Nat from here to kingdom come. Of all the places to hide a diamond the size of a man's fist. In a newel post! And there I was two years ago, or is it three years now? Doesn't matter. There I was, tearing that house apart with my bare hands in search of a hiding space large enough to hold the thing and finding nothing. Nothing! And then I had to pay to put the place back in shape again. Paid for the house a second time, as if I didn't give Berinwick a veritable fortune for it to begin with.

"I wonder who found it?" he muttered, beginning to pace restlessly before the bedchamber window. "Percivall? The two fellows who took the place last year? The women who are there this Season? Lady Miranda and what's-her-name?"

But why the devil should any of them have discovered it when none of them even knew to look for it? Marley wondered, rubbing at his nose in frustration as he paced. Surely, no one would go prying the tops off of newel posts in a house they don't own just for the fun of it?

And yet—and yet—The Heart of a Queen was not there, not where Nat said it would be. But it was there at one time. He wasn't fibbing to me about that, because the pouch he said he put it in was still in the post. Indeed, it was, thought Marley, going to the coat he had just discarded and taking the black velvet pouch from one of his pockets.

"Took the jewel, left the pouch. What sense is there in that? None," Marley mumbled, tossing the pouch onto a tabletop as he paced by. "Unless Nat merely thinks he hid the diamond and hid only the pouch? No, no, Nat hadn't drifted as far from reality then as he has now. I had just gotten him started drinking the stuff mixed with water. He'd not even thought to get it raw and smoke it then. But what other explanation can there be?" Marley ceased his pacing and thought long and hard. "Josiah Elliot," he muttered at last. "Devil if that's not the answer."

That's why Josie came here to London, Marley mused. I'll wager he rode to wherever he hid the thing at first and when he found it gone, he assumed Nat had taken it. Though how he got inside the house to look for it—

"Well, he broke in, you fool," Marley snapped at himself. "No one living there from the time he departed Crystal Pond until two weeks ago. Who knows how long Josiah has been here in London pretending to be Blazingame's valet? He broke into the house, checked in the newel post, discovered the blessed thing and—and—and what? Took it away with him, certainly," Marley said, beginning to pace anew. "But then what? If he sold it, he'd certainly not be pretending to be anyone's valet. He'd be living in Grosvenor Square with a valet of his own."

Marley might have continued to mutter to himself and pace for an entire hour if Lady Marley did not just then enter the chamber from her own dressing room and bring both actions to a halt. She looked most fetching in a trailing negligee of deep green silk that came very close to matching her eyes.

Theophania, Lady Marley, had always been an exceedingly good-looking woman and Marley had always been aware of it. He was aware of it now as she stood before him in that tempting ensemble with her guinea-gold hair unbraided, gathered merely, by one deep green ribbon at the nape of her neck.

"Are you coming to bed, Marley?" she asked quietly, slipping between the sheets herself.

Marley groaned.

"What is it? Aristotle? Are you not feeling just the thing?"

"Yes. No. I—I have this vile headache, m'dear, and I cannot seem to make it go away."

"It's because you're so upset about the veritable fortune that fluttered out of your reach tonight, I imagine," she said, slipping back out of the bed—an action performed with such exquisite movements that Marley groaned again.

"Will you ever learn not to let things set you so on edge? Come with me, Aristotle, and I'll make your headache go away," she promised, crossing the room to him and taking his hands in her own. She led him to his side of the bed and urged him in and tucked the bedclothes up around him. Then she took a hand-embroidered pillow with lace trim from behind the door in the bottom of the nightstand and placed it behind his head. Whispering tender words of encouragement, she sat down beside him on the edge of the bed, leaned gently forward across his chest, and began to massage his temples. "You will feel better in a while," she told him. "I promise you will."

But Marley doubted it. Doubted it heartily, because as gentle as she was, she was nevertheless leaning on parts of him that must be completely black and blue by this time and the pain was mounting with each moment. And yet, her fingers, soft against his temples, performing their little circle of a dance, and the fragrance of lavender wafting up to him from the pillow were certainly soothing to his mind.

If only I did have nothing but a headache, I would be close to painless now, he thought. Close to painless and near to heaven.

And then Theophania readjusted herself just a bit on the edge of the bed and two bones that seemed to connect at Marley's left knee came jolting together. He gritted his teeth to keep from groaning and when the pain lessened, he allowed himself to sigh, instead.

I will have my revenge on you for this, Josiah Elliot, he thought as Lady Marley continued to massage his temples. It's your fault that I'm lying here aching all over instead of doing what I ought to be doing at the moment. All your fault. Why you couldn't die at Talavera as I told Nathaniel you did, I can't think. But you'll die in London if I discover that you broke into my house and stole The Heart of a Queen. I promise you that.

# FOURTEEN

Elliot stared down into the deuceit with considerably mounting hope. "Empty," he said, his gaze meeting Miranda's and settling there. "I left the pouch in here, Miranda, when I took the diamond, and now the pouch is gone."

"And the lock on the door was not damaged in any way," Miranda said thoughtfully, "nor were any windows opened or broken. And Browne heard something, but it could not have been the front door opening, because the man was already descending the staircase when Browne confronted him."

"Nat." Elliot said his brother's name with suppressed joy, hoping his conclusion was correct, and yet fearing it was not. "Nat may still have a key. And who else but Nat would know to pry up the deuceit? What burglar would think there would be anything worth having inside a newel post?"

The hopefulness in his fine brown eyes combined with the joy in his voice, which Miranda could hear even though he did attempt to suppress it, gave Miranda considerable pause. A frown crept slowly over her countenance. It made perfectly good sense that the gentleman who had hidden the diamond might return for it. But to return in the middle of the night? With a pistol in hand?

"He must have known the pouch was empty when he first touched it," Miranda said, the frown increasing, her voice growing cold.

"True," Elliot agreed, wondering as the blue of her eyes

took on a frozen gleam. Like ice, they seemed to him all of a sudden. "The absence of the stone's weight alone would have told him it was empty."

"Then why, Josiah, did he shoot Browne?" Miranda asked, her tone filling with disdain. "Why hit Ariel and knock her senseless for an empty sack? What sort of a man is your brother? The memories of him that you've shared with me are of a young man with a loving, gentle nature, not this vile savage who cares naught for the lives of innocents. Do you remember him as he was then and is now, Josiah, or as you dream him to be?"

Elliot frowned and said nothing. He looked away from her, stared down into the deuceit for what seemed to Miranda an interminable time. Then, his hands trembling slightly, he replaced the top of the newel post, descended the last few steps of the staircase and crossed to the front door. His hand on the latch, he looked back up at her. "Perhaps Nat feared to be captured and hauled off to Newgate," he said, his voice low and harsh to Miranda's ears. "Perhaps he pointed the pistol at Browne intending merely to frighten the man into allowing him to leave. Perhaps, Miranda, when Miss Markum came hurtling down on him out of nowhere, *she* caused the pistol to fire and the ball to hit Browne. And perhaps, in struggling to rise from beneath her and escape before the rest of the household descended on him, the pistol in Nat's hand came accidentally in contact with Miss Markum's brow."

Miranda stared at him, speechless.

"Your footmen are awake and on guard now," Elliot continued. "No need for the likes of me to remain and protect you."

His gaze met hers and held steady. His eyes, for the first time, lacked the warmth that she thought had always and would always dwell there.

"Doubtless you will send 'round to Bow Street in the morning," he said. "Be certain to give the Runners Nat's name, won't you?" And then he opened the door and closed it softly behind him, leaving Miranda to stare after him from her place on the stairs.

Elliot struggled against the tightening in his stomach, the gravel in his throat, the very real anger that surged through him as he walked away toward Baker Street. His hands fisted in his pockets. He ignored everything around him. He kept his gaze on the pavement, not daring to blink up at any of the buildings he passed for fear he might punch his fists into their brick façades. A vile savage, he thought, seeing the disdain for Nat—and for me, as well, he thought—on Miranda's face as clearly, as perfectly, as though she stood before him yet. Nat's a vile savage and I have invented all I know of him. So speaks the duke's sister and so it must be, without the least thought as to what might truly have happened. Nat, judged, and found a vile savage without hesitation. "Like Comestock," he whispered raggedly as he crossed Baker Street. "She is much like her brother, no matter that she protests his tiresome superiority. He judges me a murdering villain and she judges Nat a vile savage, and neither of them finds it necessary to consider what might lie behind a fellow's actions. Neither of them finds it necessary to consider that their own judgment might be mistaken."

It was shortly after sunrise when Blazingame woke from dreams of Miss Feebes to the most horrendous sound. "What the deuce?" he muttered, fighting his way out of a tangle of bedclothes. "Where the devil is that noise coming from? Elliot!" he called, tying his robe around him and stumbling sleepily out into the hall. "Doughtry? Elliot? Where are you? Some creature is being slaughtered in our kitchen garden!"

*Creature. Some creature.* Blazingame halted halfway down the corridor. "Ohmigawd, the cow. Miss Feebes's cow. Susan." He turned on his heel at once, losing a slipper as he did so, and rushed back to his bedchamber. He grabbed the bell on his nightstand and rang it with the utmost vigor. He waited for two entire minutes, and when no one appeared, he made his way into his dressing room, hurried into a pair of buff breeches and a shirt, tugged on his boots without taking the time to don his stockings first, and dashed down to the ground floor. "Doughtry!" he shouted impatiently as he stalked toward the rear of the house. "Elliot! Where the deuce is everyone?"

He turned into the kitchen and smelled coffee bubbling and something burning, but he couldn't actually see anything on fire, so he assumed whatever had burned had already been extinguished and he continued onward out the kitchen door, where he discovered Doughtry, beyond the kitchen garden on the little square of grass, patting Susan's head and mumbling to the tiny cow.

"Doughtry, what is it? What's wrong with her? Oh, deuce it, don't let anything frightful be wrong with her."

"I d-don't know, my lord. But the sounds she makes are so frightful. She must be in the greatest pain, and yet I cannot see where she is injured."

"Perhaps she's not injured," murmured Blazingame worriedly. "Perhaps she's ill."

"Mmmmmmooooooohhhh!" Susan exclaimed just then. "Mmmmmmmmmmooooooohhhhh!"

"What the devil is going on over there?" shouted a gruff voice from the other side of the garden wall. And in a moment, a graying head with a nightcap askew, but still on it, appeared above the ivy-covered rocks. "Blazingame, do something about that detestable noise!"

Blazingame stared in amazement at his neighbor directly to the west, Sir Leslie Darlinton, who was a perfectly ancient gentleman and had no business to be climbing up on a ladder, which he must be doing to appear above the garden wall. "Sir Leslie, what are you standing on?" Blazingame asked at once, crossing over to stare up at the gentleman. "Get down, sir, before you cause yourself an injury."

"My ears are already grievously injured," grumbled Sir Leslie. "By all that's holy, it's a cow! Where'd you get a cow that tiny, Blazingame? And what the devil are you doing to it?"

"N-nothing. I—it—we think she may be ill. Very ill. Doughtry, send one of the grooms for a physician," he called, glancing back over his shoulder.

Doughtry merely turned and stared at him, his mouth open.

"By Juno, young man, make that dreadful caterwauling cease!" cried another voice, this one from beyond the wall on the opposite side of the yard. In a moment, the eyes of Blazingame's neighbor to the east appeared. Mrs. Collinsworth was merely a bit younger than Sir Leslie. A baron's daughter who had married a commoner—because he'd been indecently wealthy, rumor said—she was now widowed and nearing seventy. Blazingame's heart came near to stopping as she continued to rise like the sun, eyes, then head, then shoulders appearing above the wall.

"Mrs. Collinsworth, whatever you're climbing on, get down from it, do! You'll kill yourself!" Blazingame exclaimed.

"Let her," growled Sir Leslie. "Old harridan. Can't send for a London physician, Blazingame," he added. "Not for a cow. The mere thought has stunned your butler to the core. Just look at the poor fellow. He knows you can't ask a London physician to care for a cow. What the deuce happened to it? And where did it come from in the first place? Had no idea you were thinking of raising cattle in your garden. Might raise one or two if they get no bigger than that, I expect. But I warn you, I don't like the idea. Not at all."

"Good heavens, a cow!" exclaimed Mrs. Collinsworth. "Of all things. Doughtry, if your master will not do something about all the commotion it makes, then you must, and at once!"

Doughtry faced Mrs. Collinsworth, opened his mouth at her, closed it again without a sound emerging, though his hand did go back to patting Susan's head. Mrs. Collinsworth, in lace cap, skirts and all, was climbing up onto the wall. Now she was sitting down atop it, her legs dangling.

"Are you mad, Mrs. Collinsworth?" roared Sir Leslie over Blazingame's head. "Go back! Get down at once!"

Blazingame, envisioning Mrs. Collinsworth slipping from the wall and breaking into several distinct pieces, dashed from Sir Leslie's side of the yard to Mrs. Collinsworth's side.

"Mmmmmoooooohhhhhhh!" went Susan again.

"Doughtry," Blazingame gasped as he dashed past his butler, "go down to the mews and send one of the grooms for a physician at once."

"B-but, my lord."

"Do what? What did you tell Doughtry to do?" queried Mrs. Collinsworth from her perch. "Doughtry, don't you dare. Of all things!"

"But she's suffering, Mrs. Collinsworth, and we don't know why or what to do about it," panted Blazingame as he came to a halt below her. She was wearing sky-blue kid slippers, he noticed, with a puce round gown. A glimpse of her stockings proved them to be pink. I wonder if we're related? Blazingame thought, her choice of colors bringing a smile to his face despite his feeling enormously harassed at the moment.

"Well, I can hear she's suffering," Mrs. Collinsworth declared. "The entire neighborhood can hear that. Even that old grumpy-grouch Sir Leslie can hear that. She requires milking at once, Blazingame."

"Milking!" Blazingame slapped his hand against his forehead.

"Each morning and each evening," said Mrs. Collinsworth. "Good heavens, boy, it's what you do to cows. It's the reason you have them."

"I—I have never actually—" Blazingame sputtered. "Blast and damn! I beg your pardon, Mrs. Collinsworth. Didn't mean to say blast and damn in your presence. Do you—might you know how to—"

"I have never in my life milked a cow," declared Mrs. Collinsworth, clearly insulted. Across the way, Sir Leslie was laughing quite loudly. "I was born and raised a lady! Such things are not—"

"I'm sorry," interrupted Blazingame as Susan bellowed again. "I do beg your pardon, Mrs. Collinsworth. I did not mean to intimate that you had—that you ever—"

"I have seen it done!" cried a greatly relieved and excited Doughtry. "One of Elliot's nephews milked her only yesterday afternoon, my lord, and I saw how it was done."

"Do you think you can do it, Doughtry? I know the theory involved in it, but I have never actually—"

"I can," nodded Doughtry, striding confidently toward the kitchen door. "There is a stool and there are two buckets as well beside the hearth in the kitchen. I had one of the grooms fetch them yesterday. You'll see, my lord. If it is the need for milking causes this uproar, our Susan will be quiet again soon and no bother at all."

*Our Susan? No bother at all?* Blazingame gazed after his butler with a puzzled frown. *Can it be Doughtry is developing a fondness for Susan? No. Not Doughtry. Not for a cow.*


Somewhat later in the morning and far from the sound of Susan's mooing, Miss Markham began the day a bit more calmly and certainly with less noise.

"I thought you were going to send to Bow Street this morning," Miss Markum said, taking a sip of the hot chocolate that had been delivered to her, along with her breakfast, on a lovely silver tray, so that she need not leave her bed.

Miranda took a slice of buttered toast from the temptingly large breakfast provided, sat back in the chair beside the bed, took a bite and chewed silently.

"Miranda? What is it? Has something else happened?"

"Something else? Did our burglar return, do you mean? No, not another disturbance the entire night."

"Then why such a solemn look?"

"Well, because I—" Miranda's voice shivered the slightest bit. She set the partially eaten toast back on the tray, wiped her buttery fingers meticulously with a fine lawn napkin. Then she stood and began to wander aimlessly around the bedchamber, picking at things. She took a figurine of a little pug dog from the mantel, turned it upside down, then right side up, set it back in place. She ran her finger along the mantel's edge. She came to the washstand, twitched the towel out of place, lifted the pitcher, set it back down again.

"Because you what?" asked Miss Markum. "Miranda, do stand still and speak to me."

Miranda paused at the end of the bed. She gripped the smooth, cool cherrywood of the footboard tightly with both hands. Her eyes focused on the quilt lying folded at the foot of the bed and not on Miss Markum at all. She said something that was quite inaudible.

"I do beg your pardon, Miranda, but I didn't hear a word you said, dearest."

Miranda looked up and spoke more clearly. "I have wounded Josiah to the very core, I said, Ariel."

"Never. How could you?"

"By calling his brother a vile savage, and meaning it, too. He could see that I meant it. There was not a doubt in his mind. And then I suggested that he, himself, had lied to me. Had shared with me an image of his brother sewn together from dreams and wishes and not facts at all."

"Miranda! Why? Whatever possessed you?"

"We think it was his brother who came into this house last night. The deuceit was empty, Ariel. The velvet pouch that Josiah tossed back in there—the pouch that held The Heart of a Queen—was gone."

"Our gentleman burglar was not descending the staircase from this floor, or the first floor?"

"Early and I went all through the first floor and this floor this morning. There is nothing missing. Nothing but that pouch, which I expected because Josiah and I discussed the entire matter after you fell asleep last night."

Miss Markham stared at Miranda in silence.

"Well, who else could it have been, Ariel, but Josiah's brother? It had to be someone who had a key to the front door, because the fellow did not break in. And it had to be someone who knew about the hiding place in the newel post, and expected to find the diamond there. Who else could it have been but Josiah's brother, Nathaniel?"

"The two of you discussed all this?"

"Yes, and I could see quite plainly the joy rising in Josiah's eyes at the very thought that not only was this proof that Nathaniel was alive, but proof that he was definitely in London. And instead of sharing in his joy, I condemned Nathaniel Elliot on the spot for what he did to you and to Browne. And though I did not intend it, I condemned Josiah, as well, for believing in faery tales about his brother that he, himself, had invented. Oh, Ariel," she said, releasing the footboard and going to sit beside Miss Markum on the bed. "Oh, Ariel, how cold and distant Josiah grew at my words. And then he turned his back on me and departed this place."

"And he said nothing?" Miss Markum queried, setting her cup of chocolate aside and reaching out to take Miranda's hands. "He must have said something to you, dearest."

"Yes. He pointed out to me how it was quite likely his brother had not intended to harm either of you."

"He thinks my fall caused the pistol to fire and that I

was hit in the head accidentally while his brother scrambled to escape from beneath me?"

"Precisely."

Miss Markum sighed. "I have been thinking about it myself, you see, though I did not so much as consider that our burglar might have been Nathaniel Elliot. Your Josiah could very well be correct about how things happened."

"I know," said Miranda stiffly, carefully, holding back a tremendous sob that struggled to be free. "I know it could have happened just as Josiah said. I knew it the very moment he said it. But it was already too late."

"Too late? It is never too late to apologize for our mistakes, Miranda. And besides, you may not have been mistaken. I can't say if it was Nathaniel Elliot who came into this house though it appears likely, now that I know what's missing. Nor can I say what his intentions were. But neither can Mr. Browne or Josiah, dearest. Only Nathaniel can say with certainty."

"But I pronounced Nathaniel guilty on the spot, Ariel. Without the least reflection. I sounded just as Charles must have sounded when he assumed Josiah was threatening his life—"

"When Charles assumed what?" asked Miss Markum, amazed.

"Yes, yes, that's why Josiah arrived at Manchester Square such a long while after Lord Blazingame yesterday. Because Charles put him out of the coach and he had to walk home. Oh, Ariel, I spoke with such disdain. I know I did. I have listened to my words over and over in my mind the whole night through, and I was—I was—a pompous ass! After all I have said to Josiah about wishing to ignore the difference in our classes, about my birthright being of no consequence whatsoever, there I stood proclaiming his brother a vile savage and Josiah a fool not to have known it from the beginning, as though I were a queen and he and Nathaniel the dirt beneath my feet."

And then the sob Miranda had been struggling against

broke from her. Tears streamed from her eyes as Miss Markum leaned forward and drew her to her bosom, cradling her there as she had done long ago when Miranda was the old Duke of Comestock's stubborn daughter and she a mere governess who loved the girl with all her heart.


The present Duke of Comestock shoved Doughtry aside, dashed up the staircase and charged down the first-floor corridor, his blue eyes bright with anger. He caught sight of Blazingame in the morning room and stalked inside. "Where are they?" he roared. "I want them returned! At once!"

"Comestock?" Blazingame turned from the window to face the duke. "What are you saying? What do you want returned at once?"

"Not what. Who. Spinner and Jack. Ran off. Came here to their confounded uncle. Well, I won't have it! Won't have a knife-wielding villain in charge of innocents! Take charge of them myself if I must. Send them off to school. See they're raised properly. Won't have Elliot teaching them to be barbarians. No, and I'll not have my sister marrying a barbarian, either. Talk her out of it. Must. Responsible for Miranda's welfare does she acknowledge it or not."

"Elliot's nephews are missing?" Blazingame could not believe his ears. "Glory! Sit down, Comestock, do."

"No, thank you."

"They're not here, the boys, Comestock. As a matter of fact, Elliot is not here, either."

"Taken them somewhere."

"Not unless he did so in the middle of the night. Stepped out last evening shortly after I did and has not yet returned. When did the boys run off?"

"I haven't the vaguest idea," Comestock replied, removing his hat and the tan kid gloves he ought to have handed to Doughtry in the vestibule and setting them on an elegantly carved little table. "They went to their chamber last evening. Were not there this morning. Climbed out the window, I imagine. Fine lads. Left all Sophia purchased for them behind. Honest little fellows."

"Gentlemen," agreed Blazingame, "like their uncle."

"Like their uncle?" bellowed Comestock. "Like their uncle? That dastard carries a blade in his boot! He threatened *my* life while riding in *my* coach!"

"You misunderstood him, Comestock. Would have told you that you had, but there was no speaking to you about it at the time. Elliot is a gentleman. He's shared my house for months. I know him well."

"Gentlemen do not go traipsing around London with blades in their boots!"

"No, we merely carry swordsticks and canes, do we not? You ought to thank God for that particular blade, Comestock. Saved your sister's life, most likely. You don't know about that little episode at the York water gate, eh? Lady Miranda and Elliot wandered down there to look at the Thames and some ruffian followed them. Planned to assault the both of them, I should think. But Elliot pulled out his knife. Sent the dastard dashing for cover at once."

Comestock's face paled a bit.

"Think, Comestock. Elliot's an ex-military man searching London for his brother. He has not the least social entree. He cannot go strolling into the finest drawing rooms. I must do that for him. He goes, instead, into some of the most horrendous neighborhoods in the city. Not that Buckingham Street is one of them, because it's not, and I was as surprised as you to hear that they'd been accosted there. Still, would you stroll the warrens of St. Giles or Seven Dials unarmed? I think not. And as he's not got a swordstick or a cane, the blade works quite nicely. And as to threatening your life. Great heavens! The man loves your sister heart and soul. Even if he detests you—which, by the way, he doesn't—but even if he did, would he risk losing Lady Miranda by so much as stepping on your toe?"

"Well," huffed Comestock. "Well. Perhaps I misunderstood his meaning in the coach."

"Perhaps?" Blazingame cocked an eyebrow in fine fashion.

"But that has nothing to do with the boys."

"It does. He's their uncle."

"No, no, of course *that* has something to do with the boys. What I mean to say is, if they did not come here to him, Blazingame, where did they go? You're certain they did not come here and he take them wherever he has gone?"

"Quite certain. They never appeared at our door. Doughtry would have mentioned it if they had. Elliot left the house shortly after I did last evening and has not returned. I highly doubt he went to your house, stood beneath their window unnoticed and convinced them to climb down to him, then took them off with him to some foreign shore."

"Well then, where the devil are they?"

"With Berinwick?" Blazingame queried, waving Comestock down into a chair and taking the one opposite the duke for his own. "Yes, Doughtry," he added, glancing at his butler who stood, frowning, on the threshold, "his grace will have a glass of port, as will I. And he does beg your pardon for outdistancing you on his way to find me. Don't you, your grace?"

"No," muttered Comestock.

"I stand corrected, Doughtry. He doesn't beg your pardon. But bring him a glass of port regardless, won't you?"

"You think they went to Berinwick?" Comestock gazed at Blazingame, a serious frown on his face. "What lad in his right mind would run off from my house to be with that devil?"

"You've a point there," Blazingame agreed. "Speaking of devils—Doughtry, you have not had sight of that carrotyhaired fellow today, have you? Apparently, he has ceased to trail about in my footsteps," Blazingame observed, taking a glass of wine from the tray Doughtry presented him. "Did not follow me last evening, nor have I noticed him anywhere about this morning."

"Not a sign of him, my lord."

"Just so. I expect my wanderings are no longer of interest to whoever hired him, eh? Most peculiar. I thought—well, never mind what I thought. Doughtry? Is that someone knocking at the kitchen door?"

"Yes, my lord," Doughtry replied after a brief pause to listen. "Perhaps it is Mr. Elliot. No, he would come right in. The door is unlatched."

"The boys!" Comestock exclaimed as Doughtry departed for the lower regions. He set his port aside and rose at once, rushing off in the butler's wake, Blazingame hurrying behind him.


Elliot stood, staring out over the river. He'd been staring out over the Thames since well before sunrise. Now, damp and chilled, tiny curls of steam rising from the shoulders of his coat, he turned away to climb the steps of the water gate and make his way back up a bustling Buckingham Street toward Blazingame's. He climbed the steps slowly, like an old man, his hands in his pockets, his shoulders hunched, his legs aching from his hours of standing still in the fog. His eyes downcast, he took one step after the other until he reached the inside of the gate. Then he stared upward and sighed. "I'm a dunderhead," he muttered. "Why ought Miranda to have thought anything but what she did? Her home was broken into. Her best friend and her butler were both injured. Anyone would have been equally judgmental. There are emotions involved in it. Deep emotions. I ought to have understood that at once. Miranda is as fond of Miss Markum as I am of Nat. How could she not be angered by the treatment Miss Markum received? Why should she seek excuses for Miss Markum's attacker?

But I must seek excuses for him, he told himself. Damnation, Nat, you can't possibly have become a vile savage, not you. Never. I know that. And I know you would never shoot Browne purposely or hit Miss Markum in the head. But I don't understand at all what it is you have become. Why did you send the boys off with Berinwick? Why are you hiding from everyone who ever knew you? From me? "What in Hades has happened to you?" Elliot whispered to himself as he continued through the water gate and descended into the street.

He was midway up the block, his head bowed, his gaze fastened on the pavement. His thoughts were turning from Nat to center once again on Miranda and his need to apologize to her for the manner in which he'd departed her house, when he noted a disgusting bit of debris on the pavement, stepped to the side to avoid it and bumped into someone. He looked up at once. "I beg your pardon," he said, and then paused. "Feebes? Is it you? What the deuce are you doing here?"

"Elliot? Well met," Donovan responded.

"You live in this neighborhood?" Elliot queried. "No, of course not. Your uncle would never think to dwell in such an old neighborhood, not so far east, not so close to the river."

"No, lives in Hanover Square, Uncle Roger. I've been sitting up all night with a friend, actually. Are you bound for Manchester Square?"

Elliot nodded.

"I'll accompany you part of the way, then. We can share a hackney if you wish."

"You look worn to the bone, Feebes. Is your friend very ill?"

"I don't know," responded Donovan, the two falling in step with each other. "I became acquainted with the gentleman only last evening. He'll not confide in me what illness makes him suffer so. Not as yet. But I'm determined to help him nonetheless. He's a most interesting and endearing fellow. It's the oddest thing."

"What is?"

"Well, when one stops to think on it—first I discovered you on the bridge and then I discovered him at the opera. It's as though I were destined to discover a Mr. Elliot who required my assistance. And though I made a mistake with you, this particular Mr. Elliot is truly in need of me."

Elliot came to such an abrupt halt that Feebes took four steps without him before he turned around and made his way back.

"Elliot? What is it? By Jupiter, you're not going to have one of those fits again, are you? Not right here in the middle of the pavement? Well, but I'll watch over you, regardless. It's only right that I should. Go ahead."

"Go ahead?"

"Yes, fall down trembling if you must. I shall stay with you until you've finished."

"No, no, I'm not about to have the trembles. At least, I don't think I am," Elliot replied. "This friend you speak of, Feebes? This Mr. Elliot? He resides here in Buckingham Street?"

"Number Fifteen," nodded Feebes. "First floor front. I say, he's not a relative of yours, is he? It occurred to me that he might be, but then I thought—"

"What's his given name, Feebes?"

"Nathaniel." Donovan stared in wonder as Elliot immediately spun about on his heel and began, with long strides, to rush back the way they had come. "He *is* a relative," Donovan whispered to himself, and set off in pursuit of Elliot.

Miranda, with Early beside her in lieu of Miss Markum's escort, stepped into Blazingame's kitchen at Doughtry's invitation. "I know it is merely half past nine, Doughtry, and I am sorry to bother you at such an early hour," she said, "but I must speak to Mr. Elliot."

"He is not here, your ladyship."

"Not here? Then you must tell me where he's gone, Doughtry, because I must speak with him as soon as humanly possible. It is of the utmost importance."

"Miranda?" Comestock paused midway into the kitchen. "Miranda, is that you? What the deuce are you doing coming into this house through Blazingame's kitchen door like some scullery maid? Great heavens! It's that Elliot, isn't it? He's made it necessary for you to skulk about—"

"Josiah has not made it necessary for me to do anything!" returned Miranda in a frenzied tone. "Do not be criticizing Josiah to me, Charles! Not ever again! You have already judged him unfairly once, and I, who ought to have known better, have done the same. But we shan't make that mistake again, neither of us! Do you hear me? Oh, Lord Blazingame. Forgive me. I didn't see you there. Where have you sent Josiah, please? I must speak to him without delay."

"I haven't sent him anywhere, Lady Miranda. He stepped out last evening and hasn't returned as yet."

"He—he hasn't returned since last night?"

The look on Lady Miranda's face was so distressing to all three of the men that they stood speechless for a full minute. And then Comestock stepped forward and put his arms around his sister. "What is it, Miranda?" he asked quietly. "What's happened to set you off? Tell me."

In a veritable flood of words, the tale of the burglary and the assault at Portman Square flowed from Miranda's lips, stunning Comestock, disconcerting Blazingame, and setting Doughtry to fidgeting most uneasily and gazing with some apprehension around his kitchen. "And when we thought the burglar might have been his brother, I said the most dreadful things to Josiah, Charles. Without in the least considering that all might well have been a dreadful accident, I judged Josiah's brother a vile savage. I spoke of him with such disdain. And then I accused Josiah of lying to me about the man. Oh, but I ought not to have done that."

"I would have done precisely that," mumbled Comestock.

"I know, which is why I ought not to have done it."

"There was a diamond in the newel post, Miranda? A diamond?" asked Comestock, struggling to sort through her story in his mind and unable to digest the crux of it.

"Not then. Josiah had already taken it out. He carries it in his pocket now. Oh, Charles, I don't wish to discuss the stupid stone. I wish to find Josiah. I must find him."

"Hush, my girl," Comestock said softly. "We'll find the man. I'll see that we do."

Miranda, her cheek resting against the V of her brother's waistcoat, which it had not done in years, thought how comforting it was to have him to lean upon at the moment. I have forgotten what solace is to be found in an elder brother to whom one can turn, she thought, somewhat amazed. "I was so utterly s-stupid, Charles," she murmured. "I behaved in the cruelest fashion. I must find Josiah and make things right between us as soon as possible."

"A search, then," Comestock said. "My coach is out front, m'dear. We will search London high and low, eh? And we'll keep our eyes wide open for those nephews of his, as well."

"The boys? Spinner and Jack? They're missing?"

"Ran off last night. But perhaps they and your Mr. Elliot have found each other by now. We'll see, Miranda. We'll find the man and we'll find the boys, too."

"Early," Miranda instructed from the shelter of her brother's arms, "go home, please, and keep watch over Ariel and Browne. I shan't require you to accompany me any farther for I have my brother to walk beside me now."

With the utmost care, Comestock took leave of Blazingame, escorted his sister to his coach and helped her inside. He sat across from her, his back to the horses. "Where first, Miranda?" he asked. "Is one place more likely than another for him to have gone? I shall command John to drive anywhere you choose."

"To the bridge, I think. Yes, to Westminster Bridge."

Blazingame watched them depart. "Do you know, Doughtry," he said, glancing at the butler who stood only slightly behind him in the doorway, "I can't help but think it odd that Elliot and his nephews have disappeared and our carroty-haired man has disappeared at nearly the same time."

"It is odd, my lord."

"Very odd. I think I shall have a look around London myself, Doughtry. I'll have one of the hacks saddled and go for a bit of a ride. No telling but, do I come upon a particular carroty-haired man, I may descend and have a word or two with him. No telling but he may know something about that burglary at Portman Square. You'll look after Susan while I'm gone, won't you?"

"Oh, yes, my lord," agreed Doughtry with a nod.

"Just so. And if Miss Feebes and her brother should appear on our doorstep, Doughtry, you will allow her to visit with Susan, will you not? I know she's a forceful sort of young woman, Miss Feebes, and the two of you do not particularly fit together like two sides of the same barn, but—"

"But, my lord?"

"But I would appreciate it immensely, Doughtry, if you could find it in your heart to strive to like her. I can't think how it comes about, but I rather fancy that particular young woman."

"The dauntless Miss Feebes, my lord?"

"Exactly, Doughtry. I fancy the dauntless Miss Feebes."

Mr. Feebes let Elliot into the front set of rooms on the first floor of Number 15 with the key Nathaniel had given him. It was a bleak, unwelcoming set of rooms, sparsely furnished with furniture far from the best quality. Elliot's heart ached to see it. Nat *has* lost everything, he thought as he followed Feebes down a short, dim corridor.

"I put him to bed," Donovan said quietly. "There was coal, so I laid a fire, lit it, and tucked him into bed, but when he fell asleep at last, he had the most dreadful nightmares. I could not leave him, not all alone as he was. He required someone to tell him what was real and what was not. He couldn't distinguish one from the other. Here. This is his bedchamber."

Elliot stepped inside. The coals still glowed on the grate. A pair of shabby-genteel curtains had been tugged across the lone window. In an ancient canopied bed, minus its curtains and with canopy sagging in the middle, lay a gentleman so still and silent that for a moment Elliot feared he was gazing at a corpse. But then the corpse took a breath and sighed. Elliot stepped closer until he could gaze down directly into the sleeper's face. His heart, which had lurched and trembled its way through the night on the banks of the Thames, the same heart which had struggled with Miranda's words, at once cringing from the sting of her disdain and fighting to understand from whence it had sprung, that well-worn heart that had denied Nat could harm anyone intentionally, especially such innocents as Browne and Miss Markum and yet did not know—was no longer certain of it—that particularly anguished heart, at sight of the lined and vulnerable face on the pillows, cracked in two.

Elliot's hands began to tremble, the smells of sulphur and copper, blood and gunpowder, rose up around him.

Donovan ran for a chair at once, set it behind Elliot, and shoved him down into it.

"No," whispered Elliot. "I'll not return to that Hades again. Not this time. Not ever. I'll not go no matter what demons come to drag me down. Nat's found a Hades of his own. I cannot go to mine and leave him to suffer his without me. Nat," he urged in a hoarse whisper, reaching out for his brother's hand. "Nat, hold my hand. Hold tight to it. Don't run from me any longer. Don't let me slip away from you, and I'll not let you slip away from me. It's Josie, Nat, and I need you. I'm like to drown in a fit of haunts and trembling if you don't tug me to you and kiss my cheek and say you're proud we're brothers as you used to do. And you are like to drown as well, Nat. You are like to drown if you don't do it."

On the bed, Nathaniel Elliot opened his eyes and turned his head. "Josie?" he said, and closed his hand tightly around his brother's. "Am I dying, then? Is it you they've sent for me? But why do you tremble so? You're the angel, little brother. I'm the one who's doing the dying. It's me ought to tremble, not the likes of you."

# FIFTEEN

"Not on Westminster Bridge, then," Comestock observed quietly as he assisted his sister back into the coach and sat down across from her. "Where next, my dear? Blazingame mentioned something to me about the York water gate. Might your Mr. Elliot be there?"

"He does love the water gate," Miranda replied.

"John," Comestock commanded, opening the hatch with his cane. "To the York water gate."

"Yes, your grace," responded the coachman, and directed his team into Parliament Street.

"Don't look so anxious, Miranda," Comestock said, reaching across and giving the hands she was twisting together in her lap a gentle pat. "We'll find the man. I promise you that. And he'll not be as upset with you as you fear."

"He will. He was supremely angry last night, Charles. He did not say it in so many words, but then, he'd no need to do so. I understood his anger at once."

"Perhaps he was angry last night, but apparently, he loves you beyond measure, Miranda."

"He did love me," Miranda replied, her voice so low that Comestock had to strain to hear it.

"No, no, not acceptable," the duke protested roundly and in such a voice as to startle Miranda from looking out the window in search of Elliot, to staring at him instead.

"What do you mean, not acceptable, Charles?"

"I mean, my dear, that men get angry. You know perfectly well that we do. But there's not a man worth his salt who, if he loves a lady before she makes him angry, is going to cease loving her just because she did or said some little thing to set him off. Do cease looking so worried, Miranda. It does not become you. Elliot will have thought through what was said last evening and by this morning he'll have discovered some reason why you had every right to speak as you did."

"I had no right to speak as I did."

"So you believe, but Elliot will discover an acceptable reason for it. I promise you that."

"How can you, Charles?"

"Personal experience, my dear," replied Comestock quietly, returning his gaze to the riders and pedestrians they passed. "You'd be surprised at how many different perspectives a man in love can adopt when he comes right down to it. Is that—no, no, not him. A woman in love develops the same talent, believe me. Ah, here we are, turning into Buckingham Street. Keep your eyes wide open, my dear. I'll do the same. Go all the way down to the gate, John," he called up through the hatch. "We'll step out there for a moment or two."

The sight of the Duke of Comestock's team prancing down Buckingham Street caused considerable astonishment along the tiny thoroughfare. Carriages came and went, certainly, in the course of the day, but a four-horse hitch composed of magnificently matched grays, and such high-stepping grays, had all heads turning.

One head in particular turned, brown eyes bright with appreciation. His feet paused just beyond his door and they could not be persuaded to take another step, though the gentleman beside him tugged at his elbow. "Josie, only look," he said, awestruck, resisting his brother's urging to step down onto the pavement. "A four-in-hand. A scarlet coach with silver spokes in its wheels and silver horses in its traces. And it's pulling up at the water gate. It will be The Buck himself, most like."

"The Buck is dead, Nat."

"But so are you and you're here."

"I'm not dead," Elliot sighed, ceasing to stare up the street after Donovan, who'd gone to fetch them a hackney, and turning to speak to his brother directly. "I thought we'd settled that nonsense, Nat. I'm not dead. I have not been transformed into an angel. And I've not come to escort you to heaven."

"Yes. I've got it into my head that you're no angel, Josie. You cursed, you know, when I explained to you about—"

"I know I cursed. I said I was sorry for it, Nat."

"Yes, but you smashed my pipe against the fireplace bricks and tossed all my parcels of tobacco into the coals, and you didn't say you were sorry for that."

"I'm not sorry for that. Not in the least."

"Just so. And no angel would do any of those things or say any of the things you said in the first place. That's why I agreed that you can't be an angel. You're a demon more like."

"Nat, I am not dead. I am not an angel. And I am not a demon."

"Methinks thou doth protest too much," quoted Nathaniel, his gaze still fastened on that tantalizing coach and four. "However, I will give some thought to the idea that Marley was mistaken about your death. I promise you I will. But just on the chance that you are dead, Josie, and a demon, I feel I should tell you right here and now that I have no intention of accompanying you to Hades or anywhere else unless you arrange to take me in a scarlet coach with silver horses just like that one."

Elliot didn't know whether to laugh or cry. It had taken him forever to disabuse Nat of the notion that he had risen from the dead and been transformed into an angel. Even with young Feebes's help, it had been a lengthy and confusing battle.

And now I'm a demon instead? he thought, a wry smile

turning his lips upward. Though, apparently, I'm a demon with considerable influence. Nat seems confident that I can arrange his departure from this life in fine fashion. He looked toward the water gate to see just how fine a fashion he was being asked to replicate. Elliot's eyes widened considerably and his pulse began a perfectly thunderous drumming in his ears. "It's Comestock," he murmured to himself. "That's the very coach he invited me to quit on the way back from Berinwick's. What the deuce is he doing at the water gate?"

"He's taken his lady to gaze at the Thames," Nat replied, overhearing and assuming the question to be intended for him. "Comestock, you say? Will he give us the loan of his coach?"

"I—I don't know, Nat."

"Look, he and his lady are back inside already and the coach is turning. Not at all a good sign."

"Not at all a good sign?"

"Well, if you're going to escort your lady to the gate to gaze at the Thames, you ought to stay for longer than a minute or two, Josie. Sometimes Meg and I would go and sit on the steps for hours. How odd. I've not thought of Meg in a goodly long time. How odd to have you appear to me and then to see the boys and now to begin to think of Meg. Perhaps she awaits me on the other side? Does she, Josie? Oh, but I should like to see Meggy again. You ought to wave them to a stop, I think," he added as the coach came rolling toward them. "I'm much too old to ascend on the run, and so are you, I think."

"Charles! Charles! Tell John to stop!" Miranda cried excitedly. "He's there. Josiah is standing right there on that step with another gentleman and he's staring directly at us. Oh, Charles, you've found him just as you promised!"

The coach and four halted a mere two houses beyond Number 15. Comestock swung open the door, leaped from the vehicle and reaching up, lifted Miranda out onto the pavement. In a shushing of silk, Miranda hurried back toward

Elliot. "Josiah," she called without the least thought to who might hear her. "Oh, Josiah, I am so sorry for what I said last evening. I was wrong to judge so quickly and so harshly and to speak to you with such disdain. Please forgive me."

Elliot was already stepping down onto the pavement, opening his arms to her, tucking her neatly away within their circle. "I'm the one requires forgiveness, Miranda," he said, cradling her against his chest. "I ought to have realized what a shocking experience it was for you. Miss Markum injured. Browne shot. I was so blinded by the idea of Nat alive, Nat in that very house, that all I could see was how frightening the entire situation must have become for Nat when I ought to have understood how frightening it was for you."

"No, I'm the one ought to have paused and attempted to understand, Josiah," Miranda said in a hushed voice, her cheek pressing against his waistcoat. "Oh, Josiah, I feared I had driven a stake through your heart. You looked so—so cold. Your voice was like ice. And your eyes—"

"Yes, well, I wasn't prepared for it, you know," he responded, leaning down, whispering the words in her ear. "I have never seen you respond like a duke's daughter before. It sent such a shock through me, the realization of just who you are, Miranda. I have been telling myself over and over since first we came to know each other that you're nobility. I have been careful of you and your reputation because of it. But I did never fully comprehend until that instant. You are—You are—"

"A condescending, self-centered shrew," Miranda said on a bit of a sob, hiding her face against his neckcloth, unwilling to look him in the eye.

"Never that."

"What then?" she asked.

"A commanding presence?" Elliot queried. "A woman accustomed to power and judgment? A pompous ass just like your brother?"

Miranda giggled.

"Ah, that's better," Comestock said, looking up at Nathaniel from directly behind the couple. "Better giggles than sobs, don't you think, sir? Of course, an entire street full of people are staring, totally scandalized, even as he coaxes my sister to look up at him and smile, but what do I care? Surprisingly enough, for me," he added, "I don't give a fig."

"Do you have a fig?" asked Nathaniel, his gaze leaving the interesting duo of his brother and the lady and meeting Comestock's.

"Eh? Do I *have* a fig?" asked Comestock, puzzled.

"Josie's going to kiss her, I think. Right here on the public thoroughfare. Will you give a fig for that—if he does?" Nat queried.

Ignoring the rather loud conversation between Miranda's brother and his own, Josiah kissed the top of Miranda's head. And when she lifted a smiling face up to him, abandoning the shelter of his neckcloth and putting her arm around his neck, he kissed her soundly and most thoroughly.

"I was right. He is kissing her," Nathaniel said with glee. "Now, will you give your fig? To me?" Nathaniel extended an open palm in Comestock's direction.

"No, of course not. Put your hand back in your pocket, sir. It's not as though I actually have a fig in my possession."

"Oh."

The two gentlemen assessed each other in silence and then returned their attention to Josiah and Miranda.

As the kiss ended, Miranda stared with wonder into El-liot's laughing eyes. "Did I hear correctly, Josiah? Was Charles actually discussing figs with someone a moment ago?"

"I'm afraid so, m'dear. Turn around a moment, Miranda, and let me introduce my brother."

"Nathaniel?" Miranda turned at once, though she did not step out of the circle of Elliot's arms. "This gentleman is your brother, Josiah?"

"The brother you've been searching for?" asked Comestock from over Elliot's shoulder.

"Indeed. Lady Miranda, Comestock, may I present my brother, Nathaniel. Nat, this is the lady I intend to marry, and this is her brother, the Duke of Comestock."

"Charmed," Nat responded, and bowed most extravagantly. "How do you marry someone when you're dead, Josie? Do you need a special license?"

"Dead?" Miranda asked, startled.

"He thinks I'm dead," Elliot whispered in her ear with an exasperated chuckle. "I'll attempt to explain it all to you after I have got him safely settled at Blazingame's. Mr. Feebes has gone to fetch us a hackney," he added loud enough to include Comestock, who was attempting to decipher Nathaniel's comment, his face a vision of bewilderment.

"Mr. Feebes? How does he come to—" began Miranda.

"I'll explain that as well once I've got Nat settled. And it wasn't Nat, by the way, who broke into your house last night."

"It wasn't?"

"Who was it, then?" Comestock queried.

"Marley."

"Lord Marley?" Miranda could not believe her ears. "Lord Marley hid the diamond in the newel post? However did he—"

"No, it was Nat hid the wretched stone, but he told Marley where it was last evening. Expected Marley to fetch it home to him. Ah, there's Feebes now. Raggedy-looking sort of hackney, but it will have to do, I expect."

"I wish to ride in the scarlet coach with the silver horses," Nathaniel declared. "Did you forget, Josie?"

"No, Nat, but they're not ours, you see, and—"

"Charles, pay the hackney driver something and tell him we do not require him," Miranda interrupted. "And ask Mr. Feebes to join us in our coach. We shall all of us escort Mr. Nathaniel Elliot to Lord Blazingame's establishment."

"Just so, Miranda," Comestock nodded. "I'm perfectly willing to do it. But Elliot's brother must sit between Elliot and this Mr. Feebes and I sit beside you. No telling but the fellow will go searching through my pockets for that confounded fig, else."

Eleanor could not be still. Not for a moment. She fairly floated around the house in Hanover Square. Her feet barely touched the carpeting. "I do wish Donovan would come home," she whispered, straightening the piano shawl in the music room. "I cannot imagine what has kept him out the entire night. However, Uncle Roger says we must none of us worry our heads over it, so I won't."

Gentlemen are the oddest creatures, she thought then. I'm sure if I went to the opera and did not return until the following day, Uncle Roger would be out scouring all of London for me. But because it's Donovan, Uncle Roger merely shrugs his shoulders and smiles the oddest smile. And Lord Blazingame is much the same. When he thought me to be the object of that hideous scandal that almost escaped into Society, he was prepared to be most angry. I could hear it in his very tone of voice. And yet, when I pointed out that the scandal concerned him, he merely smiled at me, the same sort of odd little smile that Uncle Roger smiled. Of course, then he kissed me.

"He kissed me," Eleanor whispered happily, taking a doily from one of the chair backs, intending merely to straighten it but pressing it instead to her heart. She took a tiny step, and another, and another, and in a moment she was waltzing around the music room. Lord Blazingame kissed me, she thought. After all the trouble I've caused him, after all the truly unkind things I thought of him and said to him, he stood there and smiled that crookedy smile, and kissed me full on the lips. Oh, but he is the kindest, most understanding gentleman in all the world. He is just the sort of gentleman I have always dreamed of marrying. And his kisses taste of brandy and cherries.

Do all men's kisses taste of brandy and cherries? she wondered then, still waltzing to music only she could hear. Do Papa's? Do Uncle Roger's? Do Donovan's? Or perhaps their lips taste so sweet only to the women who love them.

Eleanor's waltz ended most abruptly. "That would mean that I love Lord Blazingame," she said softly in a haze of astonishment. "That would mean that Lord Blazingame is more than just the *sort* of gentleman I would like to marry. It would make him the particular gentleman I wish to marry."

"Who is?" asked her brother from the threshold.

"Donovan! You're home at last!"

"Yes. Who is the particular gentleman you wish to marry, Nora?" he asked again, one shoulder leaning against the door frame. "Is it anyone I know?"

"Lord Blazingame," she replied, blushing a bit and hurriedly returning the doily to the chair back. "I expect you're tired, aren't you? Having been out all night and all . . ."

"Exhausted, but I'm not off to bed yet. I've come to fetch Uncle Roger. Is he here?"

"No. He's gone out. Is something wrong, Donovan? You look so weary. Certainly you ought to lie down for just an hour or two at the very least."

"Can't. I'm on a mission, Nora."

"A mission?"

"Yes. You'll not believe it, but I have a Cause of my own. Well, it turns out that he's Mr. Elliot's Cause as well, and now Lady Miranda's and the Duke of Comestock's, too. Still, I discovered him first, and I am not about to ignore him even if all those others have stepped forward to lend their aid."

"I think it's grand you have a Cause of your own. I should like to know more about him," Eleanor said, straightening the doily on the chairback with more precision than the task required.

"Well, he's Mr. Elliot's brother, actually. Turns out there is a Mr. Elliot major and a Mr. Elliot minor. Our Mr. Elliot from Westminster Bridge is Elliot minor."

"He has an elder brother?"

"Oh, yes. Been searching for his elder brother practically forever from the sound of things. It was I brought them together."

"Donovan, how wonderful!" Eleanor exclaimed, going to her brother and giving him such a tremendous hug that he laughed and wiggled out of her grasp, gasping for breath.

"Remind me not to tell you I've done anything else quite so impressive again, won't you?" he teased, his eyes merry.

"Oh, but what a wonderful thing it must be to realize that you've brought a family together, Donovan! You must be floating on air."

"Just so. But bringing them together is not the end of it. Not at all. There's a deal of work to be done, which is why I need Uncle Roger. Because I know nothing at all about it and neither does Josiah, or Lady Miranda or the duke."

"Know nothing about what?"

"Opium," said Donovan succinctly.

"O-opium?"

"Precisely. I have heard of it, of course. So has everyone else. But none of us has had the least experience with the stuff, except for a bit of laudanum when we were ill. Apparently, Nathaniel smoked an entire pipe of it, if not more, last evening, and that's what made him speak and act so oddly when we met at the opera. Yes, and it's likely the reason he continued to act oddly the entire night and is still at it this morning."

"Donovan! You spent last evening cavorting about London with an opium eater?" Eleanor was properly horrified.

"No, of course not. That is to say, Nathaniel didn't eat it and I wasn't cavorting. I simply went to the opera and Nathaniel took the seat beside me. Then he got lost and ended up right here in Hanover Square. I took him home, Nora, and remained with him, because he began to have the most frightening nightmares even though he was awake. Well, I couldn't possibly abandon him to suffer through the night alone, because I knew, you see, when he came to ask my help in finding his way back to Buckingham Street, that he was *my* Cause."

"Where is he now?"

"We've taken him to Blazingame's. Josiah and the others remain with him while I've come to ask Uncle Roger what's to be done. I expect Uncle Roger will know, don't you?"

Eleanor studied her brother closely. His eyes positively shone with triumph and goodwill. He was decidedly happy with himself and his efforts on Mr. Elliot major's behalf. "We could leave a note for Uncle Roger," she suggested quietly.

"Leave a note? We could leave a note for Uncle Roger?"

"Yes, with the butler or one of the footmen. We can't ask Aunt Caroline to pass on the word because she's gone to Gabrielle's for a fitting and she's likely to be gone until very late this afternoon, so a note would be—"

"Whoa! Wait!"

"What?"

"I have a much better idea, Nora. I have just told you everything. You can explain it all to Uncle Roger and ask him to meet me at Lord Blazingame's."

"No, but that's the point, Donovan. I mean to return to Lord Blazingame's with you."

"No."

"Is not Lady Miranda there?"

"Yes."

"Well, my own presence must be considered quite proper then. No one can look at me askance when the sister of a duke is among the company there. If anyone says the least thing scandalous, I shall simply look them in the eye and say that Lady Miranda and I went to the establishment to lend our aid to someone in need."

"No. Uncle Roger said I was never to escort you to Lord Blazingame's establishment again. Not for any reason."

"I know things about opium."

Donovan's eyes blinked in disbelief. "You? Really, Nora, what a whopper!"

"It's not a whopper. I've read about opium in some of Mama's books."

"Which books?"

"I don't remember. Perhaps it was in some of Thomas Sydenham's writings. But I know it is made from poppy seeds and that one may mix it with liquor or water or tea and drink it down, or one may mix it with tobacco and smoke it, or one may purchase it in great hunks and eat the stuff. And I know what it does to people as well—at least—I have never actually *witnessed* what it does to people, but it's said to relieve melancholy most successfully, only it—it goes too far sometimes."

"I'll be damned," murmured Donovan. "You do know something about it."

"Yes, I do."

"And I thought you wished to use this merely as an excuse to pay another call on Blazingame."

"So you will take me?"

"I am not supposed to take you there," Donovan said.

"Did you give Uncle Roger your word that you would not?"

"No, but—"

"Then you'll take me. Because next to Uncle Roger, I expect I know more about opium than any of you."

Donovan could not quite think what to do. He knew he ought not escort Eleanor to Blazingame's again. And yet, she did know things and perhaps— "Perhaps I ought just fetch a physician," he mumbled, stuffing his hands into his pockets. "A physician ought to know about opium."

"Yes, that would be just the thing," agreed Eleanor. "And the physician will take one look at your Mr. Elliot, agree that he suffers from melancholia, and offer to provide the gentleman with more opium himself."

"There is that," sighed Donovan. "And then *your* Mr. Elliot would kill the physician and we would all go directly to jail."

"We want to go to Uncle Josie's house and we want to go now!" declared Spinner with considerable vehemence. "You lied to us about Papa being dead. Papa is alive and Uncle Josie and Jack and I are going to find him, and when we do, you're going to be extremely sorry, you are."

"Am I?" queried Berinwick, leaning back in the enormous leather chair behind the desk in his study. He propped his boot heels on the desktop, cocked one knee, and took a volume of poetry from the desktop into his hands. "What makes you think that, whelp?" he asked, his fingers beginning to mindlessly tear at the edge of the volume's first page.

"Uncle Josie is a military man, and he will come here and run you through with his sword," Jack threatened, standing directly before Berinwick, hands on his hips.

"I'm shaking in my boots," replied Berinwick.

"Well, you ought to be, because our uncle Josie is bigger than you, you know, and he'll be angrier than anything when we tell him what you did. You ain't supposed to lock people up, you're not. It's—it's—not acceptable!"

Both boys had been kept under lock and key on the third floor of Berinwick's establishment until he'd sent for them this morning. The windows on Berinwick's third floor were tiny and round and opened onto nothing—no trees, no vines, no trellises, no accessible rooftops. Both Spinner and Jack had become frustrated and exhausted with attempting to formulate some plan by which to escape and by sunrise had given it up and crawled into a large four-poster in one of the chambers and fallen asleep. Well rested now, the two lads were stomping about Berinwick's study like miniature—and enraged—lords before a despicable monarch.

"You abducted us," Spinner accused, turning away from

the ground-floor window through which he'd considered bolting until he'd spied two of Berinwick's men standing guard immediately beyond it. "That's against the law."

"Um-hmmm. So it is. Except that I didn't abduct you."

"Yes, you did!" Jack exclaimed, stamping a foot on the Chinese-red carpet. "You don't even know what abducted means! You abducted us twice!"

"I did? Well, by all that's holy! I must be extremely good at it, then, eh?" replied Berinwick, a cynical smile settling over his face. "Best make a note to myself, right, lads? Must remember to think of going into the abduction business if I should ever lose everything in the funds. Not right to let a God-given talent go to waste."

"He's laughing at us," pouted Jack.

"Don't you dare sit there and laugh at us," Spinner demanded. "We are the ones you're hurting and we don't deserve to be laughed at."

Berinwick studied the boy, lines abruptly furrowing his brow. The patch over his missing eye touched his high, stark cheekbone as a frown encompassed his entire countenance. The very intensity of his bright, one-eyed gaze caused Spinner to hunch his shoulders, turn away, and cross to the fireplace, where he reached above his head to put both hands on the mantelpiece.

"No, don't turn your back on me quite yet, Spinner," Berinwick said quietly. "Because you're correct, you know. Neither of you deserves to be laughed at. I apologize for it."

"You do?" Spinner turned to face him at once.

"Indeed."

"And a good thing, too," mumbled Jack, pulling a chair over in front of Berinwick's desk, placing it backward before Berinwick, then kneeling on it, and dangling his arms down the chair's ladder back. "A damnable good thing, because I was getting ready to call you out."

"Don't say damnable, Jack," Spinner corrected. "It's not acceptable."

"Gentlemen say it all the time."

"Not Papa. Papa never does."

"Oh."

"And you don't want to call me out, puppy," Berinwick added, selecting a new page in the volume and beginning to shred that edge. "Remember that for as long as you live, Jack. You do not want to call me out. Not even when you're grown."

"Why not?"

"Because I'll kill you in the time it takes for a cat to flick its tail."

"You are the worst liar," declared Spinner. "Worse than me. You wouldn't kill Jack ever, or me, or anyone else, either."

"What makes you think that?"

"Because one time Mr. Murphy caught Guy sneaking into the stables by your castle to play with the horses. And he said he was going to tell his master. Guy was so frightened that you'd kill him for sneaking in that he was near to crying. But then Mrs. Dempsey asked what happened, and she said that you would never kill anyone, not even a grown man, not even if it came down to your life or his."

"And she ought to know," added Jack, "because she's your mother."

Berinwick came near to dropping the volume of poetry from his hands. "Mrs. Dempsey is my mother? Who told you that?"

"She did," replied the boys simultaneously.

"By all the vices on earth!" exclaimed Berinwick. "Why would she do such a thing? Now I shall be forced to murder the two of you, all the other boys, and Mrs. Dempsey to boot."

"No, shall you?" asked Spinner, a smile slowly stealing across his face.

"Don't you dare smile at me, Nathan Elliot," Berinwick ordered. "This is serious business. I can't have the lot of you running about telling the world that Mrs. Dempsey is my mother. I'm a duke, for heaven's sake, and she's the wife of a parson. And a terribly poor parson at that."

"You're a duke?" asked Jack, amazed. "You?"

"Yes. What did you think I was?"

"A great ugly old pirate who lost his ship and was saving up to buy another one."

Berinwick's lips quivered the slightest bit. The corners of them turned decidedly upward.

"Or a highwayman hiding away in the country to keep from getting hanged on the gibbet," Jack added.

Berinwick's fingers ceased to shred the pages of the volume.

"Or an evil toad made to look like a man by drinking a magic potion."

The volume sailed out of Berinwick's hands toward the wall behind him, his mouth opened and he roared into laughter.

Blazingame brushed a tiny piece of lint from O'Riley's lapel with the tip of one finger. He was standing toe to toe with the carroty-haired man in the dim interior of Aldophus Gloom's office. Watching the two anxiously from across the room, Gloom's clerk, Will, held his breath.

"I don't care to be placed under watch in my own house," said Blazingame, his voice barely above a whisper. "Nor am I fond of being followed about all over London. I find it annoys me. Annoys me to such an extent that *if* you were a gentleman, I should be inclined to call you out, O'Riley."

"I've told you twice already. I haven't a notion what you're talking about. I never in my life—"

"I do beg your pardon, O'Riley, but you have in your life and quite recently, too. And now there's been a burglary of sorts at one of the places to which you followed me."

"A burglary?" asked O'Riley, his eyes widening. "You

think I had something to do with breaking into someone's house? Why the devil would I—"

"You'd know that better than I, wouldn't you?" whispered Blazingame, his eyes narrowing. "Perhaps someone commanded you to do it, no? Just as they set you to following me?"

The click of the outer door opening on the street level set Will into action. He spun about on his heel, dashed from Gloom's office through his own little room, and down the stairs as fast as his feet could carry him. "Mr. Gloom," he cried as he came to a halt before the solicitor who had just begun his journey up the staircase. "Mr. Gloom, there's about to be a murder in your office. I swear it, sir. A murder. Lord Blazingame is going to murder my cousin Sean."

"About time someone murdered your cousin Sean," Gloom responded, hefting himself up the steps, Will ascending them backward in front of him. "Hasn't a brain in his head, O'Riley. How many different briar bushes have I had to pluck him out of since he came to London?"

"But this particular briar bush is most serious, Mr. Gloom. Most serious. Lord Blazingame—"

A tremendous thump interrupted Will, turned him around, and sent him flying up the staircase. Gloom lumbered up as best he could after him. "That had best not have been the sound of a body hitting the floor, Will," he called after his clerk. "Not in my office!"

But it had been the sound of a body hitting the floor and it was much too late for Will to do anything about it. Blazingame stood rubbing his right fist with his left hand and Sean O'Riley lay senseless on the floorboards, his body blanketed by scads of briefs and files and notes that had fallen with him when his hip had caught the edge of Gloom's desk. Some of the papers were still falling, drifting lazily down through the dusty air.

"I apologize, Will," murmured Blazingame, "but I could hold my temper no longer. I'm a patient man, a very patient man, but I could not hear another lie pass beneath that ridiculous red moustache. I've had enough of his lies. It's taken me half the day to discover his name; I've had to chase all over London after him; and I'll not stand here and be lied to over and over again. He's your cousin, you said?"

"Y-yes, my lord," nodded Will. "My cousin. Came to have a wee drink with me after work this evening, he did."

"Will, pick that flotsam up off the floor and toss it out the window into the gutter!" ordered Gloom, huffing into his office. "No, wait! Pick up my papers first, then deal with your cousin. My lord," he added with a respectful bow. "May I be of some service?"

"Not unless you know for whom this reprobate works. He would not say and I don't think he's bright enough to have thought to go after the diamond on his own. No, definitely not. But he won't say whose idea it was."

"I doubt he'll say now, either, my lord. Apparently, you've knocked him senseless."

"One punch," muttered Blazingame. "Who would have thought he'd drop down senseless from one punch to the jaw."

"What is it he's done, my lord, to set you on edge?" Gloom queried, taking a stand beside his desk, kicking one of O'Riley's feet aside with the toe of one black shoe. "What about going after a diamond? He's a born rascal, O'Riley, to be sure. Came to London six years ago and I've not had a bit of peace since. Always in trouble with someone, somewhere. Will, now, is another matter. Will knows to walk the straight and narrow or he'll be out of this office in the blink of an eye. Know that, don't you, Will?"

"Yes, sir, Mr. Gloom," returned the exasperated Will, hurriedly rebuilding the paper towers that had fallen from Gloom's desk.

"O'Riley's been following me all over London," Blazingame said. "Standing watch outside my house and following me wherever I went. He ceased to do so only last evening. And last evening, someone broke into the house of a friend of mine in search of a particular diamond. Didn't find it, of course. Wasn't there. But in the resulting ruckus, a man was shot and a gently bred, elderly woman injured."

"Terrible," murmured Gloom appeasingly. "And did anyone identify O'Riley?"

"No. That is to say, it was quite dark and neither of the two who saw him got a very good look at all. I cannot prove it was him. But I don't doubt it might have been. Someone set him on my heels and the same person might well have set him to breaking and entering."

"Who employs your cousin these days, Will," Gloom asked in dire tones, "and for what purposes?"

"Lord Marley, Mr. Gloom. Sean works for Lord Marley. Has since three Christmases ago. I don't know what it is he does, but he doesn't ever leave London, not even when Lord Marley returns to the country."

"Just so. There's your answer, Lord Blazingame. Likely following you about at Lord Marley's request, though I highly doubt that Lord Marley would have encouraged someone to—"

"Yes, well, had he said Marley's name when I asked him, he'd not be cluttering your floor at the moment, Gloom."

"Ought to have asked the question of Will."

"Ought to have done," agreed Blazingame quietly. "Never occurred to me. I thank you, Will," he added, leaning to the right to be seen around Gloom. "You'll advise your cousin not to run off and warn Marley that I know, will you not?"

"Yes, my lord," answered Will, nodding rather wildly. "I'll advise him, my lord. Advise him to find another employer, too, I will. You may count on it."

"I will count on it."

"Is there anything else we can do for you, my lord?" asked Gloom, rubbing his hands together in anticipation, the mention of a particular diamond sending his imagination off into visions of wills and settlements and the possibility of guardianships and heiresses. "Always prepared to assist, no matter how insignificant the problem."

"No, there's nothing else, Gloom. Unless—"

"Unless, my lord?"

"Unless Will wouldn't mind checking through his cousin's pockets while he's down there. I'd like to know if there's a black velvet pouch in one of them. It's about so large," Blazingame said, describing the size of the pouch with his hands.

Will's hands dipped at once into O'Riley's pockets. He brought out a pocket watch, three pennies, a guinea, a handkerchief, and a rather large square package wrapped in brown paper. "That's all," he announced, staring at the little pile on O'Riley's chest.

"What's in the package?" Gloom queried.

"Well, it wouldn't be some old pouch and I can't think I ought to—"

"Will," Gloom said, glaring significantly down at him, "this is not the time to quibble over minutiae."

"No, Mr. Gloom. I beg your pardon, Mr. Gloom," Will replied, hurriedly undoing the string that held the package together. "What the deuce is this stuff?"

Blazingame and Gloom both leaned down, both broke a piece from the square of shredded vegetable matter, both put it to their tongues and tasted it.

"Opium," whispered Gloom, astounded. "Mixed with tobacco."

"Yes, indeed," Blazingame nodded. "Amazing what people will carry about in their pockets, isn't it, Gloom? It's not what I'm seeking, however, so I'll take my leave of you."

"Marley," Blazingame said under his breath as he hurried down the stairs and out into the street. "All Marley. Most likely has Elliot, too. Most likely has the boys. Damnation, who'd have expected him to be such a villain? Wherever he is in London this day, I'll find him, and he'd best not have harmed any of them or I'll call the dastard out on the spot."

# SIXTEEN

Doughtry stood with his arms crossed and his chin lifted stubbornly in the midst of the chaos that was Blazingame's front parlor. "No," he said again, and loudly. "I will not fetch you my lordship's dueling pistols, Mr. Elliot. Never! You must wait until Lord Blazingame returns and ask him for the wretched things. But he will not give them to you, either."

"Fine. Then I'll just go and strangle the man with my bare hands," Elliot declared.

"No, you will not," Miranda said, leaving her place on the sofa beside Miss Feebes and crossing to where Elliot stood, toe to toe with Doughtry. "Do come away with me to someplace quiet and talk this through rationally, Josiah. You will do nothing but get yourself killed if you go running off without a plan."

"Oh, I have a plan, Miranda," Elliot responded. "I plan to kill the man before the sun sets today."

"Have to hurry, then," offered Comestock from a chair beside the hearth. "Sun will be down in less than an hour."

"Charles, do cease urging him to it," Miranda said with a glare in her brother's direction.

"You don't understand, Miranda," Comestock replied, rising and beginning to pace back and forth before the hearth. "Marley has all but destroyed Elliot's brother. The fiend took a sad, grieving widower and made an opium eater out of him. And he did it with malice and forethought, too. I will lay you odds on that. Such an act deserves punishment."

"Then let the law punish him. We will call in the Runners, Josiah," Miranda said, taking hold of Elliot's arm. "We will see Lord Marley brought up before his peers, and his peers will decide what's to be done with him."

"It's not their business to decide what's to be done with him," grumbled Elliot. "It's my business. It's my family he's destroyed. How am I ever going to help Nat? What am I going to tell his boys?"

"The boys," Miranda said on a quick exhalation of breath. "Josiah, we don't yet know where the boys have gone."

Elliot ceased to glower at the upward tilt of Doughtry's chin and turned his gaze to Miranda instead. "Marley has them," he said, his voice low and rumbling. "I expect Marley has them. His handiwork, all of it. Why wouldn't he have lured the boys from your brother's house in some fashion, taken them off and locked them up somewhere?"

"Because he was quite busy last evening robbing my house, Josiah."

"Afterward."

"Well, perhaps he did lure them into his web in some way when he couldn't find the diamond. Perhaps he was angry and came to the boys' window and told them he knew where their father was. I expect he could if someone told him they'd seen the boys at Comestock House and which window was theirs."

"Ohmigawd, I did!" exclaimed Comestock. "Told the whole whist table the other night at Almack's about Sophia's two little pages living under the eaves. Called them Spinner and Jack, too. Likely Marley knew precisely who the rascals were. Never let on, though. He never let on by so much as the blink of an eye."

"That settles it," Elliot declared. "I'm going to Marley's establishment at once."

"Not to challenge him to a duel, Josiah," Miranda said

in a tone very near a command but not quite. "And not to strangle him, either. And not to threaten him with that blade in your boot. Merely to see if the boys are there and to bring them home with you."

"Do I bring them home with me before or after I bash in his head with Susan's milking stool?"

Miranda could not help herself. She laughed, then sighed in exasperation. Elliot, watching the various emotions flicker across her features, laughed himself.

"I know, Miranda," he said, fighting through his own emotions to what he hoped was a reasonable calm. "I know you're right, but can't I please just have one go at him?"

"Hush," Miranda replied, putting a hand to his lips. "Come outside with me for a moment. I want to speak to you privately, Josiah."

"Don't go," warned Comestock. "She'll not only talk you out of punishing him but into helping him change his ways."

"Oh, I don't think anyone as evil as Lord Marley appears to be will ever change his ways," observed Miss Feebes.

"Marley? Evil?" asked Nathaniel Elliot softly, his gaze drifting away from the crystals on the chandelier as the sunlight left them. He blinked at the people gathered in the room as though they had quite magically appeared from nowhere. "Marley has done nothing but good to me. Whom has he harmed that this young woman calls him evil?"

Elliot turned to face his brother, and the anger, the frustration, even the tiny hint of laughter, floundered beneath the sadness that rose inside of him, but the calm remained. He took Miranda's hand gently, kissed it, held it, and led her over to the wing chair in which Nat, so thin and pale, seemed almost buried. He tugged a footstool up before it with the toe of his boot and Miranda, seeing it was what he wished, sat down on it. Then, releasing her hand and placing his arm on the arm of Nathaniel's chair, Elliot hunkered down beside his brother. "It was Marley introduced you to your medicine, Nat, was it not? I have got that right."

"Yes. What a blessing he was to me after Meggy died. I thought I would go mad without her. Always there were tears standing in my eyes and anguish crushing my heart. But then Marley brought his physician, and his physician recommended the medicine and Marley procured it from the apothecary for me. At first, there were vials of it to mix in water. When I took my drops, I felt a deal more joyful."

"Yes, but then he brought you more and more medicine, Marley did. Isn't that what you said?"

"Oh, a good deal more. I needed more and more, you know, or else the melancholy returned to such an unbearable degree! And then we discovered it could be mixed with brandy. What happiness he brought me! What freedom from grief and despair! So you can see, Josie, that Marley was good to me. I can't think there is evil in him. Has he done something to someone?"

"Yes, Nat," Josiah responded softly, not so much as noticing that all conversation around him had halted. "He's done something truly unforgiveable to someone I love."

"I expect he didn't mean to, Josie. I expect he had the best of intentions."

"When you were feeling more the thing, Nat, did not Marley or his physician tell you to cease taking your medicine?"

"No. I did think to do with less and less of it myself, though, because everything seemed to be getting muddled up in my mind. I thought I would not take any more of the drops."

"Just so. But you *did* take more of them, Nat."

"No. I stopped. It was frightening at first when I ceased taking them. My heart raced and I felt so very ill, but I wished to get well and look after the boys better. They were so little, you know, and sometimes I couldn't even remember their names. So I didn't care if I felt ill. I stopped regardless. And after a time, I did begin to understand things more clearly again. And it was then Marley came to bring me the dreadful news."

"What dreadful news, Nat?"

"About you, Josie. About you dying on some horrid battlefield. My heart shattered to pieces on the instant. First Meg gone, and then you. But I was very lucky, because Marley had more of my medicine with him, and this time it didn't need to be mixed with water or brandy at all. He'd found the most delightful way to mix it into tobacco. He brought me a splendidly odd pipe and helped me to fill it and light it up, and after a time, it didn't seem such a terrible thing that you were dead."

"I'm not dead, Nat."

"Yes, I know you wish me to believe that. But I think you're wrong. I *know* you're wrong about Marley. He has been helping me forever. He has offered again and again to take over the management of my funds from my solicitor, but I keep forgetting to arrange it. And he was going to fetch The Heart of a Queen so I could hold it in my hand and travel through it to other worlds. I don't know what happened to him. Perhaps I dreamed that part, about his agreeing to fetch The Heart of a Queen, because he didn't come, did he?"

"No, Nat, he didn't."

"No, I didn't think so, but sometimes I forget. Sometimes, I forget to eat and light my fire, too. It all seems so very difficult and so very unnecessary."

Miranda placed a hand, tenderly, on Nathaniel's knee. "Enough questions, Josiah," she whispered.

"Only one more, Miranda, because he could answer none of them earlier and he's doing a splendid job of it now. Why did you ask Berinwick to take the boys, Nat? Why did you give him your house and place Nathan and Jack in his custody?"

"Because you died. Everything got so confusing when you died, Josie. I didn't know what to do about the boys or the servants or the tutor or the house. I couldn't keep anything straight."

"And yet, you didn't give Nathan and Jack into Marley's care, or the house, either."

"There was something queer," murmured Nathaniel. "There was something I dreamed. Or it was real, perhaps. I don't know. I don't recall precisely. I think it was you, Josie. You and Dare. I think you both came to me and told me to give the boys and the house to Berinwick. Don't you recall coming?"

"No, Nat, I don't recall it. Do you know what happened to Dare?"

"Well, yes, of course. He went to fetch the diamond. I should like to go to the opera again tonight, Josiah. Do you think Marley will bring me moneys enough to attend the opera again? This fine young man adores the opera," he said, smiling benignly at Donovan, who was sitting on the arm of the sofa beside Eleanor. "And tonight, I shall introduce him to the opera house ceiling. Oh, some nights, Mr. Feebes, the ceiling is so much more entertaining than the performers."

Donovan nodded and looked at Eleanor with considerable hope in his eyes. "I can help him, can't I, Nora?" he whispered.

"Yes, I believe you can," Eleanor agreed. "It will not be easily done, but it isn't impossible, I think."

"Josiah, enough now," Miranda said softly, standing and taking his hand. "Come with me into the garden for a bit. There's something I wish to say to you."

Elliot nodded. "I shall return, Nat," he said. "Don't go off to the opera without me, will you?"

"Will you go, too, Josie? Oh, splendid!" And Nathaniel Elliot smiled the most wistful smile.

"I should like to see Lord Marley's head on a pike," Miranda said quietly as they strolled toward Susan, Elliot with a bucket in each hand and Miranda carrying the little milking stool. "Set the buckets just there, Josiah, and then go and stroke her nose and speak to her as you would Summerset. Where is Summerset? You did not sell him?"

Elliot gave her the most curious look. "Changing the subject? You don't usually avoid unpleasantries, Miranda."

"No. And I will not avoid this one, but I have been wondering about Summerset. I have not seen you ride him once since I arrived, and I know you were fond of the fellow."

"Extremely," nodded Elliot, setting the buckets down and then going to Susan's head. "He's in Blazingame's stables. And I do take him for a gallop as often as I can. But generally it's only very early in the morning that I can do so. He's not a city horse at all, you know. Not fond of the traffic. Shies at the sight of all the coaches and carts lumbering along. Good girl, little Susan. What a very good girl you are."

"Another one, then," Miranda replied, seating herself on the stool, placing the first bucket and beginning to milk the cow. "But he's at least one I planned on having."

"I don't follow you, Miranda."

"I am merely counting heads, Josiah."

"Counting heads?"

"Yes. It's a very good thing that Lord Hartshorn has kept his promise to rebuild Lavender Hill House, because we should never fit everyone into the upper servants' quarters. If you remember, dearest, you and my nephew were forced to share a bedchamber and Whethers to sleep in the attic."

"You do know how to milk a cow," Elliot observed, attempting to give himself time to digest what she was saying and not saying at one and the same time.

"You would be amazed at all I've learned to do over the years. Early taught me to milk. She taught Ariel, as well. Oh, but we had the jolliest of times at those lessons. When we marry, Josiah, we will take your brother to live with us at Lavender Hill, and we will take the boys. I don't think it would be right of us to send the boys away to school, not when they've been without their father for so very long already. Even if he is ill, they will want to be with him, and we ought to see that they are. And I will not think to send Ariel away."

"No, no, of course not. I never dreamed of asking Miss

Markum to leave us. Steady, m'girl. And I think you're correct about the boys."

"I guessed you would agree, but I thought it best to point it out. And I've no intention of putting an end to Lucy Lavender Enterprises. I am thinking of expanding it."

"We're making a profit, then, are we?"

"Yes, indeed. Thanks to your investment and your bringing the pillows to the attention of the gentlemen as well as the ladies here in London, we shall be forced to hire a number of girls to help with the sewing."

"And this conversation is leading us where, Miranda?"

"Josiah, I love you with all my heart. You know that. And I thought I would cry to hear your brother label Marley virtuous for what that fiend did to him. And right this moment, I would like to see Lord Marley's head on a pikestaff," she said, setting the first bucket aside and reaching for the second.

"But? Whoa, sweet Susan. That's a girl. What a lovely little thing you are. But, Miranda?"

"But you were the first among us to forgive Lord Hartshorn for all his trespasses at Lavender Hill. You appeared to understand what had brought him to do all that he did. It was as much for your sake as for our own that the rest of us joined in forgiving him. And now he has proved time and again that he intends to keep the promises he made to us. All of them."

"And you wonder why I haven't the same consideration for Marley?"

"Just so."

"Because I cannot see him as I do Hartshorn. I cannot envision Marley as a good man who battles against a worm of evil in his heart, who fights, again and again, to keep temptation at bay. If Marley has kept on as he began when we were young, Miranda, he is, by now, evil incarnate."

"But perhaps he has not kept on as he began, Josiah."

Elliot nodded slowly. "Perhaps."

"You will never know if you shoot him dead straightaway.

No, and not if you challenge him to a duel, either. You cannot know what lies behind what he's done, not actually, unless you take the time to converse with the man as we did with Lord Hartshorn."

"You're merely afraid I'll be hanged for a murderer, Miranda, do I shoot him straightaway, or that I'm the one will lie dying on the grass do I call him out."

"Those particular possibilities do exist," Miranda said to the accompaniment of the rattle of milk into the bucket. "You must admit they do, Josiah. And I don't care how selfish you think I am, I don't wish to be parted from you by a gibbet or a pistol ball. I don't wish to be parted from you at all."

Elliot stood silent for a long moment, stroking Susan's nose, allowing the cow to poke at his stomach. "Very well," he said at last, "I'll listen to what Marley has to say for himself, Miranda. I give you my word on it. I'll meet with him and listen to what he has to say. I'll attempt to understand. And I will think what's to be done that's best for his family and for ours. And then I'll shoot him dead," he added with a grin.

"Our family," smiled Miranda. "Our own little family to bring Lavender Hill House to life again. What a perfect jumble of a family we'll prove to be, Josiah, the lot of us. There, she's all done with giving for today." Miranda placed the second bucket safely out of the way of Susan's hind legs, stood, and stretched a moment. "I don't know what it is, Josiah," she said. "I simply cannot conceive of the gentleman being evil incarnate. Certainly he has some virtue, something that makes him worth saving."

"Elliot! Elliot!" Comestock called from the kitchen doorway just as Elliot picked up the milk buckets. "Come here at once. You, too, Miranda. Hurry."

"Charles, what is it?" Miranda called back, seizing the milking stool and rushing with Elliot in her brother's direction.

"I cannot bring myself to believe," declared Comestock

loudly. "You'll not believe it, either. But we must. We cannot afford to doubt a word of it. Not a word."

"What's happened?" asked Elliot, his breeches wet with spilled milk as he drew up before Comestock. "Here, let me set these buckets inside. What's happened now, Comestock?"

"This," said Comestock, shoving a much-folded paper into Elliot's hand the moment he turned from setting the buckets down.

"Josiah, what is it?"

Elliot lowered the paper so that they could read it together, she standing before him, he reading over her shoulder.

"Oh!" gasped Miranda. "Oh, no!"

"Blazingame?" muttered Elliot. "How the devil?"

"We don't know how the devil, Elliot. Doughtry may know, but he's lying senseless on the sofa in the parlor. Miss Feebes was nearly overcome at first herself. Loves Blazingame, she says. Did you know? At any rate, Miss Feebes pulled herself together admirably and is ministering to Doughtry at the moment. Poor old fellow collapsed in the vestibule with this note open in his hand. Addressed to him. Delivered to him at the door. Young Feebes went to see what had happened when Doughtry did not return from answering the door in a reasonable time and found the poor man stretched his length on the floor tiles."

"And Miss Feebes is attending to him?" Miranda asked. "Oh, dear!"

"We'd best go to them at once," Elliot said, crumpling the paper in his hand and tossing it angrily to the floor. "Doughtry's an old man. Loves Blazingame like a son," he mumbled, taking Miranda's hand and starting toward the parlor. "Blazingame is Doughtry's whole reason for living. His heart might well have given out with the shock, and what does Miss Feebes know to do for that?"

"Just so, Elliot," Comestock replied, following them at once. "I thought perhaps he'd not just fainted and so sent young Mr. Feebes off in my coach to fetch Hadley, my physician. But right now, the poor old fellow's life is in Miss Feebes's hands."

"By all that's holy! How dare Marley!" Elliot exclaimed as they hurried up the corridor.

"What will you do, Josiah?" Miranda asked.

"Just as the note says. I'll meet Marley on Westminster Bridge at midnight and give him The Heart of a Queen. Damn the man! I never wanted the thing anyway! He need not have destroyed my brother's life to get it. Certainly he need not have assaulted Blazingame and abducted him to get it! Years ago I told him where I stowed it when I left to join the fighting. I told them all—Nat, Dare, Marley—precisely where I put it. Why didn't Marley simply go and fetch it for himself while I was gone if he wanted it so badly?"

"Because Nathaniel went and fetched it and hid it in the newel post?" Miranda suggested quietly.

"What did you say, Miranda?"

"I said, dearest, perhaps Lord Marley could not fetch it because your brother had already done so. And it's likely Lord Marley doesn't have the boys as you thought, Josiah."

"I hadn't thought of that. Something, at least, for which to be grateful. If Marley had them, he'd not have bothered holding Blazingame for ransom, he'd have ransomed Spinner and Jack instead."

"Then, where have the boys gone?" asked Comestock, his eyes betraying more anxiety over the entire situation than he had felt in years.

"Berinwick, I'll wager," muttered Elliot as the three of them turned through the doorway into the parlor. "I'll do what must be done to rescue Blazingame, Comestock. You go to Berinwick's and see if the lads are there. Don't back down from him, eh? No, you wouldn't. Ask him if he has the boys, and if he hasn't, then he'll join you in searching for them. I promise he will. He gave his word to Nat to keep them safe."

* * *

As darkness, damp, and chill settled once again over London, the gathering in the parlor of Lord Blazingame's establishment had swelled by two more. Lord and Lady Newcombe now sat on the brocade sofa, one to each side of Eleanor. "You did a fine job of it, my dear," Newcombe said quietly, putting an arm around his niece's shoulders. "Why, you likely saved that butler's life this Dr. Hadley said."

"His name is Mr. Doughtry, Uncle Roger," Eleanor sobbed softly. "And he is the dearest old fellow. Truly he is. I have treated him very cavalierly in the past, but I shall never do so again. I vow I shan't. I will listen to his words and do just as he wishes, if only he will live."

"He will, dearest," whispered Lady Newcombe, brushing a stray strand of shiny dark hair from Eleanor's heated cheek. "His grace's physician has assured us that he will. He merely needs rest and tender care. You mustn't continue to cry over him, Eleanor. You did all you could and you did it most admirably, too, darling."

"I—I am not c-crying merely over Mr. Doughtry," Eleanor managed. "It is—it is the terrible danger in which Lord Blazingame stands, as well, Aunt Caroline. Oh, I cannot believe all this is happening. All I wished to do from the first was to prevent Mr. Elliot from taking his own life, and now s-see all that has happened. And he w-was not even going to k-kill himself in the first p-place, Mr. Elliot."

"No, he was not," offered Lady Miranda, who sat on the low table before the sofa, holding a glass of wine for Eleanor to sip. "But Josiah was most impressed with you, Miss Feebes, for attempting to help him. Why, the very first thing he told me about you was that you were strong and courageous and quite capable. He said you reminded him of me."

"He—he did?"

"Yes, and I am very proud to think it, too, now that I

come to know you better. Please take just a sip of this, darling. It actually will help you."

Eleanor took the glass into her own hand and took the tiniest sip. She wrinkled her nose and handed the glass back to Miranda. "Do you think—Do you th-think he will be all right?"

"Lord Blazingame?" asked Miranda. "Yes, of course," she replied, pretending a confidence for Eleanor that she could not feel herself. "Josiah will go to the bridge exactly as it says in the note. He will give Lord Marley the diamond and Lord Marley will give Josiah Lord Blazingame. They will both come home safe and sound. There is nothing to worry about, dear one. Honestly."

"G-good," said Eleanor, leaning back and resting her head on her uncle Roger's shoulder while clutching her aunt Caroline's hand tightly. "B-because I l-love Lord Blazingame. I love him with all my heart, just as Mr. Doughtry d-does."

Elliot's heart ached as he brought the plate into the dining room and set it down before Nat. He hadn't put much on it. He'd not had the time to cook anything especially tempting. He would have done. He would have done anything for Nat, including cook him an entire deer, but the hour of twelve was fast approaching.

They had discussed what was best to do over and over again, he and Miranda and Comestock. It had taken hours for them to devise a plan of sorts—because Miranda had insisted she would accompany him to meet Marley. She would not be deterred from it by anything Josiah or Comestock said. She would not go to ask Berinwick about the boys and at the same time request his aid against Marley. No, she'd said, her brother must do that. She would not be the one to go for the Runners, one of her brother's grooms could do so more swiftly than she. She had insisted that her presence on the bridge would give Josiah and Blazingame the advantage against Marley, that the mere fact of her womanhood might well cause Marley to hesitate long enough to bring all to a peaceful end. Elliot attempted to believe it, but he could not help but think that Miranda's presence beside him would also present Marley with an opportunity to kill the person he loved more than anyone in the world, and thus he would be the one to hesitate. Comestock had understood his fears. Miranda had not. "If you die by your cousin's hand on Westminster Bridge this night, Josiah Daniel Elliot," she'd declared at the last, "I will die beside you. We will live or die together. There is no other choice." And that had brought an end to all further discussion of the matter.

Marley will attempt to kill me, Elliot thought as he sat down beside Nat. He's hated me forever and he'll not take the chance that I won't speak out against him and have him arrested. Nor he won't allow Blazingame to live either. And Miranda—he'll kill Miranda without a second thought if he kills the two of us. Lady or not, she will have witnessed his villainy.

"I realize it's not exactly the best dinner, Nat, but you've got to eat something," Elliot said, attempting to shunt all thought of the approaching confrontation from his mind and to give all of himself that he could to his brother for what might well be the last time. "There are carrots, though. You always liked carrots. And an apple, a slice of bread with butter, and one lamb chop. A rather sad lamb chop, but it's cooked through and will likely do you good."

"Yes, indeed," agreed Donovan, who had taken the seat to Nathaniel Elliot's left. "Do you worlds of good. You'll fade away to nothing, Mr. Elliot, if you don't eat something."

"I feel ill," protested Nathaniel weakly. "Josie, go away. Cease torturing me. You broke my pipe, you know. You broke it on purpose. I am very unhappy with you."

"I know, Nat, but I'll tell you what. If you'll eat some of this—which I cooked for you with my own hands, mind— I'll give you money to go to the opera tonight."

"No. I'm not well enough to go to the opera."

"Tell him he will be," whispered Lord Newcombe in Donovan's ear as he settled into a chair beside his nephew.

"Uncle Roger! I thought you were in the parlor with Aunt Caroline and Nora."

"I was, but Eleanor is feeling better now and your aunt and Lady Miranda are taking excellent care of her. Tell Mr. Elliot major that he will be well enough to go to the opera once he eats all that's on his plate, Donovan."

"But he won't be."

"He will, because we'll give him ten drops of laudanum in a bit of brandy."

"Dare we?" asked Donovan quietly.

"Oh, yes. The duke's physician, Elliot minor and I discussed it before Dr. Hadley departed. It's as I remember. A habitué of opium cannot have it taken away all at once or he'll become frightfully ill. He must be given less and less each day."

"Why doesn't Elliot minor tell him, then, that he shall have his medicine?"

"Because Elliot minor wishes you to do it. And then he hopes you'll be kind enough to accompany his brother to the opera."

"But I cannot, Uncle Roger. Not when Elliot minor and Lady Miranda are to go out to save Lord Blazingame. I must remain here until I'm certain all three are safe."

"You would be much more help if you accompanied Nat to the opera," said Josiah, peering at them from behind his brother's back. "He likes you enormously, you know, Feebes. And he trusts you. More than that, I trust you. I will feel a great deal better if you say you'll look after him tonight."

Donovan's gaze met Josiah's, and what he saw there amazed him. "You are depending on me, Mr. Elliot?"

"Indeed, I am. We're both pleading for you to take up our causes tonight, Nat *and* I."

"Very well. I'll do it," Feebes replied with a determined

nod. "You must eat up, Mr. Elliot," he said then, addressing Nathaniel, "for once you've finished, I've some of your medicine to give you, sir. And then you and I will be off to the King's Theatre for an evening of pleasure."

"Don't have any medicine," pouted Nathaniel. "Josie burned it all up. Nasty demon. The others will come for me now. The haunts will be rising up all over London to torture me."

"Well, perhaps the tobacco is gone, but we've some laudanum drops to put in your brandy," Donovan told him at once.

"You do?"

"Indeed."

Nathaniel Elliot looked vaguely toward his plate and remained silent for a full minute. "Will you skin the apple for me, Josie?" he asked then. "I'll eat it if you will skin it and cut it into pieces with your little Italian dagger. I should like to watch you do that."

"The Italian dagger was stolen, Nat, but I have this," Elliot replied, reaching down and freeing his knife from his boot. In a moment he was peeling the skin from the apple while his brother watched each and every glimmer of light on the thin, narrow blade. On Nathaniel's left, Donovan picked up a knife and fork and began to cut the gentleman's lamb chop for him.

Across the way, on the threshold, Miranda paused and watched. We will be victorious tonight, she told herself. And we'll be equally as victorious in weaning Nathaniel away from the opium. But neither battle will be easy. Nothing will be easy for Josiah and me at first, she thought as the apple peel came off in one long, uneven string and Nat clapped his hands like a child. It will be a struggle to deliver Nathaniel from the edge of this cliff onto which Lord Marley has escorted him. And we shall have to explain to Spinner and Jack, help them to understand what's happened to their father. And we must be there to dry their tears should their father frighten them from time to time.

"God," she whispered, "I need Your help tonight and I trust You will help me on the bridge. But I'm going to need Your help tomorrow, too, and for months and months to come. I'm going to become a bride, a surrogate mother, and the keeper of a Bedlamite all at one and the same time, You see. You've already given me Josiah and all his love, and I do thank You for that. But please give me whatever else I'll need to make life wonderful for Josiah and Nat and Spinner and Jack. Please do. Because I intend to take them all under my wing, and I intend to love them all forever, no matter what."

"Miranda?" Elliot had just handed a slice of apple to Nathaniel and looked up to see her standing there. "I thought you were in with Miss Feebes."

"My brother's coach has returned, Josiah. When Nathaniel has finished his dinner, it will be time for us to go."


Fog covered Westminster Bridge like a grimy shroud. So dense it was that all the sounds of the night were stilled by it. Not a breath of air stirred the fabric it stitched this night over Elliot and Miranda as they stood, waiting, listening for Marley's approach. Midnight had come and gone but Marley had not. With one arm firmly around Miranda's shoulders, Elliot reached into his breeches pocket and touched The Heart of a Queen lying there. Cold and dead, he thought. What does it possess that so many men have killed for it? That so many are willing to die for it? Why die for something cold and dead and cursed. To die for the lady beside me, for Blazingame, for Nat and the boys, that I understand, but this—this stone—has nothing, gives nothing, is worth—nothing. He shivered the merest bit as a cold chill rushed through him and he pulled Miranda more tightly against him. "I will give Marley the stone and he'll give us Blazingame, and nothing more will we do," he said, his voice gone hoarse with the dampness. "Once we have Blazingame, we will walk from this place to the spot where your brother's coach awaits us, drive to Manchester Square and nothing more. Pray for it, Miranda. Pray that we are wrong and that all that happens this night is a simple exchange."

"Yes," Miranda murmured, her cloak clinging dank and listless to her, without a breeze to make it billow. The warmth of his arm around her was the only warmth she felt. Her hair had grown heavy with the moisture suspended in the air and had fallen from its pins down over her shoulders, had tumbled down her back, a tawny mane surrounding her, invisible, as invisible as she and Josiah in the fog. She had one arm around Josiah's waist, beneath the tails of his coat, kept there easily by her thumb placed inside the waistband of his breeches. She tucked her free hand inside the pocket of her cloak and felt the small pistol her brother had sent her resting there. It felt, to her, like death. "Perhaps Marley isn't coming," she said after a long silence. "Perhaps something has happened to him along the way, Josiah."

"No. He comes. Listen."

The click of boot heels, hushed by the fog, reached Miranda's ears then, and an eerie, almost otherworldly jangle of spurs. And a shuffling, a whispering of cloth on cloth. And then a groan.

"Be still," growled a low voice filled with impatience. "Josiah Elliot, where are you? Are you here? You had best be here and with The Heart of a Queen in your hand, or your friend is a dead man."

"Here," said Elliot. "Right where you told me to be, Marley."

The boot heels clicked farther out onto the bridge. The shuffling accompanied it. Miranda listened closely as they approached. Her hand closed around the grip of the pistol in her pocket. She did not know Lord Marley. She had never met the man, nor did she wish to meet him now. But meet him she must and with a steady eye and, Lord help her, a sure aim if all did not go as planned. She recalled what Josiah had said about him. If Marley has gone on as he began, she thought, he will be evil incarnate. I am about to make the acquaintance of evil incarnate.

There was a sober clanking sound, very near, and then a faint flame set the fog alight—thick and yellow and without radiance, the fog. Marley had set a lantern down and unshuttered one side of it directly before them. They stood in pairs, Miranda and Elliot, Marley and Blazingame, with merely six feet separating them and the lantern between. Blazingame, a rope tied tightly around his hands, his feet hobbled, leaned precariously on a makeshift crutch, bent nearly double with pain.

"A woman?" Marley drawled quietly. "You've brought a woman with you? Taken to hiding behind skirts now, have you, cousin?"

Elliot ignored the comment. "Miranda, my cousin, Marley," he said most quietly. "Marley, Lady Miranda Wesley."

"Ah! My renter, eh? How do you do, your ladyship? *Most* unwise of you to join us. Is there a coach nearby to take you home? If so, I believe this would be an excellent time for you to leave us. We have business to discuss."

"I intend to remain, though I thank you for your advice, Lord Marley," Miranda replied, her tone soft but strong.

"Elliot, if you have a bit of sense left to you, you will force her to go. Now. This is not the time or the place for a lady's presence."

"I am not merely a lady," Miranda replied. "I am Josiah Elliot's lady."

"Not merely my lady, Marley," added Elliot, "but a woman grown who controls her own life. She will do as she sees fit."

Marley shrugged his shoulders languidly. "Then I am not responsible for what happens to her, eh?"

"Why ought anything at all happen to her?" Elliot asked

quietly. "I came here to exchange The Heart of a Queen for Blazingame. You give me one, I'll give you the other, and we shall call it a draw. I can see Blazingame. Would you like to see your prize, Marley?"

"Indeed."

Elliot took his hand from his breeches pocket and opened it.

In the dim, bitter night, the stone sought and found the weak rays of lantern light that bounced off the fog and like a dead thing brought to life, it began to sparkle.

"How do I know it's not paste?" Marley growled.

"Come now, Marley. What jeweler do you know could make a paste copy of this stone in the few hours between your message and this meeting?"

"None," Marley acknowledged, wetting his lips with his tongue, his gaze focused on the diamond. "Step forward and give it to me, Elliot. No, by gawd! As long as she's here, let the lady make herself useful. She will bring it to me."

Elliot shook his head slowly from side to side. "I think not, Marley. I'll not have Miranda touch this cursed thing. You'll take it from my hand or not at all."

"You still believe it's cursed? You're a fool, Josiah Elliot. A madman and a fool. Always were. Still are. Give it to me, then."

Elliot took his arm from around Miranda's shoulders and she took hers from his waist. Now that she could see Lord Marley, hear him speak, Miranda understood the distinction between Lord Hartshorn, her neighbor in Yorkshire, who dwelled in a state of temptation to do wrong but battled against it, and a gentleman, this gentleman, who welcomed evil into his heart. Marley *was* evil. Evil permeated him as the fog did the night.

And he'll allow none of us to leave this bridge alive if he has his way, she thought. Her grip on the pistol tightened.

"Allow Blazingame to step around on this side of the lantern, Marley, before I give you the stone."

"Josiah. You amaze me. Where is your trust, old fellow? I've said he's yours for the stone. Give it to me." It was then that Marley took his left hand from his box coat pocket, and cocked and pointed the little three-barrel box lock pistol directly at Miranda's heart.

"No," Blazingame groaned on the instant, and he stood up as straight as he could and took a swipe at Marley with the crutch.

Miranda was astonished at the swiftness and the grace of Marley as he caught the makeshift weapon before the blow could fall, tugged it from Blazingame's hands without so much as removing his gaze from Miranda and Elliot, sent Blazingame tumbling to the cobbles and the crutch clattering against the bridge rail behind him. "Young men," Marley said with the cock of an eyebrow at Miranda. "They are always so impulsive, are they not? The stone," he added, extending an open palm in Elliot's direction.

Elliot stepped forward and placed The Heart of a Queen in Marley's palm.

"And now you're a dead man," Marley drawled as the barrel of the pistol ceased to point at Miranda and pointed instead straight at Elliot.

"You don't want to kill me, Marley," Elliot murmured.

"I do. I've this lovely little gem now, you see, and I have Nat. Of course, once I finally convince your brother to sign over all of his holdings to me, I shan't have any use for Nat. But killing him will not be nearly as pleasurable as killing you, Josie. Not nearly as pleasurable. Not even killing Dare made me feel half as glorious as I do at the moment."

Slowly, carefully, Miranda took the pistol from her pocket and pointed it, beneath the cover of her cloak, at Marley.

"You killed Dare?" Elliot asked, his eyes meeting Marley's dead-on.

"Oh, yes. One little squeeze of a trigger and bang! Dead! Although I really ought to have made certain he had The Heart of a Queen on him before I did it. He didn't, you know. Ha!" Marley exclaimed. "By Jove, I can see it in your face, Josie. You never once suspected it was Dare went to fetch the stone!"

"Nor do I care that he did," whispered Elliot.

"But you ought. You ought to care, Josiah. Had he never gone looking for it, had you simply given it to me in the first place, Dare might be alive today. Of course, then again, he might not."

It happened with such speed, Miranda could not be certain that it was happening at all. Marley squeezed the trigger. The gun popped and Josiah twisted aside at one and the same time. Miranda fired her own pistol merely a second afterward. Marley lurched back out of the light into the cover of darkness and the fog.

"Miranda, he's got two more shots in that pistol. Get down!" she heard Josiah shout. And then she saw him dive into the fog after the villain. She rushed after Elliot, tripped on Blazingame's outstretched arm, and fell to the cobbles beside the lantern. As she began to rise, she heard Marley shout and then a second pop and a third. "No!" she screamed as a figure came spinning out of the darkness toward her. It was Marley. It was Marley alive and reaching down, tugging her from the cobbles, trampling on Blazingame as he did. Marley's hands circling her throat and squeezing, harder and harder. "I want it back!" he shouted, shaking her as though he were a terrier and she a rat. "I want my diamond back!" And then he ceased to strangle her, turned her away from him, and put his arms around her from behind. He kept her before him though she struggled and kicked. He held her, arms pinioned, tightly against his chest.

"Let her go, Marley. It's ended," said a voice Miranda did not recognize at all. Or was it Josiah? Did the blood pounding in her ears make his voice seem so different? Oh, God, please let it be Josiah, she prayed, attempting to catch her breath, attempting to kick free of Marley. Please let Josiah be alive. Please. Please.

And then a form emerged from the fog into the lantern light. Not Josiah. A man all in black, a devilish-looking man with a patch over one eye and a gleam in the other.

"Give it to me! I want it back!" Marley bellowed. "I'll kill her. I swear I'll kill her."

"Will you?" growled another voice, and Miranda ceased to move as Josiah stepped out of the fog and the darkness to stand beside the man in black.

Josiah was bleeding. Miranda could see blood dripping down his arm. She could hear blood dripping onto the cobbles. And Josiah held his knife in his left hand, not his right. She could see the blade flicking back and forth in the wrong hand. Her stomach lurched wildly.

And then Josiah fairly roared. "Will you have it back, Marley? Go fetch it, then!" And he raised his right hand and sent something soaring through the fog.

Marley shoved Miranda from him and she stumbled straight into the one-eyed devil himself, who caught her with one hand and lifted the lantern from the ground with the other just in time to illuminate Marley as he leaped into the air, his hands extended above his head, to catch the diamond cutting through the fog above him. He grasped it in his hand. He yelled in triumph.

And then he disappeared. He disappeared. Miranda could not believe her eyes. Marley had disappeared completely.

"Are you all right, Miranda?" Josiah asked, his arms around her. When had his arms gone around her? She didn't know. She couldn't recall.

"Miranda?" his breath whispered tenderly against her cheek.

"Josiah? Oh, Josie!" She turned in the circle of his arms and buried her face in his neckcloth.

"Do you want me to go in after him, Elliot?" she heard the devil ask. "I really prefer not to. He's likely drowned by now, and the water smells to high heaven on nights like this."

# SEVENTEEN

It was nearing five o'clock the following afternoon when Lord Newcombe leaned back in the chair beside Blazingame's bed, crossed one knee over the other, held the newspaper out before him at arm's length, and gave it a bit of a shake. "Now, where is it?" he mumbled. "Ah, yes. Here. *A Dreadful Accident,* the headline says."

"Accident?" Blazingame, tucked neatly into his bed in a fresh nightshirt, his back supported by a multitude of pillows, his brow bandaged and his ribs as well, stared at Newcombe in disbelief. "They are calling it an accident in the newspapers?"

"Just so, in each and every one of them, even the scandal sheets. Well, my lad, there were two dukes, an earl, and a viscount involved in it. I expect the Runners dared not give out the truth or even write down the whole of it in their own records. Had it been merely a valet and a viscount, it would be an entirely different story, no? Do you want to hear it or not?"

"Yes, please."

"Very well, then." Newcombe gave the paper another shake, directed his attention to the printed page before him, and began to read aloud:

*A most dreadful and distressing accident occurred sometime Tuesday evening at Westminster Bridge. Ac-*

*cording to Mr. John Stafford of the Bow Street Office, two of his Runners this morning discovered the body of Aristotle Gaylord Marley, Viscount Marley, entangled in considerable debris near one of the footings of the bridge. His lordship apparently had dropped something of value into the water and gone in to fetch it, said Mr. Stafford. Lord Marley then became trapped among the offal and drowned.*

*The Runners were most astonished to discover a large diamond clutched in one of Lord Marley's hands and assume this is the object he went into the water to recover. The diamond has been given to Lady Marley. Lord Marley is survived by his wife, by the Dowager Viscountess Marley and by his daughter, Miss Marley.*

"And that's all they say," Newcombe finished.

"Lady Marley is keeping The Heart of a Queen?"

"Apparently," nodded Newcombe. "I expect Elliot felt sorry for her ladyship and the daughter, and thought it only right to give up all claim to the gem on their behalf."

Blazingame sighed. "No. Elliot believes The Heart of a Queen is cursed. Probably hopes never to see it again as long as he lives and this seemed the best way to rid himself of it. I'm beginning to think he could be right about its being cursed. Ow!" he exclaimed as he attempted to move a bit in the bed and a fire seared through his broken ribs.

Newcombe looked up and then toward the doorway, rose from the chair, and tucked the newspaper under his arm. "Done petting the cow, are you? Well, don't stand there with such anxiety in your eyes, m'dear. Come in and take my chair."

"I—Aunt Caroline says I ought not, Uncle Roger."

"Is your aunt with you?"

"You know she isn't. You and Donovan and I came together and Aunt Caroline remained at home to finish her letter to Mama."

"Precisely. And since your aunt Caroline is not here, I'm responsible for you, Eleanor, am I not? And I say you may come in, be seated, and hold a polite conversation with our invalid here. Eleanor saved your man Doughtry's life, Blazingame, in case you didn't know."

"I do know," Blazingame said with a shy smile. "And I thank you for it, Miss Feebes. My cousin Wilde told me all as soon as I was able to grasp the meaning of his words this morning. I have known Doughtry longer than anyone else in my life. I cannot think what I would have done if I had recovered my senses to learn that my own folly had been responsible for his demise."

"Oh, please do not think any of it your fault, my lord," Eleanor said, entering the bedchamber and taking the chair her uncle offered her. "It was not you caused the shock that set Mr. Doughtry's heart to stuttering, but that frightful Lord Marley by sending him such a cruel note."

"Yes, but it was I who discovered Marley in his stables and confronted him about the burglary without so much as considering that he and his grooms might rise up against me. I was so angry, Miss Feebes, I didn't stop to think. Miss Markum was injured in that burglary, you know, and her butler shot."

"Yes, and you wished to find the man responsible and take him to task. I am very proud of you for thinking to do it, Lord Blazingame. Mr. Doughtry is proud of you, too. He says you are the most splendid earl in all of England."

Blazingame blushed, and Newcombe, who had gone to stand beside the hearth, smiled quietly at the sight of it.

"I—I am not in the least splendid, Miss Feebes," Blazingame stuttered.

"Yes, you are. You are merely too humble to admit it. Why, you even attempted, as injured as you were, to save Lady Miranda and Mr. Elliot from that fiend on the bridge last night."

"I merely—"

"Do not attempt to deny it, my lord. Both Mr. Elliot and Lady Miranda told us that you did. You have the heart of hero, Mr. Elliot says. The heart of a hero."

Blazingame studied her shining eyes, her sweetly tempting lips and the pride for him that sat boldly on her countenance, and thought what a wonder it was that such a rare young woman as Miss Eleanor Feebes existed—and even more of a wonder—this same Miss Feebes was determined to find him admirable.

"Susan!" he exclaimed abruptly. "By Jupiter, Miss Feebes, I've forgotten all about Susan! She must be milked and Doughtry cannot—"

"She was milked first thing this morning," Eleanor assured him, her admiration for him increasing twelvefold because he should think of the cow's needs at such a time as this. He has been through such horror and is in such pain and yet he remembers our Susan, she thought, placing her hand atop his on the coverlet. "Lady Miranda's cook came to milk her this morning," she said. "And Mrs. Harriot assured me that she will return to do so for as long as it is necessary. It is not the least bit of trouble, she says. About— about our Susan, my lord—"

*Our* Susan? mused Blazingame. She thinks of that little beast in the backyard as *our* Susan? And he turned his hand beneath hers so that he might clasp hers most tenderly. He held to her hand just so, gently but firmly, for the remainder of her visit.


Later that same evening, just as the sky was growing dark, Miranda stepped into Blazingame's kitchen, stared for a moment, and then leaned back against the kitchen door and laughed uproariously.

"I fail to see what's so amusing," Elliot observed, hiding a grin and turning toward her with the most aloof expression he could manage. "May I point out to you, madam, that I'm doing admirably well under the circumstances?"

"Oh!" Miranda gasped. "Oh!"

"What?"

"Your face and tone just like Charles's! But l-look at you," Miranda said, attempting to catch her breath. "What do you think you're doing?"

"I'm making my breakfast, my love," Elliot drawled, folding his arms across his chest while holding a wooden spoon aloft in one hand and leaning one hip against a counter. "I'll have you know that I've already fed Nat, Doughtry and Blazingame and none of them has died of it—yet. Thank goodness Wilde went home to dine at his own establishment and Lord Newcombe and his charges have done the same."

"B-breakfast? Josiah, it's dinnertime."

"Is it? Well, fancy that. I expect I'm making my dinner, then, eh? Will you join me, my lady? It will be delicious. I give you my word on it."

"I must be convinced of that," Miranda replied. She crossed to him, took the spoon from his hand and set it aside. She licked her index finger, touched it to his brow, brought it down and licked it again. "Flour," she said with a nod. "Just as I thought. And this?" she asked, taking hold of the top of the apron he wore and tugging him down to her. She licked his right cheek, tentatively at first, and then licked it again. "Uhmmm, wonderful. Caramel?"

"Nat wanted caramel sauce on his eggs. He wouldn't eat them otherwise," Elliot replied hoarsely, his arms encircling her. "Caramel sauce is not the simplest thing in the world to make."

"No, I'm sure it isn't. And what's this on your chin, dearest? Let me have a taste. Oh, my! Whatever it is, it's glorious."

"You're driving me mad, you know," whispered Elliot, his breath tickling her ear.

"And you're making me exceedingly hungry," responded Miranda, licking the very tip of his nose. *"You* are absolutely delicious."

"Think I'm dinner, do you?" Elliot chuckled, lifting her up, swinging her around and setting her, with a hushed swishing of her skirts, on the little counter beside him. He found that now he must look up to her and discovered he rather liked that angle, Miranda just a tiny bit above him. Their eyes met and held for a silent moment, and then Miranda's arms were around his neck and she was kissing him and he returning her passionate assault with abandon. "To the devil with dinner!" he exclaimed breathlessly when their lips parted. "I'll eat tomorrow."

"No, sir, you will eat tonight," ordered Miranda, sitting back a bit and tugging tenderly on both of his ears at once. "You are coming with me to Portman Square. Early has beef roasting on the spit, and a Yorkshire pudding beneath it, catching the last of the drippings."

"If only I could," whispered Elliot hungrily, pulling her against him once more and hugging her mightily before setting her free again. "I can't leave, Miranda. There's no one to look after the troops but me. Berinwick has the boys, but— Are you certain you're all right?" he asked, one long finger going to tickle along her cheek, sending distinct tremors through her. "I thought Marley meant to kill you last evening right where you stood. My heart stopped when I saw him with his hands on your neck. Could I have thrown my blade through his heart without harming you, I'd have done it then and there."

"I will admit to having a bruise or two beneath the collar of this gown, Josiah," Miranda replied, "and in other places as well. However—"

"What other places?"

"Never mind."

"Please tell me," he pleaded huskily, his eyes brimming with laughter.

"No. Never mind, Josiah! Cease teasing at once. I am worried about you, dear one. Do you know, at first I imagined that villain had shot you—twice. And then, when you appeared all covered with blood, I was sure of it."

"Um-hmmm. Except, I told you, Miranda, he missed me. And it wasn't blood at all. It was some vile muck I fell into while we were wrestling about, Marley, Berinwick and I. It was Berinwick made Marley miss both shots."

"Thank the Good Lord for that particular devil, then."

"Yes, but it was also Berinwick knocked me into the muck. And he landed a solid right hand to my midsection."

"Oh, for shame!"

"He did beg my pardon, though, at the time," Elliot grinned.

"I did not," growled a low voice. "I beg no one's pardon. Ever."

"Lord! Berinwick, who let you in?" Elliot exclaimed, spinning about to face him. The unexpected sound of his voice had startled Elliot and Miranda both.

"No one let me in. You ought to learn to lock your front door, Elliot."

"I did lock it."

"Not well enough. Introduce me to that wench now."

Miranda stiffened at the word and the tone, but then Elliot turned to her and winked. "What? Didn't I do so last evening, Berinwick?"

"No. You shoved me aside like a filthy rag, and after all the help I provided you, too."

Elliot grinned. "Lady Miranda Wesley, His Grace, the Duke of Berinwick, or as you pronounced him on the bridge, The Devil Incarnate."

Miranda began to acknowledge him, but Berinwick cut her off the moment her lips parted.

"Never mind," he growled. "I don't require good manners of anyone. I overheard the two of you. Yes, Elliot—you needn't glare—I did eavesdrop. I do it often. I do it because

I'm good at it. At any rate, you ought to listen to her. She's right. Clean him up, woman, and take him away with you. Feed him. I've come to visit Elliot major and I'll look after the rest of the household while Josie's gone. Elliot, I did as you asked. It's not there."

"What's not where?" Miranda asked as they strolled together toward Portman Square.

"I beg your pardon?" queried Elliot.

"His grace—goodness, it seems most extraordinary to use such a word as grace in reference to that—that—"

"He was a friend of my youth, Miranda. Apparently, he's remained my friend, mine and Nat's. I ought to have gone to Twickenham and sought his aid at once, I expect, but he never popped into my mind. Well, but it's twenty years or more since last he and I had any dealings together. You needn't fear to insult Berinwick or me, m'dear, if you mean to call him demon or devil or something like. In some ways he is."

"And in some ways he isn't," Miranda replied. "I expect one can grow accustomed to him. At any rate, he said he had done as you requested but something was not there, and I merely wondered what it was and where you thought it to be."

"The Bible, Miranda. I asked him to go to Nat's rooms and see if he could find the family Bible. I truly hoped to make myself more acceptable to your brother through the records in it, but I can't think where else it could be."

"Josiah Elliot, you are already more than acceptable in Charles's eyes. He told me last night when he took me home that you are everything a gentleman ought to be and a fierce warrior besides. He admires you and he hopes to be invited to our nuptials. Might it not be in the house in Portman Square?"

"What? Our nuptials?"

"No," Miranda giggled, "the Bible."

"I doubt it," Elliot replied with a chuckle, his arm going

around her shoulders, pulling her so close that their clothing whispered together as they walked. "Marley took the place apart looking for that blasted diamond. I can't think that the Bible could have been there and Marley not taken it. No, wait. There is a place. Perhaps—"

"Don't tell me. There's another deuceit."

"Not exactly, Miranda, but there is another place that Nat knew of and Marley might not have discovered."

"Where?"

"I'll tell you after you feed me, woman," he laughed, and leaned down to kiss the top of her head.

Miss Markum opened the door to them when they arrived. "And about time, too," she said. "I was about to send Early out in search of you. Dinner has been ready for a good quarter hour."

"You are looking as though nothing happened at all, Miss Markum," Elliot said, assisting Miranda with her cape.

"Except, of course, for the abominable bruise on my brow and a distinctive limp."

"A limp?"

"It's her toe," Miranda informed him. "She stubbed her toe and says that it is the worst of all her injuries."

"How is Mr. Doughtry?" Miss Markum asked as she led them to the dining room. "I was horrified to hear he had collapsed in the vestibule. What a despicable human being Lord Marley turned out to be."

"Doughtry's doing quite nicely, thank you," Elliot replied, usurping one of the footman's duties by pulling out chairs for each of the ladies and then seating himself. "I have no doubt he'll be up and around by the end of the week."

"No, do you think so, Mr. Elliot? That is very soon."

"Yes, but I cooked for him today, Miss Markum, and I intend to do it again tomorrow and all the days to come until he's recovered," Elliot said with the most endearing smile. "Mr. Doughtry will make a miraculous recovery, I promise you."

They dined at a leisurely pace, the conversation centering on plans for Lady Miranda and Elliot's wedding. It would be on the evening of the twenty-seventh of July, they decided, at the newly restored Lavender Hill House in Yorkshire.

"That will give everyone time to get there without a great rush," Miranda declared. "Daxonbury and Dessie intend to be back in London by July second."

"And the moon will be full, then, on the twenty-seventh," Elliot added.

"The moon? Josiah, whatever has the moon to do with—oh, Josiah, will we?"

"If it is not yet harvested, we most certainly will."

Following dinner, Miranda, Miss Markum, Early and Elliot all climbed the servants' staircase to the fourth floor and Elliot led them the length of the corridor to the chamber at the front of the house.

"Why, this be my chamber!" Early exclaimed in surprise.

"Is it?" Elliot responded. "When I was a boy, Mrs. Harriot, it belonged to one of the parlor maids. Her name was Agnes, and people were always coming and going from it. She was—"

"What?" asked Miranda with the cock of an eyebrow.

"I can see what you're thinking," chuckled Elliot, "but that's not at all what I was going to say. What I was going to say is that Aggie was a bit of a Bedlamite and collected the oddest things. May we go in, Mrs. Harriot?"

"Aye, ye may."

"Thank you," Elliot replied, opening the chamber door and stepping inside.

It was not a large room, but comfortable, with two little windows looking down on the square and a little fireplace on the wall opposite the windows. It was furnished in remarkably fine fashion for a servant's room, with a white sleigh bed, a matching washstand, a chest of drawers painted Chinese red and an armchair comfortably upholstered in red and white brocade.

"I can see your talents are well appreciated by these two ladies, Mrs. Harriot," Elliot smiled. "And rightly so. The Yorkshire pudding alone is worth the price of the bed and the chest of drawers."

"What is it we're looking for, Mr. Elliot," asked Miss Markum.

"A particular stone."

"A stone? What kind of stone? Where?" asked Miranda, her excitement beginning to build. It was a bit like hunting for buried treasure with her brother when she was child, and she was surprised how much she enjoyed the feeling even now.

"In the fireplace."

*"In* the fireplace?"

"Below the grate."

*"Below the grate?"*

"Precisely." Elliot strolled to the hearth, knelt down and removed the empty grate, setting it to one side. "Let me see. I believe it's the third fieldstone from the right and two back." He counted the fieldstones. "This should be it." And then, as the women watched, Elliot slipped his blade from his boot, pried up the stone and set it atop the grate. Then he replaced the dagger, and, stretching, slipped his hand under the fieldstone behind the one he'd removed. He stretched farther and farther until his arm disappeared up to his elbow.

"It be swallowing him down," Early observed, standing behind him with hands on hips.

"It certainly is," agreed Miranda. "Josiah, there cannot be a hole that deep. You must be putting your hand through the third-floor ceiling by now."

"It's not actually deep, but low and long. The fireplaces on the third and fourth floors have separate chimney stacks, and they are placed counter to each other with an empty space between. It goes a goodly long way, this space, Miranda. We were used to fetch things out of it with a stick with a hook on the end of it. So far, all my fingers are grasping is air, I'm afraid. No, wait a moment."

"What?" asked Miss Markum, her voice brimming with hope.

"Is it a book?" Miranda queried. "Can you tell if it's a book, Josiah?"

"Odd place to be keeping of a library," Early murmured. "And a very good thing I did not think to lay a fire tonight."

"A very good thing," Elliot agreed. "And also extraordinarily good luck that Marley didn't think to pull up the floors of the fireplaces. He fiddled with the bricks to each side of this particular one. I can tell that he did. Ah! Got it!"

He had to keep moving his arm from one side of the opening to the other to tug his prize safely out of its hidey-hole, and at one point he almost lost it. And then again, for a moment, he began to lose his balance and his head came close to meeting the chimney bricks, but Miranda grabbed him around the waist and pulled him back in time.

"What on earth did she keep in there, this parlor maid?" asked Miss Markum in wonder. "What did she collect?"

"Oh, just things," Elliot replied.

"What kinds of things, Josiah?" queried Miranda. "Now we're all curious, you know."

"There was a copy of *Fanny Hill* and several issues of a magazine called *The Bawd* and—"

"Erotica?" squeaked Miss Markum.

"That, too," Elliot agreed. "I do hope it's not *Fanny Hill* I've got at the moment."

"Or *The Bawd*," Miranda said.

"No, it's too thick to be that. Besides, I do think Aggie took those with her when she left. M'mother dismissed her finally."

"And rightly so," declared Miss Markum.

"No, no, she didn't dismiss her because of the erotica. It was because she had a penchant for collecting things she found lying in and around the house—the butler's studs, the cook's favorite stirring spoon, one of the footman's wigs. One day she discovered a dead hedgehog in the yard, collected it, and stuffed it away down here with the rest. Got to smelling something fierce. All the other servants complained loudly, and Aggie was let go. By George, Nathaniel was not so lost to the world as to forget to protect the Bible as well as the diamond, I think!" Elliot had at last maneuvered his prize into the open and reached down with his free hand to bring it out of the hole. "Thank gawd," he sighed, sitting back on his heels and staring at the sooty leather-bound volume.

It was a great, heavy old thing that he'd tugged through the space by a corner of its cover, and Elliot carried it back down the stairs and into the parlor with such deference, Miranda thought it might well be the Ark of the Covenant. "I understand," she said, laughing a bit as Early turned off into her kitchen and they proceeded to the front parlor, "that it's precious to you, Josiah, but it's not sacred. It's merely a book."

"Ah, but it's what the book contains, m'dear."

"I know what it contains, and I'm pleased you've discovered it, but I've told you, Charles can be no more impressed with you than he is already. He's granted you your birthright without so much as having seen it."

"But I should hate to lose what's in here, Miranda. It's a history barely anyone knows. The history of my family. Only sit down and look at it."

Miranda, smiling, seated herself on the sofa and urged Miss Markum down beside her. She opened the volume and found what Elliot wished her to find—a sheaf of baptismal records. She smiled more widely as she unfolded the first and the second of them. "Elliot, John," she read, and then, "Elliot, Nathan. And this is yours, Josiah." She grinned up at him as he peered down over her shoulder. "And this is Nat's. And this will be your mother's. And this . . ." Her voice faded away after a time. The paper upon which the records were written altered in thickness; the ink and the style of writing altered as well.

Miss Markum's eyes grew rounder and rounder as the names and dates continued to appear. "Great heavens, Mr. Elliot, when do the records cease and the Bible begin?"

"Well, a goodly portion of the Bible's pages are missing, I'm afraid. Had to be cut out to fit the records in. There— that's the last of them," he said with the most reverent tone Miranda had ever heard.

"Sixteen forty-six," Miranda murmured. "Salamander, Cressida. Her parents were Priscilla Salamander and— George Villiers? Josiah, is this real? It cannot be real."

"It is. The records go back no farther because The Buck and Priscilla Salamander weren't married. Priscilla had no right to The Buck's family records, and she, well, she did not come from a family who kept copies of records at all, though she did keep this copy of her daughter's, and all the children kept copies from then on. Priscilla kept this one most likely to use as a prod to get whatever she required of The Buck when he became obstinate.

"It's a great secret, Miranda, Miss Markum," he added with a serious frown. "It's a family secret. I trust you'll honor it and not go spreading it about everywhere. Well, I know you'll honor it. The Buck never acknowledged Cressy publicly. No one else knew, I expect, except Priscilla's parents and the clergyman who baptised the infant and made the entry in the parish records and this copy. None of our family has ever made a push to be acknowledged by the other branches of the family, you understand, and never will. We've no right to claim anything but what The Buck himself put aside for Cressy and Priscilla. I think it was a devil of a lot, though, what he put aside for them, because up until Nat disappeared and my life and my funds with him, my family never wanted for anything."

* * *

It very nearly broke Elliot's heart when two weeks later Lady Miranda and Miss Markum departed London before him to prepare for the wedding at Lavender Hill House near Toadscuttle in Yorkshire. He had grown so accustomed to the sight of Miranda, to the sound of her voice and the sweet security of her presence at his side, that he was constantly aware of her absence. But his heart repaired itself admirably when he rode up to the place beside Blazingame's traveling coach on July twenty-fourth, dismounted, and caught Miranda up in his arms as she ran out to him.

"Oh, but I have missed you," he murmured. "I thought I should die in London without you."

"And I could think of no one but you, Josiah, every waking moment. I came near to drive Ariel mad for thinking of you and speaking of you and wondering if you would like this or that. She's ready to part your hair with a milking stool, poor man, when you did nothing but remain to settle things in Town."

"Is this where we're going to live forever?" asked Jack, as he and the others exited Blazingame's coach.

"Yes," Elliot replied, setting Miranda's feet once more upon the ground. "Well, not forever, because you'll likely want to have a house of your own one day, Jack, and Spinner will, too. But this is the place we'll all live together until you do."

"Good afternoon, Lady Miranda," Spinner said, leading his father by the hand up to her. "Papa, you remember Lady Miranda, don't you?"

"Indeed," Nathaniel replied, bowing a courtly bow. "Charmed to see you again, my dear. What bit of paradise have you brought us to now, Josiah?" he added.

"I believe it's called Toadscuttle," offered Lord Blazingame, grinning. "Or, rather, the environs thereof. Good afternoon, Lady Miranda. I thank you for inviting me to see this valet of mine married. You're going to have an interesting life, I think, with four Elliot men to look after."

"Exceedingly interesting," Miranda grinned as she took a step forward and stood on her toes to kiss Blazingame's cheek. "I can never thank you enough for all you did for a perfect stranger, my lord. You shall always hold a prominent place in my heart. Did you not bring Mr. Doughtry?"

"Yes, but he's riding in the second coach with all our trunks. Elliot and I got a bit out of hand, I'm afraid, purchasing clothes and things for the two rapscallions and Nat. Berinwick's men will bring the boys' other things from Twickenham after the wedding. 'Once the woman has got him securely leg-shackled,' Berinwick said, actually. He did send you his best wishes on the occasion, though."

"He did? I should never have expected it of him," laughed Miranda. "The leg-shackled part I did expect. May I ask what you've done with Susan, Lord Blazingame?"

"She's in Liverpool," announced Jack, overflowing with energy from sitting still through such a long journey and unable to keep silent any longer. "Lord Blazingame escorted her to Liverpool and I escorted her with him. She was carried in an open dray all tucked up with straw and she had a big cherry-red ribbon around her neck, and Lord Blazingame and I pretended to be her outriders. Oh, but it was splendid! Everyone thought she was extremely beautiful and practically a queen."

"Took her to the Feebeses," Blazingame explained. "Lady Newcombe and Mrs. Feebes arranged it. Going to provide milk for the children at Mrs. Feebes's penny school. From what I saw, she's going to be a pet for the children, as well."

"And how is Miss Feebes?" Miranda inquired, holding Elliot's hand tightly as she strolled beside Blazingame and urged the boys and Nathaniel toward the house.

"Heavenly," Blazingame replied without thinking, and Elliot grinned as the young earl blushed.

"He requested her papa's permission to court her, Miranda," Elliot said. "Planning on going off to Liverpool for the entire month of August, aren't you, Blazingame?"

"Yes. Yes, I am. And September if necessary."

The following day, the Duke and Duchess of Comestock and Lady Sophia arrived together with Miranda's nephew Richard and his wife. And the day following that her nephew Daxonbury and his bride of almost a year, Desdemona, came racing up the drive on horseback, Dessie riding astride and outdistancing Daxonbury by a yard or more. Desdemona whooped when she saw she'd won, but then waited patiently until Daxonbury caught her up, dismounted, and came around to lift her down. And then she was running toward the doorway and Miranda's open arms, Daxonbury at her heels.

"Miranda! We are moving here to Toadscuttle," Desdemona announced with a broad smile. "Well, not into Toadscuttle exactly, but the Bradleys wish to sell off Bradley Grange and Daxonbury is going to purchase it."

"Has already purchased it," Daxonbury corrected his wife. "Only waiting for the final papers to be recorded. Good day, Aunt Miranda. And fair warning, eh? You and Elliot are going to have us around again—probably forever. Where's Elliot? Are The Graces here? Do The Graces know about Lucy Lavender Enterprises or are we to keep mum about that?"

"You're to keep mum about that for as long as you live, Dax," Miranda replied, laughing. "Great heavens! Your father has been through enough in the past month to make a gin drinker of him. Don't you dare mention a word about our association with Lucy Lavender Enterprises to the man."

"Remember that, Dessie. When you ladies are all together twittering away, don't say a word about Aunt Miranda, Miss Markum, you, and Elliot being business partners. If Her Grace hears of it, His Grace will, too, and then there'll be a brawl, not a wedding. Whose coach is that coming up the drive behind ours?"

"That will be Lord Hartshorn bringing Josiah's stepsister and her husband. They came on the mail as far as Lillenham. Dessie, do go in and tell Josiah they're arriving. He's in the study, I think. He'll want to be here to greet them. I want to thank you, Daxonbury, for everything," she added as the Marchioness of Daxonbury rushed off. "And I wish to thank Whethers, too. Did you bring Whethers with you?"

"In the coach with the baggage," Daxonbury grinned, "and hoping beyond hope that Mrs. Harriot has not lost her heart to some elegant London butler."

It was very early on the morning of the twenty-seventh when Blazingame came down to discover Elliot ignoring his breakfast and pacing the length of the morning room instead.

"Nervous, are you?" Blazingame asked.

"Yes. No. Not about marrying Miranda, no."

"About what, then?"

"Oh, nothing. What if Nat jumps up in the middle of the ceremony and declares I can't be married because I'm dead, Blazingame?"

"He won't." Blazingame took a plate from the sideboard and began to peer under the covers of the serving dishes. "Have you got the special license?"

"I gave it to Henry already. What if Comestock decides he won't be related to Lily and Henry, Blazingame? What if he makes a great to-do over Miranda marrying into a parson's family?"

"He won't," Blazingame replied, helping himself to a beefsteak, three coddled eggs and a pint of ale. "Your stepsister is a kind, lovely sort of person, Elliot, and her husband a gentleman. And you ought not be ashamed of them."

"No, no, I'm not."

"Then cease worrying. Everyone got along famously at dinner last evening and afterward. You're seeing obstacles where none exist. Jupiter, but you're a jumble of nerves this morning."

"That's another thing. What if I have the trembles, Blazingame? I've not had the trembles since you took the cow to Liverpool. What if, instead of saying I do, I fall down in a fit in the middle of the drawing room?"

"Then we will all wait until you recover yourself and get on with it," Blazingame said around a bite of beefsteak. "There'll be no one here this evening who doesn't know about your trembles, Elliot. You aren't changing your mind about marrying Lady Miranda, are you? Not after all we've gone through to make it possible?"

"No, no, of course not! I am merely—merely—I can't lose her, Blazingame. Not now. Not when we're so very close to having each other for the rest of our lives. And yet, I can't think why she will have me. Not only am I a commoner, but there's my trembles to contend with, plus Nat and the boys. And our families, Blazingame, no matter how pleasant they attempt to be to each other, will never fit together properly—"

"Wipe it all from your mind," Blazingame urged, taking a sip of ale. "Think of this, Elliot. Today you're marrying the woman you love with all your whole heart and your whole soul. Nothing beyond that truly matters, does it?"


At ten o'clock that evening the Reverend Mr. Henry Davidson stood before the long windows in the drawing room of Lavender Hill House, lamps twinkling all around him and the full moon beaming in at his back. He was prepared to marry his wife's stepbrother to Lady Miranda Wesley. He was as filled with joy for Josie and Miranda as were all of their family, neighbors and friends and he began thus: "Dearly Beloved, we are gathered here in the sight of God and in the face of this congregation—though why for such a Godly purpose at such an un-Godly hour I can't imagine—"

People began to giggle and chuckle and Elliot thought he was going to swoon. No, no, please don't attempt to be amusing, Henry, his mind cried out, but his lips remained sealed and he directed his gaze to the lady beside him. She was more beautiful than he had ever seen her. In an undergown of deep blue, topped by a robe of fine Bruges lace, she stood holding a bouquet of pink, yellow, and blue wildflowers in her hands and her blue eyes sparkled up at him with love and laughter. Her tawny locks, curled and pinned with a string of deep blue sapphires threaded through them, shimmered in the lamplight, and everything about her seemed somehow magical, mystical, to him.

"—to join together by special license this man and this woman in holy Matrimony, which is an honorable estate instituted of God in the time of man's innocency," the Reverend Mr. Davidson continued.

Miranda smiled up at Elliot. He was very pale and looked as though he wished nothing more than to take off the absolutely gorgeous blue long-tailed coat he wore, strip away his neckcloth, undo the buttons of his blue-and-white-striped waistcoat—Lord Blazingame will have picked that out for him, she thought—and run out into the cool air of the night.

Josiah Daniel Elliot was all she had ever wanted, all she would ever need. With this man, with this extraordinary gentleman, she would join together body and soul, and they would never be parted from one another, never, so long as they both did live. Miranda's heart thrilled at the very thought of it.

Nathaniel did not rise up from the rows of chairs behind them and say Josie couldn't marry because he was dead; Comestock did not protest against being drawn into a relationship beneath his dignity; and Elliot himself did not lose his senses and fall down to the floor in a fit of the trembles. He took Miranda's hand into his own and slipped a plain silver band onto her finger. He vowed every vow and she vowed them back quite plainly, though her cheeks dimpled with laughter each time she gazed at him. And in the end, they found themselves well and truly married. They were kissed and hugged; champagne was poured; toasts were made all around. And then, just as the servants were bringing in trays of food and drink to set upon the sideboards at the rear of the room, a very subdued Spinner stepped up to the bride and groom to ask, "Now, Uncle Josie?"

"Yes, I think now," Elliot said. "Run and fetch your violin, Spinner, and step out onto the balcony, won't you. Your aunt Miranda and I will be—well, but you know where we'll be. I've told you that."

"Told him what? Josiah? Ought we? Now?" Miranda stared up at him, her eyes filled with love.

"Yes. Now," he replied, taking her hand and leading her out onto the drawing room balcony, helping her down the balcony stairs, and tugging her, laughing, down the hill, toward the field of blooming lavender below the house.

By the time they reached the edge of the field, the fine, vibrant tones of Spinner's violin echoed down to them from the balcony. Elliot led Miranda in among the blossoms that billowed on the breeze, that rose and fell like a fragrant sea, welcoming their entrance. Not until they reached the center of the rows did he halt. And then he stood for a moment, gazing wistfully down at her, like a glistening shadow in the moonlight. He bowed gracefully, elegantly, like the cavalier he had once pretended to be. He took her hand into his and kissed it tenderly. "I have been blessed beyond belief to have found you, Miranda," he said softly. "God was gracious enough to have given me the most precious of all the gifts He held it in His power to give. You are everything I could ever dream of having. You are everything worth having. My dearest lady, my first and always love, my wife— shall we dance?"

# AUTHOR'S NOTE

My darling Kate, editor extraordinaire, says I ought to explain just who The Buck was. I asked if I could write an entire book about him, but she hasn't given me an answer to that as yet. So, I expect those of you who are interested will have to settle for this shortened version for now, or research him for yourselves.

The references in this book to Buck, The Buck, and Buckingham refer to George Villiers, Duke, Marquis, and Earl of Buckingham, Earl of Coventry, Viscount Villiers, Baron Whaddon, whose positions included, among others, Lord Lieutenant of the West Riding and Groom of the Royal Bedchamber. Having been enthralled with him for some twenty-five years, I generally just call him Georgie. He's not to be confused with his father, "The Duke of Diamonds," who makes an appearance in *The Three Musketeers,* or with those holding the more recent creations of the title. My Georgie, sometimes called the Madman of the Restoration, was born February 1, 1628, fought against Oliver Cromwell to restore Charles II to the throne of England and died without legitimate heirs at Kirkbymoorside in April of 1687. Whereupon, as he had requested of his monarch, his title was made extinct.

The Heart of a Queen actually did exist. It was a love token bestowed on Georgie's father by Queen Anne of France. Its whereabouts during the Regency and even today is a mystery to me, but why would I let that keep me from writing about it? I wouldn't and I didn't. This is fiction, after all.

A brief word about Mrs. Harriot. If you didn't read *My Fair Quiggley,* you may be somewhat confused. Mrs. Harriot and Early are one and the same person—Lady Miranda's cook. Circumstances in the previous book produced a closeness between Miss Markum, Lady Miranda and Mrs. Harriot that brought them to adopt a particularly unusual informality.

I love to hear from readers. Your opinions and suggestions mean a great deal to me. You may write to me at: 578 Camp Ney-A-Ti Road, Guntersville, AL 35976 or send me e-mail at http://it.uwp.edu/lansdowne.